The Wiccan Chronicles Trilogy

D. A. Barney

The Bewitching Of
Camille

PROLOGUE

1692 - Derwentwater Lake; Keswick, England

"It was the perfect day, wasn't it?" the young man murmured, his voice almost dreamlike, as he gazed at the young woman lying beside him on the checkered blanket. They were just off the quiet shore, their place of peace and privacy nestled near the water's edge. The gentle ripple of the lake mirrored their easy contentment, and the world felt still, holding its breath with them.

Together, they watched the sun as it began its journey into the loving embrace of Derwentwater Lake. Its golden rays cast long shadows across the landscape, deepening the outlines of the trees that guarded the secluded woods where they had found refuge. The woman smiled, her gaze soft as the last fading light reflected her companion's image in her loving eyes, capturing the photographic moment in quiet perfection. Time seemed to still, just for them. "Yes," she answered.

It had been the perfect day, and it had all the makings for the perfect night. With a playful grin, he rolled over, pinning her gently beneath him for just a moment before she, with a burst of laughter, shoved him off. Her movements were fluid and light, and in an instant, she was up, darting toward the shelter of the nearby woods. Her laugh echoed, teasing him, inviting him into the game. The trees stood tall, their darkened silhouettes beckoning like the gates to a hidden realm.

"Come and get me!" She laughed.

He was more than willing to oblige. He chased her to the wood's edge, where she abruptly stopped. She seemed disoriented and short of breath.

"Unhh," she grimaced as she grabbed her stomach and doubled over. "GALEN!" She screamed for the young man before she collapsed.

"Elvira?!" Galen yelled as he raced to her side.

She remained conscious, but the agony was evident in every strained movement, her body twisting and contorting on the ground as it sought an escape from the pain. Galen knelt beside her, his heart pounding with helplessness. He reached out to comfort her, but the moment his fingers brushed her skin, he recoiled—it had turned a ghostly pale, almost translucent, as if all life was draining from her.

Her body was ice-cold to the touch, a sharp contrast to the violent shivering that wracked her frame. Yet, despite the coldness, rivulets of sweat poured from her skin, drenching her in a cold, clammy sheen, as though her body could no longer regulate the chaos surging inside her.

"Uhn, no…" Galen gasped as anguish and sadness overtook his face.

His first instinct was to flee, to distance himself from the horror unfolding before him. He took a few panicked steps before stopping abruptly. His breath hitched in his throat, and he squeezed his eyes shut, forcing back the tears that threatened to spill, the weight of this decision bearing down on him heavily. With a deep, shuddering breath, he made his choice—he would not leave her. Not now, not ever.

He hovered, caught between action and fear, as a single tear slipped down his cheek. That tear carried with it all the weight of the life they had shared and the love they had known. Then, without another thought, Galen acted. He scooped her frail, convulsing body into his arms and ran toward the shore, each step driven by desperation and a fierce determination to save her.

"…You stay with me, El... Ple-ease... Stay with me."

He laid her on the blanket and patted her forehead with a napkin. He grabbed a container of water, and as he brought it to her lips, her eyes flew open, and what he saw stole the breath from his lungs. The vibrant crystal blue of her irises—so familiar, so loved—was gone, replaced by a chilling, sinister, blood-red glow. It wasn't just her eyes that had changed; something far more ominous had shifted within her, as though the woman he loved had been replaced by a dark, malevolent force that now stared back at him with an almost predatory hunger.

Her unblinking stare seemed to penetrate his soul. The smallest gasp escaped his lips - an almost imperceptible mistake, but it was enough. A strange force seemed to animate her, for even though the air was still, her hair suddenly lifted and whipped around her face as if stirred by an unseen wind. It moved with an unnatural life of its own, framing her now otherworldly visage in a wild, terrifying display. The sight left Galen frozen in place, gripped by fear, as the woman before him transformed into something he no longer recognized. He fell backward as she sat up and took a breath. She cocked her head slightly as if puzzled by the sadness that contorted his features, but that fleeting confusion was quickly replaced by something far darker. His fear was palpable—it rolled off him in waves, filling the space between them with a tangible tension. She inhaled deeply, savoring the scent of it, her lips parting slightly as a thin line of drool dripped from her mouth, driven by a hunger that Galen could neither understand nor escape. Tears poured from his face as he tried to scooch away.

"Elvira,… Please…" he whispered as he shook his head.

A smile curled up on her face as a soft, throaty exhale escaped her mouth.

"No,…" he pleaded as she stalked toward him. "No, no, no, don't. Don't… PLEASE!!" he screamed as she lunged. "NOOOOAAAAAHHHHH!!"

His scream echoed through the woods until he screamed no more. A long, uncomfortable silence followed, then a wicked cackle filled the forest with fear.

TABLE OF CONTENTS

CHAPTER 1

1693 - Lincolnshire, England

"It's the only way," Philippe thought.

As Philippe's black carriage thundered down the narrow cobblestone streets of Tattershall Village, doors and windows slammed shut in rapid succession. Curtains were drawn hastily, and candles extinguished as if the very light dared not witness his passage. The village seemed to hold its breath, steeped in dread, though a few brave souls could not resist the temptation to peer through cracked shutters, watching in fearful curiosity as the carriage wound its way up the hill toward the looming silhouette of the old, abandoned Tattershall Castle.

Philippe smirked at the drama of it all. He knew they were afraid of him, and they should be. Anyone foolish enough to venture toward this unholy place should be feared - or pitied. Tattershall Castle had stood since 1450 A.D., a curious anomaly among fortresses of its time. Ralph, Third Lord of Cromwell, had ordered it built entirely of brick—an unusual choice when stone was abundant. But Ralph's intentions had gone beyond mere aesthetics. He had believed that brick, unlike stone, could somehow repel the dark magic of the infamous Abramelin le Mage. A quaint notion rooted in superstition and one that had failed spectacularly. Philippe flicked his hand, and the curtains of the carriage magically closed.

"Do not worry," Philippe said. "They will listen to me."

"I pray you are right, my friend," said Tomas, Philippe's unnaturally pale traveling companion. "For both our sakes."

"They will listen this time. They have no choice," Philippe thought as the carriage slowed and pulled up next to the abandoned castle.

The driver, an imposing figure with muscles taut beneath his modest frame, moved with an unnatural grace as he sprang from the carriage. His feet struck the earth with a solid thud, but his movements were fluid, almost inhuman. His nostrils flared wide, inhaling deeply as though he could scent something hidden in the stillness of the air. His senses were sharp and predatory, and every fiber of his being was attuned to the dangers that lingered in the shadows. He cocked his head and peered over his shoulder to a darkened corner next to the castle entrance. His nostrils continued their marathon-like twitch until a tall, unassuming figure partially emerged from the shadows. The Driver watched the silhouetted man with a careful eye as he opened the carriage door for Philippe.

Though only twenty-five, Philippe carried himself with a weariness that spoke of battles fought and victories hard-won. His tall, lean frame radiated strength, but there was an arrogance about him, etched into the sharp lines of his classically handsome features, that warned against underestimating him. As he stepped out of the carriage, the cool night air washed over him, but he barely noticed. His eyes followed his driver's gaze, locking onto the figure half-concealed by a shadow near the castle entrance, aware that the moment of greeting carried more weight than it appeared.

"David?" Philippe asked.

David Jones stepped through the shadows of the castle into the light. A proud smile overtook David's face as he looked over the top of his glasses at Philippe. They clutched each other's right forearms in greeting.

"It's good to see you, my friend. Your presence here has been missed," David said.

Philippe raised his eyebrows.

"Well, by a few of us, anyway," David grinned. The two men burst into laughter and embraced.

"I was worried you would not come," David said.

"Because of the Elders?" Philippe asked.

"That and the war with France has made it nearly impossible to travel."

"Aaahh. The wars of man do not impede me! Let them exterminate themselves so that we do not, one day, have to," Philippe said with a disdain that David did not appear to share.

"Philippe,--"

"Tell me you were not thinking the same."

"I had always hoped one day you would learn that thinking something and saying it are two entirely different,--" David's admonishment was cut short as he felt the driver's continued stare burning into him. There was a danger in his eyes that Philippe knew David recognized and would not tolerate much longer.

"My colleague, Mr. Vincent," Philippe said to David. "His stare is not meant to antagonize. It is simply his way. But a stranger holding *his* eyes for a prolonged period of time would be taken as a sign of aggression - a challenge. One that he will readily accept every time."

David exhaled as he lowered his eyes from Mr. Vincent, but the discountenance in his sigh was not lost on Philippe. David's eyes darted to the carriage window, just catching a glimpse of the long, sharp nail on Tomas' pale finger as it pulled back from the curtain. Philippe saw the displeasure on David's face.

"You spoke of Galen in your letter," Philippe said, trying to pull David's focus off the carriage and back toward him. "How is he? Is he here, as well?"

"…Galen is dead."

Philippe's manufactured smile vanished.

"How?" he asked.

"He had recently married. A young witch, Elvira of Keswick. They had a cabin west of Castlerigg off the Borrowdale road."

"When?" Philippe asked, his anguish simmering into rage.

"Nearly a year has passed."

"Damn! Damn them! I warned them!"

"Threatened,--" David interjected.

"Two years ago this very month, I stood before the Elders after that mockery in Salem and begged them to hear me!"

"Demanded! And they did!"

"Did they?!" Philippe asked, as his blue eyes burst into a glowing blood red. "Galen is dead, along with countless others! Whose voice did they hear?! What have they done to stop these meaningless killings?!"

"They formed The Council of Warlocks," David said, "then they asked for you."

Philippe exhaled, trying to contain his rage as the red faded from his eyes.

"How many more of us need to die over this, Philippe? Talk to them again. Explain this… plan of yours," David said, eyeing first the carriage, then the driver. "I am certain this night they will be more inclined to listen, but you must bridle your emotions, my friend, or I promise you they will be your undoing."

Philippe nodded and turned to Vincent at the carriage.

"Take refuge in the forest," Philippe said to him. "I will find you."

Vincent nodded, with his eyes still fixed on David. He took a step and leapt backward onto the carriage as Tomas' silhouette shifted slightly behind the curtains. David watched the carriage race off before he turned and entered the castle with Philippe.

The crumbling walls of the castle groaned with the weight of time; their once-imposing structure now reduced to a skeleton of its former grandeur. The entryway, long since claimed by decay, led to the main chamber, where a shaft of moonlight pierced through a gaping hole in the ceiling. The light cast an eerie glow over the room, illuminating the dust and debris that had accumulated over centuries, giving the air a ghostly quality as if the castle itself breathed with the memories of its cursed past. Philippe continued into the room until he heard David's whisper over his shoulder.

"You are the strongest of us all, but you must humble yourself. Show them respect and some contrition. They are the elders: The Council, Philippe. I beg you, take heed this night, my friend. Take he-e-e-ed…."

Philippe turned to respond, but David was nowhere to be seen. Philippe inhaled and gathered his thoughts before he continued into the center of the dark room. He stepped into the circle of moonlight and waited a few uncomfortable moments. Nothing.

"You have sent for me?" Philippe asked and received no reply.

Then, a low buzz of whisperings began. Soft and Indistinguishable at first, but with every passing second, the hive noise grew. It seemed to be all around him, a constant conversation between the unseen council members, as if oblivious to Philippe's presence in the room.

"He is not strong enough to,--" a voice said.

"He is the strongest of us all," said another.

"Not strong enough to defeat a witch," another voice added.

"They cannot be defeated," another voice chimed in.

"They can! I have a way!" Philippe said.

The cacophony of voices started again.

"They are stronger than us,--"

"Faster."

"Three times more powerful,--"

"They cannot be defeated."

"Listen to me," Philippe said. "We are no match for them by ourselves. Warlocks cannot do this alone, but with the help of vampires and lycans we,--"

"What?!"

"Hear him!"

"This is lunacy!"

"Werewolves are volatile; unpredictable,--"

"Temperamental!"

"And vampires cannot be trusted."

The intensity of the voices had grown to a disturbing level and was causing Philippe discomfort.

"No, wait. Listen!" Philippe pleaded.

"He is mad."

"This may be our only hope!"

"He will destroy us all!"

"Lunacy!"

"LISTEN TO ME!" Philippe's eyes and hands flashed red.

A pulsing surge of energy coursed through Philippe's body, a tangible force that crackled in the air with every breath he took. His life force—his Qi—glowed faintly beneath his skin, a soft light that radiated from his core. With a deep, controlled inhale, Philippe gathered the energy into his hands, the power thrumming like a heartbeat between his fingers. When he slammed them together, the resulting shockwave reverberated through the room, shaking the very foundations of the castle. In an instant, the chaotic whispers fell silent, the air thick with the lingering resonance of Philippe's power.

"…You will talk *to* me."

Philippe's eyes and hands returned back to normal, and the energy in the room dissipated. Suddenly, a cloaked figure with an unfamiliar symbol on his chest appeared on the staircase to Philippe's left. Illuminated only by the incandescent glimmer of the red in his eyes that pulsated down through his chest to his glowing red hands, the warlock on the stairs stood firm and ready. Then another appeared, floating just off the ground, to Philippe's right. Philippe turned and saw two more cloaked figures hovering behind him, their eyes and hands glowing red like the other two. Philippe was neither alarmed nor afraid. His arrogance would never allow it.

"Will we fight amongst ourselves now?" Philippe asked, knowing at these odds, it wouldn't be much of a fight. "Are the witches not sufficient enough killers that we must help them with their task?..."

"Vampires? Werewolves?"

Philippe turned to find a fifth cloaked figure standing in front of him. The figure tore back his hood to reveal an older man, possibly in his late seventies.

"This is the hope you offer us?!" The Old Man asked with a bitter tongue as the other four cloaked figures floated around Philippe, ready to strike.

Philippe knew this was his only chance to make his case and perhaps save his own life.

"Vampires are strong and powerful warriors, and, as you know, their toxin is poisonous to our kind. Lycans - they don't like the term werewolf - are essential because of their speed and tracking ability. Especially the alphas, who, after all, are the only Malafecs who can smell a witch." Philippe stated with a calm that did not befit the moment. "They are perfect soldiers, and unlike us, they have proven very difficult to kill. We must put aside our differences and work with them. It is the only way. We cannot do this alone."

"And why would they help us?!" The Old Man asked.

"As fourth century Sanskrit would tell us: The enemy of my enemy is my friend,--"

"WITCHES ARE NOT OUR ENEMY!" The Old Man yelled.

"THEY'RE KILLING US!" Philippe yelled back.

The energy between the four men surrounding Philippe intensified as The Old Man's eyes and hands flashed red.

"...I'm sorry." Philippe exhaled as he tried to curtail his temper.

He bowed his head in a show of respect, hoping those would not be his last words. The Old Man's hands faded to normal while his eyes still pulsated red. The four others remained vigilant as they floated around Philippe.

"Forgive me, but do you really believe we are the only ones who suffer from this onslaught? Witches are a threat to us all."

With great fervor, Philippe paced through the confined area as he preached, seemingly to himself, ignoring the imminent danger around him.

"They do not discriminate in their hatred." Philippe continued, "They are pure evil, and if we do not join together and destroy them, they will kill every living creature on this planet."

"Destroy witches, and we destroy ourselves!"

"No. We only need to destroy the ones who have come of age," Philippe stopped pacing and faced The Old Man. "They cannot be controlled. The younglings, however, can be cultivated and bred safely, then quietly disposed of before the madness sets in. I would suggest directly after they've given birth when they are at their weakest,--"

"Do you know what you are asking?!"

The Old Man seemed appalled at the request. Philippe understood that it wasn't necessarily the request that angered The Old Man, but more so, the requestor.

"I'm asking for this Council's permission to stop the eradication of our species."

The Old Man glared at Philippe, his eyes gleaming red. Philippe stared back, obstinate of any intimidation, waiting for a response. He knew The Council did not want to agree with him, but after a few intense moments, it seemed they no longer wished to kill him either. One by one, the four cloaked men disappeared into the darkness.

The Old Man clenched his teeth as the red slowly faded from his eyes, though the abhorrence he held for Philippe was still evident as he stepped backward into the darkness and disappeared.

* * *

Philippe sat alone outside of the castle, waiting for The Council's decree. Hours had passed before David exited the castle with their decision. Philippe rose to meet him.

"Well?" Philippe asked, the arrogance ever present in his voice. "What is their decision?"

"…You seem to have earned the blessing of The Council," David sighed.

"Ha! I knew they'd,--"

"But," David interrupted, "they will not authorize killings under the age of twenty-one."

Philippe exhaled his displeasure, which David duly noted.

"They have daughters, Philippe," David said. "And we do not know for sure at what age this so-called sickness takes hold. No killings under twenty-one."

"Very well. If that is their wish," Philippe sighed and shook his head. "I would only ask that they have emissaries sent in every direction detailing my plan. Make them know of my coming and how they must view their daughters and wives from this point forward. Tell them of Galen and what will surely happen to them if they do not. The older these witches get, the more crazed and powerful they become."

David nodded. "I will see to it."

Relief washed over Philippe like a long-awaited reprieve, loosening the tight grip of tension that had coiled within him. Unable to suppress the triumphant smile that broke across his face,

10

he stepped forward and embraced David. The gesture, though brief, carried the weight of their shared history and the burdens they both bore. For the first time that night, the gravity of the moment seemed to lift, if only for a fleeting second, as Philippe allowed himself to savor the victory.

"Thank you, my friend. For everything," Philippe said.

"You needn't thank me. I did nothing to,--"

Philippe pushed back the sleeve of David's right arm, revealing the same symbol as the one embroidered on the cloaks, newly branded onto his forearm. Two crescent moons, just touching each other - waxing on the left, waning on the right - superimposed over a full moon, with the four pointy tips of the crescents extruding from the circumference. A black snake, formed in the shape of a 'W' - head on the left, tail on the right - intertwined through the two crescents: This was the symbol of The Council.

"Thank you," Philippe repeated with a nod.

David snatched away his arm and yanked his sleeve down as he glared at Philippe. He was none too happy with Philippe's discovery and perhaps at what he, himself, had done.

"I don't know that I deserve thanks," David said with a certain bitterness. "I stood up for you this night, 'old friend,' but if you're wrong and all witches do not turn evil, I will be responsible for the unjust oppression of an entire species!"

"No, my friend. I will," Philippe said.

He knew what David had done, and he did not wish him to suffer because of it. He embraced David one last time, then turned and walked into the forest.

"Where will you go first?" David asked.

"To Castlerigg, of course," Philippe said without stopping. "To pay my respects to Galen… and his bride."

CHAPTER 2

1723 - Louisiana Territory – 30 years later

Philippe moved cautiously through the bayou, each step sinking slightly into the muck beneath him. The air was thick with decay—the pungent stench of rotting vegetation and methane rising from the stagnant waters clung to his senses like a suffocating blanket. Above the murky gloom, the croaking of green tree frogs mingled with the shrill cries of screech owls, their cacophony forming a haunting, unrelenting soundtrack that nearly drowned out the oppressive silence of the swamp.

Philippe halted abruptly, his senses on high alert. Beneath the incessant clicking of the cicadas, there it was again—a faint voice, barely discernible over the natural chorus of the bayou. He spun around, his eyes scanning the thick, mist-laden underbrush for any sign of movement. But the swamp was still, a shadowy expanse of twisted roots and hanging moss, offering no clues to the eerie sound that had reached his ears.

Philippe pressed on, his footsteps careful against the soft, yielding earth, when suddenly he froze. A sound—deep, resonant, unmistakably deliberate—cut through the bayou's dense atmosphere. Boom. It reverberated through the air, shaking the very ground beneath his feet as if something immense had shifted in the dark depths of the swamp. It pounded the earth, and the bayou became silent. Philippe remained still. Then, another was heard. Boom! This one louder - closer than before. Boom! Boom! The pace quickened as leaves quivered and the ground shook. BOOM! BOOM!

Before Philippe could react, a hulking figure exploded from the dense foliage, its naked, grotesque form barreling into him with the force of a battering ram. The impact drove him hard to the ground; the air knocked from his lungs as his back slammed against the cold, damp earth. The creature's immense weight pinned him, and its claws, jagged and dripping with filth, pierced through Philippe's shoulders like hot knives, pinning him mercilessly to the earth. The searing pain shot through his body as the creature's talons sliced through muscle and bone, anchoring him in place with a terrifying finality. A guttural scream tore from Philippe's throat as white-hot pain surged through his body, but the creature would show him no mercy. Its eyes, glowing with a malevolent crimson light, bored into his own as it loomed over him. Saliva dripped from its jagged, yellowed teeth, splattering onto Philippe's face in thick, warm droplets, the sickly sweet stench of decay clinging to every breath. A soft, purring growl came from deep within its throat. Then it struck.

"AAHHHH!" Philippe screamed as he woke from his dream, disoriented and wet with sweat.

His heart raced, his breathing - heavy and labored. He frantically clutched at his shoulders, relieved to find no wounds. He exhaled and tried to gather himself until he noticed Vincent, Tomas, and three others around the campfire staring at him.

"She was in your dream?" Tomas asked.

Philippe didn't answer, but he didn't have to. His eyes could no longer hide the truth. For nearly three weeks, he had been tormented by the dreams and voices. He suspected they all had, but he was their leader; he needed to appear strong, unfazed by the mental assault, but she was unrelenting and so much more powerful than any witch they had come across in this crusade.

"I have heard her tauntings as well," Vincent grunted.

"We must end this, my friends. Tonight," Tomas said, ever so softly, through a misplaced smile on his face. "For I fear none of us will live to see the morrow if we do not."

"We are tired, Tomas, and our numbers have been depleted," Philippe said. "We need time and more men to fight this one."

"What number of men can save us from our dreams?"

Tomas' words were met with silence. What could anyone possibly say to that?

With no answer, Philippe resigned and solemnly nodded at Vincent, and it began. Vincent raised his nose and sniffed twice. He hesitated a moment, scanned the area, then closed his eyes as his nose flared and sniffed again. A long, deliberate inhale, his nostrils twitched feverishly as he took in all the scents around him. The moss on the north side of the trees, the mahogany embers of the crackling fire, a jackrabbit eight hundred yards away, just east of them — and her.

"She's near," Vincent said as he opened his eyes. "Come."

Philippe and Tomas exchanged a weary glance before standing to follow Vincent, the three beta lycans trailing silently behind them. They pushed deeper into the bayou, the thick humidity of the swamp clinging to their skin while the ground beneath them grew more treacherous with each step. The darkness felt alive, thick, and suffocating, as if the bayou itself was conspiring to hinder their every move.

As evidenced by the many lines on his face and the not-so-subtle gray in his hair, this quest had taken its toll upon Philippe. Although Tomas and Vincent had not aged physically, the mental strain was more than apparent in their eyes. Thirty years ago, a secret war began the night a lone warlock, a vampire, and an alpha lycan set aside their differences and walked into the woods west of Castlerigg to do battle with a witch - Elvira of Keswick. The twenty-two-year-old proved to be more than a worthy adversary for them. In a matter of minutes, she'd broken Vincent's arm in two places and nearly ripped Tomas to shreds before the three of them could regroup to vanquish her. An older, more experienced witch would have easily killed them.

They had learned invaluable lessons from that first brutal encounter. Chief among them was the sobering realization that survival in this war would require far more than just the three of them. To stand a chance against the witches, they needed soldiers who could fight on the so-called 'front lines' while they executed their more intricate maneuvers. So, they began to 'recruit' humans. Fortunately, there was an abundance of these involuntary volunteers. Over the years, Vincent sired more than a hundred humans into beta lycans, each bred for one purpose: to lead a relentless charge against the enemy. These ferocious attacks were essential to occupy the witches and buy time. Philippe, meanwhile, wielded his magic to counter that of the witches, using every ounce of his power to hold them at bay until Tomas or one of the other vampires, whom he had 'turned' throughout the years, could close in and deliver the fatal strike of venom into the witch's blood. It was a risky, brutal strategy, but it worked—and it worked well.

They soon discovered that defeating an average witch required not just brute force but a precise combination of power: a warlock, an alpha lycan to track them, two or three betas, and a vampire. The betas, as the first wave of attack, suffered the highest casualties, but Vincent could replace them with relative ease, 'turning' random humans to fill their ranks. Vampires, however, were an entirely different matter. While their numbers were not in short supply, finding one who could be relied upon in the heat of battle was a challenge of its own. After all, everyone knows they cannot be trusted.

For ten years, they crisscrossed Europe and Asia, moving from town to town, vanquishing rogue witches. Then, one night in 1701, in the Black Forest just outside of Freiburg, Germany, they confronted a witch who was so much more than average. At night, it was said, she would sneak into the outlying villages to steal babies from their cribs and eat them for supper. She would use candies and cakes to lure young children into the forest, who were never seen or heard from again, and she would kill anyone who tried to stop her. She was **Brun-Hilda: The Evil One** - known throughout modern warlock lore as one of the five most powerful witches in history, or one of **The Five Great Ones** as they are known today. Not once in the nearly ten years of this still very young war had Philippe and his men encountered anyone like her.

Believed to be around forty-seven years old, she had an ethereal, almost ghost-like appearance, and her tenuous stature led them to underestimate her. That mistake nearly ended their quest. She was twice as fast as any witch they had encountered. She destroyed four betas and a vampire, took Vincent's arm off at the shoulder, and nearly ripped Tomas' heart out of his chest before Philippe got off a single blast.

He quickly understood that her blinding speed was not a natural gift but a product of her mastery over an ancient ability called **Moo-Tone-Wah** - the power to move within the refraction of light. She bent the very laws of nature, her form flickering faster than the eye could follow. Had Philippe not been the strongest of his kind, that encounter would have been his last. Death had brushed against him that day, but by sheer force of will and a tiny bit of luck, he, Tomas, and Vincent managed to escape with their lives. The battle had left them battered and broken, and it took weeks for their bodies to heal and regenerate from the nearly fatal injuries they had sustained. That night proved that this war of theirs was far from over. They needed to recruit more soldiers and build a force strong enough to battle a witch as skilled as this one. So they did.

Five months later, in the winter of 1701, beneath a full moon that bathed the north reaches of the Black Forest in a cold, silvery glow, they lured The Evil One into a clearing and cornered her. With the betas in their ferocious full-lycan form and no shadows for her to move within, they attacked - eleven against one. Even with overwhelming odds against her, she held them off with savage fury for nearly a full minute before she was slaughtered. They say more than half of the ninety-six lives she had claimed during her reign were children under the age of ten.

Twelve years had passed, and hundreds of rogue witches had fallen beneath Philippe and his legion. They were relentless in their mission and driven by a singular purpose: to eradicate all adult witches – all the ones the warlocks could not control. In 1713, they traveled to the Americas and continued their quest in the place where most believe it began – Salem, Massachusetts. It was here they confronted another who would later be labeled as one of The Five Great Ones – **Tituba: The Wicked One**. Born in Venezuela around 1660, Tituba had been a South American Indian slave and, ironically, was the only true witch involved in the infamous trials. She actually confessed to witchcraft, but in reality, it was all part of her ploy. Her greatest talent lay in her ability to manipulate the minds of others, bending their will to her own. Using her powers, she cast a spell on her accusers, tricking them into setting her free.

Not long after her release, the true horror of Tituba's deceit unfolded. She pointed her finger at thirty-seven other women, accusing them of witchcraft, and her word was accepted without question. These women—innocent in every way—were executed swiftly, their lives claimed by the fear and hysteria she had manipulated. After her accusations led to the deaths of those women, Tituba disappeared, vanishing from the public eye for nearly twenty years. Her legend grew in the shadows until Philippe and his crusaders finally located her in Boston, where she used her mind tricks to create chaos and anarchy. A riot broke out near Boston Common, causing Philippe's men, along with two hundred humans, to fight amongst each other. History remembers this as the Boston Bread Riot of 1713, but in actuality, Tituba had caused the riotous ruckus in an attempt to escape. The scene was chaos incarnate, with brother turning on brother and blood soaking the streets. It wasn't until Philippe and Tomas cornered her in a warehouse near the docks that they finally ended her reign of terror. But by then, her tally of death had climbed to seventy-two, that we know of, each life a testament to the sinister power she possessed.

In the thirty years since their crusade began, Philippe and his band of hunters had brought down over one thousand rogue witches across the globe. They had fought and bled across continents, slowly dismantling the evil they claimed threatened all humanity. Tonight, there was but one more - and she knew they were coming. Kingsley, Leon, and Andre, the latest betas sired by Vincent, followed closely behind him, their youthful energy bubbling beneath the surface. They were oblivious to the true danger that awaited them, too excited by the thrill of the hunt to understand the gravity of what lay ahead. Even though they couldn't shift into their lycan forms, they were eager to engage in battle, their confidence a mere mask for their ignorance.

Together, they trudged through the thick, cloying muck of the bayou, each step heavier than the last, until they heard the sound—a cackle that would send chills through even the most hardened of warriors. A cackle, sharp and eerie, echoed through the trees and reverberated through the still air. It was the unmistakable cackle of the only witch in history who could stop six inhuman warriors in their tracks. She was the last and, by far, the most powerful of her kind believed to be well over one hundred years old and responsible for ending nearly one thousand lives and, after tonight, perhaps six more. Her laughter seemed to come from everywhere and nowhere at the same time, slithering through the night like a predator. It was the laugh of the monster who scared other monsters. **Hagatha: The Old One**.

"There," Vincent said, pointing to the entrance of a cave.

A soft breeze exhaled from the opening, and a light deep within faded. The torches they carried extinguished, leaving them in darkness. Philippe raised his hand and magically relit them.

"All who enter here shall die," Hagatha or someone's voice was heard.

Then, an evil laugh bounced off the wind and echoed through the darkness.

"We should wait for the full moon when we are at our strongest," Vincent said. "My betas cannot change."

"No! She will disappear, and our torment will continue! We must strike now and end this while we have the chance," Tomas implored.

"Then let's go. What's the problem here?" Kingsley asked.

"There are many," said Philippe. "One is this cave, my young friend."

"Yeah, what about it?"

"We are in the flatlands. There are no caves here."

"…Well, there is now, isn't there?" Kingsley said with a smile.

To Philippe, there was nothing to smile about. He alone knew what awaited them inside.

Kingsley entered the cave. The rest followed, letting the cruel laughter guide them.

"She's near. I can feel her. Can you feel her?" Kingsley asked Vincent.

He took one step further, and as his foot descended on a small branch, thorn-like needles shot from the cave wall, hitting Tomas on the neck and face. Philippe raised his hand, stopping the rest of the needles in midair, then waved them to the ground. Though he was out of range, Vincent roared as if he were in pain, then collapsed to the ground. Philippe rushed to his side.

"No! Not me! KINGSLEY!" Vincent roared.

Philippe knew what he meant. Alphas empathically experienced the exact pain of their betas at death. Vincent rose and ran to Kingsley, whose back was turned to them. His entire left side was covered with thorns. Blood spilled from his wounds as Hagatha laughed. Kingsley turned and faced Vincent.

"You said... I would live... f-forever..." Kingsley murmured as he coughed up blood.

He fell to the ground and convulsed. Vincent dropped to his knees in agony as he watched his beta take his last breath. Philippe could feel the group's resolve weaken.

"Tomas?" Philippe asked, concerned.

"I am fine," Tomas said as he flicked off the thorns. "Silver."

Vincent howled from anger but was silenced as the ground began to shake.

"Earthquake?" Tomas asked.

"No. It's her," Philippe said.

The ground-shattering footsteps quickened. Vincent sniffed. He turned to see a pair of red eyes in the darkness behind his second beta.

"ANDRE!" Vincent screamed.

Andre turned, and the figure vomited bright green acid onto his face. Both he and Vincent screamed, but Andre soon went silent. Leon leapt at the figure, but it was gone - vanished into the shadows. The green vomit melted Andre's face into a dripping mass, making it impossible to breathe. He squirmed and died a slow, painful death by suffocation. Hagatha again laughed as a breeze once again doused the torches.

"Philippe!" Tomas shouted.

With a sharp clap of his hands, the cave blazed to life, revealing the depths of Hagatha's lair. Philippe's heart pounded as he realized she was there. She had been there all along. She was the embodiment of every human nightmare and the dark monster who had invaded his dreams. Towering just over six feet tall, she was an ogre-like figure, her skin a sickly green that seemed to pulsate in the flickering light. Razor-sharp talons extended from her gnarled fingers, and her matted white hair floated around her like the tendrils of some ghostly creature, moving of its own accord. Thick, viscous mucus oozed from her jagged, rotting teeth, and her eyes—flaming red orbs of malice— pierced straight through to Philippe's very soul.

She stood motionless behind Tomas, and before anyone could breathe, she lunged and bit a chunk from Tomas' shoulder. Tomas screamed as blood erupted from the wound. Vincent charged, but Hagatha, with a thought, repelled him into the wall with bone- shattering force. Philippe's eyes blazed red with fury, but the cave was far too unstable for him to unleash his full power. Instead, he gestured sharply with his hands, sending a wave of kinetic energy that knocked Hagatha away from Tomas. The force of her impact shook the cave, her massive form crashing into the wall and sending cracks splintering through the stone. Tomas fell limp to the ground, his blood pooling beneath him.

Philippe again thrust his hand forward, hurling a large stone toward her. Extremely agile for someone her size, she avoided the stone as it smashed into the cave wall. She menacingly hissed at them, then pounced onto the wall and clung to it. Like a monstrous spider, she scuttled up to the ceiling, her long limbs clinging effortlessly to the jagged rocks above. Her head swiveled grotesquely, twisting around with inhuman flexibility before she spat a stream of acidic venom down upon them. Philippe reacted in an instant, inhaling deeply before exhaling a cold mist that froze the deadly liquid in midair. The acid particles crystallized and shattered harmlessly to the ground.

Leon charged up the right side of the cave to the ceiling as Vincent charged up the left. Hagatha turned her venomous breath into a searing inferno, blowing flames in Leon's path. Leon ran directly into the fire, his body engulfed in flames as he let out a terrible scream. He burst into flames and fell to the ground. Vincent screamed from the pain of his beta, but he did not slow down. The alpha morphed into his lycan form and leapt, sinking his nails deep into her back. She screamed as they crashed to the ground and engaged in a vicious grappling bout. For pure fighting skills, there is none better than an alpha wolf, but the witch matched him blow for blow. Still, on her stomach, Hagatha's head spindled one hundred and eighty degrees, and spit her acidic vomit into Vincent's face. She then hurled his limp body at Philippe, who flung up his hand, stopping Vincent inches away from impact. Philippe looked into Vincent's eyes, the pain and suffering etched deeply in them. The slow melting of his once-fearless friend's face was more than he could bear. With a heavy heart and a gesture of his hand, Philippe ended Vincent's misery in a flash of combustion. The alpha 'Lycan's body turned to ash and smoke, then curled up into the loft of the cave.

As the smoke dissipated, Hagatha was revealed. She stood there, wounded, dripping blood, and angry. She stabbed Philippe's torso with her nails and pulled him closer, opening her mouth to spit.

"Consuendi oris eius!" Philippe incanted.

Thread and an invisible needle sewed Hagatha's mouth closed and trapped her acidic vomit within. She launched Philippe to the other side of the cave, bouncing him off the wall. Philippe spit up blood as he tried to stand but could not. Hagatha ripped the stitches from her bleeding lips, and a few teeth fell out as she opened her mouth. Enraged, her scream built into a piercing crescendo that threatened to topple the cave.

"Hold on," Philippe thought to himself. *"Just… a little… longer…"*

Hagatha aimed at Philippe, and her breath again turned to fire. Unable to stand, Philippe raised his hand, creating a force field that protected him. As the flames dissipated, he used the last of his mental strength to hurl loose rock and rubble at her. She deflected it with ease, then charged to finish him. Tomas, covered in his own blood, rose up from behind her and tackled her to the ground. He sank his teeth into her shoulder at the base of the neck and released his deadly toxin into her body. Philippe could not move. His body felt empty. He watched helplessly as she grappled with Tomas to the very end. His last thoughts were of his legacy and witches.

"I hope… my sacrifice… was enough… That I did not fight this war… in vain."

His breaths grew further and further apart as he stared at Hagatha's monstrous body.

"When they are young,… they are so innocent,… so pure,… so… beautiful! But this,… THIS is who they truly are-e-e-e….

CHAPTER 3

May 1994 - Morgan City, Louisiana

Fifteen-year-old Camille St. Croix sat perched on the large, weathered rocks just off the shore at Lake End Park. Her gaze was distant, lost in the rhythmic ripple of the water as it lapped gently against the beach. At five foot seven, with long, cascading brown curls and piercing green eyes, Camille possessed an ethereal beauty, a rare and almost unsettling allure that seemed far beyond her years. Clad in a sleeveless, pixie-printed floral sundress, she looked more like a model from a high-fashion photoshoot than a teenager wrestling with thoughts that often left her feeling like an outsider. It was a feeling she knew well—being alone in a world that never quite seemed to fit.

As she let the sound of the water calm her restless mind, something curious happened. Several droplets of water leapt up from the lake, twisting and folding into one another as they hovered just above the surface. Mesmerized but not alarmed, Camille watched as the droplets fused together, forming a larger orb that glided gracefully through the air toward her. It twisted and morphed as if sculpted by invisible hands. Camille smiled, amused but unsurprised by the display of magic. She had seen strange things before—strange things she herself could do. The orb floated closer, taking the shape of a heart, perfectly formed, no larger than a silver dollar.

She leaned in, her curiosity piqued as she watched the water pulse through the heart-shaped droplet, almost as if it were alive, beating softly before her eyes. Giggling, she reached out and gently touched it with her index finger. In an instant, it crystallized, shimmering in the afternoon light. She glanced around, expecting to see her father—the only person she knew who could summon such magic. But instead, she found herself staring at a stranger.

Standing just beyond the shore was Julien Dumont Gerard, a striking figure who looked almost too perfect to be real. He was the spitting image of his great-great-great-grandfather Philippe, though Camille did not yet know that. Her breath caught as the tall stranger strode toward her with a confidence that seemed both regal and otherworldly. His white dress shirt, buttoned just below his neck, fit him perfectly, tucked neatly into coal-blue suit pants that complemented his lean frame. His jet-black hair, long and wild, seemed to float around his head as if they, too, were alive, moving with an energy all its own.

Camille didn't know what to think. She had never seen anyone like him before, not even her father. In her mind, he was as close to perfection as a man could be, so striking that she found herself unable to move. Paralyzed by the intensity of the moment, all she could do was stare into his eyes—eyes that glowed with an unnerving, crimson light. To anyone else, the sight of those burning red eyes might have been terrifying, but to Camille, they were nothing short of beautiful.

She had always known she was different. Growing up in the sparsely populated north end of Morgan City, she had realized at a young age that she was not like other children. Her father had often told her she was special and gifted but that her abilities were a secret no one else could know. He had promised that one day, when she was older, he would teach her how to control her magic. But for now, she was forbidden from using it. Of course, being a child, she couldn't resist. Every chance she got, she found hidden places to practice, honing her skills in secret. And by her own account, she was getting good.

But what she saw before her now—this display of magic—was beyond anything she could do. The deftness with which this handsome stranger wielded his power was extraordinary, far beyond her own abilities. She had almost forgotten about the crystalline heart floating beside her, lost as she was in the depth of his gaze—those glowing, blood-red eyes that seemed to draw her in deeper with every second. He, however, was focused on something else entirely. Kneeling beside her, Julien continued his work with careful precision, crafting his creation with the skill of a master. His presence was commanding, yet his touch was gentle, as if the very air around him bent to his will.

"It's very beauti…,--" Camille started.

"Wait. It's not finished yet," he interrupted. With a quick gesture, he pulled a pocketknife out of thin air and made a small incision on the palm of his hand.

"NO! What are you,--"

"Shhh. It's okay." He smiled.

They locked eyes for a quick moment, and somehow, she knew it would be. He tossed the knife into the air, and it vanished. He grabbed the floating heart with his cut hand and squeezed it hard as he whispered a few words of Latin into his palm. He opened his hand as his eyes faded to their natural cobalt blue color, and a vibrant red crystal heart emerged, hovering above his palm. She squinted and saw what appeared to be an illusion, but when she focused her eyes, she could see the water and blood still churning inside the heart – The Blood Heart. He had given it life.

"What do you think?" He asked.

"…It's the most beautiful thing I've ever seen."

"Then it's yours. If you want it."

Camille stared as deep into his eyes as she could without falling in.

"You're giving me your heart?" She asked.

Julien smiled. She fell in. She reached for the heart, and Julien stopped her.

"Whoa. Easy now," he said. "A heart's a fragile thing. Gotta be careful with it. Give it lots of love, or it'll break."

She nodded and cupped the beating heart in both hands and pulled it close to her chest.

"I'm Julien, by the way." He said as he extended his hand. "But my friends call me JD."

Camille stared at Julien's outstretched hand, her heart pounding in her chest. It felt as though time itself had slowed, stretching the moment into an eternity. For so long—too long—she had lain awake at night, haunted by the feeling of isolation, yearning for someone, anyone, who understood what it was like to be her. Her father was the only other person in her world who shared her gift, and even that bond had its limits. She had always hoped, dreamed, of finding a kindred spirit—someone who was like her in ways that went beyond blood. And now, here he was.

Her breath hitched as her eyes lingered on his hand, the offer of connection both thrilling and terrifying. A slight tremble ran through her fingers as she lifted her own hand to meet his, the weight of the moment pressing down on her. But there was no going back now. Summoning every ounce of courage she possessed, Camille extended her hand and, without a second's hesitation, grasped his firmly. She squeezed his hand with everything she had, her grip strong, filled with a mixture of desperation and determination.

Julien's reaction was immediate and unmistakable. His eyes widened in shock, and he gasped, caught off guard by the sheer power that surged through her touch. The air between them crackled with energy, an undeniable force that passed from her to him. His eyes flared, igniting with an intense, glowing red, the flames of his power flaring to life as if in response to hers. For a brief moment, the world around them seemed to disappear, and it was just the two of them, connected by something far greater than either of them could have anticipated.

Camille's breath caught in her throat as she felt the shift. Without thinking, she blinked, and when her eyes opened, they, too, had turned a vivid, burning red, mirroring his. It was as if a door had opened within her, unlocking something that had always been there but had never been fully realized—until now.

"I'm Camille," she said with pride.

Today, her dreams had been answered.

CHAPTER 4

Even in a crowded courtyard, he always knew exactly where she was.

November 1994 – New Orleans, Louisiana

Six months later, a now sixteen-year-old Camille sat in the grand courtyard of the Cabrini Girls' Catholic High School, blindly caressing the Blood Heart, now hanging from a gold chain around her neck. She was amused by her overly hormonal counterparts as they engaged in their rudimentary after-school rituals. She loved it here. New Orleans was so much more exciting than Morgan City. So many more people. So many more opportunities to, perhaps, find another girl like her.

She waved at an acquaintance who passed by. The girl awkwardly waved back, trying her best not to stare but failing miserably. Perhaps the stares and whispers should have bothered Camille like they would any other teenage girl, but Camille was far from the average teenage girl. In normal circumstances, she could have easily been the most popular girl in school, not that it would have mattered to her. It was enough for her to be here, living and socializing amongst all these people. She loved people, and the magnetic buzz of their energy was a rush,… or maybe it was something more.

She smiled when her bodyguard entered the courtyard. A tall, brooding man, imposing not so much in stature as in disposition. He had an eerie severity in his eyes that caused an unsettling fear in those upon whom his glare was cast. Most would not dare hold his gaze for more than a few seconds. Camille, however, was not one of them.

"Tirin!" Camille called out unnecessarily.

Even in a crowded courtyard, he always knew exactly where she was.

"Let's go. I'm hungry," he said.

"What else is new?" Camille replied as Tirin scanned the courtyard. "You know it's okay to smile every now and then, right? It wouldn't kill you. Or would it?" Camille joked.

She knew he'd never engage in this type of banter, but teasing him never got old, and every once in a while, she would swear she caught the slightest hint of a smile.

"You go ahead. I have a meeting with my advisor. Grab yourself something to eat, and I'll meet you at the office in an hour."

He looked at her, and the meaning was clear: 'I don't like that plan.'

"It's okay, T. I'll be fine. You don't have to wait. Besides, you scare my friends."

Tirin released a soft, sustained sigh, which came off like a low growl. This was normal conversation between these two. He glared at her in a way most might find disturbing until she playfully matched his intensity and glared back. He sighed/growled again and turned and left.

"Oh, and grab me something, too, please!" She called out. He, of course, did not respond. "Thank you!" She laughed.

Camille placed her hand on her almost unnoticeable stomach protrusion and smiled. She looked around to see if anyone was watching, then, with a thought, moved the branch of the tree next to her ever so slightly to give her more shade.

* * *

"Camille, understand that I simply want what's best for you," Ms. Mayes said.

Camille sat across from her advisor in the counseling office. Her enthusiasm slightly hindered by the present conversation.

"I know that, Ms. Mayes, but I'm allowed to stay in school for at least another 12 weeks."

"I'd be remiss if I did not make you fully aware of the sacrifices that await you," Ms. Mayes said in her habitually proper-by-example method of address.

"I totally understand," Camille replied.

"Have you spoken to your legal guardian, Mr. Gerard, about this yet?"

"Yes, Ma'am, and both Mr. Gerard and his son Julien are extremely supportive of my decision to keep the baby."

"What about the father?"

"We spoke to the Gerards together, and it went very well."

"And your aspirations to become a doctor? You're an outstanding student, Camille, but you should know that seventy percent of all women who become pregnant in high school never continue on to any form of higher education."

"Was this something she looked up in preparation for this specific meeting," Camille wondered.

Or, perhaps it was just embedded in her counseling brain, along with a myriad of other statistical data on troubled teens.

"Yes, ma'am, I know, but the Gerards are behind me one hundred percent. I'm going to be homeschooled through graduation. By that time, my baby will be old enough for me to attend Tulane, which has an awesome medical school, and it's only thirty minutes away."

Ms. Mayes' eyebrows flexed, more from concern than disapproval.

"I've thought this through," Camille said. "I have, Ms. Mayes."

It wasn't Camille herself who truly unsettled Ms. Mayes in this situation—it was the man. Not a boy, but a man. There was a difference, and it was that difference that gnawed at her, leaving her uneasy. In Louisiana, the law was clear: a sixteen-year-old could marry with parental consent, and from what she could gather, the Gerards were perfectly fine with the arrangement. That technicality left Ms. Mayes with little recourse, and yet, the discomfort persisted.

Camille had never explicitly said that he was older, but Ms. Mayes could tell. The way the girl deftly dodged direct questions about him, the subtle hesitations in her voice, the careful wording—all of it pointed to one truth. This man, whoever he was, was older. How much older, Ms. Mayes couldn't say, but it was clear from the way Camille danced around the subject that the age gap was significant enough to raise alarms. And yet, Camille seemed calm, unbothered, as though she didn't fully grasp—or care about—the implications of her situation.

There was a maturity there, a sense of certainty in her words that was unusual for a girl her age. It was as though Camille was already operating on a level far beyond her peers, something Ms. Mayes couldn't quite put her finger on but recognized instinctively. This wasn't the typical infatuation of a teenage girl with an older man— this was something else entirely, something deeper, more calculated. And it made Ms. Mayes feel powerless.

"And the father? How does our mystery *man* feel about all this?" Ms. Mayes asked as she crossed her arms and leaned back in her chair.

It wasn't at all difficult for Camille to pick up on the attitude that Ms. Mayes wasn't really trying to hide. She knew Ms. Mayes truly cared about her and had nothing but her best interests at heart.

"He's not a mystery, Ms. Mayes," Camille said as she toyed with the Blood Heart dangling from her neck. "The choice to keep him a secret is mine, not his. He completely supports my wish to continue my education, and I know he's going to be an amazing dad. It seems like I've known him all my life. We're very much in love, and I assure you, we plan on spending the rest of our lives together."

"So, I guess this is it then, hmm?" asked Ms. Mayes.

"No, Ma'am. It's just the beginning," Camille said.

CHAPTER 5

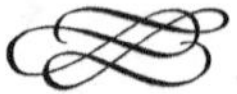

"*...I can't take away the pain.*"

Julien exited the elevator, looking every bit the executive that he was. Less than a year ago, the 21-year-old had taken over the family business, and despite the naysayers, the young prodigy was doing extraordinarily well.

"Afternoon, Mr. Gerard - I mean JD," said Serena, Julien's twenty-four-year-old Executive Assistant, as she pushed up her oversized glasses that were doing their best to try and hide the befuddled face behind them.

She lowered her head with a sheepish grin stuck on her face.

"Afternoon, Serena."

She plopped a stack of files on the counter between them that instantly changed Julien's disposition.

"I was told to tell you this all needs to get sorted out by 4:00 p.m."

Julien sighed as he opened a single file, then grimaced at the contents displayed in it.

"Really? Are you and I the only ones who work here?" He asked, shaking his head. Serena was well prepared to answer his question before his boyish grin stopped her.

"You don't have to answer that." He said as he handed the file back to her. "Set up a meeting for next Wednesday with Mr. Robertson and make sure both Ms. Rayna and our lawyer are present."

"Okay."

"And have accounting double-check these numbers. Something's,--" His brow furrowed as he studied the documents again.

"Is something wrong?" Serena asked.

"What is this, 'Malaffections?'" He asked.

"I'm not sure. I think it's some kind of club, maybe?"

"These charges are outrageous," he said. "Who authorized this?"

"Uhm, your…" she hesitated, "your father, I think. Do you want me to,--"

"No," Julien said. "I'll handle it." He closed the folder and shoved it under his arm as he turned toward his office.

"Uh, sir?" Serena asked.

He turned back to her and followed her eyes down to the last three remaining files. He grimaced again as he moved to address them.

"…Done…Done…Done," Julien said as he signed off on the last three files. "And make sure Ms. Rayna looks at all these before you send them out."

"Oh, yes. Right."

"Is Tirin here with my wife?"

"No, sir, not yet."

"Serena, seriously. I'm trying to create a more relaxed atmosphere around here, so just call me JD. Please?" He smiled. "If you do it, others will too."

"Okay... JD. Got it." Serena replied as she tried, unsuccessfully, to relax.

"My father still around?"

"Upstairs in his office with Mr. Cecil."

"Have them come down, please. I need to talk to them about this document." He said as he moved down the hall toward his office. "And send Tirin and my wife in as soon as they get here."

"Yes, sir." Julien stopped. "I mean Mr. Gerar-- JD... Sorry." She sighed as both her spirit and shoulders dropped.

Julien turned and walked back to his despondent deputy.

"I'm so sorry, I just,--"

"I know," Julien said. "It's a lot to get used to."

And it was. As one of the only humans in the office, Serena enjoyed the unique experience of being a minority - unique for her, anyway. Until eighteen months ago, the brown-eyed LSU graduate was completely unaware of the monsters with whom she shared the world. She knew about the mundane ones: rapists, murderers, pedophiles... ordinary monsters. What no one had prepared her for, what no one *could* have prepared her for, were the not-so-ordinary ones.

* * *

Baton Rouge, Louisiana - LSU campus, *Eighteen Months Earlier.*

Serena stood with her back against the wall in the middle of a dark, deserted alley. Her body contracted through an extended moan that shifted between excruciating pain and overwhelming ecstasy as she both clutched and pushed against the handsome young man she had met earlier in the bar. She was 'Mesmerized,' oblivious to everything around her. Lost in the painful rapture of a Vampire's Kiss.

"Leave now and live to see another night," she thought she heard him say.

She couldn't be sure and, at that particular moment, didn't know if she really cared. It was like she was in a dream. Things were cloudy and muddled, and although she was awake, she couldn't seem to open her eyes or want to.

"Funny, I was gonna say the same thing to you." Another Voice echoed by her.

Though muffled, the voice was familiar—its tone nagging at the edges of her consciousness. She struggled to place it, her mind grasping at the elusive memory, but no matter how hard she tried, she couldn't quite recall to whom it belonged. Then, in an instant, everything shifted. Her body seized, contracting violently as she felt something being extracted from her neck. A sharp twinge of pain followed—subtle at first, like the sting of a spider bite. But with every second that passed, the pain intensified, radiating outward in waves.

For the first time, she became acutely aware of the cold rain pounding against her skin. It seemed to grow louder, almost deafening, as it echoed around her, the droplets exploding on the pavement and bouncing off the metal trash bins that lined the alley. The sound of the rain hitting the metal door at her back reverberated in her bones, a relentless percussion that only added to the chaos unfolding inside her body. She winced with each impact, every sensation heightened as the numbing effects of the mesmerization wore off.

Her breath came in ragged gasps, each one sharper than the last, as the pain from her neck blossomed into something more sinister. With trembling hands, she reached up, her fingers gingerly touching the tender spot where she had been bitten. Her eyes fluttered open, her vision blurred and disoriented, but she strained to focus. Slowly, as the haze lifted, her fingertips brushed against something warm and slick. She pulled her hand away, and her stomach lurched at the sight of blood smeared across her fingers.

"Wha—" she whispered, not yet believing what her eyes were telling her.

As her vision sharpened, the world around her came into horrifying focus. Standing directly in front of her was the handsome young man she had met earlier in the bar, but now, with fresh blood dripping from his lips, his allure had withered into something monstrous. His once-charming smile was twisted into something dark and predatory, and the realization hit her like a tidal wave—her blood was on his mouth.

She tried to speak, her lips parting in a desperate attempt to form words, to demand answers, but nothing came. No sound, no plea, just a hollow gasp as the grim reality of the situation sank in. Her heart raced, the thundering beat growing louder in her chest, drowning out all else as her body began to tremble. What had started as shock quickly morphed into sheer, unrelenting terror. Her muscles tensed, and instinct took over. She screamed—a raw, primal cry— and tried to tear herself free from his grip.

But before she could break away, the man's expression darkened. He hissed, a low, menacing sound that sent chills racing down her spine. His hold on her tightened, his fingers digging into her flesh, restraining her with effortless strength. The pressure intensified, trapping her in place, and her scream grew louder, more frantic, as fear surged through her, overwhelming her senses. Every fiber of her being urged her to escape, but the more she struggled, the tighter his grip became, suffocating her hope with each passing second.

"Serena!" The familiar voice yelled, and although she could not see him, she now recognized the voice to be that of her friend Julien. "Stop screaming, or he will kill you!"

"I *am* gonna kill you," the Vampire said with a smile, feeding off her fear and sending her into another screaming frenzy.

He swung her around and placed her between Julien and himself as he lapped up the blood spilling from her neck.

"JULIEN!--"

"NO, HE'S NOT!" Julien said, trying to reassure her.

"HELP ME! PLEASE!"

"Serena, look at me!"

"SOMEONE HELP!--"

"LOOK AT ME!" Julien ordered, and Serena obeyed.

For the first time, she actually saw Julien. He was standing alone in the middle of the alley, soaking wet from the rain.

"See. It's me... It's just me. Your old buddy, Julien, from the bar." Julien spoke to her in a calm, confident voice that quieted and reassured her. "And I'm not gonna let anything happen to you."

"It's not up to him," the Vampire whispered into her ear.

"Don't listen to him. Just stay with me. Everything's gonna be fine," Julien said as he watched the vampire lap up more of the blood that oozed from her wound. "Okay. You've had enough. You fed, now let her go, and I promise I won't kill you," Julien said to the vampire. "But if she dies, I swear you'll never see another night."

The vampire smirked. "I dun' survived over a hundred years in this territory. Gonna take a lot more than some warlock boy to scare me."

"Wa-Warlock? What,--" Serena began, but Julien raised his hand, interrupting her.

"Ohhh, you didn't know your boyfriend was a warlock? TELL HER!" The Vampire yelled to Julien. "Tell her you a monster, just like me!!"

Julien's eyes overflowed with anger, but the time for lies had passed.

"Let her go," Julien ordered the vampire. "Now."

"Why don't you come over here, real close, and make me?"

Julien's eyes flared a vivid, glowing red as his hands began to emit an eerie, pulsating light. His long, dark hair floated wildly around his shoulders, moving as if caught in an invisible wind. Then, defying gravity, his body rose a few inches off the ground, hovering in the air. Serena, wide-eyed and frozen in shock, could only gasp at the sight. What she would later come to know as Mactrouge, a terrifying transfiguration, was unfolding right before her eyes. Horrified, her scream pierced the air, but the chaos that followed happened so fast that she barely had time to comprehend it.

In an instant, Julien snapped his left hand forward, a small yet powerful energy blast exploding from his palm. The blast struck the bottom of the fire escape beside the vampire, shattering a bolt with pinpoint accuracy. The ladder, now dislodged, came crashing down with brutal force, smashing into the side of the vampire's head. The impact was enough to make him loosen his grip on Serena, sending her tumbling toward the ground.

As she fell, Julien acted quickly. With a swift slicing motion of his right hand, he summoned a force that slid Serena across the alley floor, away from the danger. The invisible wave of energy whisked her out of harm's reach, leaving her breathless and disoriented on the ground.

But the vampire wasn't down for long. He recovered with terrifying speed, his form blurring as he charged straight at Julien. In a desperate attempt to create distance between them, Julien thrust both hands forward, trying to push himself back. His movement alone wouldn't have been enough, but the simultaneous blast of high-powered energy that erupted from his hands turned the tide. The force was immense, disintegrating the vampire in an instant, leaving nothing but ash in its wake.

The blast, however, was too powerful for the narrow alley. The shockwave sent Julien hurtling backward, his body slamming hard against the brick wall behind him. He groaned as the impact knocked the wind from his lungs. The red glow in his eyes flickered briefly, then faded, leaving him weakened. Struggling to his feet, Julien staggered forward, every step unsteady as he made his way over to Serena, the battle was won, but at a cost he hadn't anticipated.

"NO! Get away from me!" She screamed as she scooted backward away from him into the opposite wall.

"Serena,--"

"LEAVE ME ALONE!"

"SERENA!" Julien yelled, silencing her. He dropped to his knees a few feet away from her. "It's just me, the same dorky guy you've been illegally serving beer to for the last few years."

"...What are you?" She asked, sobbing.

"...Your friend," he said.

Serena was petrified. Julien extended his hand, and she flinched. She was pale, and she looked weak. Her wound needed to be closed, and the bleeding stopped.

"Sweetie, you lost a lot of blood. Please. You gotta let me help you."

Serena gave in and tentatively nodded. Julien crawled closer.

"Okay. Now, my eyes are gonna go red again. It's a little scary, I know, but I promise I won't hurt you. Okay?"

Again, she nodded. Julien's eyes flashed red. Serena flinched, then closed her eyes. Julien placed his hand on her neck, and in seconds, the wound closed and disappeared as if it had never existed. Julien quickly faded his eyes back to normal.

"There. You're gonna be okay now," he said.

"It still hurts," Serena said as she opened her eyes and stared at him.

"Yeah. I know. I'm sorry. I can heal the injury, but I can't take away the pain."

She stared at him for a few moments as the tears continued to flow. She tried to rise, but she was dizzy and weak from the loss of blood. Julien caught her as she collapsed and guided her down. Her weight pushed him off his knees to a sitting position. He leaned back against the alley wall and grabbed the back of his head only to find a hand full of blood.

"What happened?! Did he get you too?" Serena asked.

"Naw. I just,… smacked my head up against that wall there. I'm fine."

"You can't heal yourself?"

"Yeah, I just don't wanna scare you no more."

"…It's okay."

"You sure?"

"Yeah." She nodded. "It's a lot of blood."

Julien's eyes flashed red, and he quickly healed himself, then faded them back to normal. This time, Serena watched.

"Come on," Julien said, trying to alleviate the tension. "You still need to go to the hospital." He tried to stand, but he felt lightheaded and plopped back down. "Maybe—maybe we should just rest here for a minute, though," he said as he closed his eyes.

"Am I gonna be a vampire now?" She asked in a panicked, small voice.

Julien tried to hide it but couldn't help smiling a little.

"Naw, Sweetie. It don't work that way. He would've,… had to infuse some of his tainted blood with yours. Which would have killed you, by the way… Day or two later,… you'd rise up from the dead. Then you'd be one. This one here, he just,… drank a little too much, is all. You'll be… you'll be fine."

His speech slowed and was a bit slurred. Something was obviously wrong with him.

"You saved my life. Thank you," Serena said. Julien nodded as Serena continued to stare at him, trying to make sense of it all. "Why? Why would you risk your life for me?"

Julien shrugged. "We're friends. I'd like to think,… you'd've,… done the same for me, if… you… Uhhh. I don't, I don't feel so…"

Julien's body gave way as consciousness slipped from him, his form collapsing heavily onto Serena. For a moment, she stiffened, instinctively recoiling at the sudden weight of him. Her first impulse was to push him away, to free herself from the burden. But as her hands moved, they hesitated. Instead of pulling herself away, she found herself gently shifting him, adjusting his position with a tenderness that surprised even her.

Slowly, carefully, she maneuvered him into a more comfortable spot, cradling his head in her lap. The rain fell steadily around them, its cold drops soaking through her clothes and his, but she barely noticed. The alley, which had moments ago been a battleground, was now silent except for the soft patter of rain and the quiet rise and fall of Julien's shallow breathing.

She sat there, alone in the dim light of the alley, her arms wrapped protectively around his slumped body. The weight of him against her felt both foreign and oddly familiar as if, in this strange, quiet moment, they were bound by something deeper than circumstance. The world around them faded into the background, the rain becoming a steady rhythm that seemed to match the slow, steady beat of her heart. Alone, in the dark, in the rain, Serena held him—unsure of what would come next, but for now, not willing to let go.

* * *

New Orleans - *Eighteen Months Later*

"Gonna take some time, that's all," Julien said. "It's only been eighteen months, but if it's too much for you to handle,--"

"You know I'd never tell anyone about you, JD," Serena said.

"I know."

"--I owe you everything."

"Mmmm. No, you don't. You don't owe me a thing, and I didn't give you this job as a payoff to keep my secret. I think you're brilliant, and you're making me and this company better. But I don't want you to feel like you're being held hostage here because nothing could be further from the truth. If all this is causing you undue stress,--"

"It's not, it's just… I… I'm…" Serena teared up. Julien placed his hand on hers and gave her a comforting squeeze. "I'm scared. I don't wanna be, but I am. I see them walking around, and when they look at me,--"

"I know. But you gotta understand, all vampires ain't like that one. A few of them are actually pretty cool, and some, well… not so much," Julien said. "That one, that night, he was a 'not so much,' but ain't nobody like that 'round here, I promise you, and if there's ever one that does anything inappropriate or makes you the least bit uncomfortable, you tell me, and if I'm not around, tell Ms. Rayna, and we'll take care of it right then and there."

Serena nodded, but it didn't stop the tears from falling down her face.

"Serena, if you don't want to work here no more, it's okay. You'll still be my friend, and you'll still be brilliant. You'll just be my brilliant friend somewhere else." He smiled and winked at her. "And as for you keeping my secret, if I ever thought it was an issue, I would have just cast a spell and erased your memory right then and there, and that would have been that."

"You can do that?" She asked as she stared deep into his eyes.

Julien nodded. He didn't like to admit it, but he was an extraordinarily powerful warlock. Less than one percent of the warlocks in the world could do what he proposed.

"Sometimes I wish you would've. Just so I could forget."

A sadness washed over Julien's face at the thought, but he understood.

"…Do you want me to?" He asked.

The finality of that question eluded neither one of them, and there was a long, uncomfortable pause as she contemplated the possibility.

"No," she said softly. "I'll be all right."

Julien silently exhaled his relief.

"Yeah, you will." He smiled. "I'm glad. You're one of the few people around here I can actually depend on."

"I'll make sure to remind you of that when it's time for a raise." They shared a smile and a brief laugh, then he continued down the hall to his office.

CHAPTER 6

One day, a ten-year-old warlock boy brought home a full-grown woman - and she never left.

The blinds were drawn tight, casting the room in a thick, oppressive darkness as Julien stepped into his large corner office. The usual spaciousness felt smaller, more confined, with the absence of light. The door clicked shut behind him, its sound muted by the heavy silence that filled the room. As Julien moved further inside, a faint rustle caught his attention—something swift and unrecognizable darting just behind him. He turned, his eyes scanning the shadows, but whatever it was had vanished, melting back into the darkness.

As he neared his desk, the figure came into view, but not in any place one would expect. It clung to the ceiling, crawling in near-silence like a spider stalking its prey. There was no sound, no warning as it dropped silently to the floor, a dark shadow against the dim light, its movement too fluid, too predatory to be human.

Julien remained unaware of the danger as he placed his briefcase on the desk, his back still turned. The tall, imposing figure straightened, rising behind him like a nightmare brought to life. It was massive, a hulking presence that loomed just inches away, silent but menacing, its intent clear in every subtle movement. Its hand reached out, fingers stretching toward him, but Julien remained oblivious as he crossed the room to the blinds. With a swift motion, he pulled the cord, flooding the office with light.

The sudden burst of illumination chased away the shadows, lighting most of the room. The figure recoiled slightly, its form now starkly visible in the newfound brightness, yet its presence remained—waiting, watching, ready to strike.

"I'm tired, Ray. No mood for games today," Julien said as he slumped into his seat behind the desk.

He looked up to find Ms. Rayna, a strikingly beautiful woman of Creole origin, lying seductively on the sofa in the shadowed part of the room. With the outward appearance of a woman in her late twenties, she was absolutely intoxicating in her long, form-fitting ankle-length dress slit up to her hip.

"Awww. Sounds like someone had a rough shareholders meeting."

"They're all frigging idiots."

"Mmm hmm," she said, dangling her outstretched toes just outside the patch of sunlight from the window.

"Apparently, in the past twelve months since I've taken over for my father, increasing productivity by forty-eight percent and giving this company over two hundred million dollars in sales for the first time in its history is cause for complaint."

"Yes, but in that same amount of time, you decreased the profit margin from twenty percent to seventeen-point-eight."

That was not really the response the sullen son of the CEO was seeking, and he lashed out and let her know.

"You know we can't increase sales or productivity any further without automation, and those idiots won't even consider my plan!"

Rayna rolled her eyes, which irritated Julien even more.

"You said my plan was genius, now you roll your eyes?"

"I said it was genius *IF* you acquired Douglas Industries' refineries to process the ore. Without those refineries, your plan looks like you're trying to build a ladder to the moon. Maybe if you'd have graduated summa cum laude instead of magna,…" She smirked, pushing him further over the edge.

"You think that's funny?" Julien said. "Maybe you and the board liked this place better when my father and his idiot friend had run it into the ground!"

Rayna sighed deeply. She had heard this ballad a hundred times before.

"I worked my ass off to graduate early, WITH honors and WITHOUT using magic to even tie my fucking shoes so I could save this place, and I needed to do it the right way! AND I DID! Look at what I've done in only twelve fucking months!"

"You decreased the profit margin from twenty percent to seventeen-point-eight," she said solemnly, with no sympathy whatsoever toward his plight.

Defeated, Julien sank back into his chair, the weight of his frustration pulling him down. He waved her off, his silent sulking taking hold. The anger bubbling inside him was not directed solely at her—he was angrier with himself. As usual, she had been right. That was the most infuriating part. But it wasn't just her correctness that grated on him; it was the way she wielded it. She had a way of cutting through his defenses, exposing his vulnerabilities in a way that no one else could. She seemed to relish getting under his skin, twisting the knife just enough to leave him simmering. And worse, she knew it.

Every day, she rankled him, stretching herself out comfortably in the space between his pride and his self-doubt. She spoke her mind with a directness no one else dared, challenging him at every turn. Yet, despite the frustration she caused, there was no one more loyal or devoted. He knew that. Deep down, he understood that without her by his side, he wouldn't have achieved half of what he had in the last twelve months. She had been integral to his success, standing with him through every challenge and guiding him when the path seemed unclear.

Her mind was a match for his own—perhaps even sharper in ways that unsettled him. She was more than an advisor; she was his counsel, his protector, and something far more complicated. There were times when he could barely contain the urge to strangle her, with her unrelenting honesty and sharp tongue driving him to the brink of frustration. But when it came to matters of real importance, there was no one in the world he trusted more. She was his confidante, his safeguard, and as much as she exasperated him, he couldn't imagine navigating this world without her.

"Fine. So why don't you give me some good news then? How'd the meeting with Douglas Senior go? And please tell me you did not wear that."

"I thought you liked this dress!"

"Jesus Christ, Ray, you can't dress like that when you're doing business for me!"

"Oh, relax! It wasn't a board meeting. It was a lunch meeting, and other than the jambalaya, this dress was about the only thing Douglas Senior was interested in talking about. He doesn't like you very much."

"Great," Julien said wearily.

"He thinks you're a spoiled brat whose father gave him a Fortune 500 company to play with."

"The man never even met me."

"Good news is, like most, he does fear your father. We can use that."

"Unbelievable," Julien said as he ran his frustration-filled fingers through his hair.

Rayna stood up and elegantly moved toward him with her long, ebony hair draped over a single shoulder like silk. At nearly six feet tall, with a lean, well-toned, and curvaceous physique, this statuesque wonder was incredibly intimidating and abnormally alluring at the same time.

"It's the south, Julien. Deals are done in the back rooms of private clubs over a handshake and a cigar."

"A cigar laced with arsenic," Julien mumbled to himself.

"Well, you could use your powers like he did," Rayna suggested to Julien's obvious displeasure as he winced and wrinkled up his face. "I'm just saying, you'd make all these little problems just fly away."

"You know I'm not gonna do that." Then, again, as if he needed to reassure himself, "I'm not gonna be like him."

Rayna perched herself on the corner of the desk next to him.

"Then be patient. Make them money. They may never like you, but make them enough of it, they will respect you."

Julien relinquished a single nod as he fingered through his messages. He stopped on one from The Council that brought a certain uneasiness to his already distressed disposition. He briefly hesitated before he balled it up and threw it away.

"Where's Tirin? He should be here by now," he asked, trying to hide his apprehension. "You talk to him today?"

Rayna smiled. "Hmm. You more interested in where he is or with *whom* he is with?"

"He's supposed to be with Camille. Whatever other company he keeps is neither my business nor my concern." Julien answered, already becoming agitated by her unwelcome inquiries.

"Then why does it concern you so?" Rayna continued.

"It's a simple question, Ray!" Julien exclaimed. "Damn! Why you always gotta make everything so fuckin' difficult?"

"Well, for beings like us," Rayna said as she crossed her legs in front of him, "nothing is ever really simple. Is it?"

Despite his façade of indifference, Julien was anything but immune to her charms, and she knew it. But in all the years they had been together, this was one line they both knew, all too well, they could never cross. There were many stories and rumors about how they met and what their relationship truly was, but no one other than the two of them knew anything more than that one day, a ten-year-old warlock boy brought home a full-grown woman - and she never left. The intercom buzzed.

"Felix Neely on line one. Says he's from The Council," Serena announced over the intercom.

Rayna smiled at Julien's restlessness as he awkwardly paused before he answered.

"Tell him I'm in a meeting, and I'll get back to him."

"You do know you gon' have to talk to that man eventually," Rayna said, igniting Julien's ire as he glared at her.

"Don't get mad at me, I'm just the messenger."

The door creaked open, and in walked Julien's father, Barrett. He was a huskier, more imposing version of his son, but where Julien carried an air of quiet intensity, Barrett exuded something far darker. There was a simmering malevolence that radiated from him, a mischievous cruelty lurking just beneath the surface, always ready to boil over. His presence filled the room, and with it came the sense that trouble was never far behind.

Wherever Barrett went, it was safe to assume his timorously timid sidekick, Mr. Cecil, was trailing close behind. True to form, Cecil appeared, stepping into the room with a nervous energy that clung to him like a shadow. He was the CFO of Gerard Enterprises, but anyone who observed the pair could tell his role extended far beyond financial matters. Cecil always seemed to have something important to say, though it was a well-known fact that his confidence only appeared when Barrett was standing beside him. As long as Barrett was nearby, Cecil would speak up, delivering his words with an air of significance. But the moment Barrett left the room, his bravado would vanish just as quickly.

Cecil both idolized and feared Barrett, a dynamic that had existed long before Julien was even born. They had been partners for decades, bound together by shared ambition and a loyalty that was rooted both in fear and respect. Barrett thrived on this power, wielding it with calculated precision, and Julien knew all too well the storm his father could bring into a room. The tension was palpable, and as Barrett stepped further into the office, Julien braced himself, knowing that wherever his father went, disruption followed.

"This a bad time, JD?" Cecil joked, eyeing Rayna as if he'd caught them in a compromising position.

Barrett, however, found no amusement in the invalid indictment. Never once did he try to hide the fact that he didn't like Rayna and the unprecedented influence she had on his son.

"Apparently, that joke never gets old," Rayna mumbled under her breath.

"You say something?" Barrett barked with his usual look of disdain.

"Ahhh, no, sir," she responded, trying not to laugh.

"Why don't you two make yourself a drink, and we'll get this started," Julien said.

Embarrassed, he glared at Rayna.

"Oh, lighten up, Julien." She sighed as she hopped off the desk. "Don't make it so easy for them," she whispered so as not to spark Barrett's wrath. "As for your concern for Tirin,--"

"I wasn't concerned," Julien said in a hushed voice. "I just,--"

"I know you miss his company."

"Rayna,--"

"And even though he'll never say it, he misses yours too. But you have Camille, and now he has Dane. Doesn't mean you're not best friends anymore, but these intimate relationships come with priorities and commitments that may sometimes supersede that friendship."

Julien sighed, and he rolled his eyes.

"Aww. My boys are growing up," Rayna joked.

"What the hell are we waiting for? Where's Camille and that alpha of yours?" An annoyed Barrett asked.

Rayna knew Barrett's tone and aggression made Julien nervous, but in her mind, there was nothing for him to be nervous about today. She would make sure everything went as planned. That was her job, and there was no one better.

"You really need to get more control of that alpha, Julien. You give that boy way too many liberties," Cecil added for no other reason than to give Julien added grief.

Julien pursed his lips. Rayna knew he wanted to comment but held back because of his father's presence. Cecil knew it, too. That's why he said it. Julien did give Tirin a lot of liberties, but Tirin was more than just his alpha, as Rayna had stated. So, with both grace and diplomacy, she answered for him, inserting herself between Julien and impending trouble - as she always did.

"They're on their way, sir, but if you'd like, we can get started without them."

"Well, just how the hell are we gonna do that?" Barrett asked with his usual aggression.

"We're gonna do this a little different, Pop," Julien answered.

Julien gave a subtle nod to Rayna, who moved with an almost unnatural grace toward the dimly lit corner of the office. The space was strewn with plush cushions and pillows, creating a serene, almost mystical ambiance. She sank onto the cushions with a fluidity that defied her size, crossing her legs in a yoga-like seated position. Cecil, sitting nearby, could barely conceal his shock. He had never seen someone of her stature move with such ease, and though Barrett would never voice it, even he was quietly impressed by her poise.

With the playful spark in her eyes now gone, Rayna struck a long match and lit the two candles on the small, rectangular table before her. The flickering light cast shadows across her face, transforming her demeanor into something far more serious and reverent. She reached for a deck of Tarot cards, handling them with a deftness that was nothing short of mesmerizing. Her fingers danced across the cards as she shuffled them with an agility that seemed almost otherworldly.

Barrett and Cecil sat on the sofa, watching the scene unfold with a mixture of confusion and curiosity. Neither of them had expected this—certainly not from Rayna, who had always struck them as unpredictable, but not like this. They exchanged glances, equally baffled by the silent ritual before them. Meanwhile, Julien stood by the corner of his desk, arms folded, his gaze fixed on Rayna as she laid out several cards with meticulous precision. One by one, she turned the cards over, her expression growing more focused with each reveal.

It wasn't long before Julien noticed the shift in her demeanor. Her brow furrowed ever so slightly at first, but enough for him to realize that something in the cards had unsettled her. The tension in the room deepened as she continued her silent reading, her fingers hovering over the last card as if reluctant to reveal the final truth hidden within the deck.

"What is it?" Julien asked quietly.

Rayna avoided both Julien's eyes and an answer to his question as she swept up the cards and began again. Barrett's patience, or lack thereof, was on display as he sighed and folded his arms across his chest. Whatever was supposed to happen had better happen soon.

"Y'all do know there's a much easier way to do this, right?" Cecil asked and received no response from either Rayna or Julien, so he implemented a more aggressive strategy to get his question answered. "What the hell's going on?" He whispered loudly to Barrett. "I don't understand what we doing here? Why don't the boy just use his powers?"

Barrett shrugged and winced as if he had just drunk a glass of spoiled milk.

"Nowadays, he just lets this 'thing' do whatever it is 'it' does," Barrett replied.

"Don't start that, Pop. Just let her do her work, okay?" Julien said.

"I didn't realize I was stopping - what is 'it' anyway, Ceese?" Barrett asked in an effort to needle Rayna. She shot him a look that could have killed a small child but kept her mouth shut.

"I-I-I don't know, but I do think you offended it." Cecil timidly replied.

"Damn it, boy, what the hell is all this?!" Barrett erupted. "I just wanna know what my grandbaby's gonna be!"

"As do I, but,--" Julien started.

"Then stop fucking around with all this card flipping, mumbo-jumbo shit, and cast a goddamn spell!"

"Dad, spells don't work on witches! They can't penetrate their wombs!"

"Bullshit! We used one on your momma, and we were right about you!"

"You had a fifty-fifty chance!"

"You saying this thing's magic's more powerful than mine?" Barrett asked, offended by the mere thought.

Rayna didn't appreciate being referred to as an unwanted object, and as much as it angered her, she knew better than to challenge Barrett. She would have to depend on Julien for that.

"No, I'm-- 'She,' Pop, 'she'! And stop doing that! SHE doesn't use magic. She's a seer. She reads the cards, and they tell her of things that will come to be."

"Fiddle-lee-dee! Only a virgin has the gift of sight," Cecil retorted.

It was true. Of all Rayna's gifts, and there were many, there was one she could not share. Julien didn't respond with words, but his glare told Cecil everything he needed to know.

"What?! You mean to tell me in all these years she ain't never...? Ever? With nobody? Really?" Cecil whispered.

"Julien..." Rayna said softly, trying her best to ignore the foolishness going on across the room. They all turned to her as she looked up from the cards with a tear in her eye.

CHAPTER 7

"Warlocks been doing this for over three hundred years."

The elevator opened, and Camille danced through the doors.

"Hey na', Serena!"

"Afternoon, Mrs. Gerard." Serena laughed. She was always happy to see Camille.

"Serena, you always have the cutest dresses. Where do you get them?"

"Aww, thank you! One of my old roommates from college has a tiny little boutique downtown. We should go some time. I think you'd really like her more casual line."

"Oh, I would love that!"

"Then it's a date." Serena smiled. "They're all down there with your husband."

"Thanks," Camille said as she headed down the hall.

She was happy and living what she thought was the dream as the corners of her mouth twitched into a smile, but as she got closer to Julien's office, that smile began to fade from the shouting she heard from within.

"--We're putting everything on what 'she' says?!" Barrett yelled from inside. "What is it, damn it?! What do you supposedly see?!"

"Stop yelling at her, Pop! Let her be!"

Camille crept up to the door, took a breath, and concentrated. In an instant, her eyes and hands flashed red. She placed the palm of her right hand on the door, and magically, she could see within the room. She watched as Julien moved from his desk over to Rayna and knelt down beside her.

"What is it? What's wrong?" Julien asked, ignoring Barret and Cecil's rumblings.

"I'm sorry," Rayna said as she stared at the cards with a blank expression on her face.

"Come on, na'. You and me been friends way too long for that. Just tell me what you see."

"Boy or girl?!" Barrett yelled.

Rayna looked up and sadly stared into Julien's eyes. He nodded.

"Spit it out, Goddamnit!" Barrett hollered.

Camille was confused by all this. She didn't understand why Mr. Gerard seemed so angry.

"Both!" Rayna blurted out. "You have both,"

Camille felt her stomach and smiled.

"*Twins*," she thought to herself.

"Twins?" Julien said awkwardly.

Camille watched Julien carefully in this moment. It bothered her that he didn't seem to share the same exuberance over the news as she did.

"Yes. A boy and a girl," Rayna replied.

Barrett scrunched his face into a frown as he looked at Cecil.

"Well, you know who her great-grandma was," Cecil said softly. "You put them genes together with his? Yeah. It's possible,"

"What else?" Julien asked. He could see the look of dismay in her eyes and knew there was more.

"Your firstborn son will be a superior warlock. Unorthodox and eccentric, but ultimately the strongest of his time." Rayna replied with a look that implied she was confused by that notion.

Barrett sank back into the sofa with a sly smile fixed on his face. Outside the door, Camille continued to listen.

"And my daughter?" Julien asked.

Rayna looked down at the cards and paused for what seemed to be a half-lifetime. Her mouth was open and ready, but she didn't want to release the words resting on her tongue.

"Rayna,…" Julien prompted her, and painfully, she released them.

"She will be the most powerful witch ever to set foot on this planet… And on her twenty-first birthday," Rayna again paused as she looked up at him with a tear in her eye. "She will destroy you."

Julien's face remained a perfect mask, betraying none of the emotion swirling beneath the surface as he absorbed Rayna's startling, wanton words. Not a flicker of surprise or anger crossed his features— his expression was as unreadable as stone. He gave nothing away. Across the room, Cecil wasn't so composed. His hands trembled, and his glass slipped from his grasp, crashing to the floor with a sharp clatter that echoed in the tense silence. Barrett, meanwhile, fixed Rayna with a hard, contemptuous glare, his eyes narrowing at the pragmatic seer. It was clear that her boldness had crossed a line with him, though he made no immediate move, his rage simmering just beneath the surface.

Outside the room, Camille could only listen in stunned silence, her breath shaky as the weight of the words reached her. She felt the color drain from her face, leaving her pale and trembling. A ragged exhale escaped her lips, the sound barely audible as she tried to steady herself against the sudden wave of shock. Every drop of blood seemed to vanish from her body, her pulse slowing as the enormity of what had been spoken settled over her like a heavy fog.

"I'm sorry," Rayna said.

"Ch-Ch-Check it again," Cecil stammered.

"I checked three times."

"Then check it four, five more times if you have to, goddamnit!" Cecil yelled. Then to Barrett: "I'll put a call in to The Council."

"NO!" Julien exclaimed.

"Hold on now, Ceese," Barrett said with what seemed to be a misplaced calmness. "I don't think we need to bother them with this." Cecil opened his mouth to speak, but Barrett quickly cut him off. "Nah, nah, nah, it's fine. We'll just kill the second baby right after Julien kills the momma."

Camille began to hyperventilate. She was trying to suck air into her body quicker than she could dispel it. In truth, she wasn't really doing either one. All her attention had gone to that one word.

"*Kill.*" It echoed in her head over and over again. "*KILL the baby; KILL the momma. KILL; KILL; KILL.*"

She felt dizzy as the corridor began to spin around her. She stumbled and thought she might faint as the red faded from her eyes. The spell was broken and she could no longer see into the room, but she could still hear the faint, calm, confident words of her father-in-law.

"Easy. C'mon, na'," she heard Barrett say. "Warlocks been doing this for over three hundred years. I'll be goddamned if a witch makes it to twenty-one on my watch."

The elevator bell in the foyer chimed and roused Camille from her state of bewilderment. She took a deep breath and tried to fight off the panic that was beginning to overtake her.

"Afternoon, Mr. Tirin. Mr. Dane," she heard Serena say.

Camille clenched her eyes shut, forcing her thoughts into focus. She needed control—needed to harness the power swirling inside her. When her eyes flicked open again, they blazed with a deep, unnatural red, glowing with the intensity of her magic. Her long hair began to float, rising and twisting around her as though she were submerged underwater, every strand charged with the same eerie energy coursing through her veins. With a single thought, she vanished, her form dissolving into the shadows just as Tirin and his top beta, Dane, rounded the corner.

Her heart pounded in her chest as she pressed herself against the wall, holding her breath and willing herself to remain unseen. Tirin strode past her without hesitation, his steps measured and confident. For a moment, Camille thought she had succeeded, that he had sensed nothing. But then, a few rebellious strands of her hair, still suspended in the air, brushed lightly against his skin.

Tirin froze mid-stride, his brow furrowing in confusion as a faint touch registered against his heightened senses. Ahead of him, Dane had already reached the door, turning the handle and pushing it open without a second thought. But Tirin lingered, his instincts prickling at the edge of his awareness. Something wasn't right.

Dane entered the room, oblivious, but Tirin remained in place. His eyes closed, and he took two quick, sharp sniffs, followed by a long, deliberate inhale. The soft growl that escaped his throat was barely audible, but its meaning was unmistakable. He turned slowly, his nostrils flaring, twitching with an almost unnatural speed as he sifted through the scents in the air. His eyes snapped open, narrowing with predatory focus as they locked onto the very spot where Camille stood, invisible but now unmistakably detected.

"Oh my god. He can smell me," she thought.

She watched Tirin's eyes dart from one spot to another, his nostrils working rapidly as he scanned the hallway, trying to make sense out of what his senses were telling him. From what he could see, there was nothing there, yet his nose kept bringing him back to that same spot. He took a step in her direction,

"Tirin!" Julien yelled from inside the office. "What are you doing? Get in here!"

Tirin stopped, but his nose was still in overdrive. He squinted his eyes with what seemed to be a look of confusion before he grudgingly turned away and entered the room. The door closed, and the still invisible Camille carefully quietly exhaled and took a few cautious steps backward before she turned and sprinted down the hallway. She stopped, fell out of the mactrouge, and reappeared in front of Serena's podium, startling the astute assistant.

"Mrs. Gerard!" Serena gasped.

With a flick of her hand, Camille gestured toward the office, locking Julien's door, then again, her eyes flashed red as her hair lifted and began to float off her shoulders.

"Ilfra of the damned, let me be clear; neither I nor my scent were ever here." She whispered.

Serena's eyes fluttered and she faintly nodded as Camille faded into nothing, her form vanishing from view as Serena returned to her tasks. Camille carefully backed away from Serena's desk. In her haste, her shoulder brushed against a tall vase perched on a floor stand. The vase wobbled, teetering dangerously, and Camille quickly spun around, catching it just in time to steady it before it could crash to the floor.

Serena gasped audibly, startled by the sudden movement of the vase, unaware of the invisible figure mere feet from her. To anyone else, it would have seemed like the vase had moved on its own, an unsettling occurrence in an otherwise quiet office. Camille froze, her heart pounding in her chest. Outside of herself, only one other person could have possibly heard Serena's gasp—and Camille silently prayed that he hadn't.

But just as the thought crossed her mind, she heard it. Down the hall, the distinct sound of Julien's doorknob rattling reached her ears, confirming her worst fear. He had heard. There was no more time. They were coming for her.

Camille's pulse quickened as she darted toward the elevator, her invisible form moving swiftly. She slammed her hand against the call button, willing the elevator doors to open faster than they ever had. Time seemed to stretch, every second feeling like an eternity as the soft hum of approaching footsteps grew louder. She didn't have long. If she couldn't escape, they would find her.

"*They cannot know I'm here,*" she thought as the panic began to creep in.

She became aware of a trembling within her body that nearly turned into a scream when she heard Julien's office door explode outward. Tirin leapt into the corridor and sped down the hall, stopping in front of Serena's podium. Serena was terrified.

"What happened?" Tirin demanded.

"Uhh, the vase,… It was about to fall, but then it righted itself... I-I-I'm sorry, I didn't mean to,--" Serena stammered.

Tirin sped over to the vase and sniffed.

"Who was just here?"

"S-S-Sir?"

"BEFORE ME. Who was here?!" Tirin asked in a way that would have frightened just about anyone.

Tirin wasn't the least bit angry with Serena. It was just the way he talked. To say he was intense would be an understatement of epic proportions. Alphas are aggression personified and even though it wasn't always the case, their questions were often misconstrued as threats.

"Settle down, you're scaring her," Julien said as he came up behind him. "'The hell's wrong with you?"

Tirin didn't answer. He was still searching for something that had not yet been found. Camille fought to maintain her invisibility as her blood-red eyes watered.

"Who-o-o-o?" Tirin asked Serena again in a softer, less dramatic way, although still just as intimidating as before.

"N-N-No-one, sir. Just Mr. Gerard, Mr. Cecil, and,--"

A tear rolled down Camille's face and hit the carpet. Tirin whipped his head around at the sound of it, silent to everyone else, but a train wreck to an alpha enrapt in the hunt.

"Shhhhhhhhh," Tirin said, holding his finger, almost tensed into a claw in Serena's face.

Serena put her hand over her mouth, muting herself, as Tirin listened. The elevator dinged, and the doors opened. Camille carefully backed into it and edged toward the corner. Another tear rolled off her face and hit the floor. It echoed like thunder in Tirin's ears. He raced to the elevator just as the doors were closing.

"He hears them," Camille realized and willed no more tears to fall.

Tirin's hand shot out, stopping the elevator doors just before they could close. He stepped inside, his nostrils flaring and twitching with unnatural speed, his sharp senses scanning the air for any hint of a presence. His eyes moved methodically over every inch of the elevator, pausing momentarily as if they could see through the veil of invisibility that cloaked Camille. His head tilted slightly, a calculated, deliberate movement. His nose might have missed her scent, but his ears—his ears would not fail him.

Camille's pulse raced as she realized how close he was to discovering her. She closed her eyes, focusing all her energy inward. This was no longer a simple game of cat and mouse—this was a lethal game of chess, and she could not afford to make a single mistake. With a single thought, she suppressed her breathing, slowing it until it was imperceptible. Her heartbeat followed, its rhythm tapering down to almost nothing, a quiet hum of life buried deep within her chest.

When she opened her eyes again, she found herself staring directly into the eyes of the alpha—Tirin, angry and on the edge of a revelation. She remained motionless, her body locked in place, her gaze unwavering. She couldn't afford a slip, not even the smallest twitch. The silence of the moment was broken only by the buzz of the elevator alarm, its mechanical noise slicing through the tension. Tirin turned slowly, silencing the alarm with a quick swipe of his hand.

Then, his gaze dropped to the floor, where a single teardrop had escaped Camille's control. It shimmered faintly on the metal surface, almost invisible, but not to him. Tirin crouched down, his movements precise, and dabbed his finger into the tiny droplet. He raised it to his nose, sniffing it with a focused intensity, and then, with calculated deliberation, tasted it on the tip of his tongue.

His tongue flicked across the back of his front teeth as if savoring the information the teardrop had given him. Slowly, he looked up at the mirrored ceiling of the elevator, his eyes narrowing. A low, throaty growl rumbled from deep within him, barely audible but unmistakably dangerous. Camille remained frozen, knowing that any movement now could be fatal.

"Why is he angry with me?" Camille wondered. She didn't understand as these rampant thoughts raced through her mind. *"How stupid was I? Have they always been against me?"*

Tirin stood up very close to where she was standing and inhaled a long, vibrant sniff. He took in everything he possibly could through his nose before he reluctantly backed out of the elevator and turned away. Julien's confused face was the last image she saw as the elevator doors closed. Camille painfully exhaled as the elevator descended, tears freely falling from her face.

She hung onto her invisibility until she was safely clear of the building, then she ran until she could run no more. Exhausted, she found herself wandering through the warehouse district, tears still flowing freely. She jumped into the first phone booth she saw on the corner of an abandoned building next to an alley and frantically started dialing the only number her shivering finger allowed.

"Operator," the voice on the phone said.

"I need to make a collect call to this number from Camille, please," she said as she snorted back her tears. Instinctively, her hand moved to her chest, where she found the Blood Heart necklace and began to massage it between her fingertips. It always seemed to give her comfort and focus.

"One moment while I connect you." The Operator said.

A moment later, the phone began to ring.

"Pick up… Pick up, pick up, please, pick up," Camille pleaded.

After the third ring, she was connected to a recorded message:

"The number you have reached, 337-981-9161, has been disconnected,--"

"NO!" Camille screamed as the message repeated. "No, no, no!"

"I'm sorry, ma'am, there is no one at this number," the Operator said.

"But there must be something else! Another number? Anything," Camille begged. "Sorry, ma'am, there was no new number left. Who is it you're trying to call?"

"George St. Croix in Morgan City."

"One moment while I check for that listing."

Camille continued to plead quietly to herself as she waited, her fingers feverishly rubbing the Blood Heart.

"I'm sorry, ma'am. There is no listing for a George St. Croix in Morgan City or anywhere in Louisiana," the Operator said.

"But there must be something! An address? Anything; we lived there my whole life!"

"I'm sorry, ma'am. There is no address for a George St. Croix."

"No, Daddy, NO!" she cried over the operator's voice as she slid to the floor of the phone booth.

"Is there anything else I can do for you, ma'am…? Ma'am?" The Operator asked.

Camille didn't answer. She couldn't. She had begun to hyperventilate. Then her eyes rolled back in her head, and her hair lifted up off her shoulders. She seemed irritated with the sound of the operator's voice as her eyes rolled forward and flashed red, along with her hands, and began to glow.

"Thank you for using A T and,--"

Camille crushed the receiver of the phone in her bare hand, and it shattered into pieces. Her face contorted into a perverse pout, and with a wayward rumination, the phone exploded. She released a wicked scream that shattered the glass in the booth all around her. She rose to her feet and noticed two homeless people sitting in the alley, petrified by the horrid sight in front of them. It made her smile, and she began to salivate. She could almost taste their fear, and it was intoxicating to her. She stepped toward them, savoring the terror on her tongue.

"These people," she thought, with a malicious smile. *"These people... ARE peo-ple..."*

Suddenly, her saliva-filled smirk shifted to sadness, and she stopped. She clenched her fists so hard that it caused her body to quiver. She closed her eyes and stood motionless, strained - wavering in the wind. She seemed to be locked in a battle within herself against something that was so much more than evil.

"RU-U-U-UN!" She screamed, and they obligingly obeyed.

The two vagrants, who likely hadn't run in years, now sprinted down the alley with a speed and desperation that suggested their very lives depended on it—and perhaps they did. Fear drove their legs faster than they had ever moved before, the urgency of escape clear in every frantic step.

Behind them, Camille stood still as the adrenaline slowly ebbed from her body. Her wild, floating hair settled back onto her shoulders, and the fiery red that had consumed her eyes and hands dimmed, fading back into normalcy. The power that had surged through her moments before left her disoriented, her mind clouded with confusion. She felt unsteady, both physically and emotionally, as the intensity of the moment slipped away.

Without fully understanding what had just happened, Camille turned and bolted in the opposite direction, her heart still racing. She had to escape, to get away before more questions piled on top of her already tangled thoughts. Her father had given her his blessing to move in with the Gerards, offering it as a chance for her to have a better life—a fresh start. He had wanted her to be safe, to thrive.

But now, as she ran through the dark streets, that promise of a "better life" felt distant, almost elusive. She couldn't help but wonder what kind of life this truly was and whether the path she had chosen would lead her to the safety and peace she had once envisioned. The truth weighed heavily on her, but for now, all she could do was run—away from the confusion, from the power that had frightened her as much as it had saved her, and into a future that felt increasingly uncertain.

CHAPTER 8

Truth be told, malafecs were just as afraid of humans as humans were of them.

The Gerard estate sprawled across twenty-five acres of lush land, its grandeur rooted in nearly three centuries of history. Built just off the banks of the mighty Mississippi River in 1749, the plantation home stood as a testament to time and tradition, its presence both imposing and timeless. The front gate opened to reveal a breathtaking entrance—two rows of towering oak trees lined the quarter-mile road leading up to the main house. The trees, nearly as ancient as the estate itself, stretched their majestic branches high above, intertwining to form a natural canopy. The effect was like stepping into another world, an arboreal tunnel that shaded the entire drive to the grand two-story mansion nestled securely behind them.

The mansion, with its colonial charm and hints of decay, had an aura of quiet authority. Black curtains hung like sentinels over the two enormous windows flanking the stately front door, the darkness of the drapery contrasting sharply with the whitewashed exterior. Above the entrance, a wide balcony stretched across the second floor, though its four matching windows were sealed behind permanently closed shutters as if guarding long-buried secrets within the house's walls.

To the west, some four hundred yards from the main house, stood a row of six small buildings—'slave quarters' from a bygone era. Weathered but still standing, the structures now served as supplemental housing, a stark reminder of the estate's fraught history. Their presence cast a long shadow over the otherwise idyllic grounds, a whisper of the lives that had once toiled in the shadow of the mansion's towering walls.

The estate, though stately and serene, seemed to carry with it a heavy sense of memory, the echoes of the past lingering in the air, woven into the fabric of the land itself.

"This was my home; my haven... Now, I don't know," Camille thought as she ran through the front door, which seemed to magically open on its own.

Inside, two guards, who always managed to avoid the sunlight, flanked the door and closed it as she ran past them up the stairs into her room. She scrunched up next to the bed, taking caution to protect her belly, as she cried hysterically. This was all too much for her to process right now.

"Oh my God! What's wrong?" A young black woman burst into the room and knelt down next to Camille. "Are you okay? You're shivering," the woman said.

"I won't have to deal with this alone," Camille thought.

Whenever something wasn't right, whenever Camille was in a bad mood, or sick, or just needed someone to talk to, Kaitlin Morrison had always been there for her.

Six years her senior, she was the big sister Camille never had - the *human* big sister. The two were actually raised together and had been friends for Camille's entire life. Kaitlin is the primary reason Camille never had any ill feelings toward humans. Being raised like one for so many years had a wonderful effect on her, but most malafecs didn't share the same love she had for the human race. They tolerated them. They dealt with them when they had to or when it was profitable, but truth be told, malafecs were just as afraid of humans as humans were of them. What made Kaitlin different was that, for some reason, she never seemed to be afraid.

She was the one person, other than Camille's father, who had known her mother. Camille's father never spoke of his late wife, but Kaitlin always had a wonderful story to tell. She was only eight when Camille's mother, her babysitter at the time, passed away, so stories of her were slight, but Camille treasured them along with her own scattered memories.

Camille often found herself wondering why she was allowed to take up so much of Kaitlin's time. Human men were drawn to her like moths to a flame, adoring her with wide-eyed fascination, while malafec men coveted her in ways that made their intentions all too clear. Even the vampires and lycans in the house, though bound by a silent rule never to touch her, whispered about her in hushed, envious tones. Camille sometimes overheard their murmurs, their voices filled with desire and intrigue. Kaitlin, too, must have been aware of it—how could she not be? Yet, if those whispers ever bothered her, she never showed it. She seemed impervious to the attention, carrying herself with a calm, effortless grace that set her apart.

Kaitlin moved through the house with a quiet confidence, navigating both the human world and the darker, supernatural one without a trace of fear or concern. She was a fixture in both realms, belonging fully to neither yet moving freely between them as if the rules of either didn't apply to her. Always with a smile on her face, she seemed immune to the weight that burdened others in the house. Camille couldn't recall a single moment when Kaitlin wasn't smiling—her smile was like a constant light, radiating warmth and positivity no matter the situation.

She had a magnetic charm, drawing people in without effort, her presence both comforting and uplifting. She made everything feel just a little less overwhelming, a little more bearable, and in a world filled with uncertainty, that was no small gift. She was the kind of person everyone wanted as a best friend, and on this day, more than ever, Camille was grateful that Kaitlin was hers.

"Katie… Katie…" Camille mumbled.

Kaitlin grabbed a blanket and wrapped it around Camille, then helped her onto the bed. "What's happened? Are you okay? Is the baby—"

"Baby is fine… You remember my momma, Katie?" Camille asked.

"Course I do."

"How'd she die?"

Kaitlin paused a moment. She found the question to be a curious one but chose to answered it anyway.

"From a gas explosion in the house." Kaitlin said. "You were with me. At my house. You don't remember that?"

Camille got more upset with every word, constantly twirling the Blood Heart Necklace between her fingers.

"How... old?" Camille asked between sobs.

"Baby, I don't understand,--"

"How old was she?"

"Nineteen, I think. Maybe twenty, I'm not sure, why?"

"You know anybody else like me?" Camille asked, even though she already knew the answer.

"What do you mean? White?" Kaitlin said, trying to make light. Camille's eyes flashed red for a second, then faded to normal. "Oh. That. No, but, well, there's no way of really knowing, is there?" Kaitlin asked. Camille shook her head as the tears kept falling. "Baby, you're scaring me. Please tell me what's wrong."

"I'm gonna die."

"Okay. I'm calling JD."

"No! You can't say anything about this!"

"About what?"

"Especially to JD! You can't! Please! You can't!" Camille whispered loudly.

"Okay, okay. It's okay. Just... Shhhh."

Camille worked hard to control her breath as she kneaded the Blood Heart necklace between her fingers. It always seemed to bring her peace, and Julien would be home soon.

CHAPTER 9

"A baby boy for you and a pretty little girl for me."

A guard opened the not so magical mansion door as Tirin and Dane walked in, with Rayna and Julien a step behind.

"Give me fifteen minutes, then meet me in the study," Julien said.

"Wait!" Rayna called out before changing her tone to a whisper. "What if she heard?"

"She wasn't there," Julien said.

"But if she was, and she did?" Rayna asked.

"We've been through this. You're making a lot of assumptions over a drop of water on the,--"

"Tear," Tirin interrupted. Julien paused, annoyed. "It was a tear," Tirin said.

"How do you know?" Julien asked.

"Salty," Tirin said.

"So is sweat. Serena said the UPS man was there twenty minutes before me with eight packages. Now, can them heightened senses of yours tell the difference between sweat and a tear?" Tirin didn't answer. He just stared at Julien in a way that would make most uncomfortable. "Uh-huh," Julien said, in his mind, proving his point.

"Well, considering who her great-gramma was..." Rayna said before she ran past Julien up the staircase. "Camille!"

Now it was Julien's turn to whisper. His was just a lot louder than hers.

"Rayna!"

"Better to be safe than sorry, don't you think?" Rayna whispered down to Julien, then, "Camille, honey, you here?!"

"Rayna!" Julien shouted.

Rayna signaled for the two guards at the front door to follow her as an angry Julien took off after her. Tirin released a frustration-filled sigh before he and Dane brought up the rear.

"Goddamn it, Rayna. Stop!" Julien ordered.

She did, but she had already reached her destination - the bedroom door. She knocked before Julien could stop her.

"Baby, I'm here with Julien and Tirin," Rayna said in as nice of a voice as she could muster.

Julien pushed through two guards to face her.

"What the hell are you doing?" Julien angrily whispered.

"My job." Rayna smiled as he glared at her, but the deed was done.

Julien had no choice but to finish Rayna's twisted game.

"Sweetie, you in there?... Cher?... Cherie?" Julien asked.

He carefully opened the door to their bedroom. Camille was sitting yoga-style on the bed. Kaitlin sat next to her with her arm around her, holding her free hand as Camille toyed with the Blood Heart necklace in the other.

"Scuse me, Cher. Alright, if we come in?" Julien asked.

Camille nodded, but her body language spoke louder than any words could. The tension in her posture; the way her shoulders slumped slightly made it clear that she was upset. Her puffy, red-rimmed eyes told Julien the rest of the story—she had been crying. He took a step forward, intending to enter, but before he could, Rayna slid past him, eager to reach the room first. Julien exhaled sharply, pursing his lips in an effort to suppress the frustration that threatened to rise. He hated being outmaneuvered, especially by Rayna, but now wasn't the time for that.

Behind him, the two guards instinctively stepped forward, ready to follow. Rayna, without so much as a glance in their direction, waved them off with a casual flick of her hand, her focus entirely on Camille. They hesitated briefly before retreating, positioning themselves just outside the door, their presence lingering but unneeded.

Rayna moved with a measured grace, cautious, almost predatory as if she were weighing every step. Her eyes never strayed from Camille, though Camille refused to meet her gaze. Instead, Camille's eyes were fixed on a seemingly random point on the floor in front of her, distant and detached. But despite her outward appearance, it was clear that Camille was acutely aware of everyone in the room, of every subtle shift in the air. Her silence was thick, almost palpable, creating an invisible barrier that no one seemed able to breach.

Julien watched the exchange, his own emotions simmering just below the surface. Rayna was calculating, as always, while Camille remained in a quiet, impenetrable shell. The tension in the room hung heavy, unspoken but undeniable, and Julien couldn't shake the feeling that something was about to break.

"Rayna," Julien warned, but Rayna was on a mission, and she would not be deterred.

"Hey, baby. We just wanted to check and see how you we're doing?" Rayna said, ignoring Julien.

"Wow. That's a nice dress," Camille said without so much as a glance in Rayna's direction.

"Why thank you, Sugar."

"It's very pretty," Camille said, looking at Julien.

Julien knew what that look meant and where this was going, but he wasn't going to engage in this with her right now. At least, that's what he had hoped. Tirin sighed. He also knew. He signaled Dane to stay outside with the guards as he entered and closed the door behind him. Kaitlin looked as if she hadn't breathed since the door first opened. She tried her best not to move in hopes that everyone would forget she was even there, as the tension in the room rose with every word.

"Hey, JD. Ms. Rayna… Tirin," Kaitlin said. Something about the way she said Tirin's name gave Camille pause.

"Hey, Katie. What's going on in here? Everything all right?" Julien said as he walked past Rayna and sat on the bed next to Camille.

"She's just feeling a little sick, is all. She'll be fine," Kaitlin said.

"I thought this only happened at the beginning?" Julien said.

Kaitlin smiled. "This is the beginning, JD."

Julien kissed Camille's forehead. Camille gave him no response.

"We waited for you at the office, sweetie," Rayna said. "Remember the big meeting we was supposed to have today?" She just wasn't going to let up until she got whatever it was she was looking for.

"I wasn't feeling well," Camille said, as her eyes moved away from Julien, back to that fixed point on the floor. "Figured you could handle things just fine without me."

"Yes... well, you know how we worry. Especially you being in such a... delicate state and all," Rayna said.

It became apparent to everyone in the room that Rayna's last comment didn't really sit well with Camille as her eyes fluttered from that fixed point on the floor and, for the first time, found Rayna's. Julien sighed as he lowered his head and searched for that fixed point on the floor that Camille had recently abandoned.

"Just saying, a phone call would have been the mature, decent thing to do, don't you think?"

"Rayna, just,--" Julien tried to say, but his attempt to disarm this situation had failed miserably. Now it was here.

"Yeah, so would wearing a bra and some stockings, but that didn't happen either," Camille snapped back.

"Okay,--" Julien interrupted as he stood up and moved in between the two females, blocking each of their view of the other.

Kaitlin's view was clear—there was nothing obstructing her vision. She could see everyone in the room, and she could take in every detail if she wanted to. But she didn't want to. She didn't know where to direct her gaze, unsure of who or what deserved her attention in this moment. Instead, she followed a familiar habit, her eyes drifting down to that favored, fixed point on the floor, a spot made quite fashionable by both Camille and Julien when they, too, sought refuge from uncomfortable stares.

Tirin, on the other hand, had no patience for the subtleties of floor-gazing or for the conversation that was unfolding around him. His mind was elsewhere, still stuck in the elevator at the office, replaying the earlier events. His gaze, however, never left Camille.

He studied her intently, his attention solely on her, even as the others navigated the tension in the room.

In the grand scheme of things, this was just another day in the Gerard household. The small, unspoken battles between Camille and Rayna played out like clockwork, the undercurrents of their interactions so routine that they barely registered anymore. For Kaitlin, Tirin, and the rest, it was business as usual—another day filled with unspoken tension, veiled looks, and the ever-present feeling that something more was simmering beneath the surface.

"Why don't you two give me fifteen minutes, then I'll meet you in the study," Julien said to both Tirin and Rayna, but his eyes never drifted from Rayna when he said it.

"Of course," Rayna said, answering more to his glare than to his words. She leaned to the right, just far enough to again engage Camille's eyes. "I do hope you feel better."

Rayna smiled as she said it, but no one, for a second, believed that she meant it.

Camille twitched the corners of her mouth into a pseudo-smile. "Thank you."

Everyone believed that even less. As Rayna left the room, Tirin walked toward Camille and removed a paper bag from his coat pocket.

"A Po' Boy. From Avery's," Tirin said.

He started to place it on the nightstand next to the bed and hesitated as he saw a teardrop on the nightstand. Camille found Tirin's eyes and followed them to the droplet, then quickly shifted her eyes back to his nose as it twitched ever so slightly. He set the bag down on the droplet and turned to leave, just catching her eyes.

"It's catfish. Your favorite," he said, then walked away.

"Thank you," Camille whispered.

He nodded without turning back and exited the room.

"JD, I'm so sorry," Kaitlin said as she finally found the courage to speak. It was her job to fulfill the number one prerequisite for any true best friend, "I'm the one Ms. Rayna should be upset with." To lie for them. "Camille called me after school and said she was feeling poorly and asked me to relay the message, but in my haste to get over here, I,--"

"It's fine, Katie. No one's upset. Rayna can sometimes be a bit,--"

"Of a bitch?" Camille finished.

"Come on now, Cher, that's not fair."

"Why do you always defend her?"

"I'm not. Didn't think I needed to for a simple misunderstanding."

"Oh, I understood her perfectly."

"Katie, can you give us a moment, please?" Julien asked.

"Of course." Kaitlin grabbed the paper bag with the sandwich in it. "I'll just warm this up for you."

"Thank you," Camille said.

"Uh, this sickness thing," Julien asked Kaitlin. "Anything we can do about that?" For a second, it seemed as if he had forgotten about what Rayna had seen in her cards.

"Just love her like you do," Kaitlin said as she closed the door behind her.

"Well, 'na, that's easy." Julien kissed her, but again, Camille didn't respond. "Come on, Cherie, let's not fight. Not today."

Camille laid back on the bed. "I'm sorry. I'm just not feeling well at all. That's why I came home."

Julien laid next to her and touched her barely protruding belly. "It's okay, of course. It was just a big day, is all."

"I know. I missed it. Sorry. So… Wha-What happened? What did Rayna say?"

"Drumroll, please," Julien said, softly tapping her belly. "Twins."

"Really?" Camille said, trying her best to sound surprised, but she wasn't at all convincing.

"A baby boy for you and a pretty little girl for me."

Camille started crying, and it gave Julien pause.

"Did she know? She couldn't've heard. Could she?" He frowned as the idle thoughts rambled through his head.

"I'll be honest with you, Cher. I was kinda hoping for a more exuberant response," Julien said, trying to joke with her to ease his own tension.

Camille smiled through the tears. "No, no! I'm happy. It's just these hormones. I think. They gonna be okay… our babies. Right?"

"They gonna be just fine," Julien said, surprised by the question.

Camille grabbed his hands and squeezed them hard as she looked into his eyes.

"Yes, they will."

"Of course they will," Julien said with a curious look.

He returned the firm squeeze and rose from the bed. Camille pulled him back down.

"Can you believe we're here? All the way from that lakeshore to here," she asked.

"I promised you a fairytale, and we're having it, aren't we?" Julien said as his eyes searched her face. Something seemed off.

"Yes. We are." Camille said. Then, she changed the subject. "What about your dad? Was he excited?"

Julien didn't like lying to her, but in this case, "Of course. He's gonna be a granddad."

Camille smiled and patted his hands, then released them.

"Good. I'm tired I,-- I think I'll sleep awhile."

"Go 'head, darlin'."

Camille shifted, turning her body to face the wall, creating a barrier between herself and the world behind her. Julien leaned down and pressed a soft kiss to the top of her head, his lips lingering for just a moment before he moved toward the door. But as he reached it, he paused. Something held him back. He turned and stared at her for a long moment, his eyes full of unspoken thoughts, questions, and uncertainties. He wondered—about her, about them, about the silence that now stretched between them like an invisible wall.

Camille felt the weight of his gaze pressing on the back of her head, and for the first time, it unsettled her. There was something different about the way he looked at her now, something that made her skin prickle with discomfort. It wasn't the familiar warmth she had once known but a gaze filled with a complexity she couldn't quite unravel. Julien, too, was unsettled, though for reasons he couldn't fully articulate. His mind was clouded with conflicting emotions, an internal storm he wasn't yet ready to confront.

Without another word, he turned and slipped quietly out of the room. The soft 'click' of the door closing behind him seemed louder than it should have been, breaking the stillness that hung in the air. Camille exhaled slowly, realizing only then that she had been holding her breath the entire time. The tension in her body was released, but it didn't bring her any comfort. She closed her eyes, a single tear forcing its way through the corner of her left eye, sliding down the bridge of her nose before disappearing into the delicate silk sheets below.

CHAPTER 10

"*She could have been there...*"

Julien charged into the study past Tirin and Dane and bee-lined straight for Rayna.

"You ever pull a stunt like that again,--"

"I was trying to protect you," Rayna said. "If she was planning on going all Esmerelda on us, she would have had to go through me first. That is one of the reasons why you pay me, remember?"

"I don't pay you to antagonize her!"

"Technically, you don't pay me at all," Rayna indicated with a little more attitude than Julien needed right now.

"I mean it, Ray! Let her be!"

"Of course, you take her side; you always do."

"She's my wife!"

"Right, and she's never wrong and can do or say whatever she wants."

"No, but,--"

"I'd like to see how understanding you'd be if I was supposed to meet the two of you someplace and then just didn't show up or call because I wasn't feeling well. How do you think that conversation would go down?"

"ALL RIGHT!... Jesus Christ! Why can't you just try to get along with her?!"

"Hmmmm." Tirin exhaled a soft, low growl.

"Something you wanna add to this conversation?" Julien said as he swung around to face him.

Tirin gave no response.

"She was sick, and she came straight here. Okay? 'Cuz, if she was there, you'd have picked up her scent, right?" Julien asked, more and more belligerent with every breath. "I mean, you'd have picked it right up, yeah? But you didn't, did you?" Julien asked, almost as if he were daring Tirin to respond. Tirin just stared at him, weary of this line of questioning. "Because she wasn't there!" Julien shouted.

"Least not that we could see," Rayna said softly.

Julien whipped back around to Rayna, ready to finish what he came in to do. Perhaps he and Tirin were done with this conversation, but Rayna still had some seeds to sow.

"The hell's that supposed to mean?" Julien asked.

"What are the Five Forms of Magic known to this world?"

"You know goddamn well,--" Julien tried to say as he stalked her.

"Incantation, Potion, Thought, Levitation,--"

"None of which can accomplish what you say!"

"--And Transformation! The highest form of Magic."

"Which she cannot do!"

"Which *you* cannot do. She can."

Julien stopped and considered it for a moment.

"Warlocks cannot perform Transformation Magic, but witches can," Rayna said as Julien shook his head. "She could have been there, Julien."

"No."

"How do you know?" Rayna asked, now taking a step toward him.

"Rayna--"

"How do you know?" she asked firmly.

"She's only sixteen! Transformation Magic is the highest form of magic for a reason - 'cuz it's fucking hard! She can't even get off the goddamn ground yet, and now you got her disappearing?"

"Her great-grandma did."

"Esmerelda was like...what, twenty-six, twenty-seven? And one of The Five Fucking Great Ones, for Christ's sake – which is the only reason why she lived to be that old. They tried to kill her when she was twenty."

"And that girl upstairs is her direct descendant. You don't think she's capable?"

"Oh, I know she's got skills, and one day she will be a force to be reckoned with, but that day ain't today. She's sixteen! Four years younger than what Esmerelda was! She can do Incantation and stir up a mean Potion, and I've seen her do Thought Magic when she didn't know I was looking, but she can't Levitate, and she can't Transform! Not yet."

The weight in the room was making it difficult to breathe. Julien exhaled deeply. Rayna sighed with him. He couldn't - wouldn't - see what she saw, and not because he needed spectacles.

"Look, I know y'all are just doing your jobs, and I appreciate it, I really do, but I think we're all barking up the wrong tree here. We need to relax and focus and get back in sync. The three of us have survived - shit, flourished - because we've always been of one mind. One goal. One objective. I think deep down inside, we all know that Camille's not really the problem here."

"It's your father," Tirin said.

"Yeah," Julien said.

"Regardless of whether or not I'm right - which I am, by the way, he's never gonna agree to let her live," Rayna said.

Funny how the truth could always silence a room.

"I'll deal with him," Julien said.

At that moment, an ill-timed, inappropriate giggle slipped from Rayna's lips. It cut through the heavy tension in the room like a sharp blade—briefly dissolving the unease, only to create an entirely new one. Rayna had a talent for that. She had always loved to dance, not just in the metaphorical sense but in a way that made her stand out. In another life, with a bit of formal training, her tall, statuesque frame and long, muscular legs would have easily set her apart from the most elite performers. She could have balanced gracefully between the worlds of jazz and ballet, her every move poised and purposeful.

But today, Rayna wasn't gracefully navigating the stage of art and performance; she was tap-dancing on a dangerous line with Julien—a line that most in the room would never dare to cross. Everyone knew the unspoken truth: Julien had never stood up to his father before, and bringing it up was a risk no one was willing to take. Except Rayna, of course. She was, after all, Rayna. She thrived in spaces where others hesitated, testing boundaries with a mischievous spark that only she could pull off.

But even she knew when to stop. The moment stretched, and the laughter that had dared to escape her lips quickly faded as Julien crossed the room with deliberate steps, his eyes fixed on her. He stopped just inches from her face, the space between them charged with unspoken tension. Rayna's playful demeanor vanished as quickly as it had appeared, silenced by the weight of his presence, the line she had danced so close to now feeling far more dangerous.

"What's funny? Hmm? Tell me, 'cuz I wanna know," he asked.

At that distance, or from any distance, really, Rayna could see in Julien's eyes that any word spoken by her in this moment would be received as an act of war. So, instead of speaking, she shook her head. He held her stare for a few moments, well past uncomfortable, daring her to dance upon that line again, but she stood strong and held both his eyes and her tongue.

"You just better make sure, when that day comes, you're prepared for anything he brings into this house. Hear me?" Julien asked. Again, she chose to hold her words and, instead, nodded her understanding.

"And you..." indicating Tirin, "you and your betas have one job here - one: to protect her. Don't ever leave her alone like that again," Julien said as he eyed Dane before he left the room, taking a great deal of the tension in it with him. But there was still a bit left between the remaining participants.

Rayna paced a few steps as the wheels in her head spun.

"Locked doors, falling vases, tears, sweat..." She stopped and looked Tirin directly in the eye. "An alpha wolf can smell a witch from two miles away." She declared. "So, was she there or not? Yes or no?"

Tirin paused before he answered. He never rushed anything. Even the smallest phrase that escaped his lips was well thought out and precise.

"Her scent was not there."

Rayna stared at him, her brow furrowed in a way that was uncharacteristic of her usually composed self. She knew he had a soft spot for Camille—anyone with eyes could see it—but she also knew where his true loyalties lay. His devotion would always remain with Julien and herself, unwavering and absolute. That was the way of things. And more than that, she understood one crucial truth about him: he would never lie, not to her, not to anyone. It wasn't in his nature—it wasn't the alpha way. His word was as solid as the ground they stood on, and that alone carried weight in her mind. With a subtle nod, Rayna acknowledged him, though her thoughts were still spinning in different directions. She sank into the leather sofa, the cool material pressing against her as she settled into its embrace, yet her mind remained far from relaxed. There was much to consider, much that still didn't sit right. As Tirin and Dane moved toward the door, ready to leave, Rayna remained where she was, lost in her contemplations. The room around her seemed to blur, the conversation fading into the background as her focus shifted inward. There were things she needed to figure out—pieces of the puzzle that hadn't yet fallen into place. And even as the door creaked open, her thoughts stayed anchored to the questions she couldn't yet answer.

"All the time I've known you, I've never seen you bug out like that before. What spooked you? Hmm? What'd you smell?" she asked just before they exited the room.

Again, he paused and chose his words very carefully before he spoke.

"Coriander. Wild berries. Orange honey… and Tuberose," he said over his shoulder, his eye just caught hers as he left the room.

Like a computer, her mind went to work, her eyes flitted feverishly as she processed this puzzling new data, repeating the meaningless words silently to herself over and over again. Suddenly, the corners of her mouth curled upward into that familiar, dark, beautiful smile.

"Perfume...."

CHAPTER 11

"$\mathscr{T}$*here's one case of someone like, 'you' havin' twins, and trust me when I tell you, that didn't turn out well for anyone..."*

Camille laid curled up on the bed, staring blankly at the wall. The knock on the door startled her out of her trance.

"Come in, Katie, I,--" She turned over, expecting to see Kaitlin with her food, but instead, a grinning Barrett slipped into the room and closed the door behind him.

"Mr. Gerard," she said as she sat up in the bed.

"How you feelin', Sugar Plum? I ain't wake you, did I?" he asked.

"No, sir, I,--"

"Come on, na'. You and me need to be well past that Sir nonsense," he said as he sat down next to her on the bed. "In light of everythin' going on, I think it's about time you officially started calling me Dad, don't you think?"

She tried her best to act normal but could not bring herself to look him in the eye.

"Yes… Dad. Yes."

"That's better." Barrett laughed. "Well, I'm sure you've heard the news by now."

"Yeah," Camille said as she looked him in the eye. "I heard everything,"

Probably a little too pointed and definitely not in her best interests, as it caused Barrett to furrow his brow and his attitude shifted ever so slightly.

"Well, you don't really seem all that excited. Somethin' wrong?"

Camille realized her faux pas and quickly pushed down the anger boiling in her belly. She couldn't let anything show – especially to him.

"I'm just really not feeling well today. 'Dad'." She forced out of her mouth. "I honestly don't know what's come over me." She giggled, trying to remove the tension she had created.

"Aw, it's only natural to feel a little strange," Barrett smiled and relieved the room of the tension from the previous moment. "And you probably tired, too."

"Yeah. I am. It's been a very stressful day."

"I can imagine. Why don't you get some rest," Barrett said as he rose from the bed and moved toward the door. "And you not going to that school anymore will relieve a lot more of that stress."

"W-What do you mean?" Camille said, stopping Barrett at the door. "I still have six more weeks before I have to start my leave of absence."

"Yeah, but under the circumstances, we thought it be best if you started that leave, effective immediately."

The last thread of that perfect life Camille saw in her future unraveled.

"*We* thought it was best?" She asked.

"I've already notified the school."

"*We?*" She again stated.

"Well, your father and I, of course."

"You spoke with him?"

"Called him right after we found out the good news. I always like to keep him abreast of all the goings on with his little girl."

Whatever air remained in Camille's lungs seemed to vanish in an instant, as if it had been forcibly sucked out of her. Barrett's words hit like a punch to the gut, leaving her reeling. She didn't know if he was lying—couldn't tell if this was another one of his twisted manipulations or a bitter truth—but that hardly mattered now. The reality that settled over her was far more suffocating. The fact was undeniable: she hadn't spoken to her father since the wedding. And now, as the weight of Barrett's statement sank in, a cold realization gripped her. She might never speak to her father again. That thought, once distant and unthinkable, now loomed large and inevitable. A void opened inside her, dark and heavy, as the finality of it all took hold. There was no more hope, no more possibility. All that was left was the empty space where her father's voice should have been.

"But Julien and I agreed that I would finish out this term and then,--"

"That was before we found out you were havin' twins," Barrett interrupted. "And that right there's a game changer. See, people like you don't normally have twins."

"How would you know that? I mean, just how many people like me have you come across? Cuz for the life of me, I don't think I've seen a single other,"

Camille, again, let her anger and frustration slip into the light, and this time, it brought with it a darkness. Barrett closed the door and turned back to face her. His smile was gone, replaced with a dark and terrible cast.

"No. I wouldn't think you would. See, you, my dear, are a very rare breed, but I can tell you, with all honesty, that I have most definitely come across a few in my time. And as far as I know, there's one case - one, of someone like, *'you'* havin' twins, and trust me when I tell you, that didn't turn out well for anyone involved. So, this time… this time, we gonna do it right. Hmm? World's a dangerous place, Camille. Especially for someone like, *'you.'* Now it's my job; my responsibility, to keep you safe, and in my mind, ain't no place safer in this entire state than right here. So, under these… delicate circumstances, I think it's best if, for the rest of your pregnancy, you stay right here where we can watch you and help you. Anythin' we can do to relieve you of stress and keep you safe. And I ain't forget about you. I even got you the best tutor money can buy so that when this is all over, you can get right back to becoming the best lawyer the state of Louisiana ever did have."

"Doctor," Camille said, dejected, as she reached for the Blood Heart Necklace.

"What's that, 'na?"

"I wanted to be a doctor," she said softly.

She now knew that would never come to be.

"Ah. Well… You can get on to being that, then. Sugar Plum, when this pregnancy is over, and you done gone and made me and your daddy the two proudest grandpappies this side of the Mason-Dixon Line, you can do or be whatever you want."

"Think I'll call Daddy, too. Tell him the good news. I'm sure he'd want to hear it from me, don't you think?" She asked, fishing for a sign of uncertainty in his voice or, perhaps, a glimpse of a weakening resolve in his eye, but Barrett gave her nothing.

"Don't you worry 'bout 'dat, na.' He knows," Barrett said. "I left a detailed message for him earlier this afternoon. Took a while for him to get back to me, though, but he did leave a message expressin' his sheer joy and delight by your present condition and promised that he would come for an extended visit once the children are born. Oh, and uh, if you do try to contact him, don't be discouraged if you don't hear from him right away. That new job that I arranged for him keeps him fairly busy and constantly on the move." Barrett winked at her. "Get some rest, and don't you worry about nothin'. From this point on, I will personally see that you are taken care of."

His smile could not hide the deadness in his eyes as he turned and left her alone in the room.

CHAPTER 12

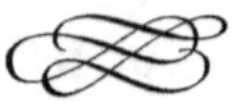

...*One long, sustained sniff,...*

Three Weeks Later:

Camille sat in the study at Julien's desk, her attention buried deep in one of the many books spread out before her. The soft rustle of pages turning was the only sound breaking the heavy silence of the room. She had been engrossed in her reading for hours, determined to keep her focus on the pages rather than the growing tension nearby.

Tirin, however, was a constant distraction. He paced back and forth across the room like a restless, caged animal, his gaze fixed intently on her. His movements were relentless, his energy crackling in the air, and though she had pretended not to notice at first, Camille was all too aware of him. The silent, unspoken pressure he was exerting had been building steadily, and though she had held her tongue, her patience was fraying with each passing second.

She said nothing, her eyes still scanning the lines of text, but the tension in her body was unmistakable. Her jaw tightened ever so slightly, her fingers gripping the edge of the book just a little too hard. She had endured his pacing long enough, and her tolerance was nearing its breaking point. One more step, one more glare, and the silence between them wouldn't hold for much longer.

"I can feel your eyes on my head," Camille said without looking at him. "It's annoying."

"It's Saturday," Tirin said sharply.

"I'm well aware of the day, date, and time," she whispered so faintly that even a dog wouldn't have heard her, but she knew he did.

"The tutor left two hours ago. Time for a break."

"Not if I want to go to med school," Camille said, with a sarcastic tone that did not go unnoticed.

"We should be outside," he said, with his eyes still glued on that single spot on her head.

"Then go! I'm not stopping you,--"

"Enough!" He commanded, then reached over and slammed the book shut.

"What are you doing?!"

"I want to go outside." His tone was even, controlled, but still commanding.

"GO. I have work to,--"

"With you."

Her anger softened as she looked up at him. There was a time not long ago when she would have jumped at the offer to go for a walk with her often-misunderstood friend. But now, trying to hold back her sadness, she reopened her book.

"I have to study."

"You've done nothing but study for weeks. You must exercise your body on equal parity with your mind." Again, he closed her book.

"Tirin, stop it!"

She looked up, meeting his eyes, but something was different this time—they weren't staring back at her. Instead, his gaze had drifted downward, settling on the closed book resting on the desk between them. Camille followed his line of sight and felt a knot tighten in her stomach. For the first time, Tirin seemed to notice the true age of the book, his fingers tracing its worn cover with a newfound curiosity. Much to her dismay, he carefully turned it around to examine the title. His eyes lingered for a moment, reading the embossed words: Ancient Spells and Magic.

He released the book, letting his gaze slowly return to hers. But by then, Camille had already snatched it up, her fingers gripping the fragile tome tightly as if protecting it from his scrutiny. She refused to meet his eyes again, her focus fixed firmly on the old book, the barrier it now represented between them. Her refusal to re-engage didn't faze him—Tirin wasn't the type to be discouraged by something so minor. In fact, there wasn't the slightest flicker of emotion on his face.

He simply sat, sinking into the chair opposite her, his eyes still locked on her with that unsettling calm. He didn't need words to convey what was building between them. The silence in the room thickened, the unspoken tension growing rapidly, swallowing the air around them. Each passing second felt heavier than the last, the weight of his presence pressing in on her like a force she couldn't ignore.

"What?!" She said as she clutched the book like a shield in front of her chest.

He said nothing. Gave her nothing. He just stared at her in a way that suggested he knew something she didn't. Or, perhaps something she didn't want him to.

"This is just as important as math or science," she answered to a question that had not yet been asked.

"Is it?"

"Yes!"

"Why?"

"…Because knowledge is power, and power is strength, and I need to be stronger!"

"Do you?"

"Yes!" She said with much more emotion than she had intended.

"Why?" His intensity increased to equal hers.

For weeks, she suspected he knew something was bothering her, and for weeks, she wanted to tell him.

"Because I,--" she began, then stopped herself before she started.

She wanted, so badly, to tell him what she had heard that day at the office and ask him why. Ask him if he was still truly her friend or if they had become enemies. Were they ever really friends at all, or was everything just a charade, an elaborate ruse to keep her guard down? A part of her still believed that the bond between them was real and that he could never hurt her, but there was too much at stake, too much to lose if she was wrong.

"--Because I'm giving birth in a few months. It will require all of my strength and more."

Tirin seemed disappointed with her answer and looked away. The disappointment in his face did not go unnoticed on the innocent young enchantress, who seemed to take much offense to his apathetic attitude. It stoked a fire within her that should have probably remained dormant.

"And you may not always be around to protect me," she said, with an attitude that was uncharacteristic for her. "When that day comes, know that I will protect myself."

A threat. Small and thinly veiled, but a threat just the same. Tirin tilted his head as she held his eyes like only a few could.

"Hmmmm," he growled, "and you think reading this book will teach you to fight?"

"I already know how to fight."

"Do you?" he said, mildly amused.

She refused to be baited by him. She knew he was trying to anger her, and she had no plans to let it work, even though it was.

"Good. Then come outside," he said. "Spar with me. Show me what you think these spells of yours can do."

"I told you," she said matter-of-factly, "I'm not going outside now. I have to study."

"So, you're afraid?"

"I'm not afraid of anything!" She snapped.

"Uh-huh," he growled as he sat back in his chair and crossed his arms, daring her.

Camille's eyes flashed red. "Sedens sella depositum confringet."

The chair beneath Tirin splintered, sending him crashing to the floor. Any normal person would be angry or embarrassed over what she had done, but Tirin was far from normal. His expressions rarely changed. He looked up at her as her eyes faded back to normal and nodded as if he approved.

"Four seconds," he said.

"What,--"

Before she could even finish the word, Tirin was up and, in the blink of an eye, around the desk and behind her with his index finger on her neck. A long, razor-sharp talon emerged from his fingertip and pressed against her jugular.

"It took four seconds for you to cast your spell," he whispered in her ear. "Versus a human, that may be sufficient time, but if you were to ever find yourself face to face with someone who was almost as fast as me-e-e-e," he growled. "Outside of becoming invisible…" He took one long, sustained sniff from her shoulder, up her neck, to the top of her head, and filled his nose with her very essence before exhaling. "Nothing in that book of yours would save you."

The talon retracted back into his finger as he released her. She spun around in the chair to face him with a horrified look in her eyes. She quivered as she looked up at him.

"Oh my God," she thought. *"He knows."*

She could see it in his eyes. But how? Hard as she tried, she couldn't stop herself from shaking as he slowly circled away from her, his eyes locked on hers. In an instant, he had broken through her tough-as-nails exterior and exposed the scared little girl hiding inside. She felt sick and light-headed as if she could pass out, or maybe vomit, or both. She was defenseless. Standing outside of her body, watching, waiting helplessly.

"Achieve balance," he commanded. "You must exercise both your body AND your mind, witch!" He said gruffly as he made his way to the door. "There is a clearing half a mile behind the trees in the back. That is where we train. That is where you will find me if you wish to… exercise."

"But I… I am forbidden to leave the compound," she whispered.

"We won't. The Gerard estate is vast and has many secret places. This is but one of them." He exited without looking back.

"Did he know? If so, who else does," she wondered. *"Julien? Rayna? Maybe it was a test. Maybe they didn't know. Obviously, he suspected, but maybe he was just trying to get me to reveal something,"* she thought.

Or maybe… Maybe he was simply trying to be what she believed he had always been. Her friend. Her heart was beating so hard she thought her chest would burst. She started hyperventilating as the anxiety of the situation rushed over her.

"Where was Kaitlin? She would know what to do. She would tell me," she thought, as her eyes began to water. *"But I can't even tell her. If she knew, her life would be in danger as well, and I can't do that to her – I won't."*

She moved slowly to the sofa, sinking into its cushions with a deliberate, measured grace. Once seated, she closed her eyes and began taking deep, controlled breaths, trying to steady herself. Her fingers instinctively found the Blood Heart pendant hanging around her neck, and she began to gently massage it between her fingertips, grounding herself in the familiar sensation. She had to calm down— not just for her own sake, but for the children growing inside her. The tension swirling around her felt heavy and suffocating, but she knew she had to control it.

Concentrating deeply, she focused on channeling the negative energy, transforming it into something more useful, something she could manage. Slowly, her eyes opened, and in an instant, they flared a bright, fiery red. The energy coursing through her body was palpable, and as it surged, her hair lifted, floating above her shoulders as if carried by an unseen force. She raised her hands, watching as they, too, turned a vivid crimson, the energy flowing like molten fire from her eyes, through her chest, and out into her fingertips.

She moved one hand down, resting it gently on her stomach, her touch soft but deliberate as she carefully felt for the right spot. Her breath slowed, her concentration deepening, and she began to chant softly, her voice barely more than a whisper. The energy pulsed through her, protective and nurturing, as she focused all of her attention on the lives she carried, channeling her strength toward them.

"Ut puella, sed puer videbunt."

She repeated it over and over. It calmed her to believe that, somehow, she was helping her unborn children, and her breathing became normal again. Then, with a thought and a quick wave of her right hand, she reassembled the splintered chair without losing the rhythm of her chant. Her children would live - no matter what.

CHAPTER 13

Camille stood at the edge of the small, private clearing. It was a serene setting surrounded by various types of trees and shrubbery. She came as he knew she would.

"Tirin!" She yelled. No response. She looked around suspiciously and took a few timid steps forward. "Tirin!"

He was there – somewhere. He could hear the fear growing in her voice, and still, he gave her nothing. She turned to leave. After two steps, she turned back, scanning the area until she focused on a tree fifty yards away to her left.

"What is she doing?" He wondered.

Then, in a soft voice only he could hear, she whispered, "I know you're there. I can feel you."

Tirin emerged from behind the tree and moved toward her.

"How did you do that?" he asked. "I know *you* cannot hear me. How did you know?"

"I don't know. I… I just did." She seemed ashamed by that fact.

Nonplussed, he growled. He stared at her a moment, then quickly removed his shirt and pants and let loose his ponytail.

"What are you-- What are you doing?" She asked, not believing her eyes as he stood in front of her with nothing more than his undershorts on. "Put your pants on!"

Tirin raised his hands in front of his torso, and her eyes grew big as he instantly willed his nails to grow into razor-sharp talons.

"Now let's see how much you know."

"What?! No! I thought we would just,--"

"I'll charge. Half-speed. You divert - if you can," he said as he turned and walked away from her.

"No. I didn't come out here to fight you." Tirin continued to walk away from her. "I don't want to do this," she said as her body began to tremble. "Someone could get hurt."

"Someone might," he said over his shoulder.

"I mean it, Tirin, I'm not doing this!" She yelled, trying to show some strength, but she could not hide her fear from him. He could smell it. It permeated through her clothes.

"Then someone will!"

He turned and charged - his movements fluid and precise. Even at this speed, he moved twice as fast as any human could.

"Nooo!" Camille screamed as her eyes flashed red and her hair floated wildly.

She gave ground as she matched his speed. She bobbed and weaved at an amazing pace, barely avoiding his attack. She caught his hand and flipped him. He somersaulted in midair and landed on his feet.

"GOOD!" He yelled, holding his ground, excited by this exchange.

All the fear that WAS in Camille had been exorcised and was now replaced with anger.

"What the fuck is wrong with you?!" She screamed as her eyes faded to normal.

"Fear is your trigger."

"I'm pregnant!"

"Mmm. Survival instincts. Naturally," he said to himself, ignoring her cries.

She looked down and noticed a clean rip in her shirt.

"OH MY GOD! You almost cut me!"

"You need to get off the ground, or this time I will."

He slowly began to circle her, all the while sizing her up.

"You could have injured my babies! We're done! Asshole!"

"Anger. Good - if you can control it. AGAIN," he ordered as he continued to circle her.

"Stop it, Tirin, or I swear to God,--"

"What? What will you do, witch?"

"You're fucking crazy. I'm outta here."

"It is unwise to turn your back on an opponent."

"Fuck you! I'm telling Julien," she said as she turned to leave.

Tirin roared from the disrespect, and he transformed into his full alpha wolf state. He knew Camille had never seen one before. She looked both frightened and in awe of this grand display.

"FIIIIIGGHHTTT!" He roared at her and charged.

"Tirin, stop it! STOP!!"

Even in this form, Tirin moved with the same fluid grace and precision that defined him. Every motion was calculated, deliberate, as if he were anticipating her every move. Camille's eyes and hands flashed a deep, fiery red, her hair whipping wildly around her as raw energy surged through her body. Instinct took over. Without thinking, she thrust both hands toward him, releasing a blast of pure, charged power from deep within her core, sending it hurtling down her arms and out through her palms. The force was immense, far greater than she had expected, and the strain of it immediately showed on her face. It hurt—her body wasn't prepared for the intensity of the energy she had unleashed.

Tirin, with his lightning-fast reflexes, leapt out of the way just as the blast exploded against the ground where he had been standing. The force of the impact sent shockwaves through the earth, and his body hurtled toward her. Camille shifted, her instincts still in overdrive, and with a swift motion, she threw her hands to the side. A powerful wave of energy followed, catching Tirin in mid-air and hurling him into a massive tree several yards away. The impact shook the ground, and leaves and branches were raining down around him.

In an instant, Camille powered down. The red faded from her eyes, her hair settled, and the energy that had surged through her vanished as quickly as it had appeared. She stood frozen, horrified by what had just happened. It had all unfolded so quickly, too quickly. Her heart raced as she stared at the spot where Tirin lay, struggling to make sense of the chaos. What had she done?

"Tirin?..." She meekly muttered.

He transformed back into his human form. Naked, he sat up and leaned against the tree. His shoulder was separated, and his arm was broken. She ran and grabbed his pants and shirt. His underwear had been destroyed in the transformation. Timidly, she moved over to him and knelt at his side.

"I'm sorry. I didn't mean to. I was just really scared, and then something just… happened," she said, as the tears began to flow.

"No. Fear is a useless emotion that you cannot control. What was supposed to happen, happened."

Camille winced, slightly sickened, as she watched him reset his own arm. He grimaced as he continued to talk, but the pain did not interrupt his thoughts.

"It is what was created from the fear. Adrenaline. That can be controlled; that is your trigger. Go-o-o-od," he growled.

With a swift motion, he grabbed his dislocated shoulder and slammed it back into place with a resounding crack. The pain surged through him, eliciting a deep, primal roar that echoed through the space—a release of both agony and relief. His chest heaved for a moment as he steadied himself, his body momentarily shaking from the strain. With his arm now set, he reached for his pants, wincing slightly as he gingerly pulled them on, careful not to aggravate the injury further. When he looked up, his eyes fell on her. She was sobbing, her shoulders trembling with each ragged breath. The sight of her in such distress hit him in a way he wasn't prepared for. He froze, unsure of what to do next. Consoling someone? Offering comfort? These weren't skills he had ever mastered, let alone encountered often. This was unfamiliar territory, and he was completely out of his depth. His instincts, honed for battle and survival, were useless here. He sat there, awkward and uncertain, his mind scrambling for something—anything—to say or do that might help. But the truth was, he didn't know where to begin. Empathy wasn't part of his usual repertoire, and the vulnerability in front of him left him feeling powerless in a way that bruises and broken bones never could.

"Stop crying. It accomplishes nothing," he growled.

"I'm sorry," she sniffled.

"Stop!" he ordered.

"I can't just stop! I cry when I'm upset, and I'm upset because I just almost killed you, and I don't know what's going on or why this is happening to me!"

He raised his injured arm and winced as she buried herself in his chest. He held her as she cried. After a few moments, she regained some control.

She looked him in the eye and earnestly asked, "Why?"

He stared back at her, expressionless. He wanted to tell her the truth, but it was not his truth to tell.

"As you said, I may not always be around to protect you, but I shall take great pride knowing that you can protect yourself."

"Can I?" she asked.

"Mmmm. You're a witch." He nodded toward his rapidly healing shoulder. "You are stronger than you know."

"Have you ever seen a witch before me?"

He sighed deeply and, as he always did, chose his words carefully before he answered.

"No… but I have felt their power."

"How?"

"When I was young, little more than a pup, my mother left me one night to do a job and never returned. That night, she was killed by a witch."

"I'm sorry."

Tirin shook his head. No apology from her was necessary.

"I was orphaned. Alone… My mother was a warrior. A superior fighter. Much of what I have learned comes from my lessons with her. It would have taken someone with great power to put her down. From that moment on, I became a student. I studied, read any book I could find, listened to stories of the old, sought out any piece of knowledge - anything that would help me learn more about witches so that one day I might exact my revenge. Two years later, I went looking for her, only to find that she had died minutes after killing my mother," he said as his eyes found hers. "They had killed the witch after they used my mother to distract her. She had been nothing more than bait." He paused a moment before he continued. "They moved away shortly after that, but I would not rest until I hunted each and every one of them down. Then, one night, at age twelve, I found them all in a decrepit bar in the Little Woods area of New Orleans: a warlock, a vampire, an alpha wolf, and his two betas."

"Oh, my God. You took on all of them?"

"Yes," he said.

"And you won?"

"No. Five minutes more, and I would not be here to tell this story. I was bloodied and badly beaten, and the vampire had just gotten hold of me when, from out of the darkness, came a young warrior floating, effortlessly, on air. It was like nothing I had ever seen. His eyes and hands glowed blood red, and his long black hair floated wildly about his shoulders. I watched in awe as he pulled pure energy from his soul, shaped it in his hands, and launched it at the vampire holding me down."

"Like what I just did?" she interrupted.

"Yes, but with so much more power," he answered. "The vampire was instantly destroyed. I had never witnessed such a thing. The power he harnessed and the fluidity of his movements were astonishing. Momentarily, the others scattered, awestruck, or perhaps they were merely in shock by the courage of this brazen young boy just a hair shorter than me. I remember the look in his eye and the smile on his face as he helped me up," Tirin said. "By this time, the boldness of his intrusion had worn off my mother's killers. They had regrouped and, again, were preparing to attack. 'What's your name, dude?' he asked me." Tirin almost smiled. "'I am Tirin!' I roared with pride. I wanted this wild boy to know who he had temporarily saved. I wanted him to know that I was proud to die at his side, for we were still badly outnumbered. 'Well, Tirin,' he said, smiling as they moved toward us, 'If we're gonna fall today, let's make them remember our names!' That was the night I met your husband."

"Julien?! That was Julien?! Fight?! No, he… he hardly ever uses his magic and certainly not to fight," Camille said, aghast at the thought.

"Mmmm. He was forced to become… a different person, but make no mistake, it still lives within him. He suppresses it, but he is a fighter, second to none."

"So, the two of you were able to defeat them?"

"No. We were still badly outnumbered until Rayna finally chose to step in."

"Rayna? My God, really?" Camille shook her head. "Seriously, what's her deal? How long has she been with him? I heard that one day, she just appeared at the front door or something stupid like that."

"I have heard the stories," Tirin said. "But I feel this truth, whatever it may be, is a mystery that neither one of them will ever be compelled to reveal. All I can tell you is that she had been his protector long before that day. She is quite unique. One of the most skilled and ferocious fighters I have ever witnessed." Camille rolled her eyes. "You should not antagonize her so."

"I'm not afraid of Rayna, and I don't antagonize her."

Tirin softly growled at that statement.

"Well, I wouldn't if she would stay away from my husband," Camille said.

"You misunderstand her. She is protective of us both, but not unlike any mother would be."

"That may be true for you, but trust me, the last thing she wants to be is Julien's momma."

Tirin, not interested or comfortable in taking this conversation any further, continued with his story.

"She tipped the scales much closer to our favor that night and made it one that none of us will ever forget. I have been indebted to them both ever since. Come. You should eat."

"Yeah. I am tired and a little light-headed. Maybe being pregnant and all, this wasn't such a good idea," she said.

"Nonsense. You're a witch. What you feel is the result of you calling upon your Qi."

"What?"

"The energy that witches and warlocks expel from their bodies is drawn from their soul, their life force - Your Qi. Using it weakens you. That is the cost of wielding the power you possess. If a runner never became tired, how would he ever be defeated?"

"If I'm weakening myself, then I'm hurting my babies. I should stop."

"NO, you must train! For the runner, the longer the race, the more training required to strengthen endurance. It is the same with magic practitioners," he explained. "As they tire, their magic diminishes. Training and building endurance increase's your ability to sustain your powers."

"How fast can I grow if I train properly?"

"Mmm," he grunted. "Growth is dependent upon the ability to maximize one's natural gifts. One runner's gift may be his speed. Another may have superior endurance. Another recovers quicker than the other two,--"

"Who wins?" she asked anxiously. Tirin's brow folded into a frown from the question. "All things equal, who wins?"

"All things are never equal in a fight."

The disappointment in her face was evident, and he found her impatience and desperation curious, so he gave her something.

"The one who possesses the greatest combination of the three." He sighed. "But you must always remember using your power costs something. It is the third of the Three Laws Of Magic."

She had a look of surprise on her face as she had never heard any of this before.

"Three? Wh-What are the other two?"

He released a long, sustained grunt. "Time is a constant that cannot be changed. I have heard fables of a chosen few that can stop it or slow it down temporarily, but no one on this earth possesses the power to move forward within it or turn it back. And you cannot bring back the dead. Once a soul has left this place, it cannot be retrieved."

Tirin rose and helped Camille to her feet. She stood there a moment and thought about all she had learned as Tirin headed toward the estate.

"The witch in your story," she called out to him, "am I to become like her?"

The question stopped him in his tracks. He exhaled heavily as if the question itself had weighed him down. He turned and answered her the only way he could.

"Whether it be today, tomorrow, or the next, we will all fall. When your day comes, make them remember your name. I shall be here for you tomorrow and every day after if you wish to continue… exercising."

He turned and sped away, leaving her standing there, alone with her thoughts.

CHAPTER 14

"*It'll only hurt for a second. Then it's just gonna feel soooo gooood...*"

March 1995 - *Twenty weeks until birth*

In the Gerard house, one might struggle to tell the difference between noon and midnight. The perpetual presence of vampires demanded that the interior remain sealed against even the faintest sliver of sunlight. Every window was blackened, thickly covered to block out any trace of day, creating a world where the sun's influence never reached. Candles lined the darkened windowsills, casting their soft glow in place of natural light. More candles hung suspended above doors and tables, their flickering flames providing the only warmth in the otherwise shadowed halls. Two candles stood on each step of the grand, winding staircase, illuminating the path from the base to the second floor like silent sentinels.

At the heart of the home, a towering six-foot, two-sided fireplace blazed constantly, casting light and heat into both the living and dining rooms. The firelight flickered across the walls, adding a soft glow to the otherwise dim rooms. In the study and kitchen, a smaller version of the same fireplace offered comfort, particularly to those in the house who still preferred a hint of warmth in their surroundings.

Though the house had electricity, and Julien and Camille often relied on it for convenience, most of its inhabitants preferred the natural dimness of candlelight—or, more fittingly, natural darkness. The modern comforts of the home were there, but they meant little to most of the malafecs who occupied it. Except for one thing: refrigeration. In a house full of vampires, it was an absolute necessity.

Blood had to be readily available at all times. It was their sustenance, and the old days of vampires prowling the streets in search of victims were becoming a relic of the past. They couldn't just hunt and kill humans indiscriminately anymore, not like they used to.

But they were still allowed to walk the night. Permission had been granted to hunt the fringes of society—the homeless, the old, the lonely, and the occasional wandering tourist. With the hypnotic effects of the mesmerize, they could feed without leaving a trace. The victims would be left weak, their minds foggy but otherwise unharmed. The puncture wounds would heal, often explained away as a snakebite or a dog attack. All might not be forgotten, but then again, who truly listened to the whispers of the homeless or the elderly?

This was a new age, and these were domesticated vampires who were strictly forbidden to kill anyone unless sanctioned by Rayna, Julien, or Barrett. This was Rule One, and it was certain death – or re-death in this case - to anyone who disobeyed it, but they were vampires, after all. Everyone knows they can't be trusted. So they kept refrigerators full of blood to help curtail their animalistic instincts, both in the house and in the outer quarters. A luxury that the Gerards could easily afford, or, as it were, one they could not afford, not to have.

Rayna, however, had a penchant for a different type of luxury. She liked nice things. She was a girly-girl at heart, who liked to shop for shoes, try on dresses, be pampered at the spa, and get her nails done. She toyed over which option would fill her time this afternoon as she lounged on the veranda just off the left side of the house, the mighty Mississippi River in her view.

With an empty carafe of her specially mixed Bloody Marys and a stack of her favorite magazines, she was, at the moment, content to remain here. Barring some emergency, Saturdays were hers to do as she wished, and right now, all she wished for was another carafe.

"Jimmy Lee, bring me,--" She stopped herself and sighed deeply.

It was Saturday morning. Outside of Tirin, the only ones here who could come out and serve her were the ones she served. A slight sigh of irritation escaped her lips as she slipped on her flip-flops, grabbed the empty carafe, and trudged back inside. She heard the front door close as she made her way to the kitchen.

"It's probably just Kaitlin," she thought. *"Who else would come over here on a Saturday morning?"*

"You looking awfully good this morning, Ms. Morrison," Rayna overheard one of her front door guards say, confirming her summation, which couldn't help but make her smile. But something in his voice gave her pause.

"Thank you, Leo," Kaitlin said.

"Downright tasty," Leo continued.

"Knock it off, Leo," Jimmy Lee, the other guard ordered.

"Shut up!" Leo fired back.

Leo was what most would consider a brute. He was the newest and easily the biggest, most intimidating vampire on Rayna's staff, and he still possessed a lot of his human self.

"This is an 'A' and 'B' conversation between me and Kait," Leo added.

He was a bully, a man used to taking whatever he wanted, but in order for him to survive in this environment, these habits would need to be purged.

"Yeah, well, Ms. Rayna finds out about this,--" Jimmy Lee tried to explain.

"Rayna ain't here," Leo replied before Jimmy could finish. "So why don't you just 'C' your ass out of it, hear me? You keep your mouth shut, and she won't. Ain't that right, Kait?"

Rayna pursed her lips. Respect was something upon which she placed a great deal of emphasis with her employees. *Especially* the ones who were allowed in the house, and right now Leo had just crossed a line into a place he did not want to be.

"Huh? And what you think about me calling you Kait?" Leo asked.

"I think Ms. Morrison would probably be better," Kaitlin said confidently. "Excuse me, please."

As angry as Rayna was right now, she was much more titillated by the complete absence of fear in Kaitlin's voice. This intrigued her, so she decided to let these unpleasantries play out a bit longer.

"Aw, you a spicy little girl, ain't you?" Leo said. "Look at her, Jimmy Lee. She act like she ain't even scared."

"Should I be?" Kaitlin asked.

"Naw. It'll only hurt for a second." Leo smiled as his fangs began to emerge. "Then it's just gonna feel soooo gooood to you."

Kaitlin nonchalantly pulled out the cross dangling from her neck, hidden behind her shirt, and dropped it on her chest. She stared at him with an indifferent defiance.

Leo smiled. "You know, if I listen real hard, I can hear the blood rushing through that long, sexy neck of yours," he said, ignoring the cross.

"You should put your tongue and teeth back in your mouth and walk away."

"I don't think you want that. Little human girl walking around all these mal'fecs like you, one of us. Maybe you wanna be one of us, huh? You wanna be my little groupie?" Leo laughed.

Rayna was mortified, yet still, she continued to listen.

"I don't wanna be a vampire, Leo, but if you wanna continue to be one, you should step away while you still can."

Rayna smiled at her audacity. Something about this girl she just liked.

"Or what?" Leo asked, losing his smile. "What you gonna do, little girl?"

If Kaitlin was at all intimidated, she certainly wasn't going to let him know it now. If she did, just like with any bully, the harassment would never stop. Rayna knew this and had heard more than enough. She stepped out of her flip-flops and moved into the room.

"Huh?" Leo continued. "You think I'm afraid of that little cross around your neck? Or maybe you think I'm afraid of what you think Rayna might do?"

"Oh, I think you should definitely be afraid of at least one of those," Rayna said as she strolled up behind Leo. "Morning, Katie-Kane."

"Ms. Rayna." Kaitlin nodded.

Rayna smiled back at her. She could see the relief in Kaitlin's face and was very proud of how she handled the situation, but now it was her turn.

"Rayna, I-I…" Leo stuttered, trying to defend himself, but Rayna quickly cut him off.

"Hush."

"I'm just sayin',--"

In the blink of an eye, Rayna tore his ear clean off his head with a swift, brutal motion. There was no hesitation, no mercy. Leo's hand instinctively shot up to the side of his head, clutching at the sudden void where his ear had once been. The pain hit him like a wave, and he drew in a sharp breath, preparing to unleash a scream that would have shaken the walls—had Rayna not moved just as quickly to silence him.

Her fist connected with his throat in a devastating strike, cutting off the scream before it could even escape his lungs. The force of the blow sent his massive body crashing to the floor, the impact reverberating through the room like a sledgehammer slamming into concrete. Leo lay there, writhing in agony, his face contorted in silent pain, unable to make a sound as his throat spasmed from the vicious hit.

Rayna bent down over him, her presence looming as his body squirmed beneath her, powerless. The silence that followed was thick and suffocating, broken only by the faint, ragged gasps Leo managed to draw through his crushed windpipe.

"You and I gonna have a long talk about interruptions, manners, and a few other things." Then, to Kaitlin, "You okay, Sugar?"

Kaitlin was in a bit of shock. She had witnessed many things in her time, things that most people would never see, but it had been a while since she had seen effortlessly quick violence like this. And even though it was on her behalf, Rayna could tell it disturbed her.

"Uhh… Yes, Ma'am. I'm… He was just trying to scare me."

"I know, but apparently, he didn't do a very good job of that either," she said as she grabbed Leo's hair and pulled him up to his knees.

"And the next time you address me, you better damn well put that, 'Ms.' in front of 'Rayna,' you hear me with that one ear you've got left?"

Leo, with one hand on his throat and the other on the side of his head where his ear used to be, could barely gasp out a response.

"Nod if you understand," she commanded.

He did, and she released him.

"Jimmy Lee, take him down to the cellar and put him in the playroom for me." She smiled at the thought of what was to come. "I will join you shortly."

"Yes, Ms. Rayna," Jimmy Lee said as he quickly removed Leo.

"Oh, and here." She tossed him Leo's ear. "Put this in my collection for me, please."

"Yes, ma'am."

Jimmy Lee disappeared around the corner with Leo. Rayna noticed Kaitlin's dumbfounded look.

"Don't worry 'bout him. It'll grow back," she said, studying Kaitlin.

"I know. I just..." Kaitlin exhaled deeply as she closed her eyes and shook her head as if she were trying to avoid a sudden dizziness.

"It's just the pheromones from the attempted mesmerize. Vampires release ten times more than other beings. It's what makes them virtually irresistible to humans," said Rayna as she stared at Kaitlin. "You, however, seem to be more immune to their effects than most."

"Ah, well, again, thank you, but it really wasn't necessary," Kaitlin said. "I knew he wasn't going to do anything."

"How do you know?"

"Because no vampire in this house would dare do anything you didn't tell them to," Kaitlin responded.

"Hmm." Rayna smiled. "Still, Leo's a big boy. Even Jimmy Lee's a little afraid of him. And you didn't even flinch."

Kaitlin shifted uncomfortably.

"We work with a lot of humans who know who and what we are. I don't know that I've ever met one as comfortable around mal'fecs as you."

"Mal'fecs just like humans, there's good ones and bad ones," Kaitlin said. "Excuse me." She turned and tried to head for the stairs, but Rayna's curiosity needed to be fed.

"Julien told me that you were attacked once. Almost died."

"Yes. I got myself into a… bad situation my freshman year in college."

"Tulane, right?" Rayna asked.

"Uh, yes."

"Not many people get attacked by a vampire and live to tell about it."

"It was a lycan, actually," Kaitlin said.

Rayna had a puzzled look on her face.

"Really? You got attacked by a lycan who didn't sire you, and he left you unscathed?"

"It was a female, and,--"

"You got attacked by a female?! And she left you looking like this?" Rayna could not contain her amazement.

"She left her mark." Kaitlin hesitated, then lifted up her shirt, revealing two inch-long scars on either side of her lower abdomen.

The wheels in Rayna's head spun.

"*There's something here. Something more that needs to be mined,*" she thought.

Rayna's instincts were as keen as her wit, and when she locked onto something, she clung to it like an old dog with a new bone.

"Interesting," Rayna said, almost to herself, as her eyes flitted back and forth across Kaitlin's stomach. "So precise."

Kaitlin uncomfortably lowered her shirt. Rayna's eyes drifted to Kaitlin's, looking for a response. Kaitlin quickly looked away as if she was purposely avoiding Rayna's eyes.

"Lycans are exceptionally focused and extremely temperamental individuals. *Especially* the females," Rayna said. "For the life of me, I can't imagine why she would leave you alive."

She asked to prolong the conversation as she slowly moved closer and closer, trying to catch Kaitlin's eyes.

"I guess I was lucky."

"Like standing under a tree holding a lightning rod in a thunderstorm, lucky. Baby, to my knowledge, luck like that doesn't exist."

"Guess you could say I had a guardian angel watching over me that night."

"Mmmmm. Was he cute?" Rayna asked.

Kaitlin couldn't hide her smile.

"He thinks so," Kaitlin said. The genuine affection she held could not be kept from her face.

"Sounds like a very interesting young man. Someone I surely would like to meet." Rayna's eyes began to sparkle as she finally found Kaitlin's eyes and locked in.

"What the hell are you doing?!" Camille yelled from the stairs.

Kaitlin blinked and shook her head as if she were coming out of some sort of trance. Rayna grunted, irritated. She did not like being interrupted, but she tried her best not to show it.

"Morning, Sugar. How are you feeling today?" Rayna asked.

Camille walked down to them. "What were you just doing?"

"Just having a little chit-chat with Katie-Kane, making sure she's all right."

"All right from what?" Camille asked Kaitlin, concerned.

"It was nothing. Really," Kaitlin responded.

"What happened?" Camille continued to press.

"One of the guards was just messing around,--"

"Who?!"

"Leo, but, really, it was nothing." Kaitlin tried to explain, but Camille wasn't having it as she whipped around to Rayna.

"Where is he?!"

"Leo's in time-out. I'll deal with him shortly," Rayna said. She didn't appreciate Camille's tone but tried to be civil. "I was just seeing to Katie first."

"You were trying to read her," Camille said, squaring up with Rayna.

"I'm sure I don't know what you're talking about," Rayna said.

"Camille, it's all right. We were just talking. That's all. I'm fine," Kaitlin said, trying to stop this before it got started.

"No. This is why I told you to never look in her eyes," Camille said to Kaitlin, still glaring at Rayna. "She has this power where, if she catches your eyes just right, you fall into a little trance, and she can see your thoughts and secrets without you ever knowing. It only works on humans. Julien told me all about it, so don't even bother trying to deny it."

Whatever pretense remained in Rayna hiding her anger, fell away at that moment.

"You wanna read somebody's thoughts? Try reading mine," Camille said as she stepped in Rayna's face. Her eyes flashed red, and her hair floated wildly off her shoulders. "Tell me what I'm thinking."

Whether you were human or a malafec, there weren't many things scarier than a witch in mactrouge, but at nearly six feet tall, Rayna looked down at the five foot-seven inch sixteen-year-old and laughed. Not a snicker, not a giggle, not even a chuckle, but a straight-from-the-gut belly laugh.

"Seriously?" Rayna said, looking down at Camille. Many emotions danced in her eyes, but fear was not one of them.

Before anyone could utter another word, Tirin stormed into the room, a blur of movement as he wedged himself between Camille and Rayna. His massive frame created an immediate barrier, forcing both women to instinctively step back. Kaitlin gasped, her eyes wide with surprise. Without so much as a glance, Tirin stood tall, and before their eyes, he shifted into his full alpha form. His already imposing body expanded, muscles rippling as his size increased, driving Camille and Rayna to take another step back, the space between them growing as his transformation completed.

Rayna's sharp gaze flicked to Kaitlin and, for the first time, noticed the fear clouding her eyes. Vampires never unsettled her, but lycans clearly did. The tension thickened, and in that charged moment, Dane came rushing in, his posture tense, ready for action. A bewildered look crossed his face as he took in the scene, unsure of what had sparked this sudden confrontation.

Tirin let out a howl—not the deep, aggressive kind that signaled an impending fight, but something different. It was two sharp bursts followed by a longer, higher-pitched cry that reverberated through the room. The unusual sound cut through the tension like a knife, its meaning lost on most, but it held a purpose that stopped everything in its tracks.

From the second-floor landing, Julien appeared, a T-shirt in hand, his face marked by confusion as he took in the scene below. Kaitlin, moving with a practiced calm, placed her hands gently on Camille's shoulders, offering her quiet reassurance. Camille, her hands still crackling with latent energy, slowly powered down, the red fading from her eyes as her body relaxed. The immediate threat passed, but the air was still thick with the weight of what had just happened.

CHAPTER 15

"What's wrong?!" Julien yelled, pulling the T-shirt over his head as he quickly descended the staircase.

Barrett marched toward the railing on the second-floor landing.

"What the hell is going on down there?!" Barrett yelled, "Julien! Why is that boy doing full alpha in my house?!"

"I got it, Daddy," Julien said as he hit the bottom stair. He looked to Rayna. "What's wrong?"

"Your *wife* flashed her eyes at me," Rayna said calmly, her eyes still locked on Camille.

"Wh-What?" Julien said, not knowing whether to look at Camille or Rayna.

"She did what?!" Barrett yelled.

"I got this, Daddy!"

"If you got it, then why is that boy still in full alpha in my entryway?!" Barrett yelled.

Julien gave a subtle nod to Tirin, who responded instantly, morphing back into his human form with practiced ease. Now fully naked, he stood his ground between the two women, his stance wide and firm, arms crossed over his chest. His eyes remained fixed ahead, deliberately avoiding the gaze of either Camille or Rayna, his expression unreadable, as if he were a silent barrier holding back the storm.

Kaitlin quickly averted her eyes, her discomfort evident in the way she turned her head, trying to put distance between herself and the scene unfolding before her. Camille, on the other hand, reacted differently. She lifted her gaze toward the ceiling, her jaw tightening as she exhaled sharply through her nose, the sound a clear signal of her rising frustration. She shook her head, visibly perturbed by the entire situation, her anger simmering just beneath the surface. The interruption had derailed the moment, and the tension that lingered was an unwelcome distraction she had no patience for.

"Julien," Barrett muttered between gritted teeth.

"Dane," Julien said, calling for the beta to do something.

Dane took off his shirt and quickly wrapped it around his sire's waist, then moved to the side. Tirin never flinched, and Rayna never took her eyes off of Camille.

"Y'all know better! You wanna roughhouse, you take that shit outside!" Barrett yelled.

"All right, Daddy!" Julien yelled back. His irritation resonated in both his face and his voice. He paused a second and calmed himself. "What happened?"

Both Camille and Rayna started talking over one another in a cacophonous shrill.

“Stop.” Julien nodded to Camille.

“I caught her reading Kait.”

“I did not read Kaitlin.”

“Liar!”

“Rayna?” Julien asked.

“…Okay, maybe I tried, but I didn’t do it.”

“Ms. Rayna!” a dismayed Kaitlin blurted out.

“You don’t get to do that to my friends!” Camille added.

“I like her too, Camille! Maybe if you didn’t treat her like a China Doll all the damn time, she and I could actually have a conversation or two,” Rayna said.

“Like the one she was having with Leo?” Camille turned to Julien. “He tried to intimidate her.”

“He did what?!” Julien exclaimed.

“Say what, na’?!” Barrett echoed simultaneously.

“I’m already dealing with the matter,” Rayna told Julien.

“When did this happen?” Julien asked.

“A few minutes ago. He was just talking smack. I knew he wasn’t going to do anything,” Kaitlin said, trying desperately to de-escalate a situation that had escalated to a point that was well out of control.

“I want him banned from this house!” Camille demanded.

“She’s right!” Barrett yelled down. “Rogue vampire in the house,--”

“He’s not rogue,” Rayna interrupted.

“His ass needs to be put down!” Barrett continued.

Rayna rolled her eyes. "He's just new, Julien. Trying to get a reaction from her. That's all, but it's no excuse for what he did. He crossed the line, and he will be punished, but I still believe he can be of some use with more… extensive training."

"All right, if you think you can control him. Otherwise, put him down," Julien said. "Either way, he's banned from the house."

"Agreed," Rayna said.

"You're leaving that up to her?!" Camille asked.

"Yes," Julien responded.

"Why?"

"Because that's her job."

"One of her guards threatened one of my friends," Camille said.

"And she will deal with it, as she has always done. Did you flash your eyes at her?" Julien asked pointedly.

"…Yes," Camille answered, a bit taken aback.

"Why? Were you provoked? Did you feel threatened in any way?"

"I told you, she was trying to read Kaitlin,--"

"That's not good enough."

"Julien,--" Camille tried to plead her case, but Julien had heard enough. He turned to Kaitlin.

"I'm sorry, Kait. I know this was an invasion of your privacy, and I apologize for that. Rayna was out of line and shouldn't have done it," he emphasized as he glared at Rayna, "but a lot of that fault comes back to me. From a business aspect, it gives me a powerful advantage over my competitors, and I push and encourage her to do it all the time. It's second nature for her." Then, again, to Rayna. "But she shouldn't be doing it here." He said with a displeasure in his voice that he did not try to hide. He then turned back to Camille. "However, that doesn't mean *you* get to threaten her life."

"I didn't,--" Camille exclaimed.

"That's exactly what you did! What'd you think would happen next? You're a witch, I'm a warlock, when we mactrouge, we show ourselves, and we are saying with mortal finality, 'here I am, now what do you wanna do about it?'"

"That's right!" Barrett added his unwanted opinion. "And you had better have your big girl panties on, 'cuz any mal'fec or human with half a brain is gonna try and take you out right then and there, 'cuz they know that's what you ready to do to them!"

"DAD!" Julien yelled, then looked to Camille. "This… this thing between you and her has got to stop."

"She provokes me!"

"I did nothing to provoke anything," Rayna fired back.

"You tried to read my friend!" Camille yelled.

"ENOUGH!" Julien shouted with a forcefulness he didn't normally show. "I am sick, physically sick of having to be in the middle of you two, and, damn it, I'm not doing it anymore! I can't." He glared at Rayna. "You are too old to be playing this high school shit with her!"

"Why are you yelling at me? I did nothing this,--"

"This time! You did nothing this time! What about all the rest?! You constantly go out of your way to agitate her and, at times, to make her feel stupid! That ends today. SHE'S MY WIFE!… You need to show her the respect that comes with that title."

Rayna said nothing. She just stood there glaring at Julien, angry and embarrassed. He then turned his wrath on Camille. "And Rayna is my family. She's the closest person in the world to me, next to you."

"What the hell am I, chopped liver?" Barrett chimed.

"Goddamn it, Daddy, you know what I mean! Could you please just let me handle this?!" Julien yelled. He focused back on Camille. "You don't wanna talk to her, fine. Don't. I don't care, but this is her home, too, and she's not going anywhere - EVER. You need to accept that and get over it."

The front door opened, and Cecil entered with the normal obliviousness that seemed to follow him wherever he went.

"Why am I opening the damn door myself? Where's these so-called guards at?" he asked.

"One of them got pissy with the little human girl," Barrett answered.

"Jesus, Daddy," Julien said as he shook his head from frustration and embarrassment.

"You put him down?" Cecil asked Barrett.

"Cecil, I'm handling this,--" Julien said.

"That's what I woulda done," Barrett said, talking over his son. "Right then and there."

"Damn right," Cecil agreed. "Can't have a rogue vampire roaming around the house."

"He's not rogue!" Rayna yelled, and Cecil jumped. The frustration was taking its toll on her as well.

"Then Camille flashed her eyes at this one here," Barrett said, jerking his thumb at Rayna as he descended the staircase.

"Uh-oh," said Cecil.

"That's why she mad," Barrett finished.

Julien, flustered by the constant interruptions, had no words, and even if he did, it no longer mattered. This was the Barrett and Cecil show now.

"Sweetie pie, you shouldn't be flashing anybody around here. Especially not your family," Cecil said.

"Okay, if you two got some place to go,--" Julien made one final attempt at corralling the situation. He failed.

"It's about respect!" Barrett shouted out as he reached the bottom step. "Sometimes I wonder if your generation truly understands that. We an eclectic group, to say the least, and I'll be goddamned if I approve of all the nonsense that goes on around here. I got two male lycans tinkerbelling in the room down the hall from me," he directed toward Tirin and Dane. "Little human girl running in and out of here at all times of day and night," to Kaitlin, "and this one here," he emphasized, pointing at Rayna, "thinking she running the goddamn house! I'll tell you what, Ceese, I don't like any of it!"

"I don't like it either," Cecil added.

"But we don't have to, Ceese, and neither does any one of you. But y'all damn sure better learn how to respect it, 'cuz like it or not, all of us right here in this room, we are a family. We may not always approve or even like each other, but we gonna have to learn how to respect one another, or else shit gonna have to change around here, and I mean quick!" Barrett turned to Kaitlin. "What you experienced today is truly what a vampire is: nasty, vile creatures, every last one of them. Everybody knows they can't be trusted."

"Daddy," Julien grimaced disapprovingly.

"Aw, you know it's true! That don't mean I ain't friendly with some of them, I'm just calling a spade a spade." He turned back to Kaitlin. "So if you can't handle that, then you don't need to be fooling around here, 'cuz we house a mess of them, and they ain't going anywhere soon. This one here," he pointed to Rayna, "may think she's running shit, but this is still my house." He turned to Tirin. "And the next time you think about going full alpha in here, it better be for a better reason than breaking up a fight! Still stinks in here!"

Barrett then walked up on Rayna and looked her dead in her eyes. She fidgeted from the uncomfortableness he knew he was causing her.

"When's the last time one of these vamps disobeyed you?" He asked her directly, but he didn't receive an answer to his inquiry as quickly as he would have liked. "WHEN?!"

"I don't, I don't,--" Rayna stuttered.

"NEVER," Barrett answered for her. "Put him down. If for nothing more than as an example to the others."

He turned away from her to Camille. Something in his eyes made her as uncomfortable as it did Rayna, but for a much different reason.

"Flashing your eyes is serious business, little girl. You got lucky today. Next time you do it, you better hope you're strong enough to take whatever comes back at you." He glanced at Julien, and there was an air of disappointment in his eyes before he turned away. "C'mon, Ceese." He said, and then the two men left the room.

Julien was pretty hot after being upstaged in such a manner, but at this point, an egg could be fried on any one of the faces in the room.

"Are we done?" Camille asked with a very controlled anger in her voice.

"…Yeah," Julien said.

He turned to her, but she wouldn't look at him. She just kept rubbing the Blood Heart necklace between her index finger and her thumb. He reached for her hand, but she jerked away and moved to the stairs.

"We'll be fixing up the nursery," she said.

Camille looked back to Kaitlin as she ascended the stairs and instead caught Rayna's eyes. There would be no forgiveness in either one of these two today. Kaitlin felt horrible, and not just from what Barrett had said, even though she could not help but wonder if he was right.

"I'm so sorry. I feel like this is all my fault," Kaitlin told Julien.

"It's really not," He reassure her.

"Things just got blown way out of proportion, and I never should have let it," Kaitlin said.

"Kaitlin," Rayna called. "Julien's right, sweetie, none of this is your fault, and I am truly sorry for what I tried to do. Your story was just so compelling, I… I just got lost in it. Forgive me."

Kaitlin gave her an understanding smile and headed for the stairs.

"And, Sweetie," Rayna continued, stopping her again, "for future reference, crosses don't really work."

Kaitlin paused as she processed this information and her mistake.

"Holy water does," Camille said, the anger still heavy in her voice.

Rayna pressed her lips together, forcing herself to hold back the sharp, biting retort that teetered dangerously on the edge of her tongue. The words were there, impatient and venomous, but she swallowed them down, keeping her expression cool and controlled. Julien, standing nearby, let out a soft sigh, barely more than a breath, and gave the slightest shake of his head—so subtle that only Tirin caught it. This was not a conversation meant for human ears, and Julien knew it. These were things they preferred to keep out of sight, far from the world of those who didn't understand their lives.

But Camille didn't care. She held Rayna's gaze with an unflinching intensity, her eyes locking onto hers for a few moments longer than necessary. The tension between them hummed in the air, silent but tangible. Without a word, Camille finally turned and ascended the staircase, her footsteps deliberate as she headed for her room, Kaitlin quietly following in her wake. The others remained in place, unmoving, the silence heavy as the tension lingered like an unspoken weight over the room.

It wasn't until the sound of the upstairs door slamming shut reverberated through the house that anyone moved. Julien exhaled loudly, the breath escaping through his nose in a clear sign of exasperation. Before he could even begin to speak, the weight of what had just transpired hung between them all, unspoken but understood.

"Am I excused?" Rayna inquired. The softness of her query did little to hide the harshness hidden behind her eyes.

"Rayna,--"

"I have business I need to attend to downstairs, unless you wish to yell at me some more."

Julien sighed. He knew both Camille's and Rayna's feelings were hurt, he just wasn't sure how this phenomenon became his fault.

"Yeah. You can go."

Rayna turned and headed for the cellar.

"...I'll be at Club Dallas for a few hours if you need,--"

The cellar door slammed shut. The slamming of doors was a pretty good indication that neither of the two dominant women in his life needed nor wanted anything to do with him for at least that amount of time. Julien looked to Tirin who released a long, deep exhale.

"Thank you, my friend," Julien said. "Funny thing is… different time, different place, those two would be best friends."

"Urrrm, maybe," Tirin grunted. He wasn't sure he agreed with Julien's affirmation, but he wouldn't completely discount it. "But not this time. Not this place."

Julien didn't want to, but he couldn't help but smile.

"Come on, get some clothes and come to the club with me. I got to inventory the liquor, and I'm interviewing a new manager. It'll just be a few hours. Neither one of them's gonna have anything to say to me for at least that long, anyway."

"You think it wise for both of us to leave them here alone?" Tirin asked.

"Probably not," Julien responded, "but I think we could both use a drink or two."

Tirin grunted. That affirmation he agreed with.

"It's been too long." Julien looked to Dane, then back to Tirin. "You think he's ready?"

"For what?" Dane asked apprehensively, still a little shell-shocked over what had just transpired.

"Mmmm," Tirin growled. "To be ready for something, one has to have an understanding of what is to come next."

"Well… You're part of this family now. Time for you to carry some of the load," Julien stated.

"What do you want me to do?" Dane asked nervously.

"Stay out of their way and, at the same time, don't let them kill each other," Julien said.

Tirin growled softly and nodded his approval, then bounded up the stairs. Julien nodded and headed for the door.

CHAPTER 16

"*That is the point where you will meet your vampire, and that is when you shall die.*"

April 1995 - *Sixteen weeks until birth*

Time had passed, and while the tension of the past seemed to have faded into the background, the intensity of Tirin and Camille's training sessions had unmistakably escalated. Even now, five months into her pregnancy, Tirin showed Camille no mercy. He pushed her hard, giving no concessions for her condition. And true to her nature, Camille didn't ask for any. She met every challenge head-on, the fierce determination in her eyes never wavering.

After a grueling session, they took a break beneath the shade of a large tree that stood at the edge of the training clearing. Camille, visibly fatigued but energized by the workout, eagerly dug into her snacks, devouring them in a bid to restore her drained energy. Despite the physical toll, there was a quiet satisfaction in her posture, a sense of accomplishment that showed in the way she breathed deeply, regaining her strength.

But as she reveled in the success of their session, it was equally clear that Tirin did not share her contentment. He sat a few paces away, his body still tense, his expression hard. There was a storm of frustration brewing beneath the surface, though he said nothing. Camille may have felt proud of what they had achieved, but in Tirin's eyes, it wasn't enough. The unspoken conflict simmered between them, the intensity of the training reflected in the unyielding looks they exchanged.

"That was an awesome session," Camille said, quite happy with herself.

"You need to get off the ground. It's been too long," he snarled.

"Hey, it's not like I'm not trying. Who are you comparing me to, Julien? Just 'cuz he was a prodigy and did it at twelve or whatever,--"

"It has nothing to do with that. Warlocks mature much faster than witches. Julien was not special because he could float at twelve. Nor was he special simply because of the power, but rather, the *command* of the power he possessed at that age."

"Okay, calm down. Maybe it's just not my time yet."

"No, you're ready. I can feel it. You're holding yourself back. Why?!"

"I'm not! Besides, I'm still moving really fast," she said. "You remember that time when you were coming at me from the side, and I spun around, and it was like I was this matador who had just ole'd the bull, and you went flying into the bushes?"

She laughed and raised her hand for a high five, but Tirin had no interest in indulging in her self-indulgence.

"Understand, the first wave will be betas," Tirin explained. Camille sighed as she lowered her hand and continued to satisfy herself with her snacks as she listened. "They are pack animals. They will not attack alone. They will try to surround you, and they will be relentless."

"How do you know all this,--"

"These things are secret to no one!" He yelled. "This is who we are and how we fight! We all must discover the demon inside of us and learn how to use it."

Camille shivered. That got her attention.

"The alpha and the vampire will be close by – observing; looking for weaknesses, and watching for openings.

"How will I be able to tell the difference between the alpha and the vampire?"

"The alpha will be the one staring at you, waiting to see how you fare against his betas. Waiting to see if there's anything left of you with which to even bother."

"And the vampire?"

"…The vampire you will never see. They are ruthless assassins, killers who lurk in shadows and hidden corners. They have no desire to fight you; their only desire is to kill you, and they are exceptionally efficient at this. They are the strongest of us, and once they lock up with you, there is no escaping their hold. You will die. A predicament, however, you will never see because you would never escape the betas as you cannot GET OFF THE GROUND!"

"I'M TRYING!" She yelled. Tirin growled his disapproval of her tone, and she lowered her voice. "Under the circumstances, I think I'm doing pretty fricking good," she mumbled under her breath.

"Do you?" he asked, with just enough sarcasm in his voice to spark a flame.

"Yes, I do,"

"Mmm. How long do you plan on using this pregnancy of yours as a crutch?"

The flame was ignited, and a fire began to smolder within her.

"For maybe another four months or so."

"You do not get to rest on the laurels and deficiencies given to human women, witch."

Her brow furrowed deep within her forehead, and her tone began to rise.

"It's not a deficiency, it's a fact! I'm carrying not one, but two lives in me! TWO! Two more people that I'm responsible for that I have to protect!"

"Which is exactly why you need to get off the ground,"

Camille let out a sharp, frustration-laden exhale, the sound carrying with it a noticeable release of tension. Along with the breath, a considerable amount of her pent-up anger seemed to dissipate, the edge softening just slightly. Tirin watched her closely, finding it fascinating—perhaps even perplexing—how she always managed to push her anger down when it reached a certain threshold, finding a way to control and release it before it consumed her.

But now, as he observed her with keen interest, an unsettling thought crossed his mind. What would happen if she didn't release it? What if she allowed that anger to build, unchecked and unrestrained? The idea intrigued him, the possibility stirring a dark curiosity. He had seen glimpses of her power, but there was something deeper, something raw and untapped, lurking just beneath the surface. And now, more than ever, he wondered what might happen if she let that power—along with her rage—run free.

"What if you are injured? What will *trying* get you then?" He asked in an attempt to mock her.

"What does that even mean?" she asked, clearly annoyed.

Tirin reached across and scratched her forearm with the sharp nail on his index finger, leaving her with a nice-sized cut. Camille screamed from the pain. She was livid. There are lines, and, in her mind, he had just crossed one.

"Goddamn it, Tirin!"

"Heal yourself," he said calmly as he continued his observation of her.

Her eyes flashed red as she placed her hand over the cut, giving him an earful the entire time.

"You can't just do shit like that! We were having a fucking conversation, not sparring! That's not fair!"

"No fight is fair. Have you learned nothing from me?"

She removed her hand after a few seconds, and the wound was gone, but her anger remained as her eyes faded back to normal.

"I've been matching you step-for-step for weeks, and alphas are faster than betas and vampires, you said so yourself! Would it kill you to give me an ounce of credit?!"

"You think you deserve it?"

"I almost killed you on my first fucking day, so, yeah, I think I do."

It seems as if lines were being crossed on both sides with no regard to the feelings of the other, but crossing lines with lycans can be dangerous, and Camille was teetering toward a testy place.

"I was moving at far less than full speed for your benefit," he said as he glared at her in a much different way than he had before.

Camille held his glare, absorbed it, and then spit it right back at him.

"Really?" she said, not believing the excuse that was offered. "Then maybe next time you go all out, and let's see what happens."

Tirin released a low growl as he stood up and removed his shirt. Camille had moved well past the line and had unknowingly challenged an alpha.

"Rise."

And he readily accepted it. Camille rolled her eyes and, again, exhaled her anger and frustration. This time, it was a bit too late.

"Come on, T, save it for tomorrow. I'm tired,--"

"RISE!!!" he roared.

The ferocity in his tone caught her off guard, and she jumped a little. Then she rose from the blanket and glared at him with defiance and an indifference that did nothing to soothe the tension of the moment.

"You think you're ready?" he asked. She did not answer. "Then let us see."

He turned and walked away from her. She shook her head and released another sigh, then attempted to soothe the overly serious situation.

"Tirin, look, I'm sorry if I offended you, okay? I was just saying,--"

Tirin raised his hands to shoulder height so Camille could see the talons rise up from his fingers as he continued to move away from her.

"You would do well to protect yourself at all costs," he said, then slowly began to jog away from her, zigzagging back and forth.

"Tirin! Come on!" She called out as she watched him gradually pick up speed; then, like a blur, he accelerated into the wooded area where she could no longer see him.

"Whoa," she gasped.

She had never seen him move that fast before. Her instincts kicked in immediately as she dropped into a defensive stance, her eyes flashing a vivid red and her hands glowing with the same dangerous energy. Sharp talons sprouted from her fingertips, and her hair lifted, floating wildly around her head and shoulders like a storm brewing just beneath the surface. Despite the surge of adrenaline, she forced herself to calm down, focusing her mind, listening intently as her gaze swept across the tree line.

But all she could hear was the deafening thud of her own heartbeat pounding relentlessly against her chest. It unnerved her—this creeping sense of unease—and she couldn't quite place why. Her confidence, usually unshakable, wavered for just a moment. Then, in a blur of movement, he shot past her from behind so fast that she barely registered it. Off-balance and caught off guard, she instinctively fired an energy blast in his direction, but it flew wide, just missing its target.

Her heart raced faster now, and her nerves frayed as she realized just how close he had gotten. There was no time to dwell on the near-miss; she knew he was circling, waiting for the next strike. The tension in the air grew thick, and for the first time, she felt a flicker of genuine uncertainty.

"They will try to surround you," his voice echoed through the glade.

She turned, trying to pinpoint the sound and again, he blew by her from behind. She turned and slashed at him, and again, she missed.

"All the while searching for weakness…"

He ran past her again, this time dragging his finger across her forearm, opening up a cut. She flinched from the pain, swung at him, and missed.

"And they shall be…" He came up behind her, stopped, and scratched her left shoulder. "Relentless."

She screamed and turned to her left. He mirrored her, moving to his right, and slashed down her other arm. She spun around, firing wildly, but he was already gone.

"TIRIN!" she screamed, trying not to cry as blood dripped from her wounds.

"She must learn to hold her focus, or she will have no chance," he thought. "Heal yourself!" he yelled as he sped by again.

He dragged his finger across her back. She screamed and fired two shots in his direction and again missed horribly. "If you can!"

"Stop it! Please! I can't do this," she pleaded.

She tried to heal one of her wounds, but he gave her no time.

"They will not stop!" he yelled. "They will keep coming and coming until you kill them!"

He charged straight at her, a blur of motion, and within seconds, they were locked in combat. Camille tried to keep up, her body moving instinctively as she fought to match his speed and relentless aggression. But it didn't take long for her to realize the truth—he was simply too fast. Each move she made felt just a fraction too slow. She blocked, slashed, and unleashed blasts of energy at close range, desperate to land a hit, but even in such close quarters, she couldn't connect.

His agility was beyond anything she had ever encountered. Every time she attacked, he slipped through her defenses, his movements fluid and precise. His technique was nothing short of masterful, and she felt the gap between them widening with each failed attempt. As she swung at him, he ducked effortlessly beneath her strike, his body a blur as he darted low. In one swift motion, he slashed her leg, a stinging blow that sent her off balance. Before she could react, he was already gone, speeding away before she even hit the ground.

"Or you tire to the point where you can no longer defend yourself!"

She staggered to her feet as he zoomed in and locked up with her from behind as if he were a vampire.

"That is the point where you will meet your vampire," he whispered in her ear, then, with his talon, delivered a deep cut to her shoulder at the base of her neck where a vampire would bite her. Her scream echoed throughout the glade. He released her, and she slumped to the ground.

"And that is when you shall die." He said as he looked down at her. "For witches, vampire bites do not heal."

Camille laid on the ground below him, wailing and bleeding from her multiple wounds. Tirin stood over her with his chest expanding and contracting as he tried to inhale as much air as his lungs would allow. He was both physically and emotionally drained. Most think alphas have no emotions, but in actuality, they overflow with feelings, and he cared for her too much to allow himself to be soft on her. She had to learn, and she had to learn fast because he knew what was coming.

"This is not a day camp. This is not to be fun for you. You will learn to get off the ground, or you will bleed. Heal yourself," he said as he turned and walked away from her toward his shirt.

When he reached down to grab it, an eerie, unfamiliar voice raised the hairs on the back of his neck as it passed through him.

"AGAIN," the voice ordered.

It was cold and hollow and registered a little deeper than his apprentice's.

"I'M NOT DONE WITH YOU YET." The voice taunted.

Tirin turned carefully, his eyes narrowing as he watched Camille, still on the ground, taking slow, deliberate breaths. Her hair whipped wildly around her, almost as if it had a life of its own, caught in an unseen wind. As he observed her, something remarkable began to happen—one by one, her wounds began to heal themselves, the torn skin stitching together with an eerie, magical precision. She raised her head, and when their eyes met, the look she gave him was unlike anything he had ever seen before. It wasn't just anger—it was something far more dangerous, something primal.

In a fluid motion, Camille sprang to her feet. Her arms extended down to her waist, and her fingers slowly unclenched, palms facing upward. Her hands began to glow, a radiant energy pulsing from within as her power intensified. Then, for the first time, she rose—effortlessly lifting about a foot off the ground. The wind seemed to bend to her will, swirling around her as she hovered in the air. A dark, sinister smile curled at the corners of her mouth.

She hovered there, weightless and commanding, her presence more powerful than it had ever been. Tirin realized at that moment that something had shifted—something fundamental—and he wasn't sure if he was ready for what would come next.

"AGAIN!" She commanded.

"…No," he said, as he held his ground, taking care not to move.

In a blink, she zipped over to him within inches of his face.

"Are you afraid?" she asked, with a smile that could only be described as evil.

"…No. I'm tired. And so are you. That's enough for today," he said, holding eye contact with her.

She surveyed him, searching for the slightest sign of fear. He gave her none.

"Camille. That's enough..."

After a few more tense, drawn-out moments, the ghoulish grin slowly faded from Camille's face. The wild energy that had once animated her seemed to drain away, and her hair fell flat against her shoulders. The crimson glow that had burned so fiercely in her eyes and hands dimmed until it vanished completely. Her feet touched the ground softly, and the power that had coursed through her moments before now felt distant, like a fleeting memory.

She stood there, the silence between them thick and heavy. Gone was the fierce intensity, replaced by an overwhelming sense of discomfort. Camille couldn't bring herself to meet his gaze—her eyes remained fixed on the ground, her shoulders tense with the weight of what had just happened. Shame crept up inside her, tightening her chest. The surge of power had felt intoxicating, but now, in its aftermath, all she felt was embarrassment.

Her cheeks flushed with quiet humiliation, her fear of what Tirin might be thinking gnawing at her. The silence pressed down on her, and the shame lingered, making her feel small and exposed.

"I'm sorry," she whispered.

One by one, tears flooded her eyes and fell from her face. Tirin extended his arms and embraced her. These past few weeks, he, too, had learned something. He had learned how to properly comfort his friend.

"I don't know what just happened to me."

"...You learned how to get off the ground."

"I could've killed you."

"Shhhhh."

"No! You don't understand. I… I wanted to." She began to cry harder. "I can't do this. I can't! I can't control it!"

"You cannot control it unless you first learn to embrace it,--"

"NO, I DON'T WANT TO,--!"

"YOU MUST!!" He roared. The volume temporarily snapped her out of the sorrowful state she was slipping into. "It is who you are. There is a demon in all of us, Camille. You must learn how to embrace yours or one day it will consume and control you."

"…But I don't know how," she whispered.

Tirin sighed as he watched the tears stream down her face.

"…Then we shall figure it out - together. Come. You need to eat," he said as he walked her toward the estate.

CHAPTER 17

August 1, 1995 - *The Birth*

Nine days after her seventeenth birthday, Camille and Kaitlin strolled through the sprawling grounds behind the estate. The air was thick with an unsettling energy, the kind that made the skin prickle with anticipation. Above them, clouds moved with unnatural speed, chasing one another across the midnight sky as if driven by some unseen force. The wind whispered through the trees, carrying with it the unmistakable scent of an approaching storm.

The atmosphere felt charged, electric, as though something was brewing not just in the sky but in the very air around them. Camille glanced up at the racing clouds, her brow furrowing slightly. There was a heaviness to the night, a sense that whatever was coming wasn't just a storm—it was something more.

"We have to get in," Kaitlin said, offering Camille support as they walked.

"In a minute. I like the feel of this air on my face." Camille said, then took a long breath through a contraction. "Ohhhhh, they're going to be here soon."

Julien, Barrett, Rayna, and Dane watched from the veranda as a few unusually large raindrops began to fall.

"I think our girl time is over," Kaitlin said as a gigantic drop exploded on her head. "You feel ready?"

"Ready as I'll ever be, I guess," Camille said, gritting through another contraction. Her feet pushed into the ground, and it seemed to shake slightly.

"Whoa," Kaitlin gasped and looked at Camille.

Things were happening—strange, unsettling things that gnawed at Camille's mind. She hated keeping secrets from Kaitlin, but at this point, she wasn't sure she had a choice. There was so much Kaitlin didn't know and even more that Camille wasn't ready to share. Her nerves fluttered under the weight of those unspoken truths, and her fingers instinctively reached for the Blood Necklace around her neck. She massaged the pendant between her index finger and thumb, finding a fleeting sense of comfort in the familiar gesture.

Uncertainty hung heavy in the air. Camille didn't know how it would all play out, didn't know what was waiting on the horizon, but one thing was clear—it was almost time. Whatever was coming, whatever truths were about to surface, she would soon have to face it. The anticipation was maddening, but there was no turning back now.

"Thanks for always being here for me, Katie."

"Girl, please. Where else am I going to be?" Kaitlin smiled.

"No matter what happens tonight, I need you to know that you're my best friend, and I love you."

Kaitlin's scrunched her face from Camille's curious statement.

"What does that mean?" Kaitlin asked. "What do you think's gonna,--"

"Ahh!" Camille screamed through another contraction as lightning simultaneously flashed in the sky.

Julien ran over to them from the veranda and grabbed Camille.

"I got her from here, Katie." Julien said, then to Camille, "c'mon, Cher. We need to get you inside. You need to lie down now."

As they approached the veranda, Camille's eyes caught a subtle exchange—a nearly imperceptible nod from Julien to Rayna. It was so brief that most would have missed it, but not Camille. Her senses sharpened, and with that simple gesture, a slight panic began to rise within her chest. When they all moved inside, Rayna lingered behind, and the unease within Camille swelled.

The feeling only intensified as they reached the foot of the majestic staircase. Each step she climbed felt heavier than the last, her growing anxiety building with every creak of the wooden stairs beneath her feet. The rhythmic pounding of the rain against the covered windows filled the house, the sound eerily in sync with the anxious thrum of her heartbeat. Above it all, the deep, orchestral booms of thunder echoed through the estate, signaling the storm's arrival.

The storm was here, both outside and within, and with each step Camille took, the weight of it pressed down harder, wrapping itself around her with a sense of impending inevitability.

"Where's Tirin?" She asked as she looked around with the slightest hint of fear in her voice.

"Don't worry about him," Julien said as he ushered her into the room and tried to get her in the bed.

"No. I want him here,--"

"C'mon. There you go," Julien said as he gently eased her down.

Camille laid down on the bed and exhaled fully. It felt so good. She had completely forgotten why she was walking around to begin with. As the doctor propped her legs up, Camille's eyes fell on the grandfather clock in the corner of the room. She noted the time - 1:12 a.m. as the doctor began his examination. Camille looked at Kaitlin who reassured her with a smile. Then her eyes fell to Julien.

"You're doing great," he smiled at her and squeezed her hand.

She tried to smile back, but she couldn't. She wanted to be happy but realized at this moment she wasn't.

"Julien,--" she started.

"It's happening," the doctor shouted in a tone that just didn't feel right to her.

Whatever she was about to say no longer matter. It was time. Camille took a deep breath and began to chant, over and over, in her head.

"Ut puella, sed puer videbunt… Ut puella, sed puer videbunt…"

******

Down the hall, around the corner, Cecil had just reached the top of the stairs with two very large men in tow. He was surprised to be met by Ms. Rayna, with Leo and Dane standing just behind her.

"Wh-What are you doing? Move," Cecil ordered, even though it didn't really come off as one.

"Julien thought it would be best if we kept this a family affair tonight." She said with her ever-present smile.

Right then, Jimmy Lee and two new guards, the brother and sister combination of Tikesha and Taquan, came out of the rooms behind Cecil and his men, giving Cecil the impression that he was surrounded and outnumbered. Rayna moved next to Cecil and wrapped his arm around hers.

"Come on, Sugar. This is so exciting. We wouldn't want to miss it." She said as she escorted him down the hallway.

"B-But,--" Cecil stuttered.

"Oh, don't worry. My people will see these gentlemen out for you."

She giggled as she rounded the corner with Cecil, and her smile widened as they listened to a brief, albeit violent, commotion in the hall behind them. Cecil strolled beside her to Camille's room in shock and silence.

*****

As they approached Barrett, just outside the room, a scant scowl etched onto his face when he saw who was with Cecil and, more importantly, who was not. The scowl became more pronounced as he looked over their shoulders, seemingly waiting for someone to approach. No one else did.

"Excuse me," Rayna said as she squeezed by Barrett and stepped into the room. "This is the best part. I don't want to miss it."

"Where are my guests?" A stunned Barrett asked Cecil through clenched teeth.

Cecil did his best to avoid Barrett's unrelenting glare. He shuffled and fidgeted as he cleared his throat and lowered his head to answer.

"She, uhm,… had them escorted out."

"You let her do what?!" Barrett squawked.

"I didn't let her do it, Barrett," Cecil whined, "It just kinda happened."

"Julien!" Barrett bellowed.

Cecil flinched as Barrett busted in the room, but he was instantly halted by a blood-curdling scream from Camille that shook the entire house. Cecil nearly fainted.

"W-W-Was that her or Barrett?" Cecil thought before he fearfully raced into the room.

Inside, Camille's eyes opened, blood red eyes and lightning struck violently outside. She was fixed and focused and there was an eeriness about her that wasn't present before. As she pushed, the thunder boomed outside like artillery exploding on the ground. Everyone around her jumped. Only two in this room had witnessed a witch giving birth before, so they weren't sure if these weird coincidences were normal. Barrett and Cecil knew they were not.

"PUSH!" The Doctor ordered, and Camille obeyed. "AGAIN!"

Then, with one long, painful push, the first child had entered this world.

"It's a boy!" The Doctor yelled.

That seemed to surprise no one. Camille let out a ragged breath as lightning struck again as the storm grew. It felt as if the storm was in sync with her breath. The doctor cut the cord and passed the child to Kaitlin, who took the baby boy to a basin to be cleaned.

"You're doing great, Cher," Julien said.

Camille squeezed his hand – a lot harder than he wanted, but he took it, and he did not let go. She needed all her concentration now, all her focus – all her power.

"I see the head! When I tell you, push!" The Doctor ordered, but this time, Camille could not obey.

"No, I can't wait!"

"Not yet!"

"I CAN'T WAIT!"

"NOOOO!"

Thunder roared across the sky, and bolts of lightning relentlessly struck the house and grounds, each flash illuminating the black night in a cold, eerie blue. For brief, unsettling moments, it felt like day—harsh and unnatural. The entire house seemed to groan under the force of the storm, trembling as though it might tear apart at any second. There was no longer any question about the source of the chaos; she was doing this, and everyone knew it.

Then, with a monstrous scream that echoed through every wall and every soul within, she summoned everything she had. The power surged from deep within her core, a force so raw and primal that it felt as if the very earth beneath them was trembling in response. This was no mere outburst—this was something far greater, something unstoppable, and with every ounce of strength, she pushed it out, unleashing it into the world.

"Ut puella, sed puer videbunt!" she thought - she *willed* as a child emerged from her womb with a powerful blast that blew open all the windows and took out the lights.

The old house exhaled, and an eerie wind rushed through the room and slammed the door shut. Silence… Then, the soft, innocent cry of a child was heard, and the lights flickered back on. No one spoke. No one moved until the doctor made his highly anticipated announcement.

"It's a....... boy?"

Julien whipped his head around to Rayna, who had a look of confusion locked on her face. Both Barrett and Cecil cast their gaze upon her as well. Her eyes flitted back and forth as she shook her head with disbelief. The one who was never wrong was wrong. Rayna took a step forward to examine the baby closer.

"NO!" Camille exhaled powerfully, and the room shook.

Rayna immediately stopped as her eyes shifted to Camille. In all the commotion, no one had noticed the change in her. Her blood-red eyes pulsed, slightly more intense than some had come to expect, and a thick patch of the hair, floating wildly about her shoulders, had turned completely white. Her fingernails had grown into sharp talons that pierced the bed as she clasped it and there was a danger that emanated from her that was not there before. Some may have mistaken it for something darker.

"Give me my babies - NOW!" She demanded.

Julien stood strong next to her, but even he was slightly shaken by this display. There was a freshly moistened stain on the front of the doctor's pants that was spreading in size. His body quivered as if he had just crawled out of a frozen pond, and his eyes had grown so big that his lids could not encase them to blink. He looked to Barrett for direction, for clarity - for help.

"Don't look at him! Give them to her!" Julien yelled.

Julien's directive startled the doctor so much that he nearly fumbled the newborn, garnering the one thing he didn't want: more of Camille's attention. He nodded his apology as he bowed and carefully backed away from her.

"NOW!!" she exclaimed, with a force that nearly knocked the doctor over. He clumsily handed the child off to Kaitlin and stumbled out the door as fast as his freshly moistened legs could take him.

"Come," Camille said to Kaitlin in a still deep but much less aggressive tone.

Kaitlin couldn't keep the fright off her face. She had seen many things that most humans have not, but she had never seen this side of Camille before. No one had, except for Tirin. Kaitlin tentatively brought both babies to Camille.

"JD... I need to,--" Rayna started, but Julien quickly raised his hand, silencing her, or he tried to.

"Julien,--" Rayna continued.

"GO!" Camille's voice boomed.

Rayna glared at Camille with seemingly daring impudence that made Camille smile.

"Rayna, NO!" Julien ordered.

He shook his head at her with a look on his face that seemed to beg her to comply. After a moment, she begrudgingly turned and left the room. Barrett, however, who didn't look the least bit bothered by any of this, would not be so easily swayed.

"Well, now. Look at you," he said to Camille as he slowly moved toward her, "There's the little girl we been waiting to see."

"Pop,--" Julien said tentatively as Camille dug in, ready for a fight.

"Nah, nah. It's all right. I just wanna get a look at my grandbabies," Barrett said, waving Julien off.

"Not now, Pop."

"I'd say now's as good a time as any."

Tirin, who had been silently lurking in the shadows the entire time, finally stepped forward, emerging from his hidden corner. His movement was sudden, deliberate. Camille flinched at the sight of him, her body tensing, but she held back, resisting the urge to strike. Kaitlin, frozen with fear, clutched the babies tightly to her chest, unwilling to move a muscle.

Barrett, however, remained undeterred. His steps were bold defiant as he continued forward, ignoring the growing tension in the room. But before he could advance any further, Tirin moved with swift precision, placing himself directly in Barrett's path, his presence an immovable barrier. Barrett's brow furrowed, his eyes narrowing with displeasure, but before the confrontation could escalate, Julien quickly intervened. He stepped between the two of them, his presence commanding as he sought to defuse the situation before it boiled over.

"Pop, please... Let's just,-- let her rest awhile, okay?" Julien pleaded.

"What are you doing, boy?"

"I just think we all need to take a moment and,--"

"Get out of my way."

"Pop, you don't have,--"

"Move, God damn it!"

"NO! The second baby was a boy, not a girl. We don't have to do this now," Julien whispered.

Rayna and Cecil stood in the doorway, waiting to see what would happen next.

"Please, Pop. Please. Just... let's just talk in the morning. Okay? You can see your grandbabies in the morning. I promise you, I will bring them to you myself... Please."

Barrett stared at Julien with a disapproving scowl on his face. He glared at an unmoved Tirin, then turned and left with Cecil so close on his heels that he nearly tripped him. Tirin turned to Camille, her hair floating, eyes glowing red. His eyes calmed her, and her talons retracted. He nodded to Julien and turned to leave.

"Where you gonna be?" Julien asked.

"Close," he said as he exited the room with Rayna.

Camille let out a long, well-deserved breath.

"Katie," Julien said. "Why don't you clean them up a bit while,--"

"No! They stay with me!" Camille yelled.

"Okay. Okay. They will." Julien reassured her. "All night. We all will, won't we, Katie?"

Kaitlin nodded, her movements careful and diffident as she took the babies to the basin on the other side of the room. Julien, watching her briefly, turned his attention to Camille and sat beside her on the bed. Camille's gaze remained fixed on Kaitlin, her body trembling, fear and exhaustion etched into every line of her face.

Julien, sensing her distress, carefully draped a blanket over her shoulders, the fabric offering little comfort but serving as a small shield against the storm of emotions swirling within her. He slowly reached for her face, but at his touch, she flinched, her body tensing reflexively. Undeterred, he moved his hand toward her head, and as he did, her hair—wild and unruly—began to settle, calming with his presence.

Tears welled in her eyes as Julien gently stroked her face, his fingers brushing over the stark white streak that now ran through her hair. The tender motion seemed to soothe her, if only slightly, and for a moment, the weight of all that had happened faded into the background, leaving only the quiet intimacy of his touch.

"I like it," he said, smiling. "Yeah. You know most women tend to wait 'til after the delivery to change their hair color, but, well… you're a multi-tasker. You always were a little different, weren't you? That's one of the many reasons why I love you so much."

Tears streamed down her face as she finally noticed the multiple strands of her beautiful dark brown hair had turned white.

"No, no, Cher. It's new. It's different, but I like it. I do."

She started sobbing, and the red washed out of her eyes.

All magic comes with a cost.

Julien embraced her and held her tight.

"It's gonna be alright, Cher. I told you before. Everything is gonna be just fine."

Camille pressed her face into his chest.

"Was it fine? How long would it be? What would they all do if they knew about the spell? If they knew that the second child was, in fact, a girl?"

So many questions swirled in her head. It gave her nothing but doubt.

CHAPTER 18

"...this one is you-u-u-u,"

"Nooooooo!" Camille screamed as she sat up in the bed.

A concerned Kaitlin rushed over to check on her. The babies were also concerned, or maybe just agitated from being woken in such a way. Either way, they were now awake and crying, too.

"It's okay. It's okay now. It's just me. Shhhhh," said Kaitlin as she tried to comfort her friend.

Camille clung to Kaitlin, her arms wrapped tightly around her, as she rested her head on Kaitlin's shoulder. Her eyes remained wide open, unblinking, filled with a deep, unsettling fear. She didn't dare close them, afraid that the darkness behind her eyelids would pull her back into another dream—another nightmare. The one that had jolted her from her sleep still lingered, vivid and haunting, the images burned into her mind.

In the nightmare, her eyes were permanently blood-red, glowing with a malevolence she couldn't control. Her fingers ended in long, sharp talons, and her skin had taken on a permanent deep green tint, unnatural and terrifying. There was rage, madness, and blood—so much blood. The memory of it made her shudder. In the dream, she had become the very monster they feared she would be, a creature driven by uncontrollable violence and chaos.

Camille knew, with a sinking feeling, that this nightmare wouldn't be the last to torment her sleep. It felt too real, too close to the surface of her thoughts. And the more she thought about it, the more a terrifying question echoed in her mind—was it truly just a dream?

"Baby, I have to ask, what happened last night?" Kaitlin asked. "Was that,… normal?"

"I don't know. I don't think so. I… I just… I was so scared, and something just,… took over. I could feel my body changing, and I couldn't stop it," Camille cried. "I'm sorry." She hugged Kaitlin hard.

"Is this what you were,--"

Camille silenced her. She sensed another presence in this room. She scanned and found Tirin crouched in his corner, watching. He rose and walked toward her. Camille's eyes flashed red. Tirin stopped but did not flinch.

"Where's Julien?" Kaitlin asked. "He said,--"

Tirin raised his hand, interrupting her. "He will return shortly."

Kaitlin carefully made her way to the babies and brought them over to Camille. She could feel Tirin's eyes on her every movement, but she was too afraid to look back and confirm.

"I-I-I think they're hungry," Kaitlin said to Camille.

Camille found peace in Tirin's presence, and she let her eyes fade to normal.

"May I?" Tirin asked.

Camille hesitated for a moment, then gave a small nod of approval. Tirin moved silently around the bed toward Kaitlin, whose body betrayed her attempts to remain composed. She tried to hide her fear, but her stiffened posture and the way she quickly lowered her eyes told a different story. She dared not meet his gaze, afraid that even a fleeting glance would reveal too much. Camille had often noticed Kaitlin's discomfort around Tirin—most humans felt a certain unease in his presence—but today was different.

For the first time, in the quiet stillness of the morning, Camille didn't just see Kaitlin's fear—she felt it. It poured from her in waves, thick and unmistakably discernible, and it made Camille deeply uncomfortable. Not because her friend was terrified but because, disturbingly, she found herself drawn to it. There was something intoxicating about the way Kaitlin's fear hung in the air, and, to Camille's horror, she realized she almost enjoyed it. It was as if she could taste Kaitlin's terror, and it was surprisingly sweet.

A brief flicker of red flashed across Camille's eyes, unnoticed by anyone in the room. She clenched her fists, forcing herself to crush the dark thoughts spinning through her mind. With effort, she refocused on Tirin, who was now staring intently at the children. His gaze, sharp and predatory, made Camille uneasy in a way that was hard to shake. The tension in the room thickened as Camille tried to wrestle her emotions back under control.

"Have they been named?" He asked.

"Lucien and Dani, I think." She answered.

Tirin's brow furrowed at the second name.

"Daniel," Camille said, correcting herself.

"They're identical." Kaitlin added, "Except for their eyes."

"Yes-s-s-s… This one has your eyes, but I see his father in him." He commented before turning his attention to the second child. Again, his brow furrowed, and his eyes squinted as he tilted his head. "This one… He has his father's eyes," he said. Then he lifted his gaze to Camille. "But this one is you-u-u-u,"

Camille's anxiety level raised to new heights as Tirin's nostrils began to flare and twitch uncontrollably. She reached up and grabbed Dani from Kaitlin.

"They need to be fed," she whispered, her eyes locked on his.

He nodded to her, glanced at Kaitlin, who would not return his gaze, then exited the room to give her privacy. Camille looked deep into Dani's blue eyes to make sure no trace of the baby's true self was present.

"It's okay, baby. The big, scary man is gone," Kaitlin whispered as she gently ran her finger across Lucien's tiny, furrowed brow. "You don't have to be afraid anymore."

Camille wondered in that moment if Kaitlin's reassurance was for Lucien or herself. She knew Kaitlin's true feelings, but right now, she was more concerned about the hideous ones she had harbored.

"It's so funny," Kaitlin said.

"What?"

"The look on this little guy's face. It's like he's actually listening to me."

"He is," Camille said as she moved Dani to her breast for feeding.

"No, I was just joking." Kaitlin chuckled as Camille stared at her. "I mean, I know he can hear me, but he can't possibly understand what I'm saying."

"Not yet, but in a few months, he will."

"What?..."

"I don't know why, but our senses are a little keener than humans. They'll both be able to understand everything we say to them within a few months, and they'll be formulating sentences within the year."

"You're serious,"

"Yes. I guess it's because back in the day we had to learn spells and stuff early on. We had to adapt, or we wouldn't live very long," Camille said as she stared at Dani. "So, keep talking to them every chance you get. They're gonna need it." She said, almost to herself.

Kaitlin smiled at Lucien, not noticing the somber undertone of the statement.

"And, um," Camille said, "for future reference, you should maybe be careful what you say around Tirin. He's much more sensitive than people give him credit for, and I wouldn't want him to take anything you say the wrong way."

Kaitlin tensed. "No, I was just, I-I-I didn't mean anyth,--"

"I know,--"

"I was just whispering to the baby,--"

"Sweetie, alpha wolves can hear, clear as day, from about a hundred and fifty yards away when they focus on it," Camille said, and Kaitlin gasped. "I always suspected that Tirin could probably hear a little further than that."

Kaitlin looked pale, almost sickly, and the sight of it made Camille's stomach churn with guilt. She couldn't understand the depth of her friend's fear—was it solely because of Tirin, or did it extend to all lycans? The source of Kaitlin's dread remained elusive, and that uncertainty gnawed at Camille. She had hoped that by sharing this information, by being open, she might ease some of the tension, maybe even diminish the fear that clung to Kaitlin.

But instead, it had the opposite effect. Rather than calming her friend, the revelation seemed to amplify her terror, making it more visible. Camille could feel the weight of it in the room, suffocating and heavy. It was as though her attempt at reassurance had only served to stoke the very fire she had hoped to extinguish, and that realization left Camille feeling worse than before.

"Hey, I don't think he was listening this time - I know he wasn't, I can tell. He would've… He wasn't." Camille said, trying to reassure her friend. Kaitlin shrugged, but Camille knew it was only pretense. "I'm sorry, I didn't mean to upset you,--"

"It's okay, I'm fine."

"…I just thought you should know, is all,--"

"I'm fine."

Camille nodded and let it go and the two of them sat quietly in the uncomfortable silence, together and, at the same time, both of them very much alone.

CHAPTER 19

""*...* $\mathcal{A}$ *in't nobody ever gonna let that girl see the sunrise on her twenty-first birthday..."*

Julien burst into the study, still in the process of buttoning up a fresh shirt, his movements quick and agitated. Rayna followed closely behind, her expression sharp, the remnants of their ongoing argument hanging in the air between them like a storm cloud that refused to dissipate.

Behind the desk, Barrett sat with the same deep-set scowl etched into his face, the same one he'd worn the day before, a permanent mask of disapproval. His eyes narrowed as Julien entered, but he said nothing, letting the weight of his silence speak for him. Beside him, Cecil had taken his place on the sofa, his posture stiff and rigid as he did his best to mirror Barrett's expression. His attempt at disappointment, however, lacked the depth and malice that came so naturally to Barrett, yet he sat there, dutifully trying to match his mentor's disapproving glare.

"The prophecy was clear!" Rayna argued.

"It was false. The second was a boy, not a girl. End of story," Julien countered.

"FALSE?! She did something!" Rayna yelled.

Julien whipped around to face her.

"We've been through this. She doesn't have the power to do what you suggest. No witch her age does. Let it go."

"Well then, maybe you could explain what we saw last night," Cecil said evenly.

"Birth is a powerful thing. She was scared, that's all," Julien said.

"Of what?!" Rayna asked.

Julien looked to his father, then back to her without answering.

"I'm telling you, she was there that day, Julien," Rayna continued.

"Oh, Jesus, Rayna,--"

"At your office. Tirin said,--"

"He said it was nothing."

"He said he smelled a witch!" She said, talking over him.

"No! He said he *thought* he smelled,--"

"Smelled Camille!" She finished for him. "He smelled her perfume! Poison by Christian Dior."

"...That's what you've been basing all this on? *THAT'S* your little secret?"

"She somehow figured out a way to hide her scent, but she forgot about the perfume," Rayna said proudly. "Coriander, wild berries, orange honey, and tuberose - That's what he smelled that day! The exact notes that comprise your wife's favorite perfume,"

"And Serena's," Julien said with the confidence of a person who knows he's right - even though he's wrong.

"...What?"

"Serena would always comment on how much she loved the smell of Camille's perfume, so I picked up a bottle for her birthday - last October. That's about a month before all this nonsense started."

Rayna's eyes flittered. "But,--"

"Enough," Julien ordered. "You're wrong. Let it go."

But that was something Rayna could not do.

"JD," Rayna continued, "I'm telling you, that baby has got to be destroyed."

"*That* baby?!" Julien exclaimed. "There is no 'that' baby! There is *my* baby! My babies! My flesh, my blood--MINE! You understand that?! Now we are done with this!"

But Rayna was not. She simply could not, would not let this go. She revealed the tarot card from that day at the office.

"Julien, the prophecy specifically said that we cannot let that baby,--"

"GODDAMN IT, SHUT UP!!" Julien screamed.

The air in the room grew heavy as both Barrett and Cecil stared at Julien, waiting to see what was next. Cecil had known Julien his entire life and in all that time, he had never seen him speak to *anyone* with that tone. Especially her. Even Julien seemed uncomfortable with what he had said to her. More so, how he said it. Barrett might have actually been proud of how Julien silenced her had he not had his own bone to pick with his son. His scowl remained, along with the uncomfortableness of the silence in the room.

"That's enough, okay?" Julien said softly, embarrassed by his outburst. "This conversation is over."

Barrett and Cecil watched in cold, emotionless silence as Rayna stood frozen, her gaze fixed on the floor. The weight of their unspoken judgment hung heavy in the air, stretching time into what felt like an eternity, though only a few seconds had passed. Without a word, Rayna finally moved toward the desk, her steps deliberate and controlled. She placed the single tarot card on the edge, then, with swift precision, picked up the ornate knife-shaped letter opener. In one fluid motion, she drove it through the card and deep into the lip of the desk, the sharp blade embedding itself with a force that reverberated through the wood.

Rayna didn't look back as she turned sharply on her heel and stormed out of the room, the door slamming shut behind her with a resounding crack. Julien, anger flaring in his eyes, moved quickly to the desk, attempting to pull the letter opener free. He gripped it tightly, but no matter how hard he pulled, it wouldn't budge from its new home. Frustrated and seething, he turned, ready to pursue her. But just as he took a step, Cecil's calm, measured voice cut through the tension, stopping him in his tracks.

"Prophecy or not, you know, the longer you drag this out, the more difficult it is to cover up, right?"

"We're going to handle this one my way, Ceese," Julien said as he continued toward the door.

Barrett finally broke the scowl on his face and hurled it toward his son in the form of a question.

"And exactly what way is that?"

The question was a simple one. The answer would not be. It would be the beginning of something that superseded everything that was going on between him and Rayna. This was it. The moment that he had not been waiting for.

"Hm?" Barrett continued. "Your great-great-great granddaddy spent his life trying to put this world right, and,--"

"He spent his life slaughtering hundreds of innocent witches." Julien took a deep breath and dug in. This can had been opened; the bell had been rung.

"What'd you say?" Barrett said as he stood up.

It was a move meant to intimidate his son. It did, but Julien couldn't back down now.

"Daddy, the earth is not flat. We are not the center of the universe, and all witches are not evil. Especially not that one upstairs. Come on, Daddy, you're an educated man. How can you just believe,--"

"It don't matter what I believe! What matters is what The Council believes!"

"That's right!" Cecil chimed in. "So, you got to take care of your business, boy. 'Cuz there ain't no place on this planet that you can run and hide from them."

"I'm not running anywhere, Ceese, and I'm done hiding."

"Well, then you need to wake up and smell the coffee," Cecil countered. "'Cuz ain't nobody ever gonna let that girl see the sunrise on her twenty-first birthday, and there ain't a goddamn thing you can do about it."

"You done?" Julien said with an edge.

"Yeah."

"Good. If I'm wrong, I'll put her down myself," Julien said, "'Til then, anybody so much as look nasty in her direction, they gonna have to deal with me. There. Now I'm done, too."

He turned to leave, then stopped himself and took another deep breath. It wasn't over yet. He turned back to his father.

"Pop. You gotta promise me, no matter what, you will not interfere."

"Julien, The Council,--" Barrett started.

"I DON'T CARE ABOUT THE COUNCIL!" He screamed, and silence followed.

That was the second time he had spoken with such acrimony, and this time toward his father. This was a new day, indeed. Julien collected himself, lowered his tone, and continued.

"I'll deal with them, okay? It'll be on me, not you." He said as if he were asking for permission. "That's my wife upstairs, Pop, and I love her, and I need to know that my father isn't gonna try to kill her. So, you gotta promise me, or else…" He paused as he tried to contain the emotion that was beginning to seep through. "We gotta leave. All of us. Today… And you will never see us again."

Barrett shifted his stance. He wasn't expecting that. Julien knew how much that hurt. It hurt him, too.

"Promise me… Please." Julien asked.

Barrett's glare was sharp, filled with a mix of emotions that he fought to keep hidden. Beneath the anger that burned in his eyes, there was something else—something more vulnerable. Though he'd never admit it, not even to himself, his feelings were hurt. It was a wound that cut deeper than he wanted to acknowledge. But even with that simmering beneath the surface, Barrett Gerard was still Barrett Gerard. He was a man—no, a warlock—who didn't take kindly to being challenged, least of all by his own son.

He had built his life on control, on always having the upper hand, and the thought of losing that grip stirred something dark within him. Barrett was used to getting his way, accustomed to bending others to his will. And when that didn't happen, when someone dared to defy him, there were always consequences. Bad things had a way of following in the wake of his disappointment, and today felt no different.

"Suppose I do see this little experiment of yours through," Barrett said. Cecil tried to interject, but Barrett raised a single finger and silenced him. "Then what? You just gonna live happily ever after? Huh? What 'cha gon' do when The Council comes for her? And make no mistake, they will be coming."

"I'll explain to them,--"

"No," Barrett interrupted.

"I'll show them,--"

"No."

"Damn it, Pop,--"

"NO!"

"I'm trying to tell you!--"

"I don't give a good goddamn what you're trying to say, and neither will they! They don't care what you think, nor do they wanna hear any of your reasons. Their job is to kill that girl; well, actually, that's your job, but if you don't do it, they will go around you, over you, or through you to get it done. If you run, they will follow - if you hide - they will find you. You think they don't have alphas, too?!" Barrett yelled. "You might have done all that fancy learning at that fancy *human* school of yours, but you don't know nothin' about these kinda folk. You think The Council is five old men in robes sitting in some dark room underneath a castle in England? You think you can just stroll over there and be granted an audience because your last name is Gerard?"

"Probably could get one 'cuz of that," Cecil stated.

"He probably would, but it wouldn't be with the Governors."

"Nooo. My whole life, I've never even seen them," said Cecil.

"Ain't nobody seen them! Nobody even knows who they are!"

"So, what, you two expect me to be scared of five old men no one's ever seen? That you don't even know exist?" Julien said.

"Those five old men ain't The Council, Julien," Barrett continued. "Those five old men *run* The Council. This what I've been trying to tell you, boy, if you just open up that college-educated mind of yours and listen. The Council is a network of *millions* of people around the world, both humans and malefecs, whose single solitary purpose is to make sure that that girl upstairs, and every other witch on this planet, never sees their twenty-first birthday! They been doing it for two hundred and seventy-three years, so you can imagine they must be pretty goddamn good at it by now. You really wanna know what they're capable of? Continue down this foolhardy path of yours, and you gonna find out real quick, and then there ain't gonna be nothing I can do to help you. You will be on your own. Do you understand me?"

Julien was taken aback by this. He had never seen or heard his father talk this way. He couldn't tell whether this was another bullying tactic or something worse.

"Pop, I still need you to,--"

"DO YOU UNDERSTAND ME?!" Barrett yelled.

It was something worse. If Julien wasn't intimidated before, he certainly was now, but it was too late. There was no going back.

"Yes, sir. I do… Now promise me," he said with finality.

"…I promise," Barrett said through clenched teeth.

Julien thanked his father with a subtle nod and exited the room. He closed the door, careful not to slam it, and when he turned around, Tirin was there. He startled Julien. Tirin had a way of doing that to everyone.

"Jesus!" Julien gasped. He exhaled deeply and moved toward the stairs. Tirin followed.

"You heard?" Julien asked.

Tirin grunted in response, his usual nonverbal acknowledgment carrying a weight of understanding. They stopped at the base of the stairs, the air thick with unspoken tension. Tirin's sharp eyes locked onto Julien, studying him closely. The young warlock's face was still pale, his movements stiff, as though the words spoken in the room moments before had left an indelible mark. It was clear he was still rattled, the shock lingering in his eyes, betraying the turmoil just beneath the surface. Tirin could see it all—Julien's struggle to regain his composure, the way his breath hitched slightly, the subtle tremor in his hand as he gripped the banister. What transpired in that room had shaken him deeply, and Tirin, for all his gruff exterior, could sense that this moment had affected the young warlock more than he'd let on.

"What will you do?" Tirin asked.

"I-I-I don't know. I gotta think."

"Mmph. Then what would you have me do?"

Julien shook his head. "Just… watch her."

Tirin stared at him for a second, then bounded up the stairs until Julien stopped him.

"Hey," Julien said. Tirin turned back to him. "No matter what, okay?"

Tirin didn't respond. He didn't need to. Exhausted, Julien sat on the staircase, resting his face in his palms.

"What have I done?" He wondered. *"What do I do now?"*

Kaitlin came out of the kitchen with a plate of food for Camille. She saw Julien sitting on the stairs and moved over to him.

"Julien?" Kaitlin said, startling him out of his worrisome thoughts.

"Hey, Katie." Julien exhaled. "You getting a little too good at sneaking around here. That was vampire worthy."

"I wasn't trying to sneak, I--"

"I was just joking. What's up?"

"I'm sorry to bother you. I just - Are you all right?"

"Yeah, no, I'm fine. I'm fine. Hey, look, I know you're probably a little upset about last night,--"

"Yeah, I wanted to talk to you about all that,--"

"It got a bit dramatic; I know. See, we, uhm,… We don't usually have twins. It's only happened once that I know of, and well,--" he chuckled and shook his head. "Well, let's just say that didn't turn out so good. So, you can imagine everyone was a little on edge. I apologize if we scared you. Sometimes, I forget you're not one of us. I mean, you are, we think of you as family and all, but,--"

"I get it," Kaitlin said.

"Yeah. Anyway, it's fine now. It's all good. Everything's gonna be all right."

"Okay, I…" Kaitlin wanted to say more; ask more, know more, but thought better of it. "Thanks," she said as she continued upstairs.

Julien sighed deeply. He wasn't sure whether he was trying to put her at ease or himself. Either way, he was pretty sure it hadn't worked.

CHAPTER 20

August 5, 1995 - *Four Days Later*

Julien and Rayna stood in tense silence, each keeping their eyes fixed anywhere but on each other as the elevator of Gerard Enterprises ascended. The quiet between them was thick with unresolved tension, a conspicuous weight pressing down on both of them. Rayna, as always, was a rock—unmoved and unwavering. She could have gone days, maybe even a week, without uttering a word to him. Her steely composure allowed her to let the silence linger, unaffected.

But Julien wasn't built that way. He was a pleaser, someone who thrived on harmony, and the uncomfortable weight of Rayna's silence gnawed at him more than he cared to admit. It was suffocating, and though he tried to hold out, the pressure was too much. He couldn't stand knowing she was upset with him, and in the end, his need to break the tension, to fix whatever had been fractured between them, overwhelmed him. He gave in, his resolve crumbling under the weight of her quiet disapproval.

"Look, I'm sorry, all right? I shouldn't have spoken to you like that and... I'm sorry," he said.

He gave her a peck on the cheek and impatiently waited for his forgiveness.

"And?" she said, not giving him an inch, as the elevator doors opened.

"Don't push it, okay?" Julien said as he exited.

The smile he knew she was holding back emerged, and she followed him to the lobby, where Serena met him halfway. A nicely dressed, slender human man was sitting in the waiting area behind her.

"Mr. Gerar - I mean, damn it!-- JD," she corrected herself. "I tried to call you before you left,--"

The man pushed up his glasses and rose after hearing the Gerard name.

"Julien Dumont Gerard?" The Man asked.

"Yes?" Julien said.

The man rushed over, and they shook hands. Julien noticed a strange ring on the man's right index finger. He didn't get a good look at it, but something about it was very familiar.

"Felix Neely," the man introduced himself as.

"From The Council," Serena added. She looked as if she was going to be sick.

"Well, this day just got interesting," Rayna smiled.

"Actually, I'm one of the liaisons to the Administrator who's in charge of the southeast region. I track movement and acquisitions for him."

"I tried to call you, I really did," Serena said in an apologetic voice. "I'm sorry."

"It's all right, Serena." Julien reassured her, then, "Mr. Neely, this is Ms. Rayna, my personal counsel."

Rayna offered her hand to him, and he eagerly took it. She smiled at Mr. Neely as she captured his eyes. Her gaze was mesmerizing, and her eyes seemed to sparkle before she released him. She gave a tiny shake of her head to Julien as she walked past him toward the office. Mr. Neely blinked off the haze from the momentary trance and Julien signaled for him to follow them down the hall.

"I do apologize for not making it down here before this," Mr. Neely said, "but there has been a growing amount of activity and movement in this region."

"Really?" Rayna said.

She opened the office door, and they all entered. Julien sat behind his desk, Felix sat across from him, and Rayna perched herself protectively on the corner of the desk in front of Mr. Neely - her favorite spot.

"Well, yes," Neely continued, "just in the past months, ten witches have been born and there's still six active pregnancies going on; seven, including yours. She must be due soon. Right?" Neely asked. "I've being trying to get ahold of you to offer my services to help make the transition as easy as possible. Anyway, added to the eighteen younglings at various ages over eleven states, it's a very prosperous and exciting time."

"So, you're the liaison to the… Administrator?" Rayna asked, playing dumb while fishing for more information.

"Forgive me, I misspoke. He's a Top Administrator, actually."

"Ohhh. Goodness. That sounds important. What's the difference?" Rayna asked.

Mr. Neely crinkled up his face in a geekish manner and looked at Julien.

"Oh, he never tells me anything. Thinks it's beyond me, but I do find these topics quite interesting," Rayna said as she crossed her legs.

Felix tried hard not to stare, but he was obviously quite taken with her, as most men were.

"Uh, well, uhm, with your permission, sir?" he asked Julien.

"Wha--? Of course. Yes. Please, go," Julien said.

He didn't care. His mind was fixed on how to get out of this, and he was happy that Rayna was buying him time.

"Well, technically, I'm an Administrator. We're comprised of mostly half-breed warlocks, pardon the term, and other humans like myself. No real chance for advancement here, but, as you can imagine, the pay is quite satisfying."

Rayna's smile and leg encouraged him to continue.

"Top Administrators are pure-blood warlocks with a wide range of responsibilities. Everything from writing legislation and doctrine to enforcing policy. They deal in business affairs, finance, public relations with other malafics and humans who are keyed into this world."

"So that's who Julien would be if he wanted in? A Top Administrator?"

"Well, it is an entry-level position for most pure-blood warlocks who look for a career in The Council, but I would think someone with Mr. Gerard's pedigree and background would move directly into an Elite Administrator position," Neely said, nodding proudly. "They deal directly with the Governors."

"Wow. What are their responsibilities?"

"That's well above my pay grade, I'm afraid." He laughed. "Although, I have recently been privileged enough to make the acquaintance of an Elite Administrator. I'm told they rarely leave England, so it was quite an honor."

Julien, not so discreetly, cleared his throat. He had heard enough about The Council and wanted to get back to the problem at hand. Rayna took the hint.

"Well, that's just so wonderful, Mr. Neely. So, how on earth do you know where all those witches are?"

"Uh, well, alphas, of course. We keep one stationed within a few miles of every witch. That, along with the file of the paperwork Mr. Gerard filled out,--"

"Paperwork? I never filled out any paperwork," Julien said.

"Up until this point, your father has been in charge of that, but now, with your 'responsibility' quickly approaching, everything gets transferred over to you."

Julien's heart nearly stopped as Mr. Neely looked through his briefcase for the file.

"Well, isn't that interesting," Rayna said. "Please, Mr. Neely, tell me more."

"Ah, yes, here we are," Felix said, retrieving and opening the file he was looking for. "Camille St. Croix-Gerard. Acquired in 1988 by Barrett Gerard from George St. Croix for seven hundred and twenty-five thousand dollars."

Julien nearly choked as the air rushed out of his chest.

"My father... paid for Camille?" Julien said softly, barely aware he was speaking aloud.

"Huh. All this time, I thought he adopted her," Rayna said.

"Well, he did. That's the standard way we orchestrate getting the witch into her new environment without raising any eyebrows. My people don't take kindly to underage girls marrying full-grown men, you understand?"

"Of course," Rayna answered. "But technically, the marriage was within the law. He waited until Camille was sixteen. That's the legal age in most states."

"It is. But most people don't know that. It's one of those little details people like me go to great lengths to keep out of the public eye."

"Interesting." Rayna smiled. "So, I guess that day in Lake End Park wasn't just a chance meeting after all."

"Mmm," Felix nodded. "Your father paid a lot of money, but as you know, there just aren't enough witches to go around. We are optimistic that we will increase those numbers over the next ten to twenty years, but because they don't live that long and because they procreate once, they are a rare commodity that goes to the highest bidder."

Rayna was fascinated by all this. Julien was trying not to go into shock. Felix continued.

"Plus, you must know the pedigree of your wife is, frankly, astounding!" Felix handed Julien the file. "She's a direct descendent of Esmerelda: The Beautiful One, one of the Five Great Ones! My god! Combine that with your lineage. I can only imagine how powerful your child will be, and if it's a witch? I'd be shocked if, when her time came, she sold for anything under a million dollars."

Rayna gave Julien a knowing smile that he very much tried to ignore.

"So," Felix continued, "your father's done pretty much everything. All we'll need from you is the actual time and date of birth when that happens and the youngling's gender: warlock or witch. If the latter, we'll assign an alpha to her for tracking purposes. More than likely, it'll be the same one that is, for now anyway, being used to track your wife."

Julien's attention was locked in the file, not quite believing what he was reading and, only catching certain words and phrases out of Neely's mouth.

"Who is this alpha watching my wife?" He wondered.

"Lastly," Neely continued, "we'll need the exact time of your wife's death to close her file. Along with my other duties, I can also help in the planning of the 'accident' and the information that will be released to the press," Mr. Neely explained. "Over the years, I've put together dozens of scenarios that don't attract attention in my world and are as quick and painless as possible for both you and your wife during this sensitive time."

"Well, Mr. Neely, you seem to have everything covered quite nicely," Rayna said, enjoying all of this way too much.

"Thank you, Ms. Rayna," Felix said sweetly. "But, as you can imagine, my superiors have been doing this kind of thing for quite a long time."

"I see," Rayna said. "Now, just for conversation's sake, what would happen if a warlock chose to, I don't know… not kill his mate. What happens then?"

"Ms. Rayna! You are charming!" Felix laughed.

Rayna did not. She simply stared at him until the laughter stopped. Julien closed the file and rubbed his brow. Mr. Neely looked at him, then to her, then back to him.

"Oh, Mr. Gerard. No. No, no, no. Do you have any idea how difficult it is to plan an accident after the birth? I have a contact at the local paper, but,--"

"That won't be necessary," Julien said.

"They can keep it out of the press for,--"

"There'll be no accidents. All witches are not bad, Mr. Neely. My wife will not be killed."

Mr. Neely seemed appalled and offended by Julien's statement, and the happy-go-lucky, good-natured man who had entered the office was no longer there.

"We must all conform to the laws of society, Mr. Gerard. Even beings such as you. You, no doubt, understand how making your presence known to my kind would be, at the very least, hazardous to your kind's existence. So, if we are to keep your race out of our history books, protocols must be followed."

"I'll take responsibility for,--"

"You don't get to make that decision!" Felix said in a tone that didn't fit his disposition, and Rayna didn't particularly care for it, as the brow furrowed on her beautiful face.

"Inside voice, Mr. Neely, please," Rayna warned.

"This is absurd," Felix said. "It's unheard of. You must know that this foolish course of action will be met with great opposition from The Council."

Felix jumped up and snatched the file out of Julien's hands. Rayna caught him by his wrist and held it tightly.

"That sounded like a threat, Mr. Neely." She asked.

Felix squirmed. Rayna squeezed. Felix winced.

"Rayna," Julien sighed, and she released him.

"I do not make threats," Felix said as he massaged his wrist. "My job is to cross T's and dot I's and find solutions to problems. YOUR problems." He snatched up his case and quickly distanced himself from Rayna. "However, there is a highly specialized branch in our organization whose sole purpose is dedicated to eliminating them."

"Good day, Mr. Neely," Julien said.

Felix cautiously returned to the desk and placed his business card on the other side of it, careful to keep his distance from Rayna's powerful grasp, then quickly moved to the door. He paused and turned back to them.

"She's a direct descendent of Esmerelda. Only one witch in history has been more powerful and taken more lives. If retribution from The Council doesn't frighten you, then that fact alone should. Read your history book. Good day."

He left in a huff.

"Well. At least now we know what we're up against," Rayna said. "So, Mr. President, what do you wanna do?"

Julien closed his eyes as he moved his hands through his hair and winced.

"We gotta find that alpha."

CHAPTER 21

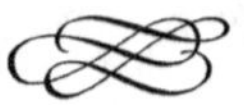

"*Hickory dickory dock,*"

June 23, 1996

Rayna's eyes tracked Julien with unwavering focus as he anxiously paced back and forth across the study. Each step seemed more restless than the last. It was clear he wasn't handling things well, and seeing him like this filled the room with an uncomfortable tension. Tirin, seated on the sofa, watched him just as intently, his gaze following Julien's every movement. Neither of them liked seeing him like this— disheveled, weary, and clearly on edge.

"This is a marathon, Julien," Rayna said, "not a sprint."

Julien stopped pacing and sank into the couch next to Tirin.

"It's been almost a year. Why can't you find that damn alpha?" He asked both of them, but the question was directed mostly toward Tirin.

"Baby, by now, he knows we're probably looking for him, so…"

"And if *I* didn't wish to be found…" Tirin added.

"It's been too long. Every day that goes by puts us more at risk. We're wide open here. Anything could happen."

"We'll find him," Rayna said with some finality as she sat on the armrest next to Julien. "We got time. It's not like they're just gonna storm up in here. Plus, she's not quite eighteen yet. We got time."

Julien combed his fingers through his hair, then suddenly popped up and moved toward the door.

"I need to tell her what's going on," he decided.

Tirin turned and looked at him. Alarmed, Rayna jumped up.

"Julien,--" Rayna started.

"She needs to know. I can't keep this from her."

"Stop," Rayna said as she darted in front of him with a speed she doesn't often show. "Think this through."

"She's my wife! She can handle it."

"It's not about 'handling it,'" Rayna said. "I get it. You want to protect her, but telling her is not the way. It's just going to make things more…"

"What?" Julien asked as he waited for her to finish her thought.

"Unstable, difficult,--"

"She's not,--!"

"No, that's not what I mean! Listen, you know how she is. She's a fighter, and she'll want to fight and that's just what they want. She'll be playing right into their hands. We can't protect her like that. We'll lose, you know this. Plus, with the kids and all, it'll be too much stress on her - on all of us. And we can't afford any mistakes. Not now."

Julien contemplated her words for a good, long time, and they made sense.

"Okay," he said, relenting.

He sat back down and took a deep breath.

"But you two better find that fucking alpha."

Rayna nodded. Tirin did not respond. He knew it was his responsibility to find the alpha, and he knew Camille's life depended on it.

* * *

July 12, 1997

It had been just over a year, and still, the alpha had not been found. Time had dragged on, and now Camille was just two weeks away from her nineteenth birthday. The Council, despite their power and resources, had yet to launch an attack. They once held the luxury of time, but that luxury was slipping away with each passing day. Meanwhile, Julien was becoming more unraveled.

He stood silently in the doorway of the nursery, his gaze fixed on Camille. She sat between the two cribs, her fingers playfully tickling the toddlers, their giggles filling the room. Her face softened with joy, a rare smile lighting up her features as she sang nursery rhymes to them. They were her light, the one thing that seemed to ground her amidst the chaos. But as Julien watched her, his heart clenched. While Camille found solace in these innocent moments, the storm outside their walls continued to rage, and the cracks in Julien's composure grew deeper. "You really are a natural at this," Julien said, startling her.

"I didn't hear you come in," she said. "They're just so beautiful, aren't they?"

He sat down next to them and picked up his 'sons.'

"That they are. And so are you," he said as he took her hand. *"And strong. How strong?"* He wondered.

He shook his head as if to rid himself of these thoughts. Camille looked at him curiously.

"Are you okay?" she asked.

"Of course. I'm fine. It's great."

She didn't believe him, but he wasn't very convincing, and the smile faded from her face.

"JD, what's wrong?"

"Nothing, Cher'. Really. I'm fine."

She studied his eyes. He held her gaze.

"I want to tell you, Cher'," he thought. *"I don't know if I can protect you."* More intrusive thoughts. *"No, I can. I will. Somehow."* "I'm just really tired, that's all." He told her and hoped it was enough.

There was a quiet knock on the door. Camille and Julien looked over. Tirin opened the door, revealing Rayna beside him. Rayna sighed and shook her head.

"Excuse me, Cher'," Julien said. "I gotta go deal with something. And don't worry, I'm fine. It's all good. Promise." He put on a smile and handed the children to Camille and they eagerly climbed into her arms as he stood up and moved to the door.

Camille's smile faltered the moment he stood, her fingers instinctively reaching for the Blood Heart around her neck. Nervously, she rubbed the pendant between her index finger and thumb, a small gesture of comfort in the midst of her unease. Her focus shifted back to the children, and though her voice continued to sing nursery rhymes, the warmth had drained from her tone.

Julien paused at the door, his hand resting on the frame as he glanced back at her. He could feel the distance between them—the unspoken doubt hanging in the air. She didn't believe him; he could see it in the way she avoided his gaze, in the nervous fidgeting of her hands. As he stepped out and closed the door behind him, a heavy thought lingered in his mind: What did she truly think? What was going through her head as he left her alone with her doubts?

"Hickory dickory dock," she sang to them, and, amazingly, the two thirteen-month-old children mimicked her. "The mouse ran up the clock. The clock struck one, and down he run. Hickory dickory dock."

CHAPTER 22

June 14, 1999

It was well after midnight in the Gerard compound as a weary Camille entered the darkened kitchen. She didn't sleep much anymore, not that many young mothers do, but it wasn't the twins that were keeping this winsome young witch up at night. She found the refrigerator without turning on the light, as witches can see just as well at night as one would on a bright, sunny day. She opened the door, grabbed a bottle of milk, and abruptly found out that she was not alone.

"Can't sleep either, huh?"

Startled by the voice she knew was Barrett's, she accidentally dropped the bottle.

Magically, it stopped just before it hit the floor, hovered a moment, then slowly moved toward Barrett's somber, silhouetted figure sitting at the table. He reached out and grabbed it from the air.

"Thank you. I could use a little more," he said. He snapped his fingers, and the lights came on. "Oooh, that's harsh." With a thought, he dimmed them to a much more tolerable tone for this time of night. "Yeah. That's better." He said as he poured some more milk into his glass.

Camille's anxiety level rose as her eyes nervously shifted around the room. She didn't know where to look. She didn't know where to be anymore, but she knew it wasn't there.

"I-I'm sorry, I didn't know you were in here." She solemnly whispered and turned to leave.

"It's fine. Pull up a chair. Join me," he said.

"No, I don't think I—"

"Come on, na'. You came down here to have a glass; have a glass." He interrupted. "It'll help you sleep."

The cabinet behind her flew open, and a glass came flying out. It whizzed perilously close past her head, straight into Barrett's hand. Then, the chair across from him at the table pulled itself out, beckoning Camille to come forward.

"I insist," he said in a tone that seemed more like an order than a request.

She reluctantly joined him as it seemed she didn't have much of a choice, and he poured her a drink. He placed his index finger on her glass, and his eyes flashed red.

"I like mine warm. Soothes this old soul," he said as he heated the glass. "Ummm. Maybe hit it just a tad too much." He removed his finger, and his eyes faded to their normal color. "Give it a minute. Let it cool."

He smiled as he sat back in his chair and took her in. Camille couldn't bring herself to look at him. She fixed her eyes on the glass in front of her and feverishly rubbed the Blood Heart ornament hanging from her neck.

"You know, it seems like forever ago when you and I would find private moments like this. On the terrace, in the garden,… over a glass of warm milk, and just,… talk. Didn't matter what it was about. We'd just talk… You remember?"

She thought about it for a moment, then looked him in the eye with her answer.

"Yes. But that was a time when you thought of me more as a daughter than a prisoner."

A sly grin broadened his face as he took a sip of his milk. He always admired her courage.

"You know; pretty much my whole life, people done looked to me as the bad guy or the bully. And between you and me, I done my fair share of things to earn those titles." He chuckled. "But this time, darling, I don't know that to be completely true."

He had a look on his face that implied that he knew something she did not. That look made Camille more uncomfortable than she already was.

"I think if we were to be brutally honest with each other, we both know that you're way more powerful than you let on to be, and if you truly wished to go, it would be difficult—not impossible," he emphasized, "but difficult to stop you."

"If we are being 'brutally' honest, I would ask you, 'Where would I go?' Where can I go? Back to my father's?" She asked, with a slight sarcasm. Her eyes fell to the table as she pondered the question herself, then slowly made their way back up and again, locked with his. "Where?" She exhaled with much more emotion than she had intended.

Barrett nodded. Camille wasn't sure if it was a nod of agreement or one of contemplation as his brow furrowed when he took another sip of his warm milk before he responded.

"Long time ago, there were these… let's call them, 'monsters,' and they were the most powerful beings on the planet. When they was young, they was nice enough and all, but as they got older, and the power inside of them grew,… it was frightening. No being on this earth is meant to possess that much power. It overwhelmed them and, eventually, drove them crazy. That's when the killing began. And it went on and on and on. They'd kill anyone and anything that crossed their path. And if nothing crossed their path, then they went looking for stuff to kill. And if someone hadn't stood up and said, 'NO!'" Barrett erupted. Camille flinched, not so much from the volume but the fury that came with it. "'This is wrong! These monsters must be stopped!' they would have killed every living thing on this planet. Everything. Then they probably would've turned on each other and started killing themselves. So, one man did just that. He stood up, and alliances were formed; enemies became friends, and a war was waged for nearly thirty years until these 'monsters' were controlled – not destroyed, but controlled. See, if you destroy all the bees 'cuz of a few stings, then the world is deprived of honey." He smiled. "So, over the centuries, that alliance or, 'Council' if you may, has stayed together to maintain balance and control. They have laid down laws set rules in place that we all must live by in order to survive. And just like in any society, they have people who enforce these rules. They are powerful, and their reach extends throughout the seven continents, stopping just outside that front door. And the reason it does is 'cuz centuries ago, the man who stood up and said 'No' was your husband's great-great-great, grandfather."

Camille inhaled deeply and painfully forgot to let it go. Barrett continued.

"He was strong, passionate, confident, and he possessed no fear. No fear! That was the only reason he succeeded in his mission, rising to the greatness that he did, and…" He paused, searching for just the right word. "*Ironically*, I see so much of him in you. From the moment I first saw you, I knew you were the one. I'd a never picked you to marry my boy if I didn't. Julien's the most important person in my life, and I love him to death, but he's weak. My fault, I suppose. I was afraid he was gonna turn out just like me, so I let him go to all these,… human schools." He said distastefully. "Tried to raise him to be a better man than me. That was the mistake. Should've just raised him to be a better warlock. He needed someone like you, with your strength and confidence. You shaped him in a way that I never could, and I see you doing the same thing with them two boys. And I like that. So, even though it may appear like a prison - sometimes we build walls, not so much to stop somebody from getting out, but maybe 'cuz we're trying to stop somebody else from getting in."

There was a warmth behind Camille's eyes, but her anger outweighed it.

"I'm not a monster, Mr. Gerard! You think I would hurt anyone in this house? You are my family. The people in this house are all I have in this world."

A single tear escaped her eye. With a slight turn of his index finger, a tissue materialized in front of her. She took it.

"When I was a boy, people used to talk about this young witch from Southeastern Texas, who, years back, had killed both her husband and newborn son," Barrett said.

"I would <u>never</u> do that!"

"How you know?"

"Because I'm nothing like her. I—"

"She was your great-grandmother."

His words hit Camille like a gut punch and took the wind right out of her.

"She killed 288 people before she was stopped. Only one witch in history has killed more."

Camille struggled to speak. She looked as if she might vomit.

"How do you know what you're capable of or what you're gonna do when the change happens? You may not want to admit it, but I know you've felt it. It's overwhelming and all-consuming. You've let go and succumbed to it for a moment or two, haven't you?" He said with a devilish grin. She could not respond because she knew it was true. "What's gonna happen the one time it comes over you, and you can't bring yourself back? Hmm? Are you willing to take that chance with Julien? Lucien? Dani? This house-this city?"

"I would die before I would hurt them or any one of you here. I would kill myself."

Again, Barrett nodded to her response, and he reached across the table and squeezed her hand.

"The Gerard name is strong and carries a lot of weight within The Council," he said, as he held her eyes, "but without order, there is chaos, and they just ain't gonna let that happen."

He stood up, touched her glass with his finger, and warmed it up again.

"Your milk's getting cold." He said with an uncharacteristically loving smile.

Barrett was many things. Most of them were bad, but the one thing he wasn't was a liar. He genuinely liked Camille. In another world, he most definitely would have loved her.

"I must be able to move freely. I will not be locked up anymore."

Barrett stopped himself at the kitchen door and, again, nodded in agreement with her.

"And if they come for me—"

"When," he interrupted.

"…I promise you, they will remember my name."

Barrett smiled and silently chuckled to himself.

"And that, young lady, is exactly what they're afraid of."

The lights faded as he left the room, and Camille sat alone at the table in the dark.

CHAPTER 23

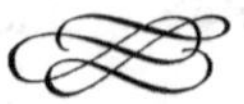

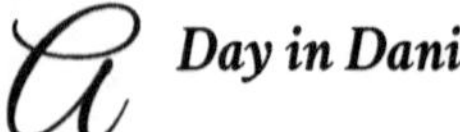 *Day in Dani*

Morning

June 22, 1999.

"It's okay, it's okay," Dani heard the muddled, almost indistinguishable voice say.

"NO!" Dani screamed.

To him, it was anything but okay.

"Shhhhhhhhhh. It's okay," the voice said, becoming clearer and more familiar with every word. "Come on, baby, wake up. Wake up."

Dani slowly opened his eyes to the sight of his mother's loving face. He seemed disoriented, shocked that she was really there.

"Momma?" he gasped as he stared at her.

"I'm here, baby," Camille reassured. Dani entangled himself in his mother's arms and held onto her as tight as he could.

"I thought you was dead," Dani said as he began to cry.

"It was just a dream, baby. Everything is fine now."

"No, it wasn't no dream, it was real! We have to go, we can't stay here no more!--"

"Go where?" Lucien interrupted.

Dani pushed himself away from his mother as he stared at his older twin, who immediately moved to take his place by climbing into his mother's now free lap.

"Where we going, Momma?" he asked as he toyed with the Blood Heart necklace around his mother's neck like she so often did.

Dani looked as if he had just been caught with his hand in the cookie jar.

"Nowhere, baby," Camille said as she kissed Lucien on the head. "He's just dreaming. You go on and wash up for breakfast while I get him up, okay?"

"No… I want to stay here with you," Lucien said as he snuggled in closer to his mom.

Camille picked him up and placed him on the floor, much to his displeasure.

"Go on, do what Momma says. Go pee-pee, and wash your face, and brush your teeth. Be Momma's big boy," Camille said as she leaned over and kissed him again.

"Yes, ma'am," Lucien said.

He offered Dani an unpleasant glare before he trudged into the bathroom.

"Momma," Dani whined but was quickly silenced with an equally unpleasant glare from Camille. He held his tongue and looked down, avoiding her eyes until the sound of the closing bathroom door could be heard. "Momma,--"

"What is wrong with you?" Camille scolded him in a hushed but firm voice.

"I saw something bad," Dani said as the tears began again.

"It was just a nightmare."

"No, it was real. The monsters was fighting you, and you didn't win."

"Dani,--"

"There was blood everywhere, and you didn't get up!" Dani yelled as the tears gushed from his eyes.

"Dani! You stop this right now."

"No! We gotta go. We can't be here no more!"

"Hush! It was just a dream. Now I need you to be a big boy and,--"

"NO! I don't wanna be a boy no more!" Dani yelled as Camille grabbed him by his shoulders.

"Stop it," Camille said.

Dani shook her off and started pulling at his own hair.

"Take it off! Get it off me! I don't want to be a boy no more!" He screamed. Camille slapped him in the face. Not hard, but more than hard enough for him.

"Shut up!" She said in a low voice, pointing her finger at him. "You shut your mouth right now!"

Dani grabbed his face as his bottom lip quivered. It was everything he could do not to cry out, but it was definitely coming. Camille's eyes flashed red as her hair began to float, and in an instant, she zipped off the bed across the room and placed her glowing hands on the hallway door, allowing her to see into the hallway. Empty. She zipped across the room to the bathroom door to check on Lucien. Brushing his teeth, the water running. Good. Then, in a flash, she was back on the bed.

Dani could hold back no longer, still holding his face, his eyes closed, and his mouth opened wide as he inhaled, taking in as much air as his little lungs could. Then, just as he was about to release this huge, delayed wail, Camille's eyes again flashed red. She raised her hand in front of his mouth as if she were catching the sound before it could be heard. She let him scream for a good while, even though no sound was ever heard. Then;

"ENOUGH!" she commanded, still in a firm, hushed voice. "That's enough."

Dani sniffed and snorted back his tears, but he obeyed, bottom lip shaking like a hummingbird's wings. Camille's eyes faded to normal as the two of them silently stared sorrowfully at each other for a few melancholy moments.

"You don't wanna be a boy no more?" Camille asked, trying hard to hold back her own tears.

Dani shook his head, 'No'.

"Would you rather be dead? Hmm? 'Cuz I would rather you not be. That would make me very sad." Camille said. "NEVER talk like that again. EVER. You understand me?"

Dani, still trembling, nodded solemnly. Camille grabbed him and held him tight.

"I love you, and I'm sorry, sweetie,… but neither one of us gets to be a little girl."

Suddenly, Lucien busted out of the bathroom.

"I'm done!" Lucien said with much enthusiasm.

Camille wiped away her own tears and got off the bed.

"Good boy. Now make up your bed, then come on down," she said to Lucien. She looked at Dani. "In the bathroom. Now. Hurry up," she said and then exited the room.

Dani sat there for a few moments more, angry, embarrassed, stoic, and still quivering. Lucien eyed his younger twin with a distasteful look.

"Why you such a crybaby all the time?" Lucien asked.

"I'm not!" Dani yelled as he started to cry.

"Wah, wah, wah, all the time," Lucien said with a child-like look of disdain on his face.

"Stop it!" Dani yelled before he ran into the bathroom and locked the door behind him.

With a sadness no one could understand, he stared at himself in the mirror as he wiped away the last of his tears, wondering if anyone would ever see what he, what *she* really looked like. Then, as he moved to the toilet.

"LUCIEN!"

"What?!" Lucien yelled from the other room.

"You pee'd all over the toilet again!

"So,"

"How am I supposed to go now?!"

"Just stand up and go and stop being such a baby!" Lucien yelled.

Dani heard him run across the room and slam the bedroom door. He was gone.

"…I can't," Dani said to himself. Tears of anger and frustration began to flow across his cheeks as he grabbed some toilet paper and began to clean up after Lucien. Again.

* * *

Afternoon

That afternoon, Dani's anxiety simmered, his eyes darting nervously between his brother and the scene unfolding before him. He could feel the tension building, the anticipation of what was to come tightening in his chest. Lucien sat rigid in a chair at the center of the study, his young face a mask of concentration. Barrett and Cecil stood about ten feet away on either side, their expressions unreadable as they focused their minds on the task at hand.

Without so much as a flicker of movement, they began launching wooden Latin alphabet blocks at Lucien, using only their thoughts. Each block hurtled through the air with precision, aimed directly at Lucien's face. The young warlock, relying solely on Thought magic, had no choice but to deflect them or be struck. One after another, the blocks came—a rapid succession of ten, sent with increasing speed and force.

Lucien, diligent and focused, deftly deflected each one, his brow furrowed in concentration as his powers moved in sync with the attacks. He didn't falter, his movements swift and seamless, but Dani's nerves remained on edge, the sight of his brother so intensely tested only adding to the tension in the room.

"Excellent! That's an excellent job, Lucie!" Barrett lauded. "Chip off the ol' block is what he is, huh? Am I right?"

"He's definitely talented, I'll say that," Cecil said, "but your daddy was doing twelve at your age." He told Lucien. "You gonna have to practice if you wanna break that record."

"He will, won't you, son?"

"Yes, Grandpa," Lucien answered.

Barrett laughed and gave him a big hug, then looked to Dani.

"Okay, Mister," Barrett said to Dani, "You're up."

"I don't want to play blocks today, Grandpa," Dani said.

"Well, how you expect to get as good as your brother if you don't practice?" Cecil said.

"Come on. Ten blocks," Barrett insisted. "One time, and you're done."

The smile quickly fell from Lucien's face as Dani trudged over and sank into the chair.

"Now concentrate," Barrett said in a serious tone.

Dani took a deep breath and prepared himself for what he knew was coming. Dani saw the first block rise up in front of his grandfather and surge toward him. A split second later, Cecil did the same. Dani concentrated as best as he could, but to no avail. The first block slammed into his face. He winced from the pain, and before he could recover, Cecil's block smacked him on the side of his head.

"Ouch!" Dani said softly as another from Barrett came flying in.

"Come on! Stop this one!" Barrett said hopefully, as the block bounced off of Dani's face again, quickly followed by Cecil's doing the same.

Dani whimpered as the pelting continued. Tears began to fall. He tried to put his hands up to block the onslaught, but with a thought, Barrett forced the child's hands down to his side and held them there.

"No hands! Concentrate!" Barrett ordered as the blocks kept coming, one after another, pounding Dani in the face and head as Lucien sadly looked on.

"Grandpa, stop! Please!" Dani screamed.

Then finally, magically, a block was deflected. Then another. Barrett immediately waved his hand, ending the game, shaking his head as Dani sat in the middle of the room sobbing.

"What you stop it for?! He was finally doing it," said an excited Cecil.

"Was he?" Barrett asked as he glared at Lucien. "Well, was he, Lucien?"

Dani looked at his brother as he sniffled and sucked back his tears. Lucien stared at the floor, afraid to look up.

"I said, was he?!"

Lucien jumped from the harshness of Barrett's tone.

"I just didn't want him to be hurt no more," Lucien replied, holding back his own tears.

"What you think's gonna happen if he ever gets into a real fight? HUH?! What if you ain't there to help him then?!" Barrett scolded. "You wanna help him, practice with him, push him to be better, that's how you help him!"

"I don't get it. The boy should be able to do at least four blocks at his age. At least!" Cecil said, shaking his head.

Barrett sighed deeply as he stared at Dani. Dani didn't want to cry, but he was embarrassed and ashamed, and his face was bleeding, and it hurt.

"Aww, now, come here. Come to Grandpa," Barrett said as Dani slowly walked over to him, not trying to hold back the tears any longer. Barrett hugged him tightly. "All right, all right. It's over now."

"I DON'T LIKE TO PLAY BLOCKS!" Dani wailed.

"Shhhhh, shhhhh… here, let me look at you." Barrett took his hand and gently moved it over Dani's face as if he were stroking a cat or a small dog. The small cuts and welts, along with the blood and tears, disappeared. "There. See? All better."

Dani sniffled. Grandpa could always wipe away the welts and physical scars, but there was no magic powerful enough to purge the mental pain left behind.

* * *

Night

"Look who came for a sleepover tonight," Camille sang as she and Kaitlin entered the bedroom.

The two women froze in place, their breath catching as they watched a wooden block slam into Dani's face with a sickening thud. He winced, a sharp cry escaping his lips, his fists clenched tightly from the searing pain. But despite the agony, Dani didn't raise his hands to defend himself.

He sat there, rigid and stoic, as blood and tears mixed on his cheeks, dripping slowly onto his shirt. The hurt was clear in his eyes, but he refused to move, to show weakness. He took it all in silence, enduring the punishment with a resilience that seemed both heartbreaking and defiant.

"LUCIEN!" Camille yelled.

Lucien, startled, lost concentration, and the remaining blocks fell to the floor.

"What the hell are you doing?!" Camille screamed as she rushed over to Dani.

She picked Dani up off the floor and set him on the bed to examine him. From the number of cuts and bruises on Dani's face, it was apparent that this session lasted much longer than the one with his grandpa earlier in the day.

"Get over here!" she ordered Lucien, who approached with fear on his face. "Look at his face! Why would you do this to him?!" Her eyes and right hand flashed red. Dani flinched as she gently healed his damaged face. "WHY?!"

Lucien jumped again from the fear of his mom's ferociousness and began to cry.

"I'm sorry! I was just trying to help him get better at blocks!" he wailed as a tidal wave of tears gushed from his eyes.

Camille was appalled by the truth of the situation, and her eyes faded to normal.

"How long have you been playing blocks?" she asked, not wanting to hear the answer.

"A long time," Lucien cried.

Camille closed her eyes and shook her head in an attempt to curtain the emotions boiling with in her.

"Is blocks some kind of weird game?" Kaitlin asked.

Dani nodded.

"Come here, baby," Camille said to Lucien.

She picked him up and gently caressed the back of his head as he continued to cry on her shoulder.

"This how you played as a kid?" Kaitlin asked, aghast at the thought, as Camille rocked Lucien to a calm state.

"...No. Not me. It's a game for warlocks. Witches can't do it until they're much, much older," she said as she stared at Dani with tears in her eyes. "How long?" she asked sadly.

"I don't know." Dani shrugged.

"Yes, you do," Camille said, but Dani would not answer. "It's okay, baby, just tell me. Please."

Dani would not say. So, Lucien spoke for him.

"Since Ray-Ray brought the new guard home," Lucien said.

"That was over two months ago!" Kaitlin exclaimed.

Camille's face quivered. She clinched her teeth and rapidly blinked her eyes, trying her best to contain the anger, the demon brewing just beneath the surface. She continued to rock Lucien as an anchor.

"Why didn't you tell me?" she asked Dani. Dani shook his head and would not answer. "Why?" Camille pressed.

Then, with an apathy and indifference that a mother would never want to see in their child, Dani looked at Camille and answered.

"I was just trying to be a big boy like you wanted me to," Dani said.

That answer was too much for Camille to bear. She closed her eyes in a failed attempt to stop a tear from escaping. She extended her left hand to Dani, he placed his right hand in hers, and they squeezed.

"I'm sorry, Momma," Lucien said.

"It's not your fault, sweetie," Camille assured him.

"I just didn't want him to get hurt no more. I didn't like to see him being hurt like that. I was just trying to make him strong."

"I know, baby, but what you were doing wasn't making him stronger. It was the same thing they were doing to him that you didn't like."

"But Grandpa said,--"

"Grandpa was wrong," Camille said, not trying to hide the anger in her words. "You two aren't supposed to fight each other - EVER. You're supposed to fight for each other. Even if you're mad or unhappy with one another. It don't matter, 'cuz you're siblings and that bond is sacred and special like no other." Then, to Lucien, "and you are doubly special. You know why?" Lucien shook his head. "'Cuz you're the big brother. You came first, which means you're bigger and stronger and faster than he is right now. He's just not ready to do the things you can do and it's gonna take him some more time before he can catch up to you."

"When will he be ready?"

"I don't know, sweetheart. Everyone's different, but until he is, it's your job to look after him and protect him when I'm not around. 'Cuz that's what big brothers do, until he's big enough and strong enough to protect himself. Even then, you're still always gonna be the big brother, that ain't ever gonna change, and it's something you should be very proud of."

Lucien started to stroke the Blood Heart necklace around Camile's neck, and it seemed to settled him down.

"That why you like Dani more than me?" he asked.

It was such an innocent question, asked without a trace of malice or ill intent. But even at nearly four years old, Dani could sense how deeply it wounded his mother. The moment the words left his lips, Camille's face crumbled ever so slightly, her efforts to hold back tears painfully obvious. The question had struck a place in her heart that not even The Council or any outside force could ever touch.

Kaitlin, standing nearby, couldn't hide her own emotion as her eyes welled up in sympathy.

"Don't cry Momma. I understand now. He needs you more right now. 'Cuz you need to protect him just like you want me to, right?" Lucien asked as he tried to wipe away his mother's tears.

Lucien's simple words held a wisdom far beyond his years, and in that moment, Camille's heart swelled with pride. She was prouder of him than she could ever express, knowing how remarkable it was that he had pieced it all together on his own. But there was a truth Lucien would never fully grasp, one known to all mothers. They love their daughters more than life itself, fiercely devoted to their safety and happiness. But the love a mother holds for her son—it was something else entirely, a love so deep, so different, that no words could ever explain it.

"That's right, but baby,… I could never love anybody more than I love you. You are my… You're *my* boy. My very, very special boy. My beautiful, big, strong baby boy. I don't know if I'll ever be able to show you how special you are to me, but I promise you that I will try. Okay?" Lucien nodded as he continued to massage the Blood Heart between his fingers. "You think a strong boy like you could come help me get some cookies and milk for you and your brother?"

"Yes, ma'am," Lucien said enthusiastically. Camille got up with Lucien on her shoulder. She nodded to Dani, who subtly nodded back. Camille gave him a fragile, broken smile as she and Lucien exited the room.

"So," Kaitlin said, trying to change the tone, "I hear someone's been having some pretty bad nightmares."

Dani nodded as Kaitlin took Camille's place on the bed.

"Well, we gonna try and make sure that doesn't happen tonight, okay?"

Dani nodded again as he curled up one side of his mouth to muster up a half of a smile.

"What's wrong, sweetie?" Dani shook his head. "Come on. You know you can always talk to me." She smiled.

Dani stared at her with a longing look in his eyes.

"You think one day I'll be as pretty as you and Momma?" Dani asked.

"Girls are pretty. Boys are handsome." Kaitlin laughed. "I swear, I'll never get over how articulate you are at three years old."

"I'm almost four," Dani said, his little brow furrowing up from the accusation.

"Sorry, yes, you are." Kaitlin smiled. "And yes, I think you're gonna be a very handsome young man."

"As handsome as you and Momma?"

Again, Kaitlin laughed at his innocence. She loved both boys as if they were her very own, but she had always felt a special connection with Dani.

"Yes," she said, "I think you will be."

Dani smiled and hugged a surprised Kaitlin tightly around her waist. He sat back when he felt her scar. He pointed to the area under her shirt and she raised it slightly for him to see.

"It's just my scar," she said. "I have one just like it on this side too, see?" She showed him the matching scars. He went to touch it, then pulled back. "It's okay," she said.

He ran his finger over it and something about it made him sad, then embarrassed, and again he pulled back. Kaitlin rolled her shirt back down.

"Does it hurt?" Dani asked.

"Not anymore."

"Why don't you make it go 'way?"

"I can't do that, sweetie. I don't have that power."

"Momma does. If you ask her, she'll make it go 'way for you. She makes all of me and Lucien's scars go 'way."

"I don't want it to go away."

"Why not?"

"You may be too young to understand this, but… the scars aren't bad. The experience in which I received them was. Took me a long time to understand and accept that. I wear them now as a sort of badge." She smiled. "It's a visible reminder, both to me and to whomever approaches me, that I am strong and no matter what you throw at me, I will endure."

Dani stared at Kaitlin, thinking hard about what was just said.

"What does 'endure' mean?"

Kaitlin tried to choose her words carefully.

"Uhmm, to survive, to continue to exist, to… to not allow yourself to be broken, even when others try to break you."

Dani reached out and touched her scar, this time through her shirt.

"Grandpa takes my scars away sometimes," he said. "You may not can see them no more, but,--" He ran his little fingers along his face. "I still feel them… I endure?"

"Yes," Kaitlin smiled to keep from crying. She scooped Dani up in her arms. "Yes, you do. Come on. Let's get you ready for bed."

CHAPTER 24

"Open your eyes for me, witch. Fight."

Lightning illuminated the night sky outside the window as Camille quietly returned a bottle of milk to the fridge. The soft sound of thunder followed, but inside, the house was still. Both the kids and Kaitlin were fast asleep, lost in peaceful dreams, but Camille remained wide awake, as she had so often these past few months. Exhaustion weighed heavily on her, the strain etched in the new streaks of white that ran through her hair. The toll of the past three years and the relentless burden of the spell was becoming more visible with each passing day.

Her tired eyes lingered on the refrigerator door for a moment, the quiet almost suffocating. Then, piercing the stillness, the phone rang.

"Gerard residence," Camille answered.

"Hey, Cher'," Julien said, on the other end of the line. "I'm packing up now. How's my boys?"

"Did you know your dad has had them playing blocks?"

"Yeah, how'd Luc do? Did he make twelve yet? Those last two blocks really make a diff—"

"Julien!"

"What?"

"You knew?"

"Well, yeah, what's the big deal? We all did it. I used to look forward to,--"

"The big deal is Dani isn't very good at it right now, so they torture him."

"Camille,--"

"And when Lucien tried to stand up for his brother, he got yelled at, then was told if he wanted to help him, he should be practicing with him."

"…Luc was sending blocks at Dani?" Julien asked.

"Yes! I walked in on them, and Dani's face was a mess, and then they both started crying and - I want it stopped. If you won't, I,--"

"I'll handle it. I'm sorry. I didn't know. How are they now?"

"They're fine now. Kaitlin's with them. They went down about an hour ago," Camille said. "I let them stay up late 'cuz they wanted to see their daddy."

"Mmm. Were they mad?"

"They'll forgive you."

"What about you?"

"Just come on home," she said as she massaged the Blood Heart.

"I'm on my way. Love you."

"I love you, too," Camille said, hanging up.

* * *

At the office, Julien grabbed his briefcase and headed for the door. He opened it and was startled by Tirin - again.

"Stop doing that! Jesus!"

"What's the emergency?" Tirin asked.

"What emergency?" Julien said. "There's no,-- wait. What're you doing here? Who's watching Camille?"

Julien's stomach sank as they stared at each other. Tirin took off like he was shot out of a cannon as Julien ran back to the phone and dialed as quickly as he could.

"Pick it up," he begged. "Please... PICK IT UP!

* * *

Camille walked into the dark hallway and was on her way up the candlelit staircase when the phone rang again. She came back down to answer it.

"Hey, Babe," she answered, then the phone went dead. "Julien? Hello?"

Then, a strong wind rushed through the house and blew out most of the candles on the stairs. Just a few weakly flickered in the now-darkened room.

"What? How did that happen?" She wondered.

A flash of lightning illuminated the room momentarily before darkness reclaimed it. Silence. Only the soft pelting of raindrops on the old house could be heard. And then there was a 'creak'. The sound someone might make if they stepped on a loose floorboard, or an old door opening on a rainy night. She quietly placed the phone down and turned to find nothing but darkness and the cause of the strong wind and the creak. The front door had been opened and was swinging freely, back and forth, in the nighttime air. The guards were always posted outside at night. They would NEVER leave the door open - if they were there. Her heart rate increased, and the air became thicker and increasingly more difficult to breathe as the hair on her arms and the back of her neck tingled. She knew she was no longer alone.

She cautiously moved toward the front door to close it and a shadowy figure, inside the house, darted past a window behind her. She looked back but saw nothing. As she turned and continued toward the door, three sets of eyes appeared in the darkness. Lightning flashed and their figures, three men, were briefly illuminated. Two stood in the background, over her shoulders, as one crawled across the ceiling above. She reached the door and jerked her head around, but the eyes on the men closed and she again saw nothing. When she turned to close the door she heard a low, menacing growl that emanated from the ceiling, just off her left shoulder. A flutter of lightning flashed and this time revealed a fourth man standing behind the other two. The man on the ceiling dropped to the floor as the illumination from the lightning flickered away the light, to darkness. Camille calmly closed the door and locked it. She blinked and her eyes flared red as her hair raised up off her shoulders and talons sprouted from her nails.

"KAAITLIIIIINNNNN!!!!" Camille screamed as she whipped around, ready to fight.

Upstairs, Kaitlin was awakened by the scream. She jumped out of bed and nervously moved for the door. Just before she crossed the window, a fanged man crawled up to it and looked in. Kaitlin stopped, out of his sight, and remained very still.

"Oh my God, it's a Vampire," she whispered so faint that she couldn't even hear it. Not seeing his target, he kept crawling across the window, out of sight. Kaitlin ran back over to the bed and grabbed the children and huddled in the corner between the bed and the wall.

* * *

Tirin raced through the streets. Nothing more than a blur. He blew by bewildered pedestrians and dodged oncoming cars, moving at a speed much faster than any lycan was thought to be able.

* * *

Back at the house, the children screamed as the vampire crashed through the bedroom window. Kaitlin jumped up and tried to insert herself between him and the children and was rewarded with the back of his powerful hand against her face. The impact sent her flying over the bed, out of the way and barely conscious. He hissed at the screaming children, then quickly exited the room. He was not there for them.

Below, Camille was surrounded by the four intruders. She looked spectacular as she floated just off the ground, feinting and dodging, just out of their clawed reach. Her movements were accelerated and lethal as she systematically took out each and every one of her attackers, save one. He was much quicker and more agile than the others. She knew he was the alpha. He managed her wrath with a skill she had only seen from Tirin, then dished out a bit of his own. If not for her training, she would have surely died by his hand.

Again, she heard the scream of her children and immediately abandoned the fight and zipped toward the stairs. The alpha pursued. Camille flew to the top of the staircase as the alpha sprinted up the wall to cut her off. He leapt and slashed her arm. She screamed and awkwardly shot off an energy blast as she fell. She missed, but it was enough to unbalance the alpha and send him tumbling to the floor below.

At that moment, Tirin busted through the door, his chest expanding and contracting rhythmically as he desperately tried to

221

suck in air. He was going to need it. The intruding alpha popped up and readied himself for battle. Camille rose and raced down the hallway to her crying children. As she passed an open door, *her* vampire appeared from the shadows of the darkened room. He grabbed her from behind with a surprising quickness and sank his fangs deep into her shoulder before she could put up the least bit of resistance.

The pain was beyond anything Camille had ever experienced, a searing agony that coursed through her veins like wildfire. She could feel the venom spreading, burning every nerve as it surged through her body. Instinctively, she jerked up to fight, but her strength was fleeting. He was too strong. The toxins gripped her, and her body grew weaker with each passing second. Just as her eyes began to flutter closed, sharp fingernails suddenly pierced the vampire's back, forcing him to release her before his task was finished.

Camille collapsed onto the floor, gasping for breath. She rolled over, her vision hazy, and looked up to see the vampire writhing in pain. Another hand, strong and unyielding, gripped his chin and twisted his head sharply, spinning it around with a sickening crack. His neck snapped, blood spurting from the wound, spraying across Camille's face just before his body burst into a cloud of dust.

As the dust settled, Rayna stood over her, revealed as her unlikely savior. Camille lay helpless, unable to move, watching as Rayna stared down at her, the faintest hint of a smile playing on her lips—or so it seemed. Camille wasn't sure. The room had begun to spin, her vision blurring as the venom continued to weaken her. In the distance, she could hear the sounds of a brutal fight. It was Tirin, locked in battle with the alpha. She wished with all her heart she could help him, but she couldn't even stand.

Her thoughts turned to her children. She had to reach them. With a desperate will to protect them, she rolled onto her stomach and began to crawl toward their room, her body trembling with every effort. Rayna followed silently, her expression unreadable, her eyes watching Camille's struggle with a strange, almost curious gaze.

"Oh, my God, NO!" Kaitlin yelled as she watched her friend crawl up to the door.

With her back to the children, she didn't notice what Camille's eyes were fixed on, behind her. Dani - the real Dani could now be seen. The spell had been broken, and for the first time, *Danielle* was very much present. A confused Lucien stared at the girl who was there in the place of his sibling.

"What'd you do with my brother?" he asked.

Kaitlin turned and, in that moment, understood what Camille had done. She staggered over and swept Danielle up in a blanket just as Rayna arrived at the door. Rayna stood over Camille and looked down at her, watching the blood ooze from her neck.

"MOMMA!" Lucien screamed as he stared at Camille.

He took a few steps toward her, but the sight of his mother, covered in blood, paralyzed him. Camille reached for his hand, but he wouldn't take it. She pulled her hand back and instead grabbed onto the Blood Heart necklace resting on her chest.

"Shhhhh. It's okay. It's okay. Auntie Ray-Ray's here," Rayna said, as she stepped into the bedroom and scooped him up. "Where's your brother, baby?" She asked, then yelled for Tirin. "Tirin, get up here!"

"I-I-I don't know," Lucien cried and sniffled. "That girl took him!"

"TIRIN!" Rayna screamed, then to Lucien, "what girl, baby?"

Camille's eyes were barely open. She couldn't move. She silently mouthed an incantation that distracted Lucien. It was a beautiful voice that came to him on the wind that only he could hear. Rayna turned to Kaitlin and started to move her way.

"Katie? You okay, sweetie?" Rayna asked.

"Don't tell," Danielle whispered.

"Yes, Ms. Rayna," Kaitlin said as she squeezed Danielle tighter.

"Everything's all right now. Is Dani okay?" Rayna asked as she continued to move closer.

Kaitlin gently rocked Danielle back and forth, trying to soothe the child's soft cries. There was an unmistakable tension in the room, but her focus remained on the tiny life in her arms. Outside the room, Tirin limped toward Camille. He looked battered, like someone who had barely survived a vicious fight, but he was alive—and for an alpha, that meant everything. Alphas fought to the death, and the fact that he was still standing, though barely, was a victory in itself.

Tirin knelt beside Camille, his expression softening as he pressed his hand firmly against her neck to staunch the bleeding. His movements were slow, careful, as if the mere act of touch could bring her some comfort amidst the chaos. Inside the room, Rayna crouched down in front of Kaitlin, who continued to cradle Danielle protectively. The child began to cry louder, her tiny voice breaking through the silence, while Rayna's sharp eyes remained fixed on Kaitlin, observing with an unsettling intensity.

"Let me take a look-see, Sugar," Rayna said as she reached for the blanket.

"T,--" Camille whispered, unable to complete the sentence.

"Open your eyes for me, witch… Fight." Tirin demanded. "FIIIIIGHT!" he bellowed. And Camille obeyed.

Camille snapped her eyes open as wide as she could, her last bit of strength igniting them in a fiery red glow. With a pained exhale, she forced out what little energy remained. In the bedroom, Kaitlin trembled as Rayna slowly pulled back the blanket, revealing a small, terrified boy—Daniel—his wide eyes brimming with tears. Kaitlin's heart sank, her amazement barely masked by the fear gripping her.

Dani screamed, thrashing in Kaitlin's arms, desperate to get to his mother. His small body fought against her tight hold, but Kaitlin knew what lay on the other side. She held him close, determined to protect him from what he didn't need to see. But what Kaitlin didn't know was that Dani had already seen it. He had told his mother about the dream—the one with the blood, and how she didn't get up. And now, he knew he was right.

As Dani struggled, Rayna stepped in to help, gently holding him still. With her free hand, she reached for Kaitlin, her cold fingers resting on Kaitlin's quivering chin. Slowly, she lifted Kaitlin's head just enough to catch her eyes, holding them in an intense, almost mesmerizing gaze.

"*No,*" Camille thought, but it was too late.

Rayna's eyes sparkled as she looked into Kaitlin's soul and smiled. A tear escaped the corner of Camille's eye and rolled down the side of her head as her eye closed and consciousness drifted away.

CHAPTER 25

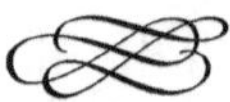

"They came to my house; now you go to his."

June 23, 1999

Camille lay motionless in the bed, her skin pale and her breathing faint. Though she had lost a significant amount of blood, it was the venom coursing through her veins that posed the real danger. The vampire's attack had been cut short by Rayna, but the damage was already done. The toxin had invaded her blood, slowly poisoning her from within. It was an excruciating way to die, and there was nothing anyone, or any magic could do to stop it.

Julien knelt by her side, his hands clenched into fists, a mix of anger, frustration, and helplessness weighing heavily on him. He was powerful—one of the most powerful warlocks alive—and yet, in this moment, he was utterly powerless. All he could do was sit and watch as Camille's life slipped away.

The door creaked open, and Rayna and Tirin stepped inside. Julien didn't even glance their way. His heart knew that none of this was their fault, but his mind refused to accept it. The weight of responsibility bore down on him—he was supposed to protect her, and he had failed. Now, as he knelt there in his torment, all he could do was direct his anger toward the only two people within reach.

"How could this happen?" asked Julien.

"They were well trained. They waited until the first shift guards in the slave quarters had left for the night, then they took out the guards in the house and on the grounds. They've obviously been studying us for some time," Rayna replied.

"You let them come into this house and do this," he said to Rayna. Then, to Tirin, "and you let that alpha get away. The one you couldn't find for almost two years."

Tirin remained silent. His guilt wouldn't allow him to respond. He just stared at Camille's lifeless body with a contained fury within his eyes and no one to release it on.

"Julien, he had to disengage. I needed him to attend to Camille while I checked out Kaitlin and the kids," Rayna said. She knew Tirin wouldn't respond, so she spoke for them both. "If he hadn't gotten to her when he did, she'd be dead now. He had to let the alpha go."

"YOU SHOULD HAVE HAD HIM BEFORE! NOW LOOK AT HER!" Julien yelled, no longer able to suppress his anger as he swiveled around to face them. "Between the two of you, as powerful as you are, with all the resources we have, you couldn't find one goddamn alpha! Well, you goddamn well better find his ass now."

"…Julien, chasing an alpha is like chasing the wind if we don't know where to look. You know that," Rayna said softly, not trying to spike his ire.

"Then go to the fucking source!"

Julien removed Felix Neely's business card from his pocket and threw it in her direction.

"They came to my house; now you go to his, and you find him. Take whoever you need, but you get it done this time."

"Okay. I'll take care of it, but Julien I... I saw something. Something in Kait--"

"Now, Rayna! I need you to do this now, yesterday - A FUCKING YEAR AGO!!"

Rayna nodded and exited the room. Her little secret would have to wait. Tirin took one last look at Camille, then turned to follow her.

"Hey," Julien said, stopping Tirin at the door in a much more reasonable, forgiving tone. "Just find him. Please."

Tirin nodded, then left.

* * *

Four days later. Julien listlessly walked down the stairs. He was tired and concerned about Camille's condition. She was a fighter, and she was doing much better than anyone expected, but the poison in her body would not be denied. It was still working, and there was no cure.

The front door slammed open, and Tirin stumbled inside, bloodied and bruised. Rayna rushed to help him, but he waved her off, refusing any assistance. Behind him, his five betas—Dane, Teddy, Micah, Cree, the sole female of the pack, and Gus, the newest—filed in, forming a disciplined line. Tirin was in rough shape, his body battered and his clothes soaked in blood, most of it his own. His right eye was swollen shut, and his left arm was tucked tightly against his chest, protecting an obvious injury.

He barely made it into the entryway before collapsing to his knees, the weight of exhaustion finally overtaking him. His betas moved to assist, but Tirin let out an angry, guttural roar, and they immediately retreated back into their formation, standing at attention. He had been through the fight of his life and lived to tell the tale. The grim trophy he clutched in his right hand—the severed head of an alpha—was proof enough that his opponent hadn't been so fortunate.

Tirin raised his head and locked eyes with Julien. Without a word, he tossed the alpha's head onto the rug at Julien's feet. The severed head landed with a thud, blood seeping into the fabric. Julien stared at it for a long moment, his eyes narrowing as he nodded in quiet acknowledgment. He stepped forward and, with surprising care, helped Tirin to his feet. Rayna stood back, her chest swelling with pride at the sight of Tirin's resilience.

Just then, Barrett and Cecil entered from the dining room, laughing, their jovial mood cut short as they saw the bloodied head lying on the floor. The room fell into a tense silence, the weight of the moment sinking in.

"What the hell is this?!" Barrett yelled over the mess the severed head had made to the expensive rug.

Rayna handed Julien a small gift box, big enough to house a bracelet.

"What's this?" Julien asked with a scrunched face.

Rayna beamed with excitement as Julien opened the box. Inside it, he found a tongue.

"What's left of Mr. Neely." She answered.

Julien looked sick as he snapped the box shut and shoved it back to her. Barrett and Cecil weren't taking the news any better.

"Felix Neely?" Barrett choked the words out of his mouth.

"Rayna,--" Julien gasped.

"You told me to start with him," Rayna said in a very defensive tone.

"Question, not kill! JESUS!" Julien cried out.

"What have you done?! What the hell have you done?!" Barrett yelled, with a panicked look on his face.

"They trace that body back to this house, we're all dead," Cecil chimed in as he so often did.

"They won't be able to trace him back to this house," Rayna said. She was more than a bit perturbed that they didn't seem to appreciate what she had done.

"Why not?" Barrett asked.

"'Cuz there's nothing else left to trace."

Julien opened his mouth but could find no words in it. Cecil looked as if he might pass out, and Barrett looked as if he could kill. He was barely able to contain his anger.

"Look at you. Talking tough 'cuz you're too stupid to be scared!" Barrett said through clench teeth.

"I beg your pardon,--"

"SHUT UP!" Barrett yelled. If looks could actually kill, Rayna would be dead. "Y'all done gone too goddamn far this time! Killing a member of The Council?! IDIOTS! ALL OF 'YA!" If they find out, all hell's gonna rain down on this house!"

"Hopefully, that vamp did enough damage, and we can cover this end," Cecil said.

"Cecil—" Julien warned.

"That girl should be resting in a six-foot hole in the backyard instead of that bed upstairs!" Cecil finished.

Julien took a step toward Cecil, but before he could get any closer, Tirin intervened, placing a firm hand on his chest. The lycan's nostrils flared as he sniffed the air, his sharp instincts pulling his attention elsewhere. He glanced upward, toward the top of the stairs. Following his gaze, the others turned to see Camille, standing on the landing, her pale form barely holding itself upright.

Her eyes, once fierce, were now dulled with exhaustion, her posture weak. She stood there for a moment, her face unreadable, then without a word, she turned and staggered back to her room, her steps unsteady, each one heavy with the weight of everything that had happened.

"One day, your mouth's gonna get you into something my daddy can't get you out of," Julien said to Cecil before he ran up the stairs.

"Julien!" Barrett hollered.

Julien stopped but did not turn.

"I warned you. I told you what would happen if you went down this path, but now you done gone too far. I ain't gonna let you and your pets bring this house down. I won't. Make this shit right, while you still can, boy."

"…I will, Daddy, I will," Julien said, and he continued upstairs.

"You better. Or I will," Barrett said, almost too quiet for Julien to hear. Almost.

CHAPTER 26

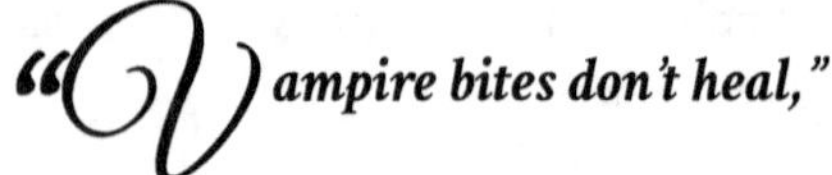

"*Vampire bites don't heal,*"

Camille locked the bedroom door. She barely made a few more steps before her legs gave out, and she collapsed to the floor, tears spilling uncontrollably as she dragged herself toward the bed. Each movement was a battle, not just against her weakening body but against the overwhelming sadness pressing down on her chest.

She was scared. Terrified, in fact. And she felt utterly alone. Alone in a house full of people waiting for her to die. The doorknob rattled from someone trying to open it. Other than the two children, that lock was useless in stopping anyone in this house from entering a room they wanted to get into. It was no more than a tool used to indicate someone's desire for privacy. The knock on the door that followed meant that desired privacy would be observed - today.

"Camille… Open the door. Please, Cher'," Julien asked, from the hallway.

Camille didn't budge. She just sat on the floor and continued to cry.

"I'm not sure what you heard, but,--"

"Just leave me alone," she said in a weakened voice. She wanted to yell, she tried to, but didn't have the strength to project.

Camille heard him mumble to someone before he walked away. A few moments later she heard another knock.

"I said, go,--"

"Sweetie, it's me," Kaitlin said.

Camille pulled herself up off the floor and staggered over to the door and opened it. Kaitlin stood there with Dani at her hip. She saw Lucien down the hall holding Rayna's hand as Rayna led him into the playroom. She locked eyes with Rayna for a moment and was gifted with her patented, deviously insincere smile as she closed the door to the playroom behind her.

Camille knew that Rayna had discovered the secret in Kaitlin's eyes, but what could she do about it now? She was weak and she was dying. All she could do was wait for Rayna to play out her malicious game. Camille had no doubt in her mind that, when it suited her needs, Rayna would deliver the final blow and reveal to all that Camille had lied and hidden Dani's true identity and when they found out, well… they would do what they would do.

"Come here, little one." Camille said as she took Dani into her arms and hugged him tightly as Kaitlin closed the door.

Camille's voice was horse, and her breath was labored. It seemed a chore for her to take one. Kaitlin sat down on the bed and hugged them both. Camille put Dani down.

"I was so scared I lost you," Kaitlin said. "Why didn't you tell,--"

Camille put up her hand and silenced her. She took a breath and painfully swallowed, gathering enough energy to flick her finger and re-lock the door, then her hands turned red, and she raised a force-field that engulfed the room. Inside the field, the illusion lifted, and Dani stood there as her true self - Danielle. She tried to run into the bathroom to steal a quick look at herself, but the force-field only covered the width of the bedroom. As soon as she crossed over the threshold and entered the bathroom, Daniel appeared. A frown overtook her/his face, and his bottom lip stuck out in sadness.

Camille's eyes faded back to normal as she looked away from the unhappy child and stared, trance-like, out the window, kneading the Blood Heart between her index finger and thumb. She breathed a bit easier without the weight of the spell upon her, but not much. Maintaining that force field was no walk in the park. Kaitlin looked proudly at Danielle as she re-entered the bedroom.

"You're so beautiful," Kaitlin assured her.

Dani frowned and shrugged her shoulders. She wouldn't know.

"How's my Luc?" Camille asked.

"He's fine. Missing his momma."

Camille grunted, not quite believing her.

"He's just scared, Camille," Kaitlin said. "It was a lot for him to see you that way."

Camille didn't respond. She just continued to stare mindlessly out the window.

"Why didn't you tell me about Dani?"

"…I'm so tired," Camille whispered, her voice raspy and weak.

Kaitlin pulled Camille's face from the window to her and forced Camille to look at her. A tear formed in Camille's eye and rolled down her face.

"I'm tired, Kait. I can't do it anymore," Camille said, then more tears followed.

Kaitlin embraced Camille and let her cry as Dani watched with more sadness in her eyes than any child her age should ever have.

"Okay. Okay… It's okay." Kaitlin said, hoping to comfort her.

"No, it's really not," Camille replied, not comforted from the attempt.

"But baby, why? Why hide her from them?"

"If they find out, they'll kill her."

"No," Kaitlin said as she shook her head. "Not JD. Not JD."

"Rayna told him about a prophecy. Dani's gonna kill him on her twenty-first birthday,"

"What?--"

"And they said not to worry 'cuz ain't no witch made it to twenty-one in over two hundred fifty years. Not my momma, not my little girl… not me. That's why I have two boys."

Kaitlin began to tear up.

"JD would never let,--"

"Anything happen to me?" Camille interrupted, finishing Kaitlin's sentence.

Camille tilted her head and revealed the still-infected vampire bite.

"Baby, no. No, no, no, I can't believe this. I won't!"

"Promise me you'll try and take care of Danielle when I'm gone."

"Camille,--"

"That's her real name. Danielle." Camille smiled. "When I die, the spell will break. She'll be exposed. Promise me you'll try to get her away from here. I can't, but maybe you can."

Danielle ran to her mother and hugged her. "Momma, no! You don't talk like that! You're strong! You're not gonna die. I don't want you to." Dani said as her eyes welled up.

"Shhhhhhh, baby," Camille said, stroking her hair. "You're right. I'm sorry." She gave her a hug and kissed her on her forehead. "I'm sorry. Now let me and Kay-Kay talk a little bit. You go on over there and do your rhymes."

"I don't want to! They're stupid!"

"Hey!" Camille said, pointedly. "They are not stupid! Don't you ever say that again, you hear me?"

"Camille." Kaitlin admonished.

"Sorry, Momma," Danielle said.

"Just,… go do what I asked, please," Camille said in a soft, hushed voice.

She was too exhausted to argue, and at the same time, it was her way of apologizing for her outburst. She leaned down, kissed Danielle gently on the forehead, and wiped away her daughter's tears, her own eyes brimming with a deep sadness. As Camille watched, Danielle shuffled over to the corner of the room, her small voice breaking the silence as she began to recite *"Hickory Dickory Dock."*.

"JD said you're gonna be fine," Kaitlin said. Camille shook her head. "But… What if we leave? Can you release the spell on Danielle and heal yourself?"

Again, Camille shook her head.

"Vampire bites don't heal on me," Camille whispered. "Promise me. Please."

Kaitlin's eyes filled with tears of both sadness and frustration.

"You know I will. But you're not gonna die. I won't let you. I won't. I'm gonna get you some help."

"Ain't nobody on this earth can help me now," Camille surrendered. "Even if there were, there ain't no one strong enough to take them on."

"There's one," Kaitlin said without an ounce of doubt in her voice.

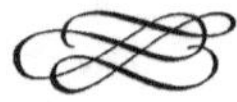

" *...ignorance, selfishness, and hate.*"

July 9, 1999

Sixty miles outside of Port-Au-Prince, nestled quietly within the mountains and deep valleys of the Central Plateau, sat the small commune of Boucan-Carre. Just under a mile north of that, laid the Sacred Heart Mission, an orphanage and school to nearly three hundred children, monks, and assorted workers. Curiously, the mission was encased inside a well-kept twenty-foot-high stone enclosure with a heavily fortified, sliding, double wooden gate. Children of all ages filled the courtyard inside and seemed content within the containment of the carefully crafted walls. As well kept as the gate and surrounding fence were, the same could not be said about the five main structures within the walls.

The school itself consisted of three separate, but identical buildings hastily erected using a low-grade cement mixture for the walls and a patchwork of multi-colored, corrugated aluminum siding for the roofs. The fourth building, similar to the school, was used for supplemental housing, and in the center of these four structures stood the fifth building: a larger, much older two-story complex made of stone, mud bricks, and cinderblocks. The first floor housed a medical facility and mess hall while the second included bunk-style living quarters for the children.

Across the courtyard, alone in a small corner of the compound, was a decrepit wooden church. There were several planks missing from the façade, like rotted-out teeth in an old, giant mouth. It was one of the oldest churches in Haiti. Cracked and scarred from earthquakes, weather, and rebellions, it stood only because it somehow refused to fall.

Inside the sanctuary, dripping wax candles illuminated the dirt floor from which the pews had long ago been removed. On the altar wall, hung a dark wooden cross, hand carved out of kajou peyi, a beautiful mahogany type wood commonly found in the surrounding forest. Mounted on the cross, was an exquisite hand-painted, life-sized sculpture of our lord and savior. Below the cross, a tall black man, in his mid-twenties, knelt before the altar. He prayed, in quiet solitude with the stillness of a sphinx, dressed in a long robe that draped effortlessly from his strong shoulders to the floor. He was Jean Laveau.

An elder monk, silent and slow, shuffled into the church with an envelope in hand. He hobbled to the altar, hampered more from wear than age, and crossed himself before he knelt next to Jean. Disciplined to a fault, Jean finished his prayer, crossed himself, sat back on his heels, and looked at the elder monk with no apprehension. The Elder, however, had much. He handed Jean the envelope, and Jeans eyes instantly fell upon the return address. It was from Kaitlin. Being all too familiar with their history, the Elder could not tell if the anxiety he felt was permeating from Jean or himself. He took a much-needed breath as Jean opened the letter, which simply read, 'I need you.' Three simple words. That was enough. Jean closed his eyes and lowered his head as he carefully re-folded the letter along its creases, placed it back into the envelope, and tucked it away within his robes.

"…Father,… I must go," Jean said.

"I know," the Elder nodded.

"I will return as soon as,--"

"No." The Elder said. Jean looked to him, not understanding the much too quick dismissal. "We all knew the day would come when you would leave our little island paradise," the Elder replied. "Even as a child, I always knew your destiny would lie in another place. The time has finally come for you to fulfill it."

"But,… what of my responsibilities here?" Jean asked.

"The children will grow; the mission will thrive." The Elder again nodded. "Your responsibilities are to mankind, my son. Not to me, the children, this mission,… not even to her."

Jean lowered his head in an effort to hide the hesitation in his eyes as the Elder continued.

"You have been given a great gift. One that allows you to fight for those who cannot fight for themselves. I fear there are many battles outside this tiny island that need the services of a warrior such as yourself. Admittedly, in my more selfish moments, I've… hoped to keep you here, but we both know this is not where your God-given talents were meant to stay."

"Father, I…" Jean hesitated as he searched for the words. They were present. He just did not wish to speak them.

"Speak your peace." The Elder replied, giving unneeded permission.

"…I am afraid."

"Of?"

"That I am not yet strong enough. That I cannot put my personal feelings aside and resist the hatred I have in me, the hatred I have… for them," Jean said, as the emotion overtook his voice. "It clouds my judgment, and because of it, I crossed a line that should have never been crossed. I have prayed diligently, every day, for forgiveness for it, for even just the strength to forget it. Yet every day my prayers go unanswered, and all I am left with is anger and fear that I will repeat it, again and again and again," Jean said.

The Elder listened with much empathy. He understood Jean's pain. He also understood that pity was not the answer to it.

"It is not the prayers that fail you, my son. It is for what you are praying for. You pray for forgiveness." The Elder shook his head. "How can you expect something from others which you refuse to give to yourself? You pray for the strength to forget; I would challenge you to pray for the strength to live with the memory. I would also challenge you to pray for the courage to release this hate. We all have lines, Jean. Yours just happen to separate the boundaries between good and evil. They are ambiguous at times and are often disguised by ignorance, selfishness, and hate. Three things that cloud all our judgments at one time or another, but for someone who must be judge, jury, and executioner, you do not have the luxury of such dalliances. Hate can never be a part of your equation, my son. Find it. Recognize it within yourself, then purge it from your soul. Only then can you be certain that these lines of yours will remain uncrossed."

Jean nodded in agreement. The monk grabbed Jean, and the two men embraced for a good while, as if they knew they would probably never see each other again.

"I love you, Father," said Jean with tears in his eyes.

"I love you too," said the monk proudly. "God be with you."

Jean nodded. "And also with you."

Jean rose, crossed himself, and exited the old, rotted church to prepared himself for his entrance into the real world.

CHAPTER 28

"*Magic man's coming,*"

July 10, 1999 - *3 Years, 11 Months, 9 Days, A. B.*

The following evening, 1,399 miles away, Rayna lay sprawled across the floor in the upstairs office of Club Dallas, an upscale dance club in the heart of New Orleans' uptown Garden District. The club, one of Julien's side ventures, existed primarily for income tax purposes, but Rayna found it more than just a financial front. Muted music reverberated rhythmically through the office walls and floor, a constant, comforting pulse that seemed to sync with her own. She relished the after-hours quiet, the post-business lull when the club was still alive with the distant throb of bass and the electric energy of the patrons below. The vibrations coursed through her body as she lay there, absently flipping her Tarot Cards one by one, her thoughts wandering, restless, searching for mischief.

Suddenly, her brow furrowed, her head tilting slightly to the side as her sharp eyes scanned the display of cards before her. The rhythmic flipping of the cards grew more deliberate. One, then another, and another. Her fingers moved with purpose now, each turn of the card adding to a picture forming in her mind. As her eyes settled on the final card, her lips curled into a slow, satisfied smile. Something devious indeed.

Without hesitation, she reached for the phone on the desk. The buttons clicked rapidly beneath her fingers as she dialed the mansion, her mind already racing ahead with whatever scheme had just been set into motion.

"Hey, it's me. Put him on. Quick," she said to the person on the other end.

She flipped another card as she waited, and her smile widened.

"What's up?" Julien asked in a faint and fatigued voice.

"Magic man's coming," Rayna said.

"What?"

She flipped another card.

"Here, to New Orleans."

"…Friend or foe?" Julien asked with much more interest in his voice.

She flipped another card.

"Don't know."

"Well, what's he want?"

She flipped another card.

"Something that belongs to you," Rayna said, slightly aroused as she flipped another card before her smile filled her face.

"And he's coming fast."

"When?"

"Have to get back to you on that one, baby. Sweet dreams."

"Rayna,--"

She giggled and hung up before Julien could finish his question, then looked over to one of the two guards with her.

"Get over to Kaitlin's place. Check it out. I want to know everything."

"Yes, ma'am," the guard said as he moved toward the door.

"And Marcus," she called out, stopping him, "be stealthy. No one is to know you were there."

"Yes, ma'am," he answered before exiting.

Rayna casually flipped over another card, her playful smile still lingering on her lips, but the moment her eyes fell on the image, the smile vanished, ripped away as if by an unseen force. Something in the card instantly unsettled her. Her brow creased deeply, and her once carefree expression transformed into one of confusion and agitation. Her sharp eyes flitted back and forth across the surface of the card, trying to make sense of what she was seeing. It was *The Lovers* card. The simple image held a weight that was impossible to ignore. What had once been a light-hearted diversion was now charged with an unexpected intensity. She stared at the card, her mind racing. This was not what she had anticipated, and for Rayna, that was deeply disturbing.

CHAPTER 29

July 11, 1999

Jean stepped off the jetway, immediately hit by the thick, humid air that clung to the city like a second skin. The scent of New Orleans at night was unlike anywhere else—a mix of heat, earth, and something intangible, almost magical. It carried an energy that stirred something deep within him, awakening old memories and a familiar, unsettling nervousness. His stomach tightened, but the sensation quickly spread, crawling up his spine and settling in his chest.

And then he saw her.

The moment their eyes met, the nerves that had begun to flutter inside him expanded, coursing through his entire body like electricity. His breath caught in his throat. She was here, and just like that, everything he had tried to keep at bay came rushing back.

"Bonjour," Jean said to Kaitlin.

"Hi," she replied, gifting him with her beautiful smile. She was genuinely glad to see him.

He didn't think it was possible for her to be more stunning than what he had remembered. He was wrong. He hesitated; his arms twitched. He didn't know if it was okay to hug her.

"Plus belle que la derniere fois," he said.

"You look great, too," she replied.

That was the permission he needed. They embraced and neither wanted to let go.

"I missed you so much," Kaitlin said.

"Are you all right?"

"I'm fine. It's not me who's in trouble. It's my friend who needs your help."

She grabbed his hands. It felt good to Jean as he had missed her touch.

"Come on, we need to talk. You hungry?" she asked.

"Eh. I had dinner, at least that is what they called it on the plane. But perhaps some,... chai tea?" He smiled at their private joke. She smiled back.

"I think I have just the place for,--"

She froze mid-sentence, her eyes widening as the tiniest gasp slipped from her lips. The shift in her expression was immediate, and Jean, who knew Kaitlin all too well, recognized the sudden wave of anxiety that washed over her. Only a few things could evoke that kind of reaction in her, and whichever one it was, it had just arrived.

He searched her eyes, trying to decipher the fear she held there. It didn't take long. The specific dread in her gaze was unmistakable. Jean quickly turned to follow her line of sight.

Coming toward them were three men and one woman. Julien, Rayna, Dane—and Tirin.

In that instant, Jean understood. He knew exactly what they were, or at least, he thought he did. But it was Tirin who commanded his full attention. Tirin was the one.

"Hey, JD. I-I didn't know you were going on a trip tonight," Kaitlin said. She tried desperately to hide the fear and anxiety that was born from this chance encounter, but she wasn't doing a very good job of it. Naturally Rayna noticed Kaitlin inch closer to this man as they approached them, and when she saw Kaitlin take his hand, it brought a grin to her face.

"I'm not," Julien said, looking at Jean. "We're just here to meet a plane." Julien offered his hand to Jean. "Julien Dumont Gerard, but most folks around here call me JD."

Jean released Kaitlin to shake Julien's hand. Unlike her, he had no fear - of any of them.

"Gerard?" Jean asked as he tilted his head slightly to one side. "Any relation to Barrett Gerard? Of Gerard Industries?"

"He's my father," Julien said, raising his eyebrows, surprised by this strange man's knowledge of his family.

"Really?" Jean said knowingly.

"You know him?" Julien asked.

"Only by reputation."

"Heh. Didn't realize Pop had a reputation," Julien said in Rayna's direction.

"Oh, his deeds are quite infamous."

"That a fact?"

"Oh yes. For instance, that night in 1975 when 28-year-old Barrett Gerard walked into a board room with John Manning and twelve minutes later walked out as president and primary stockholder of Manning Oil and Sulfur."

Julien's body tensed. Kaitlin squeezed Jean's hand as tight as she possibly could. She closed her eyes, hoping that when she opened them, she and Jean would be anywhere but where they were. Rayna, however, couldn't have been enjoying herself more as she laughed heartily over Jean's comment.

"Jean," Kaitlin accidentally breathed out in a soft gasp.

She seemed surprised by the fact that she was able to get it out at all or afraid that she actually did.

"You've heard this as well?" Jean said to Rayna, off her laugh. "How Manning literally gave his entire company to *his* father in twelve minutes. Manning left his family nothing and died two years later, in debt and impoverished in a whorehouse in the French Quarter."

"Oh, I like him, JD," Rayna said as her smile widened from ear to ear.

The air grew thicker, and it wasn't because of the steamy New Orleans' night. Finally, Rayna broke the tension as she cleared her throat, a signal to Julien. She was enjoying this man's game and she wanted to play.

"My, uh, counsel, Ms. Rayna," Julien said. "Jean, is it?"

"Yes," Jean replied.

Rayna offered her hand. Jean, again, released Kaitlin's hand, much to her dismay, and took Rayna's and kissed it. Kaitlin liked that even less.

"Well, aren't you just the gentleman," Rayna said as she smiled and locked eyes with him.

Jean smiled as her eyes began to sparkle. Kaitlin knew what Rayna was doing but could say or do nothing to stop it. Not that Jean needed her help. He was a man who was not so easily seduced.

"You have the most beautiful eyes, Ms. Rayna. Almost hypnotic," Jean smiled. "Almost."

Rayna giggled, full of fascination over this new player, astounded that her 'charms' had no impact on him.

"Ooooh, I surely like him," Rayna whispered in a lustfully, throaty voice that caught both Kaitlin and Julien's attention.

Rayna's attempt to ease tension only seemed to raise it in a completely different way. Julien didn't like whatever it was that was going on between Jean and Rayna in that moment, so he ended it by introducing the last of his raiding party.

"My chief of security, Mr. Tirin, and his lieutenant, Mr. Dane," Julien interrupted.

Everyone seemed to want to somehow diffuse the mounting tensions growing in this group with every passing second, but every failed attempt seemed to only make things worse. This attempt made it much worse. Jean held Tirin's eyes and returned his glare like no one other than Julien, Rayna, or Camille would - or should.

Tirin had all but healed from his recent battle with The Council alpha, but Jean, in his unrelenting surveillance of Tirin, noticed the tiniest scar on his face that was still visible. Jean discerned that Tirin had recently been in a fight. He knew alphas only fought to the death, and since this one was still here, he knew he was formidable. Jean acknowledged this with a smirk. He was not the least impressed or intimidated by any of this, and he would shake neither Tirin's nor Dane's hand. Instead, he again took Kaitlin's to offer her some much-needed relief. He knew the effect lycans had on her.

"You here on business or pleasure, Jean?" Dane asked, trying to break the intensity of this particular moment.

Jean sighed deeply. "Seems it's always a bit of both," he answered, still holding Tirin's eyes well past the safe limit.

Julien was also good at discerning; he had spent these last few moments wisely as he grabbed Jean's attention away from his alpha.

"Well, take note, sir," Julien said, with a pleasant look on his face, "New Orleans is a very beautiful city, but things aren't always what they appear to be. Danger could pop up in the most unexpected places. Be careful, or it could be the last city you ever see."

"I shall keep that in mind," Jean responded.

"Good. And, on that note," Julien said, "we should be going. Bye, Katie. Nice meeting you, Jean. Hope you enjoy your visit."

Jean nodded. Rayna smiled at him and lingered until Julien pulled her away. Tirin eyes lingered on Jean an uncomfortably long time as he inhaled through his nose, taking in Jean's scent and not hiding the fact that he was. He then quickly turned and followed after Julien, with Dane in tow. Kaitlin looked as though she had been oxygen-deprived. It was everything she could do to keep from passing out.

"What is wrong with you?" Kaitlin whispered.

"Shhhh," Jean said.

"Don't shush me! Are you crazy?"

"Shhhhh!" Jean puts his finger over her lips as he looked after the group. They stepped onto the escalator and began to descend.

"That one can still hear you," Jean whispered, pointing at Tirin. Then he lowered his voice to a level so soft, it seemed as if he was just mouthing words, "Can't you?"

Tirin whipped around and fixed his eyes on Jean with a purpose that was clear to both men as the escalator took him out of sight.

Kaitlin gasped. "Oh my god." She was shaken almost to tears.

"Are you sure *you're* not the one in trouble here?" Jean knew Kaitlin was severely rattled by Tirin, and he knew why.

"I... I didn't know they would... That *he* would... I-I mean, he wouldn't turn,--"

"Alphas can transform anytime they want, day or night, full moon or not."

"But not in front of all these people. H-H-He wouldn't,--"

"They're erratic and extremely dangerous. You know this."

"I know, I know," she said, almost to herself.

"And a warlock as well? Brilliant," he said. "Since when did you become so friendly with Malafecs?"

"Right around the time I met you," Kaitlin said as she glared at him, insulted by the question.

She was visibly rattled by what had just transpired. The tension from the encounter still gripped her, but what she didn't need right now was his sarcasm or the sharp edge in his tone. Without a word, she turned on her heel and walked away, her movements quick and stiff with frustration. Jean let out a weary sigh, watching her retreat. This was far from the reunion he had pictured in his mind—so far from the embrace and warmth he had hoped for. With resignation, he followed after her, knowing there was little else he could do.

* * *

Outside the airport, Julien held the limo door for Rayna as she entered. He didn't know what to think as he followed her into the car.

"What'd you see?" Julien asked her.

"Nothing," Rayna said, with an intrigued look on her face.

"He's not human?"

"Oh, he is. That's what makes him so interesting."

Julien stared at her for a moment with a perplexed look before he turned to Tirin.

"Put a beta on him."

"He knows what I am," Tirin said.

"Well then,.. put two on him, I don't care!" Julien said. He was doing his best to control his emotions, but it seemed as if they wanted to seep through all at once. "And what the hell's going on with the arrangements for us to meet with The Council?" he asked Rayna.

"I'm working on it, Julien," she said, not wishing to hide the irritation in her voice, "you know they're not the easiest folks to get ahold of."

"Well, maybe if you hadn't killed Neely,--"

"Oh Julien, please," she said as she bitterly waved him off.

"Just get it fucking done!" He yelled.

She rolled her eyes in frustration as she turned her back on the conversation, already too tired to care. Tirin's gaze remained fixed on him, unblinking, intense—as it always was.

Julien, sitting rigidly, squeezed and rubbed his hands together in a futile attempt to ease the tension coiling inside him. The anxiety was clear to everyone, radiating from him like a storm cloud. He wasn't handling the pressure well, and it showed. Unable to contain his frustration any longer, Julien slammed his fist into the limo door as they pulled away, the thud echoing his pent-up rage and helplessness.

CHAPTER 30

"I made a promise that I wouldn't interfere. You did not."

July 12, 1999

Camille sat quietly in the gazebo just off the veranda, Dani nestled in her lap. She had hoped the warmth of the early morning sun would bring her some comfort, perhaps lift her spirits. But instead, it only served to highlight the stark contrast of her fragile state. The sunlight, which once energized her, now made her gaunt face and pale skin even more noticeable. Her hair, now almost entirely white, flowed limply around her shoulders, with only a few lingering tufts of its original color—faint remnants of the woman she used to be. The harsh reality was undeniable: she wasn't getting better. And as much as she wanted to fight it, there was nothing anyone could do to change that.

"My time is almost up," she thought as she stroked the Blood Heart dangling from her neck.

Good. Bad. Did it matter anymore? Maybe not for her, but for them. She watched Lucien racing around the lawn, then looked at Dani.

"Sing for me, darling," she said as she stroked Dani's hair, her voice not much more than a whisper now.

Dani smiled and sang. "With a knick knack paddy whack, give a dog a bone, this old man came rolling home!"

"Good. Again," Camille said.

"This old man, he played one, he played knick-knack…"

Camille convulsed into a hard, wet cough. It didn't sound good at all. Dani looked at his mom with much concern.

"It's okay. Keep going," Camille whispered.

Dani frowned and snuggled closer to her. The love felt healing to Camille and helped her ignore the two men that flanked her. Her protectors.

"*Where were they when I really needed them?*" She thought.

She glanced to the house and saw Cecil as he peeked through the curtains, spying on her. Inside, Cecil dipped down a bit, wondering if he had been detected. Barrett walked up to him carrying two coats.

"She's a strong one, I'll tell you that. From the looks of her, I'd say she got about three, maybe four days tops." He said before he noticed Barrett with the coats. "Where you going?"

"I'm not going anywhere. I made a promise to my son that I wouldn't interfere. You did not." Barrett said as he tossed Cecil his coat. "Come on."

Cecil didn't know what was about to happen, but he was pretty sure he wouldn't like it. He glanced back at Camille before he followed Barrett out.

* * *

A limo dropped Barrett and Cecil off on the corner of a not-terribly-busy intersection in downtown New Orleans. Cecil's body was so tense he thought his legs might snap.

"I can't do it! I can't do it," Cecil complained in a loud whisper. "Why can't you just,--"

"Hush up!" Barrett barked at the bumbling buffoon. "You just do exactly what I told you - say it exactly the way I told you, and it'll be fine! He couldn't give two baby shits about you."

"But I can't even get there! I tried before, you know that! I ain't powerful enough to make that spell work," Cecil whimpered.

"You straighten up, goddamn it! I'm going with you, but you gotta talk to him alone! I can't have nothing to do with it! Now shut up and let me concentrate! It's almost time."

Cecil lowered his head like a berated little boy. Barrett pulled out his pocket watch and two gold coins. He seemed anxious, which was a word no one ever used to describe him. His watch read 11:45 a.m. He took a breath, closed his eyes, and focused. When he opened them, they were blood red. A thick mist rolled up, and as it dissipated, an empty trolley car was revealed. Cecil's stomach churned with nerves as the doors opened. Barrett entered and dropped the two gold coins into the change box, then waved Cecil aboard. The Driver looked his passengers up and down for a moment, then pulled The Trolley whistle twice. The door hissed closed as the mist engulfed The Trolley. When it dissipated, it was gone.

Barrett tried to relax in his seat as The Trolley slowly rolled its way through the ethereal mist - at least, it appeared to be slow. Cecil's anxiety ratcheted higher with every passing second. Then, with a quake and a thunderous boom, The Trolley emerged from the mist and rolled to an abrupt stop. The doors hissed open, and The Driver eyed the two men as they exited.

Wherever they were, this part of the city was eerie, empty, and unfamiliar. It felt as if they were in a vacuum; no sound was heard except that of the mysterious transport behind them. The Trolley doors hissed closed, startling them, then, in the blink, it jetted off with a thunderous boom and disappeared. The excess mist was instantly sucked up behind it.

Cecil surveyed his surroundings until his eyes fell upon an odd little establishment across the street. Small in size, perhaps, but somehow, it loomed larger than the bigger properties on either side of it. Above the door, dangling from two chains below a wrought iron bar hung a sign that read '*The Fat Lady.*'

Two heavy bolts slid back with the ferocity of gunshots, one after the other. Bang! Bang! In response, the large metal door succumbed and slowly opened on rusted hinges. The squeal of the hinges echoed through the otherwise silent streets. The door stood, opened and waiting, beckoning them forward.

This was the place.

CHAPTER 31

ℳr. Cifer & Archie Ray

Flashback Harlem – 1927

In the shadowy depths of the Low Down district, just east of Jungle Alley, at the end of a dark, forbidding street off 136th and Lennox Ave., stood the notorious Lap Joint and Speakeasy known as The Fat Lady. The street was dimly lit, casting long, sinister shadows that clung to the walls, and the air was thick with an undercurrent of mischief and danger.

A well-dressed white man strode confidently down the alley, his attire sharply contrasting the grim surroundings. He wore a sleek black and red pin-striped suit, carrying an air of power and purpose. In his right hand, he held a hand-carved walking stick, topped with a two-headed cobra-head handle, its ruby eyes gleaming ominously in the dim light. His left hand clutched a polished silver briefcase with an ivory handle, his fingers adorned with rings that sparkled faintly with each step.

The ruby-eyed cobra seemed to glint in the dark as he approached the heavy, iron-clad door. Without hesitation, he rapped on it rhythmically with his walking stick, Da-dot, Da-dot. The sound was sharp and deliberate, like the knock of someone who knew they belonged.

A small peephole slid open with a metallic clatter, revealing a single, suspicious eye. The eye scrutinized the man from head to toe, lingering on his extravagant outfit. Without a word, the man snapped open his briefcase, turning it to the peephole. The eye widened instantly, nearly bulging out of its socket as it took in the contents. Whatever was inside clearly impressed the watcher beyond measure.

The peephole slammed shut with a sharp clink, and a series of heavy, metallic bolts echoed through the night: one from above—Bang!—and another from below—Bang! The door slowly creaked open, revealing a large, imposing figure who filled the doorway with his bulk. He was the kind of man who looked like trouble wouldn't dare cross him—broad-shouldered, towering, and capable of handling whatever chaos came his way.

From within the speakeasy, the muffled sounds of lively music, raucous laughter, and the clink of glasses spilled out into the street. The atmosphere inside buzzed with revelry, in stark contrast to the foreboding quiet outside.

"Good evening, sir," The Doorman said.

"Good evening," said The Man.

"Bottom of the stairs. Enjoy," replied The Doorman.

The Man with the cobra-topped cane confidently stepped across the threshold and vanished as he descended down the long, narrow staircase. He heard the heavy door slam shut behind him, followed by the locking of the two heavy bolts - Bang! Bang! but he never gave it a second thought or worry as he proceeded down the darkened flight to the music and merriment that awaited him below.

At the bottom of the stairs, he was met by the Maitre d'; a tall, slender black fellow with a welcoming smile. To his left - a small bar, with seating for eight people, served bottles of low-grade, bootleg whiskey with fake labels and warm, homemade beer in ice-cold glasses. Directly behind the Maitre d' were ten wooden tables, closely bunched together, packed with patrons dressed in their Sunday best. A beautiful, young, black server in black stockings and a red skirt that was just a hair longer than too short had just enough room to squeeze by and service all the tables. The ladies didn't seem too happy about it, but the gentlemen didn't seem to mind.

In front of the tables was a small dance floor that could easily hold ten, maybe twelve couples, all bumpin', grindin', and shufflin' back and forth to the music. Just beyond stood a small stage; it was five feet tall and eight feet deep, large enough for three musicians: a drummer, a bass, a fiddle, and a piano player. To their left, a Fat Lady sat on a stool. She had a mic in one hand and a handkerchief in the other to dab the sweat from her brow as she sang torch songs under a revolving blue and red light. Four more tables on a slightly raised platform stood against the far-right wall. A little larger and roped off, these were reserved strictly for the small smattering of white patrons, celebrities, or the more upscale blacks who could afford them.

The Man had no interest in the lively crowd or the bustling activity around him. His eyes were locked on a specific booth—the only booth in the joint—nestled at the far left, tucked against the wall between the end of the bar and the stage. The booth was fitted with a velvet curtain, meant to be drawn for moments of privacy. Tonight, however, the curtain remained open. Inside sat Archie Ray, the enigmatic proprietor of The Fat Lady and undisputed ruler of that booth.

Archie was a figure surrounded by mystery and intrigue. A transplant from the West Indies, rumor had it that he had won the entire speakeasy—lock, stock, and barrel—in a marathon craps game two years prior. Whether true or not, what couldn't be disputed was Archie's unmatched skill at the craps table. He was, without question, the best craps player in the city. And that was precisely why The Man had come here tonight.

Archie Ray was a man of sharp refinement and luxurious tastes. He adored the feel of a perfectly tailored suit against his skin, and his obsession with maintaining his impeccable image was no secret. Once, he had even shot a man who had the misfortune of stepping on his polished shoes. He was not someone to be taken lightly, and his reputation reflected that.

Tonight, Archie was flanked by two stunning women, the "loveliest lovelies" in the joint, their laughter and sparkling champagne accentuating the air of decadence. They seemed to be enjoying the show on stage, their animated conversation blending with the ambient jazz. However, their laughter was about to be cut short as the Maitre d' approached with a quiet, somber urgency, signaling a shift in the atmosphere.

"Boss," said the Maitre d'.

"Not now, D, let it wait," said Archie in his deep, Caribbean accent.

"You need to hear this," D said. Archie gave him a 'This better be good' look.

"That Caucasian fellow over there in that nicely fitted suit heard a rumor about you and your infamous craps game, and he got himself an itch that needs to be scratched."

"Do I look like I'm interested in playin' craps right now? Get him some lotion or a drink or whatever," Archie said as he snuggled closer to one of the lovelies. "I don't care. Just don't bother--" D laid ten perfectly crisp, hundred-dollar bills on the table.

"He thought this might peak your interest," D said.

The two lovelies gasped. The music stopped, and the Fat Lady stopped singing. The place was silent.

"Man says there's plenty more where that came from. If you interested…"

Archie put down his glass and leaned back in the booth. He tilted his head around D to get a good look at Mr. Sharp-As-Shit, who nodded hospitably. Archie's eyes caught hold of the walking stick in his right hand. The ruby eyes on the cobra heads seemed to draw him in. He thought about it for a good while, then snickered softly to himself, downed the last of his glass, and politely excused himself.

"'Scuse me darlin'," he said to one of the lovelies as he scooched his way past her, out of the booth, "but 'dis business." He gathered up the bills and confidently strolled over to the man. Both D and the Lovely Lovelies followed. "I believe 'dese belong to you," he said, handing the man his bills. "Temporarily, anyway."

Both Archie and the man, along with everyone else in the joint, laughed at the joke.

"Boss, this here is, Mr. Cifer," said D, making the introduction. The two men shook hands.

"Mr. Ray, I have heard… so much about you," said Mr. Cifer.

"'Din you got me at a disadvantage, 'cuz I ain't 'eard nothin' 'bout you," Archie said. Mr. Cifer smiled and nodded as he looked around the place.

"I must say I love your establishment," said, Mr. Cifer, changing the subject. "Although, if it were mine I,… might have gone a different way with it."

"Ehh. Interested in gettin' in 'da nightclub business, are ya'?"

"Well, I suppose that depends on you, Mr. Ray. Unless you just happen to have a suitcase full of hundred-dollar bills lying around somewhere for collateral."

Archie smiled and laughed at the thought.

"Naw. I'm afraid I do not."

"No, I don't suppose you would," said Mr. Cifer. "How much you think it's worth?"

"Fifty, sixty grand, easy," Archie said, as his tone changed to a more serious side. "Ya' tink you can 'andle 'dat type a' action?"

"Where I come from, Mr. Ray, we play for that type of action before lunch."

"Yeah? And where, exactly, is 'dat?"

"...Down south," Mr. Cifer replied as he flashed that brilliant smile.

"So ya' came all 'dis way to throw bones with ol' Archie Ray, huh?"

Mr. Cifer again avoided the question by looking over the club.

"...Yeah,... definitely woulda gone a different way."

Archie was intrigued. There was something very much 'not right' about Mr. Cifer, but this was Archie's place, and there was something very much 'not right' about him as well, so;

"Standard rules. I'm da' house. And ya' can quit anytime ya' want, but da' money ya' loose, stays wit' me-e-e," Archie said slyly.

"And what about the money I win?" Asked Mr. Cifer, coyly.

Archie's laughter boomed through the room as Mr. Cifer offered a knowing smile, while the crowd erupted in applause. With a confident swagger, Archie led Mr. Cifer to a door off to the left of the tables, then through another behind the stage. Inside was a single, gleaming craps table, lit as if waiting for its next battle. Mr. Cifer placed his briefcase on the table and snapped it open. Inside, stacked with pristine precision, were five thousand crisp, fresh hundred-dollar bills.

Archie, as always, played the role of the house, setting the odds, while D, his trusted man with the stick, prepared to run the game. D passed the dice to Mr. Cifer, and with that subtle motion, the game commenced. The two men faced off across the felt, rolling dice through the morning and deep into the night, their concentration unshaken by the passage of time. Tension mounted with every roll.

As the final hours passed, Archie remained unflappable. One by one, Mr. Cifer's bets crumbled beneath the weight of Archie's unrelenting luck—or skill. By the end, not a single dollar of the $500,000 remained in Mr. Cifer's possession. D methodically stacked the winnings in neat piles before Archie, the crisp bills gleaming under the low light.

The room grew quiet as the massive Doorman, sitting quietly in the corner, subtly shifted in his seat. He was ready. He had seen it all before—men crushed under the weight of their losses, unable to walk away quietly. Five hundred grand was a lot to lose, and when men lost that kind of money, they usually had something to say about it. Everyone knew that trouble could be one word away.

"Well, looks like ya' might need to go back down south," Archie laughed. "Maybe ya' can make anodda' five hundred thousand before breakfast!"

"I think it was lunch, boss," D added.

"Split da' difference; call it brunch!" Archie and D had a good laugh as The Doorman watched Mr. Cifer closely. Mr. Cifer seemed amused as he eyed the two men.

"Your celebration seems a bit premature, don't you think?" Mr. Cifer interrupted.

"We got all the money, partner. Game's over," said D.

"Not quite all, I still have this."

Mr. Cifer removed a single gold coin from his breast pocket and placed it on the table. Archie's eyes got big. He could tell it was real just by looking at it but nodded to D to check it just the same. D scooped it up to examine it and his eyes told Archie what he already knew. Real. Solid. GOLD. Archie wanted it and Mr. Cifer was gonna give him a chance, but there was one, tiny little condition.

"One roll. Seven - and I win it all," explained Mr. Cifer, "The coin, the money, the club, and everything in it. Anything else, you will be a very, very rich and lucky man."

Without hesitation, Archie took the deal, not batting an eye. He never considered the fact that Mr. Cifer had just set the rules and, in this particular bet, the odds were in his favor, not the house. Archie didn't care. D pushed the dice in front of Mr. Cifer, who reached down for them then... abruptly stopped.

"What's wrong?" Archie asked, "Pick 'em up. Roll."

"If you don't mind, this time, I think I'm gonna use my dice," Mr. Cifer said with a smile.

Archie and D looked at each other and immediately broke into laughter.

"Well, my friend, I think I do mind," Archie said. "What's the matter, you don't like my dice?"

"The dice are fine," Mr. Cifer answered, before losing his ever-present smile for the first time. "It's the two tiny, little magnets inside of them I have a problem with."

The hair on the back of Archie's neck stood straight up, as the smiles fell from both his and D's faces. Busted.

"I don't know what kinda etiquette ya' got where ya' from, but 'round here, 'dere are consequences a man pays when he insults someone," Archie threatened.

Mr. Cifer reached down and picked up the dice and crushed them in his bare hand, letting the dust fall on the table; the dust and two tiny, little magnets.

"Good," Mr. Cifer agreed, as he glared at Archie, "cuz I'm feeling a little slighted right now."

Archie shot a quick look at The Doorman. Instantly, the hulking figure rose and took a menacing step toward Mr. Cifer, ready to enforce his presence—but that was as far as he would get.

Without even glancing in his direction, Mr. Cifer calmly lifted his walking stick and tapped it once against the ground. BOOM – it thundered. The cobra heads adorning as the cane came to life, their ruby eyes glowing with a fiery light that bathed the room in an eerie red hue. In an instant, The Doorman was engulfed in flames.

But these weren't ordinary flames.

The Doorman screamed in agony, writhing as the fire devoured him, yet curiously, his skin remained unscathed. The flames weren't burning him—they were torturing him. Pain, but no marks. Suffering, but no escape. It was designed to break him from the inside out.

"Sit," Mr. Cifer commanded, his voice calm and steady.

The Doorman had no choice as the all-consuming fire continued to lick at his body. With no other option, he obeyed, collapsing into a chair with a tortured groan as the flames continued to rage around him, ensuring his suffering lasted as long as Mr. Cifer desired.

"You see, where I come from, there are consequences as well."

D dropped the stick and ran for the door. With a thought, Mr. Cifer locked it. He slammed the walking stick down again and the cobra heads tongue's flicked and flitted as D grabbed the door handle. It was red hot and scalded his hands, again leaving no marks. D screamed as both the door and D's hands burst into flames.

"Stay," Mr. Cifer ordered, his eyes still fixed on Archie. D obeyed as the flames spread up his arm and engulfed the rest of his body. "There's still business to attend to, ain't that right, Mr. Ray?"

Archie was petrified. "P-Please, Mr. Cifer,--"

"I think we can dispense with the formalities now," said Mr. Cifer as his skin turned a deep red and two horns grew out of either side of his forehead. "Call me Lou."

"…Lou-Cifer,…" Archie whispered as his eyes grew as wide as the Hudson River.

Loucifer laughed heartily at the sound of his name. The flames from the door began to slowly creep around the room, sealing Archie in.

"You think you can cheat me; laugh in my face and just walk away?!" Loucifer said in a powerful, booming voice that made Archie cringe. "You think you can play me for a fool?!"

Loucifer picked up his dice, and with a flick of his wrist, let them fly. Archie watched them soar through the air and land on the table, bounce up off the wall and fall back, resting, at peace; 'four' on one die, 'three' on the other. Loucifer roared with excitement as he slammed the walking stick down again. The entire place; walls, the floor, the ceiling, everything but the table and Archie were engulfed in the living flames.

"NOW ALL THIS BELONGS TO ME!!!" He boomed.

The screams of all the people in the next room could be heard through the walls, but there was no smoke, nothing burned. There was only pain and anguish, and the screams that went with them.

"Gotta say, I like you, Archie. Dumb as a log, but you got balls, so I'm gonna make you a deal. Gonna give you a chance to save yourself and your people a lotta pain."

"Anythin', please! I'll do anythin' ya' say," Archie begged.

Loucifer raised his walking stick once more and slammed it to the ground. **CRACK.** Instantly, the craps table erupted into flames, engulfed in a violent blaze that roared to life. Now, everything in the room was on fire—everything except Archie.

The heat was overwhelming. Thick, oppressive, and suffocating, it wrapped around Archie like a noose tightening with each passing second. Sweat poured down his face, his shirt clinging to his back as the air itself seemed to catch fire. The flames danced and crackled around him, devouring everything in their path. Yet, despite the inferno raging mere inches from his skin, Archie didn't burn.

He could feel the scorching heat—an all-encompassing, unbearable pressure that seemed to squeeze the life out of him—but the fire never touched him. It was as if the flames were waiting, teasing him with the promise of agony without delivering the fatal blow.

And that, somehow, was worse.

"One chance. One roll," Loucifer said. "You lose; the suffering that ensues will be legendary!" Loucifer laughed. "People will write stories about it for generations to come!"

Archie cowered as the intensity of the flames rose. With it, the screams of his people were amplified.

"But if you win," smiled Loucifer, "there's a chance for you – for all of you, he continued. " You got this big, badass reputation for being the best craps player in the city. Can't nobody shoot the shakers; bounce them bones better than 'Ol Archie Ray! Ain't that what they say?!" Loucifer laughed. "Well now's your chance to prove it. Show me that you're more than just a worthless cheat; show me that you can put the lives of others before your own. Show me that you're the man of the hour, too sweet to be sour!" Loucifer yelled as his laugh filled the room. "All you have to do is pick up the dice and roll me an 'eight', right here, right now. And just for shits and giggles, make it a 'hard eight'!"

With a thought, Loucifer moved the flame-engulfed dice across the table in front of Archie, and waited. The heat from the table was suffocating. Archie timidly reached over the burning table and grabbed the smoldering dice, dropping them immediately as he screamed.

"Awww, them dice is hot, ain't they?!" Loucifer laughed.

Archie looked at his blistered hand, scalded from the intense heat of the dice. Not D, not The Doorman, not anyone else was left with any physical scaring or burn marks from the flames, but this was Loucifer's game now, and playing it came with a cost. Loucifer smiled at Archie's predicament.

"Come on, Mr. Man, pick 'em up and roll, or you can step away from the table; save yourself some pain. Why should you suffer anymore? Walk away and let them burn for all eternity. Either way, you belong to me!" Loucifer laughed.

Again, Archie reached over the flames on the table for the dice. He winced as he carefully tried to 'set' them in the proper position, burning his fingers with every touch. He pulled back. He couldn't do it. He couldn't take the pain. He turned away as Loucifer laughed.

Archie's gaze flickered between D and The Doorman, their faces twisted in agony, their screams endless from the torment that consumed them. The flames danced relentlessly, licking at their flesh, though it was pain without injury. Despite the horror, there was no hatred in their eyes. No disappointment. They didn't blame him for the choice he had made.

That realization struck deep. Tears welled in Archie's eyes, his heart sinking like a stone in a cold, dark sea. He knew, without a doubt, that if the others in the next room could see this, they would feel the same way. They would understand. But understanding didn't make this any easier.

His trembling hands hovered over the dice. Across the table, Loucifer grinned, his eyes gleaming with anticipation, waiting to witness the outcome of this cruel game. Archie swallowed hard, tears now streaming down his face, as he reached for the dice. The moment his fingers made contact, they sizzled and smoked, the heat searing into his flesh. His grip tightened, and this time, despite the burning pain, he refused to let go.

With a heart-wrenching scream, Archie launched the dice high, watching them arc through the air, glinting in the firelight. Loucifer's eyes tracked their movement, excitement growing as the dice clattered against the back wall of the table and rolled to a stop. His grin stretched from ear to ear, a silent promise of the chaos to come.

Archie barely had time to breathe before Loucifer lifted the walking stick, poised with devilish intent. With a swift, deliberate motion, he slammed it down. **BOOM!**

CHAPTER 32

The Talisman

With the door to The Fat Lady open, Barrett and Cecil could hear a faint memory of music from within. They moved up to the opening and the large Doorman stepped out. Cecil looked up at the considerable figure, dumbfounded, afraid to move. Barrett grabbed his arm, startling him.

"Stop it, goddamn it! That ain't even him," Barrett said as he grabbed Cecil firmly by the shoulders. "Look at me. Now when we get in there you gotta remember to say it EXACTLY like I told you."

Barrett's usual unshakeable demeanor wavered. His nerves were on edge, evident in the way he clenched Cecil's arm, dragging him forward. This was no ordinary situation, and under normal circumstances, Barrett wouldn't have entrusted Cecil with something so delicate. But nothing about this place was normal. They crept cautiously past The Doorman, whose silent, watchful eyes followed them as they slithered by. He didn't speak, didn't move—just observed.

Once they were inside, **BAM!** The heavy door slammed shut behind them, followed by the unmistakable **Bang! Bang!** of bolts locking them in. Cecil squealed like a frightened animal and attempted to scramble up Barrett like a tree, his panic turning him into a fumbling mess. Barrett growled in frustration and shook him off, pinning him against the wall. For a brief moment, he stared hard at Cecil, trying to mask his own unease. He sucked in a breath, steadying himself, and then released Cecil, who cowered back, both of them struggling to regain their composure.

They descended the narrow staircase, the sound of their footsteps merging with the growing hum of music below. With each step, the atmosphere grew heavier, as if the air itself were thickening around them. When they finally reached the bottom, what awaited them was something straight out of a different time—a time long past but eerily familiar.

They stepped into what looked like an after-hours Lap Joint from Harlem, circa the late twenties. But this wasn't Harlem. And it wasn't the twenties. Yet, somehow, it was unmistakably the same place.

The room was cloaked in shadows, a dark mist lingering in the air, though the source of the smoke was elusive. The joint was packed, just as it had been in the past—same faces, same musicians, same everything. The cute waitress moved between the tables, the Fat Lady sat perched on her stool, and the maître d' stood at his post, all as if they had never left. The only difference was the oppressive darkness, the way the smoke seemed to cling to the edges of the room, giving the place an unsettling, timeless feel.

Cecil couldn't have been more uncomfortable if he had put his drawers on backward and as his foot left the last step and landed firmly on the club floor, the music stopped, the Fat Lady fell silent and every eye in the joint turned to the two of them. Cecil thought he might wet his pants. Barrett gave the illusion of calm as he checked his watch. It was exactly 11:56 a.m., when D approached them.

"You got a reservation, partner?" D asked.

"No," Barrett said.

"Good! 'Cuz we don't take them here!"

The room laughed, and Cecil nervously laughed with them.

"C'mon, Pops. I got a table for y'all right over,--"

"How about that booth there?" Barrett interrupted.

The laughter stopped and D's smile fell from his face as Barrett flashed a gold coin and pointed to the corner booth where Archie used to sit.

"I-I-If it's available, that is," Barrett finished.

"That booth there?" D asked.

"Yes, sir."

"Well that,... that's a private booth, for... special customers. And that booth only seats one."

"Well, that's just fine," Barrett said as he shook D's hand and slipped him the gold coin. "I'll just take a seat at the bar next to that lovely young cappuccino-skinned beauty right there. Yeah." He flashed her a toothy smile, then turned back to Cecil. "You go 'head."

Cecil didn't move. Barrett grabbed him by the arm and gave him a little shake. He took Cecil's hand and put some gold coins in it.

"Exactly," Barrett said with emphasis and concern, then he nudged Cecil toward the booth.

Barrett winked at D, then sidled over and cozied up next to the cappuccino-skinned beauty at the bar.

"Right this way, Boss," D said to Cecil.

D led Cecil over to the booth as the Fat Lady resumed her song. The musicians joined in and everyone's attention slowly drifted back to the show. Everyone except Barrett, who watched Cecil with much apprehension as he enter the booth. Cecil felt like he might throw up. All bets were off on any other bodily functions at this point.

"You drinking?" D asked.

"Ah, scotch - s-single malt, p-please," Cecil stuttered.

Cecil glanced back at Barrett, his eyes wide with fear, as D sauntered over to the bar. Barrett's patience was razor-thin. He jabbed a finger into the air, motioning sharply toward Cecil, then pointed at his watch. Cecil swallowed nervously, fumbling to check the time. It was almost noon. D returned moments later, setting a much-needed glass of scotch in front of Cecil and, on the opposite side of the table, a dented, beat-up tin cup that looked like it had been through a war. Without a word, D drew the heavy curtains, plunging the booth into an even deeper shade of darkness.

Cecil stared at the cup, his stomach twisting into knots. There was something unsettling about it, something that made him want to look away but couldn't. Nervously, he checked his watch again—fifteen seconds until noon. The pressure mounted. His pulse quickened.

Closing his eyes, he tried to steady himself, mentally repeating the instructions that had been drilled into him, over and over. He silently mouthed the words, his lips barely moving. His hand trembled as he pulled a gold coin from his pocket, holding his breath as he dropped it into the cup with a soft clink, precisely at 12:00 p.m.

He waited, his heart pounding, his breaths coming in short gasps until - Nothing.

"Maybe it ain't gonna happen." He tried to convince himself. *"And, that be just fine by me,"* he thought as he picked up his drink and took a sip.

Then, from out of the shadowy side of the dark booth, came a hand, followed by an arm. Cecil choked and spit up his whiskey as the rest of a partially-shaded body appeared. Either that or it wasn't there at all. Cecil wasn't sure until the hand reached into the cup and grabbed the coin. The apparition's partially-shaded face oozed into the light and half of a smile was revealed on the face of what appeared to be Archie Ray. Appearances can deceive. Archie Ray was no more.

This was The Talisman.

"Your watch is fa-aaaaasst," said The Talisman.

Cecil was on the brink of tears.

"I'm, I'm, I'm S-S-Sorry."

The Talisman placed the coin in his breast pocket, and it crackled and sizzled.

"What can IIIII do for youuuu?" The Talisman whispered.

"I, uhm, I-I got a-- a job for you?"

"Don't neeeed a job. Got one."

"Okay, yes. Well, then, uhm, how 'bout I hire you? Yes! I'd like to hire you."

"Well now, 'dat different." The Talisman said and then moved his cup toward Cecil.

"I, uhm, I-I-I just paid you, didn't I?" Cecil politely asked.

"You paid to seeeee. Now pay to woooork."

"Okay, sure. I think I have... Yes!"

Cecil produced another coin and dropped it in the cup.

"Whooooooo?" The Talisman asked.

Cecil pulled a picture from his pocket and showed it to him. The Talisman looked, but did not take it.

"And, uhm, if it can be done quickly, that would be,--"

"The deal has been maaade; paaaaid. Know that it shall be done."

The Talisman took the coin and put it in his breast pocket. It crackled and sizzled like the last.

"Okay, okay. Oh, and uhh - one thing. A young man might try to stop it, but,--"

"Any get in the waaaay of Talisman; fall preeeey to Talisman."

"Whoa, wait a minute, na'--," Cecil tried to say as D ripped open the curtain.

Cecil jumped and looked up at him. He seemed disoriented as he looked around. The Fat Lady was on the stage, singing her songs and all was normal – as normal as this could be. When he looked back, The Talisman was gone. Other than the cup, there was no hint that he was ever there.

"That's it, Pops," D said as he picked up the cup. "Show's over."

Outside, The Trolley waited for them, surrounded by the slow-moving fog, with the doors wide open, beckoning them to enter. Finally, Barrett spoke to him.

"How'd it go?" Barrett asked.

"Ah, well… fine, I-I guess. No, it was fine," Cecil said as they stepped on The Trolley.

Barrett eyed the response carefully, his tension easing just enough for him to seem satisfied. Without a word, he pulled out two more gold coins and dropped them into the change box. The clink of the coins echoed in the eerie silence.

The Trolley doors hissed shut, sealing them inside. Slowly, almost too slowly, the Trolley began to roll backward, the world outside slipping away as if caught in a dream. The movement felt surreal like they were being pulled through thick molasses, time-bending around them.

Then, without warning, BOOM—the Trolley was gone. Vanished in an instant, leaving only the lingering echo of the sound behind.

CHAPTER 33

July 12, 1999

"You have lived in this self-imposed darkness for years! These things are not new; warlocks having been killing witches for centuries!" Jean stated, with much frustration as he paced across the small living room in Kaitlin's apartment.

"You knew this and did nothing?" A surprised Kaitlin replied.

"And what would you have me do?"

"Help them!"

Jean seemed appalled by the mere suggestion.

"It is not my fight, Kaitlin. And even if it was..." He said as he shook his head repugnantly.

"Why? Because of what happened with Hazel?"

It was more than apparent that he was unwilling to breach that subject, with her, at this time. At any time really.

"There is a reason this began three hundred years ago," he said as he tried to guide the subject back to something a little more palatable.

"There was a reason slavery began, too."

"Oh, Kaitlin, please do not play the slavery card with me!"

"They're killing women, Jean! They enslave them, exploit them and then murder them when they are done! How is that okay?!"

"Not women, Kait. Demons."

"Mal'fecs," she contradicted.

"Demons; Malafecs; Mal'fecs; put sugar on it if you wish, but it will not change the facts,"

"Then you support this oppression, this genocide?"

"You throw around these buzz words for emphasis; like they should make a difference, but they do not. Those words mean – NOTHING. For beings like them, they do not apply."

"Why, because they are not of your race?—"

"THEY ARE NOT OF ANY RACE!!"

Jean yelled with a harshness and hatred in his voice that Kaitlin had never seen before and it frightened her.

"By definition; race is a division of mankind, possessing traits that are transmissible by descent and sufficient to characterize it as a distinct human type!"

Kaitlin closed her eyes and turned away.

"You question my definition?" Jean asked.

"Only your interpretation."

"She is a witch, Kaitlin. The most powerful and dangerous demon/malafec there is. She may be friendly with you now, but when the change happens—and make no mistake, it will—there will be nothing left of the girl you know. She will become pure evil with no regard for human life whatsoever and if given the chance, she will unleash the incredible power she possesses for no other reason than to cause pain and suffering to others!"

"And you've never done that," Kaitlin said in an accusatory, caustic tone that she instantly wished she could take back.

She closed her eyes when she saw the pain she had just caused before Jean lowered his head, and it hurt her almost as much as it did him. She had rebroken something ancient inside of him that she now saw had never truly been fixed. It felt like centuries had passed in the few seconds of silence that followed.

"What do you want from me, Kaitlin?" He dolefully asked. "Have you called me all this way to poke and prod at wounds that, even without your daggers, shall never heal?"

"…I'm sorry. I… That was… I'm sorry." She said as she furiously fought to wipe away the tears that flowed freely down her face. "I'm sorry… I never realized until now how much hate you still carry with you from that night," she whispered, almost to herself as it seemed the words did not wish to leave her mouth.

"…And you do not?"

"No… I can't. I had to let it go. If I didn't it would have destroyed me like it's destroying you."

Jean had almost forgotten how wide this rift between them had become. He knew his continued silence on this matter would only increase the divide, and as much as that pained him, he had no words to offer her. So, she offered a few to him and she prayed that he would take them.

"Nothing that happened that night was your fault!" She cried. "Please, you have to know that!"

"Kaitlin..." He said, unable to take her eye. "Everything that happened that night was my fault... Everything..."

One by one the tears rolled down his face. Old tears from years long past. For so long he had held them back. Now they would not stop.

"Jean, if you hadn't killed her, she would have killed every man, woman, and child in that village."

"I thought that way for a long time; trying to justify my actions, but... maybe it was not my job to kill her but instead to, perhaps, save her... Or, to at least try. But I was... I was afraid," he admitted. It was a terribly hard thing for him to say and she knew that. "I went there in search of blood, not to help someone who was once,... my friend. I failed all three of you that night."

He placed his hand on her stomach. She took his hand in hers and gently placed it on her heart.

"You've never failed me and I won't let you continue to believe that," she said, as she shook her head. "Things happen for a reason. We may not understand the reason that day, that month or even that year, but in time; when we are truly ready to receive it, these things always become clear." She smiled. "I don't know if you could've helped Hazel that night. She may have already been too far gone, but I do know one witch you can help. Please. At least meet with her. For me."

Jean exhaled a great deal of the pain he had carried for so long. It was a good start. They both knew there was still a lot more.

"Very well." He nodded. "I shall meet this witch of yours, but... I can promise you no more than that."

Kaitlin smiled until the look on his face changed. Something seemed to draw him to the window of the upstairs apartment and a concerned Kaitlin quickly followed. Carefully, they both peeked through the curtain and gazed down to the alley across the street. Two men, careful to stay in the shadows, looked up at the building.

"Oh my God. Are they watching me?" Kaitlin asked.

"No. They are watching me."

"I have to warn Camille," she said as she moved away from the window. "She's coming over soon. If she shows up while you're here—"

"I will not be," Jean said.

He quickly assessed his surroundings, both inside the window and out, then slid himself between the heavy curtain and the wall.

"I hate it when you do this," Kaitlin whispered as she turned away.

He drew the curtain over himself, and, in an instant, he was gone.

* * *

Moments later, Jean slipped from the shadow near her building and flagged down a cab. As he climbed inside, he made sure the two men lurking in the alley caught sight of him. He wanted them to follow.

The men scrambled into their car, keeping to the shadows as they tailed the cab from a distance. Jean directed the cab driver calmly.

"Turn there, down that alley," he said, pointing to a narrow, dim-lit path.

After tossing some bills to the driver, Jean stepped out and waved the cab away, walking leisurely down the alley. He could hear the other car approaching, its engine low and predatory.

With a practiced ease, he slipped into the shadow of a nearby doorway, disappearing into the darkness. The men turned into the alley moments later, unaware that they were hunting in the wrong place, searching a building on the other side of town.

CHAPTER 34

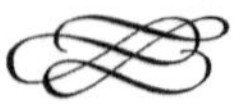

Camille and the kids tumbled into Kaitlin's home. Camille's beta bodyguards, Teddy and his younger brother Gus, followed close behind her. She moved slowly and her breath was heavy and labored. Although she put up a good front, there was as much concern on their faces as a beta could show.

"Kaitlin!" the boys squealed and ran to her.

"My little cuties! Y'all come on in!" Kaitlin said. "Sorry to bother you today, Camille. But I just received these sponsorship forms and I need to get them in the mail right away."

"Ahhhh, okay," Camille said, trying to play along. "I wanted to get out of the house for a little while anyway."

She caught a glimpse of herself in the mirror and quickly turned away, not wishing to dwell on what she already knew.

"Thanks. We can go over them in the other room," Kaitlin said.

She wrapped her arm around Camille's and gingerly helped her toward the kitchen. The beta guards pushed the door open and entered first.

"It's clear," Teddy said as he walked in, gave it a quick look and a sniff, then exited.

Kaitlin entered the room and was startled by Jean standing behind the door. She gasped, and in an instant, the two betas were there, pushing past the women to get into the room. They accidentally knocked Kaitlin to the floor in the process. Camille caught a glimpse of Jean before he vanished again behind the swinging door.

"What is it?" Teddy asked gruffly. "What?!"

"N-Nothing... I just stepped on a wet spot or something and slipped a bit," Kaitlin said. "Jesus, guys."

Teddy stooped down to help Kaitlin up as Gus continued to sniff around.

"You two go wait by the door," Camille said softly. She was tired, and everything, at this point, required effort.

"But we aren't supposed to leave,--" Gus tried to say before being cut off.

"Now!" she ordered; they both nodded and obeyed.

"Sorry, Katie," Teddy said. Gus nodded his apology as well. Kaitlin smiled and nodded back. She understood. Camille felt awful for yelling at them. That wasn't who she was. She loved Teddy and Gus and considered them both more than just bodyguards.

"Guys,... I'm sorry," Camille said softly. "I didn't mean to snap at you. I'm just... I'm just tired."

"It's okay. We understand." Teddy said solemnly. "We'll be in the foyer. Just whisper if you need us."

They struggled to mask their emotions as they left the kitchen, attempting to conceal the sadness that weighed heavily on them. But it was a losing battle. They were betas—they felt deeply, and their attachment to her was undeniable. As the kitchen door swung shut behind them, Jean emerged from the shadows. With a finger pressed to his lips, he signaled for silence, then quickly rubbed his hands together, creating a faint hum of friction.

Camille watched, entranced, as his hands began to glow with an ethereal blue light, the glow intensifying as his movements sped up. He touched the walls, and the glow rippled outward, sealing the room in a soft, shimmering aura. Camille couldn't tear her eyes away. She had seen magic before—her father, Julien, Barrett, and Cecil had all wielded it. But there was something undeniably different about the way this man did it. Something she couldn't quite name.

"We may speak freely, now."

"I hate it when you do that," Kaitlin said.

Jean did his best to ignore the comment he had heard so many times before.

"I am,--" Jean started.

The door pushed open. Jean jumped behind it as the two kids barged in. He was gone when the door swung shut.

"Momma, I gotta go to the bathroom," Lucien said.

"Top of the stairs on the left," Kaitlin replied.

Camille opened the door.

"Gussy, can you take Luc to the restroom, please? It's at the top of the stairs."

"Yes, ma'am," Gus said.

"Momma, I want you to take me," Lucien said.

"I have to talk to Katie. Go with Gussy, sweetie," Camille said.

"Momma," Lucien whined.

"Lucien. Please."

"Okay," Lucien said sadly. He touched her face. He knew she wasn't feeling well.

He darted toward Gus, who effortlessly scooped him up, bounding playfully up the stairs. Gus's laughter echoed through the house as Teddy remained by the front door, his posture alert, eyes scanning the surroundings with unwavering vigilance. Camille let the kitchen door swing shut behind her, and as it did, Jean appeared once more, silently emerging from the shadows.

"Are you a warlock?" Camille asked.

The look that Jean gave her made it clear that he was not happy by the accusation.

"Ah, no, sweetie. He's human, like me," Kaitlin said before Jean could answer.

Camille was still enthralled.

"Then how can he do,--"

"Please. Our time is short," Jean said curtly, cutting her off.

It didn't take long for Camille to surmise that this man did not like her, but she couldn't understand why someone she'd never met before could have such strong feelings against her.

"Can we speak in front of..." Jean started, but became distracted by Dani and the question was forgotten.

Jean studied Dani hard for a moment, then looked to Camille, then back at Dani. Disbelief and astonishment filled his face. Fear filled Camille's.

"He can see me, Momma," Dani said with a coy smile on his face.

"Can you? Oh God, I'm losing,--" Camille started.

"No," Jean stopped her and bent down to the child before him. "She looks like a boy, but… I can see the girl within."

"Can anybody else?" Camille asked.

"Eh. Only if they truly looked," Jean said. "What is your name, little one?"

"Dani."

"Dani? Daniel, perhaps?" Jean said with a smile. "Or is it--".

"Danielle," Dani said.

"Ahhhh, Danielle. Pretty. My name is--."

"I know who you are."

"Do you?"

"Yes. Sometimes I see you in my nightmares. You help me when the monsters come," Dani said.

Camille's jaw fell open. She had no idea how to handle this new revelation.

"Huh. She has sight," Jean said, almost to himself. He would never admit it, but he seemed almost enchanted by the child. The same could not be said for her mother, as he swiveled around to Camille with a stern look on his face. "Did you know this?"

Camille shook her head, then remembered Dani's dream the night she was attacked.

"You're here to help us get away, right?" Dani asked him. "If you don't we'll die."

A wave of fear went through Camille's body. Jean stared blankly at Dani. As much as he tried to hide it, that bothered him. Kaitlin knew, because she knew how he felt about children. They heard a bounding down the stairs. Jean winked at Dani and again placed his index finger over his lips. Dani smiled and knowingly nodded. Camille gripped Dani's shoulders. Jean jumped behind the door just as Lucien opened it.

"Y'all go play in the other room, okay?" Camille asked. "Do some nursery rhymes for me."

They both gave her that annoyed look that mothers know all too well.

"Please," Camille asked softly.

She knew she sounded like a nag, and she didn't want to be so hard on them, but there was so much more at stake than either one of these two innocents could imagine. Well, at least one of them, anyway.

"Okay, Momma," Lucien said.

Dani sighed and rolled his eyes. Camille gave him a look as the two boys exited. The door closed and Jean appeared. Now he was all business. He studied Camille up and down, knowing it made her uncomfortable and not at all caring. He looked at the bandage on her neck.

"May I?" he asked.

She nodded with hesitancy, and he carefully removed her bandage.

"Mmmm," he sighed. "Vampire."

"Yeah," Camille said. Her voice trembled a little as the emotions she'd been holding back began to slip through.

Jean moved to the fridge, surveyed the contents within, grabbed a carton of orange juice, then removed a small vial filled with a milky substance from a pouch in his coat. He began mixing the two together as he spoke.

"Your girl. A complicated spell. The very fact you were able to execute it at all at your age… and to sustain it for… three years?" Jean asked, not looking at her.

"Nearly four," Camille said, uncomfortable with his insinuations.

Jean stopped and gave her a hard stare.

"No Wiccan I have ever met has had the power to accomplish such an ambitious undertaking," he said in a curiously accusatory tone.

"How many of us have you met, Mr. Laveau? Seems like we are an endangered species," Camille quipped, no longer trying to play nice with someone who obviously didn't like her.

"Endangered or dangerous?" Jean asked.

"Stop it, Jean," Kaitlin interrupted. She didn't like the direction these two were heading.

"It's okay, Katie. It doesn't really matter anymore. This is about Dani," Camille said then expelled a painful, nasty cough that made both, Kaitlin and Jean wince. "My time is nearly up."

Jean hesitated a moment before he approached Camille with the concoction and a dishtowel.

"And if it were not?" He asked her.

They both stared into each other's eyes, seemingly looking for answers that neither had.

"Do you believe all witches turn evil at twenty-one?" Camille asked, trying hard to hide the vulnerability and pain behind the question.

She asked, not in search of his opinion, but genuinely hoping that he possessed the answer she sought. As much as Jean tried to view Camille as just another bloodthirsty malafec, all he saw before him was a frightened, innocent girl who, in some ways, reminded him of another. Again he hesitated, then poured a small amount of the concoction on the wound and quickly placed the dishcloth on top of it. It burned and she flinched and pulled away. Her eyes flashed red and her hair floated wildly about. Instantly Jean's eyes flashed blue and he jumped back and took a defensive posture. Kaitlin immediately jumped in between the two of them.

"Camille, it's okay," Kaitlin exclaimed, trying to get in front of something that she did not wish to happen.

Camille steadied her breathing and relaxed. She trusted Kaitlin with her life. She powered down, her hair settled, and her eyes returned to normal. Kaitlin then looked to Jean and begged him with her eyes. With much reluctance he followed suit and powered down. He let out a tension filled sigh and then against his better judgment, offered the glass to Camille.

"Drink the rest," he ordered. Camille didn't budge. Jean tasted it for her. "I assure you. It tastes far better than it feels."

Camille took the glass and drank it. Kaitlin let out a sigh of relief, for she knew now that her friend would live.

"Rest. Sleep long tonight. You should regain most of your strength, if not all, by morning," he said. "You are very lucky. Vampires are extremely focused and efficient killers. It would have taken something extraordinary to stop them from finishing a task."

"Hmph. Rayna seems to think so," said Camille under her breath.

"I beg your pardon?" Jean asked.

"…You never answered my question," Camille said, changing the subject.

Jean paused a moment, then moved to replace her bandage.

"I do not have the answer you seek, Wiccan, but I do know that once the calling begins, there will be nothing you can do to stop it."

"Jean," Kaitlin gasped as she moved over to comfort a dejected Camille.

"I will not lie to the child, Kait. Her destiny was set at birth. The fact that she is even alive and standing before us today is an anomaly that, from the timing of this vampire bite, would seem someone is desperately trying to correct."

"The Council," Camille said.

"Who?" said Kaitlin.

"Or your husband," Jean said.

"No. I don't care what either one of you thinks. I know Julien. He would never be a part of this," Kaitlin said.

"Whether or not his hands are soiled from this particular act is irrelevant. He is a Gerard, Kait."

"What does that mean?" Kaitlin asked.

"His ancestor is the one who started this centuries ago." Jean said. Kaitlin didn't know how to respond.

"It's true. Barrett told me," Camille added.

"Hmmm. You have acquired much knowledge. Perhaps more than you should," Jean said as Camille glared at him. "Your husband is aware of my presence now. He will make our task that much more difficult. If I am to get your child to safety - and I will do that, for Kaitlin - I will need the help of a wiccan as powerful as you. Your strength will return within a day or two, so it must be soon. Our task will be difficult enough. We cannot give them a full moon as well."

"When?" asked Camille.

"The little one, she will know when I am to come," Jean said. "Listen to her."

"And what about Camille?" Kaitlin asked.

Jean lowered his eyes and thought about how to answer this question for what seemed a very long, uncomfortable moment. He raised his head and squared up with Camille.

"It will be of little consequence IF we succeed in our task, only to fall prey to the two things that will never stop pursuing you: The Council and 'the call.' You will place both your child and Kaitlin in considerable danger and I cannot allow that."

"Jean!" Kaitlin said with much anger and frustration in her voice.

"But you will protect my child?" Camille interrupted.

"I will," Jean said.

"Even from me?"

"Enough!" Kaitlin said. "I will not have,--"

"No," Camille said, "let him answer."

Jean knew how angry Kaitlin was with him right now, but he would not lie or hide his intentions.

"The moment you become a threat to Kaitlin, the child, or other innocents,… that moment shall be your last."

Kaitlin was a volcano on the verge of eruption. Her grip on the chair in front of her was so tight she could have snapped it in her bare hands. Camille, however, showed no emotion whatsoever.

"I thank you for your honesty and for helping my child," Camille said. "I only wonder why you would risk so much to save her now if you plan on doing the same thing to her as you will try to do to me, once she reaches an age that makes you - uncomfortable. I struggle to understand how that makes you any different from The Council."

Jean was at a loss as he stared at the young girl standing before him. Then his body tensed as a look of alarm washed across his face.

"Someone is coming," he said.

He slammed his hands together, and a blinding light overtook the room.

CHAPTER 35

"*I do hope to meet this mystery man of yours before he leaves.*"

The kitchen door burst open as Julien stormed in, with Tirin following close behind, his usual intensity radiating from him. They both stopped short, finding Camille and Kaitlin leaning over Camille's shoulder with a scattered pile of papers on the kitchen table, their expressions startled by the sudden intrusion. Just before the door swung shut, Camille caught a glimpse of Teddy and Gus ushering the children quietly out the front door. Jean had vanished without a trace.

"Julien, what are you doing here?" Camille asked, doing a very poor job of masking the irritation in her voice.

"I was gonna ask you the same thing," Julien asked, not trying to mask the irritation in his. "Kaitlin," he said, acknowledging her presence, but there was something in his tone that, for the first time ever, made her uncomfortable.

"Hey, Julien," she replied. "Tirin," she said softly.

The lycan offered her no response, and she quickly averted her eyes so as to not spark his ire. Even still, she could feel his cold stare on her, and as much as she tried not to be, she was intimidated.

"Where's your friend?" Julien asked. "What's his name? Jean?"

"Ah, he went shopping and a little sightseeing."

"Sorry I missed him," Camille said. "I look forward to meeting him before he,--"

"Alone?" Julien asked suspiciously.

"I'm sorry?" Kaitlin said.

"You let him go alone?" Julien continued.

"I, uhm, I'm supposed to meet up with him in an hour, but the deadline for these papers was,--"

"What kind of papers?" Julien asked, not letting up on her, but Camille had had enough.

"They're sponsorship papers that I promised I'd help her out with. Why?"

"Sponsorship papers?" He directed this at Kaitlin. "Then why couldn't you bring these 'sponsorship papers' to the house instead of making her come out in this condition?"

"What's your problem?" Camille asked.

"You should be at home in bed resting, not running around the city. You seem to be getting better, but you're still weak and,--"

"If I was weak I'd be dead!" Her voice raised just enough to let Julien know she had no interest in playing this game anymore.

"Camille,--" Julien said, trying to calm her down, but it was too late for that.

"Kaitlin offered to come by, but I WANTED to get out. I NEEDED to get out of that house. So I got the kids ready and I left. Tirin wasn't around so I grabbed Gus and Teddy." She glared at Tirin as she rose from the chair. "And don't you even think about punishing them. It was my decision, they had no choice in the matter." Then, back at Julien, "so if you've got a problem, you address it with me and leave her alone!"

"Camille, it's okay," Kaitlin said, "I don't think he was,--"

"I wasn't accusing Kait of anything! I'm just saying you're still sick, and you need to be in bed where we can look after,--"

"I'm not sick, Julien, I was bitten by a vampire!" Camille screamed, letting all her frustrations out with it. "In my own house!... So don't you try and make it seem like I'm any safer there."

"Baby, it's just harder for us to protect you if you're roaming around town."

"Well, now that The Council has decided that Gerard's front door is no longer off limits, I don't see that it makes much of a difference at all!"

All the blood fell straight out of Julien's face.

"Wh-wh,--?" Julien tried but couldn't get the words out.

"Your father and I had a long talk over some warm milk."

Julien was horrified. He closed his eyes and exhaled completely, contemplating if he really, truly wanted to ask the next question.

"What did he tell you?" he asked softly as he opened his eyes and looked away. He didn't have the courage to look at her.

"Well, we talked about monsters and bees and my great-great grandmother. Then we talked about The Council and alliances," she said, glancing at Tirin, then back to Julien. "And what an outstanding citizen your great-great-great grandfather was."

The silence was long and heavy and seemed to swallow up all the air in the room.

"…Camille,--" Julien said, still unable to find her eyes.

"Why didn't you tell me?" she whispered as a tear fell down her face. Julien could not respond. He just stood there, shaking his head.

"…WHY?!" Camille yelled.

"What was I supposed to say?!" Julien yelled back. The words burst out of him.

"You were supposed to tell me the truth!"

"That it's against the law for me to fall in love with you because two minutes after you give birth, I'm supposed to kill you?!"

Yes. That was what Camille had wanted him to say, but actually hearing the words come out of his mouth hurt far more than she had planned. Tears streamed down her face.

"How am I supposed to say that to the only woman I've ever loved?" he asked as he took a step toward her. "All I could do is try and protect you the best way I – we could until,--"

"Until what?! They killed me for you?!"

"Until I could find a way to convince them not to." He grabbed her and held her tight as she cried hysterically. "And I will. I promise you I will. I just need to talk to them and make them understand."

"You should have told me." She said in a very small voice. She had exerted a lot of energy in the last few moments and it was beginning to show as she struggled to catch her breath. Julien moved in and took her in his arms as her body began to slump.

"I know. I'm sorry." He kissed her.

The unconditional love they shared filled her chest with optimism. She believed he was sorry, and she wanted to entrust him with her secret as well, but the words he whispered to his father at the birth still echoed in her ears:

"The second baby was a boy, not a girl. We don't have to do this now. We don't have to do this NOW. We don't have to do this. NOW." That's all she could hear.

She grabbed the Blood Heart Necklace and gently massaged it between her index finger and her thumb as she rested the side of her face against his chest.

"I can't live with these secrets between us. This is not the way we're supposed to be." She said.

"I know."

Then, she gave him a chance.

"Is there anything else you're not telling me? Anything else I should know?"

"No, just…" Julien hesitated.

Tirin, for the first time during this whole ordeal, briefly shifted his stare from Kaitlin to Julien. He, too, wondered what Julien would say.

"What?" Camille said as she raised her head to find his eyes.

"Just that Rayna finally got me an audience with The Council. We're going to London at the end of the week to make our case. After that,… after that everything'll be just fine."

Tirin masked his sigh so discreetly not even Jean would have noticed as he redirected his intense stare back to Kaitlin. Camille manufactured the best smile she could as she continued to caress the Blood Heart Necklace, trying desperately to hide her dejection.

"Okay. Good." She nodded, then turned to Kaitlin. "Well, I should get going. It was good for me to get out, but I got a little worked up and I'm not feeling so well, again. You got everything you need, right?"

"Yes. Thank you."

They embraced. Camille kissed Kaitlin on the cheek and Kaitlin gently wiped away a tear on Camille's face with her thumb and gave her the patented 'Kaitlin smile'.

"You're going to be okay." Kaitlin nodded to Camille and Julien as well.

"Bye," Camille smiled as she turned and moved toward the door, then stopped just shy of it. "Oh, and I do hope to meet this mystery man of yours before he leaves. I'd be very disappointed if I didn't."

"I'll make sure that happens," Kaitlin said. "I promise."

"I apologize for barging in on you like this." Julien said, "I was just worried."

"It's okay. I'd have done the same thing." Kaitlin smiled.

Julien acknowledged her before exiting the kitchen with Camille, leaving Kaitlin alone with Tirin, his eyes fixed on her. Kaitlin's smile faded fast. Tirin's stare was unwavering. It was as if he could feel her pulse rate rising with his eyes. He took a single step toward her. She flinched. He saw. She was terrified, afraid to move and afraid to hold her ground. It was everything she could do to stop herself from calling for Jean, but if she did, everything they had planned would be lost, so she remained still as her heart rate elevated even further.

Tirin tilted his head as his eyes slowly tracked from one side of the room to the other, then back to her. He closed his eyes and inhaled through his nose. A long, continuous sniff. His nostrils twitched with feverish intent through the massive intake of air. He opened his eyes and, again fixed them on her as he exhaled heavily through his mouth.

"Shopping," he said.

One word, but it was all he needed to chill her to the bone. He followed it with a faint but pronounced, guttural growl, just loud enough for her to hear it. She froze, her eyes locked on his. She couldn't move, too scared to even look away; a dangerous game to play with an alpha wolf. One that had cost many people their lives. But she could not move. All she could do was stand there, quivering, her eyes locked with his. He took another step toward her and;

"Tirin!" Julien called out from the other room.

Tirin lingered for a few agonizing seconds, his presence thick with unspoken menace, before finally turning and leaving. The door barely swung shut when Jean reappeared. He swiftly raised a hand, signaling for her silence before she could utter a word. Kaitlin stood there, trembling, the chill of fear still clinging to her as they listened for the sound of the front door closing. Only then did Jean rush to her, wrapping her tightly in his arms, offering comfort where words failed.

CHAPTER 36

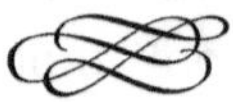

"Today, he will remember my name."

July 14, 1999

A smoky, black finger placed a needle on an old record, spinning on an even older record player. The record showed its age as it crackled and popped before "Feelin' Good" by Nina Simone began to play. The Talisman moved from the old player and continued to dress himself in front of a large bureau with a mirror on top of it. He gazed at his image with little to no opinion as he stood tall in the smoky, ragged, old bedroom that time had somehow forgotten. Like him, the room was most definitely aged, but oddly very neat and clean. The bed was made; clothes folded and put away, no miscellaneous objects lying about. Nothing was out of place – except that thin layer of smoke that drifted freely throughout the room as if it had a life of its own. He buttoned his sleek black vest, fastened the cuffs of his black shirt and slipped on a matching black suit jacket to complete what seemed to be his 'Sunday Best' ensemble. He then donned a large brimmed black hat and traced the edge with his fingers. It made him smile as he always loved the way a well-tailored suit felt on his body… Time to go to work.

He stepped out of the Fat Lady with a hand-carved, ruby-eyed, two-headed cobra staff at his side. Strikingly similar to the walking stick carried by his boss, but a little bigger. He moved to the street, where he stood curbside, motionless - waiting. All dressed up with someplace to go. A thick mist rolled in, then a 'BOOM' and The Trolley rolled out of it. The Talisman board the intrepid transport and took a seat in the very back. The Driver required no payment for this passenger. An arrangement had been brokered where this mechanical mystery provided passage, for him, from this place to the other, for free. The Trolley reversed its course and, with a 'BOOM', disappeared into the mist.

The Talisman smiled as he peered through the window. The Trolley seemed to be moving so fast that life was blurred and, at times, so slowly that they were practically at a standstill. It tickled him every time. As The Trolley rounded a wide corner, he raised his staff, hooked a snake head on the cord, pulled it, and The Trolley eased to a stop.

He stepped down onto the street, where, as always, his presence divided the crowd. Some people took immediate notice, their eyes widening in uneasy recognition, while others seemed oblivious, as if he barely existed. As he strolled past a bustling café, a man began to choke on his sandwich, gasping for air as a frantic woman struggled to administer the Heimlich. When he stepped off the curb, a car swerved violently to avoid him, crashing over a fire hydrant before careening into the intersection and colliding with another vehicle.

The Talisman smiled—a small, unsettling grin—as he turned the corner and moved toward a nearby park. Children played and shrieked in delight on the blacktop, their carefree laughter echoing through the air. He stood still, watching them, until his eyes finally found her.

Camille.

She was radiant, lifting Lucien off a swing and twirling him into her arms with effortless grace. She looked strong again—well-rested and content, her laugh echoing as she playfully raised him above her head before cradling her true baby boy close. Lucien's joy, however, was fleeting. He glanced past his mother's shoulder, locked eyes with The Talisman and instantly the boy knew something was wrong. His smile vanished, and he began to cry. Dani, sensing the same ominous presence, looked up from his swing and also started to wail.

Camille, confused by the sudden shift in her children's emotions, turned swiftly in search of the source of their displeasure. Her eyes swept across the playground until they landed on this strange, otherworldly figure standing there, entirely out of place, yet commanding the scene. Like an old, weathered photograph he stood motionless with an open pocket watch in one hand, and that mystically, magical walking staff in the other. Camille's heart pounded as she caught his eyes – fixed and focused solely on her. She had no idea who he was, but his presence was eerie and weighted. It washed over her and left her with strange sense of unease. Then, with a deliberate snap, he closed his watch and politely nodded to her as he raised his hand and beckoned her forward.

"It your time, girl." He said with the most sincere of smiles. "Come."

He took a single step toward her, and that was one too many as far as she was concerned.

"GUS!!" Camille screamed.

Gus zoomed in and, grabbed Dani and Luc, and sped them off to safety as Teddy headed straight for The Talisman. The Talisman tapped his walking staff on the ground, and in an upward motion, the dual snakeheads came alive and shot out at Teddy. They slithered around his neck and body and began to squeeze and bite at him. The humans in the park took off screaming in every direction, but Camille stood strong and readied herself for what could possibly be the fight of her life. She had been taught to never use her powers in the presence of humans, but her life was at stake and so were the lives of her children. There would be no holding back on this day as her eyes and hands flashed to red and her hair floated wildly above her shoulders.

"TIRIN!!" she hollered as Teddy went down.

She didn't know exactly where he was, but she knew he was close enough to hear. Tirin sped onto the scene just as the snake heads had recoiled back into the staff. He sped by Camille and slashed through The Talisman's torso. To his surprise, the wound healed instantly. The Talisman extended the staff and the snake heads again lunged forward. Tirin skillfully avoided them, as only he could, and charged in again. He knocked the staff out of The Talisman's hand and took him to the ground as the sky began to darken.

"MOVE!" Camille shouted.

Tirin broke free just as Camille drew from her Qi and launched a powerful blast at The Talisman, knocking him through the brick wall behind him. The sky rumbled as lightning flashed all around them. The bricks quivered and shook until The Talisman erupted from the pile. With a wave of his hand, he sent Tirin flying into the monkey bars, nearly knocking him out. The Talisman regained his smile and carefully adjusted his hat, then extended his arm out to the side. The staff flew into his outstretched hand, and he continued his march forward toward Camille.

"Now you done made me maaaad," he said in a weird, almost playful kind of way.

With a thrust of his hand, he blocked Camille's next blast, sending it back toward her with increased speed. She was barely able to dive out of the way as the blast exploded on the blacktop. The Talisman made a grabbing motion with his hand, and an invisible force engulfed Camille and held her in place. She squealed in pain as The Talisman squeezed the air.

"It time for you now, girl." He said to her. "Time for you to come with meeee,"

Camille closed her eyes and tried to concentrate, but the pain was unbearable as he seemed to be crushing her with some unknown, invisible force. As the rain from this self-made storm began to pour down, she felt her resolve weakening. Had she just gotten her life back two days ago, only to lose it again today? With her life force fading, she remembered Tirin's words:

"In order for you to control it, you must embrace the demon inside."

She understood now that it was the only chance she had.

"Uhhhh, nooooo," Camille groaned in a throaty voice.

Her eyes opened, still glowing red, but this time brighter, more focused--more evil. Talons shot from her fingers, and the sky blackened and began to swirl above the playground. The street rumbled. Manhole covers exploded high into the sky as lightning struck the ground around The Talisman.

"NO-O-O-O!" She screamed.

With a burst of energy, she broke free of the hold, forcing The Talisman's hand to open. He stared at his fingers in confusion. This had never happened before. Camille thrust her hands forward and knocked him backward. His face revealed his surprise of the power she possessed, but he would be neither distracted nor deterred. He gathered himself and resumed his trek toward her. Tirin, still dazed, staggered to his feet and zipped in to again join the fight. He tackled

The Talisman, and they grappled fiercely. She didn't think it possible for anyone to withstand Tirin like this.

"Who... What was this?" She wondered. *"No matter. Today, he will remember my name."*

The earth moved and cracked beneath her as she rooted her feet in the blacktop. She inhaled deeply as the energy swirled and formed in her chest, and she pulled up every ounce of it. The Talisman opened his mouth, and a red-orange mist was released that most likely would not be good for Tirin. Camille thrusted her right hand forward and knocked the alpha off of The Talisman and away from whatever harm came with the mysterious mist. She then forcefully thrust her left hand to the sky.

"DE CAELIS!" She yelled, and she released ALL the energy within her into the storm clouds above.

An eerie lightning crackled throughout the sky. Camille screamed as she clenched her fist and immediately yanked her hand down, bringing with it all her energy and that of the storm onto The Talisman. The immense force exploded into the open manhole, and the rainstorm funneled in behind him, down the hole. Whatever, if anything was left of him, was flushed away. Tirin stared at her in awe over what she had just done. The storm began to dissipate, and the sky lightened as her eyes returned to normal. Heat lapped through her body, much too fast for her to withstand. Her vision narrowed, and she became dizzy.

"T-Tirin..." Camille whispered as her eyes blurred and closed, and gravity took hold. Tirin raced to her and caught her in his arms before she could hit the ground and sped off, out of sight.

* * *

On the other side of town, Jean sat alone in a clearing, meditating - or pretending to, anyway.

"Why you following me, lycan?" Jean asked. No response. "I know you are only a beta, but you are close enough to hear me."

Finally, Dane walked into view.

"You've chosen some very interesting places to visit in your, supposed first trip to New Orleans," Dane said.

"I like the outdoors and since you were going to be joining me, I thought we would go someplace where you might feel more at home."

"Now, how'd you know I was on you?" Dane giggled.

"Lycans have very dry skin; poor hygiene as a result of not bathing as much as--"

Dane zipped over to Jean and released a low, lingering growl.

"Tread lightly, my friend, or you may come to find I'm not your ordinary beta."

Dane turned to speed away. After two steps, he stopped awkwardly, surprised to see Jean standing in front of him.

"And on that day, you will come to find I am not your ordinary man," Jean said.

Then his eyes flashed blue, then back to normal. Dane, both frustrated and confused by this unusual display of power, let out a roar, then sped away.

CHAPTER 37

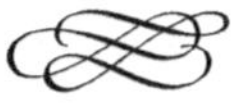

"$\mathcal{M}$*any things you do for me, my friend, 'Nicely' has never been one of them."*

"I asked you to do one thing. One thing!" Julien yelled as Dane stood before him with Tirin at his side. Teddy sat on the sofa. He was in bad shape, bruises and bite marks all over him, but he was a beta lycan - he would recover. Gus stood next to him, along with betas Micah and Cree.

"Julien,--" Tirin started.

"No!" Julien cut him off as he continued in on Dane. "You blew it!"

"I didn't lose him, Sir," Dane replied.

"Were you with the magic man at all times?" Julien asked.

"Yes,"

"Even while that thing was attacking my wife?"

"I heard the disturbance in the distance, and for a brief moment, he was gone, but,--"

"Then, no! No, you were not! Maybe he's got something to do with this, maybe he don't, but we don't know now, 'cuz you fuckin' lost him!"

"I was the one responsible for Camille. If you wish to assign blame, assign it to me," Tirin asserted in a feeble attempt to stick up for his number one.

"Oh, there's plenty to go around," Julien said as he eyed his alpha. "RAYNA!"

"I'm right here," she said as she entered the room and closed the door behind her. "Shush! Camille's sleeping, calm down."

"I thought you said The Council was gonna back off 'til we met with them this weekend."

"This is not The Council, Julien."

"Then what the hell is it?!"

Julien was an emotional wreck, and it seemed as if the pressure building inside of him was ready to blow.

"Dark glasses, cobra-head walking staff with a big black hat?" she asked Tirin, who nodded yes.

"Well,… that sounds like The Talisman," she sighed.

"A what?" Julien said.

"A who," she responded. "He's like a,… vigilante reaper. Works for pay - gold coins - and if it is him, we definitely got a problem, 'cuz once he's paid, he won't stop 'til the job's done."

"I thought you and your boys killed him," Julien said to Tirin.

"More like she killed him," Tirin replied.

"I would doubt that," Rayna said as she shook her head. "I don't know that he can be killed."

"Well, someone had to hire him. Find out who," Julien ordered.

"I can guess who," Rayna said.

"No. He promised he wouldn't interfere."

Rayna cocked her head and stared at him.

"Naw. He wouldn't lie," Julien said, trying to wave her off, but she crossed her arms and held her stare. "To me, okay?! Where is he, anyway?"

"What a coincidence, him and Cecil left yesterday on a 'business trip,'" she said while making air quotes.

Julien raked his fingers through his hair, lost in thought as he mulled over the possibilities. His eyes flicked toward Tirin, seeking a reaction or even an opinion. But as always, Tirin remained impassive, offering nothing. Speculation wasn't his domain; it never had been. His role was action, not guesswork.

"No," Julien said to himself. "He wouldn't lie to me."

"Whatever," Rayna said.

"What about this Jean fella? What'd you find on him?" Julien asked, changing the subject.

"You may not like that answer either," Rayna said.

"Cut the fuckin' dramatics, Ray,--"

"His name is Jean Laveau. As in Madame. Marie. Laveau." Rayna said.

Julien stopped cold. Everyone in the room looked at Rayna.

"What'd you say?" Julien finally asked.

"He's her son."

"Impossible. She's just a myth."

"Yeah, and there's no such thing as vampires and lycans either."

Exasperated, Julien sat on the sofa next to Teddy, shaking his head with an unwarranted smile on his face. Rayna continued.

"Allegedly, that voodoo queen had fifteen children over a hundred-fifty-year period," Rayna said, moving into the center of the room. "All of them had great powers, and all of their deaths have been documented in some way, shape, or form; all but one... her youngest, a baby boy named Jean. As the story goes, she was well over one-hundred-fifty years old when she was impregnated. Her condition was, of course, unsuitable for the trauma of childbirth, and she died minutes after the child was born. It is widely believed that, during that short time, she somehow transferred all of her power to him, making him not only the most powerful of all the siblings but one of the most powerful humans in the world."

Julien slowly clapped his hands. He was in no mood for her stories.

"All myths are based on some facts, my friend," she replied.

"Uh huh," Julien said. "So, we still don't know shit, do we? I mean, he could be here to help fight this Talisman for all we know."

"I doubt it. Rumor has it he's not very fond of Mal'fecs. He's killed plenty. Including an alpha, from what I was told." Rayna said as she looked at Tirin. He offered her no response.

"Rumors?!"

"It's also widely believed that he killed one of the Five Great Ones."

"Now that's just bullshit," Julien said. "Philippe killed Tituba, Brun-Hilda and Hagatha, and The Council killed Hazel and Esmerelda."

"The Council took credit for Hazel's death, but my sources say otherwise."

"Why would they lie?!"

"A: To cover up the fact that they fucked up and let a witch get her full powers, B: To cover up the fact that they didn't even know she existed 'til after she killed sixty-something people, and C: To cover up the fact that *one human man* killed her! I forget; how many Council members did Esmerelda kill before they finally put her down? Thirty? Or was it two hundred and thirty?"

"One man cannot kill a witch!" Julien yelled.

"Ohhh, I think we both know he's more than just a man," she said.

"Can you confirm it?! Can you confirm any of it?!" Julien yelled.

"It's not like I can just whip out a periodical and look this shit up! But the last documented records of him are six years old, from a small island in the Caribbean. Hazel was killed on a small island in the Caribbean six years ago. And as you know, Kaitlin was attacked by a female lycan and mysteriously survived - SIX YEARS AGO - and not at Tulane. Wanna guess where?" Rayna said with a little more attitude than Julien wanted to hear from her right now.

"So, what? You saying Kaitlin brought some magical witch killer here to,--"

"That is not what I'm saying, Julien! Kaitlin loves Camille. You know she'd never put her in harm's way."

"Then why did she bring him here?" Tirin asked.

He sounded angry, but with him, one could never tell. It was interesting enough that he asked a question at all, but it was really the only one that mattered. Rayna had no response.

"Oh, now you go silent," Julien said. "I need more, you hear me? MORE!! I want to know everything about this man, and I mean EVERYTHING!!" he ordered before turning to Tirin. "Seems like nowadays Camille talks to you more than anyone. What's going on with her?"

"She's afraid," Tirin said.

"Of what? The Council? Us? You think that's why Kaitlin brought this man here? To help her?"

"I think if Camille saw any of us as a threat, she wouldn't need much help," Tirin replied.

"Interesting choice of words," Julien thought as he held Tirin's stare, trying to find an answer in his eyes that he knew was not there. He then moved to Dane. "Take all the guards from the office and put them on the perimeter and a few more in the house."

"Yes, sir," Dane said.

"And you know what? Fuck it," he said. He looked at Tirin. "First thing in the morning, you go find Mr. Jean 'Fucking' Laveau and ask him, NICELY, to join us for brunch. NICELY, Tirin. I want him sitting right there, and I want Camille right next to him when we speak. All this guessing shit ends tomorrow."

"And if he won't come?" Rayna smiled.

"He'll come," Tirin said firmly.

Everyone stared at Tirin. They all knew what that meant. Julien sighed as he ran his hands through his hair. He looked at Rayna, then thought better of that.

"You know what," he said, as he lowered his head and gently massaged his temples, "I'll do it myself."

Tirin gave Julien a questioning look.

"Many things you do for me, my friend," Julien said, "'Nicely' has never been one of them."

CHAPTER 38

"*I am trying to let the hate go.*"

Jean sat on Kaitlin's sofa and packed up the last of his things. Kaitlin timidly placed her hand on the curtain to peek out the window.

"They are still there," Jean said, stopping her.

She moved away and sat by him on the sofa.

"What do you think's gonna happen?"

"Julien will not let her just walk away."

"What does that mean?"

"…You know what that means," he said. "You should get some rest. Tomorrow will be taxing."

She took his hand in hers and stood up.

"For both of us," she told him.

He took her in his arms and kissed her the way he wanted to when he got off that plane. The way she wanted him to. They shared a passion that no amount of time could ever extinguish. A love that no distance could ever erase. They undressed each other with a patience and fervor that only a chosen few on this planet will ever know. They guided each other in silence, with an unspoken language native only to them. The sensual telepathy used by the chosen two as their silhouetted bodies melded to one.

* * *

Jean navigated the thick bayou, surrounded by the constant hum of life from the swamp. He halted, certain he heard a voice, but when he looked around, the dense foliage revealed nothing. He pressed on. A heavy footstep resonated, dull and thunderous, shaking the ground beneath him. Boom. The bayou, once alive with sound, fell into an eerie silence. Jean stood frozen. Another footstep followed, louder, closer. Boom! Boom! The leaves shuddered, and the earth trembled. Boom! He spun around just in time to see a massive, naked figure crash through the vegetation, colliding with him. The creature leapt, knocking him hard to the ground, pinning him beneath its weight. It was her—Hagatha, the Old One. Her glowing red eyes bore into him, saliva dripping from her jagged teeth onto his skin and a deep, menacing growl rumbled from her throat. Just as she prepared to strike, Dani's voice rang out, "NO!" But Hagatha only smiled, her growl deepening, and then she attacked.

"Ahhhh!" Jean yelled as he woke up, soaked with sweat and breathing heavily.

Kaitlin sat up next to him in the bed, startled.

"What is it?! What's wrong?!"

"…It is time," he said.

He swung his legs over the side of the bed and threw on his clothes. She sat up on her knees and watched him for a moment before she dressed. Jean walked over to the window to check the status of the two 'men' in the alley.

"What about them?" Kaitlin asked.

"They will not be there when you leave," Jean said. "Remember, your job is the girl. Protect her. If there is to be fighting, leave that to the witch and myself. Understand?"

"Yes," Kaitlin said.

Jean handed her a few small trinkets. To the uninitiated, the trinkets looked like nothing more than a few tiny, plastic balls and some toy jacks from his coat.

"Be prudent with them." Jean nodded. Kaitlin nodded her understanding and placed them in her pockets.

"Hey," Kaitlin asked, "are you okay with this? Really?"

He moved close to her and found himself in her eyes.

"The line between good and evil is, at times, unclear, disguised by ignorance, selfishness; hate…" He said as he nodded. "I am trying to let the hate go."

Kaitlin smiled and touched his face.

"Promise me you'll be alright."

"No matter what happens this night, know that there has not been a day in the last six years that I have not loved you."

He kissed her with everything he had. Savored the essense as if it might be the last time their lips ever met. He hesitated briefly, allowed himself to become lost in her eyes. Not yet ready to sever the connection, he backed away from her, toward the shadow in the corner of the room.

"I hate it when you do this." She said pointedly, but her eyes said something different.

"Leave in thirty seconds," he smiled.

"Jean, wait,--"

His eyes flashed blue. He quickly closed them and he was gone, dissolved into the darkness of the corner of that room.

"…I love you," she whispered into the dark, empty space where he once was.

****

Across the street, Jean emerged from a shadow on the wall of the alley with a stake in each hand. Two vampires stood inches away from him. Without a word, he struck and drove the stakes through their backs. He turned, ran down the alley, jumped in the air and magically transformed into an abnormally large raven. The Raven circled around and hovered with Kaitlin's window in his view, perhaps hoping to steal a last look before he circled away and flew off, in the direction of the Gerard estate.

CHAPTER 39

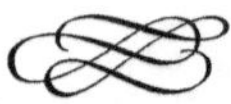

"*Understand, there will be casualties...*"

July 15, 1999

"Momma."

Camille's eyes snapped open to see Dani fully dressed at the side of her bed.

"It's time, Momma," he whispered.

Just now, he noticed that he had missed a hole on his shirt and buttoned it incorrectly. Embarrassed, he quickly tried to fix it. Camille's stomach sank. She laid still in her bed, afraid to move or even blink as if the boogey-man might see her and come out of the closet to take her away. For the first time, she understood that she never truly had the chance to think this through.

Her head was spinning with so many questions:

"Is this right? Do I really have to leave? What if I stay? Where will I go? What will he think when I'm gone?"

It was overwhelming. Three days ago, she was dying, now she had been given a second chance at life by a man who, for some reason, hated her. Yesterday, that second chance had been threatened when she was nearly killed by a stranger she couldn't even comprehend, and now - now she had to leave the man she loved under the cover of night.

"Why?"

Another question she had no answer for.

"Momma?"

Camille blinked herself back from the place she had drifted off to. Dani was still standing there, innocently staring at her. That was the answer to at least one of her questions and perhaps the only one that really mattered. She tried to quietly slide out of bed without waking Julien. She thought this might, somehow make it easier on her. To just leave without looking back.

"Wha,--? Camille?! Wha-what's wrong?" Julien said as he flopped around, still half asleep, trying to wake himself.

"Nothing, honey. Dani had another nightmare. I'll take care of it. Go back to sleep."

She placed her hand on his face and gently guided his head back to the pillow. He smiled and looked at her in the way that only he could, and just like every other time since the day they first met five years ago on the shores of Lake End Park, she melted. She ran her fingers through his long black hair, gently massaging his head as his eyes closed and he rolled over, away from her. Dani ran around to the other side of the bed and hugged his father hard and he didn't want to let go.

"I love you, Daddy," he said as the tears streamed down his face.

"Aw. I love you, too, Peanut," Julien said as he propped himself up on his forearm and wiped Dani's tears away. His brow furrowed when he noticed Dani was completely dressed. "You going somewhere tonight, kiddo?"

Dani pursed his lips and looked at his mom, afraid he might have mistakenly given something away. Julien noticed the button fiasco that Dani had not yet successfully fixed and corrected the situation by unbuttoning the top three buttons on Dani's shirt.

"Now try." Julien nodded.

Dani, again, looked to his mom, hoping she might guide him out of the predicament he seemed to have waded into, but she was lost in the weight of this night and grappling against the decisions that led up to it. She had nothing more than a nervous nod to offer her often distressed daughter. Dani looked back to his father, who gave him a reassuring nod, not knowing that reassurance was not what the young child was in search of in this moment. Dani lowered his head and delicately buttoned his shirt, careful to not miss a single button.

"Perfect," Julien smiled, "just like you." Julien ran his fingers through his son's hair and kissed him on his forehead. "It's pretty dark outside. What do think about, maybe going back to bed and leaving in the morning instead?" Dani's eyes filled with water and he sadly nodded his compliance. "Good man." Julien agreed. "Now go on back to sleep and no more nightmares, okay? You've got nothing to be afraid of, 'cuz I'm never gonna let anything happen to you."

Camille exhaled softly. It was everything she could do to stop herself from breaking down. How bewitching he was to her right then, in that moment. She too wanted to hug him and kiss him and feel his arms around her one last time, but she knew if she succumbed to this impulse, she would not leave. She swept Dani up in her arms and headed for the door. She stopped at the threshold, knowing once she crossed it, she could never come back. Dani understood the gravity of the situation and searched his mother's eyes before burying his face in her chest. Camille sighed and then left the room. Neither of them looked back.

When Camille entered the children's bedroom with Dani, she saw an unusually large raven perched outside on the windowsill. It moved into the shadow on the corner of the window and disappeared. A breath later, Jean stepped out of the shadow next to the window, inside the room, and moved toward them. Camille would never say it, but she was extremely impressed with Jean and all the things he could do. Jean knelt down to Dani and smiled at him.

"You knew," Jean said.

Dani hugged him hard. "I'm scared."

It bothered Camille how comfortable Dani was with this stranger. Honestly, she didn't like it at all. Her eyes flashed red as she threw up a force-field to block out any noise from the rest of the house. Jean loved children, but even he seemed a bit taken back by the connection he had with this particular one.

"Nonsense. You have nothing to fear," he said. "No one will harm,--"

"For *you*," Dani interrupted. "I saw you in my nightmare. I saw what that monster did to you. You saw it too, didn't you?"

"What are you talking about?" Camille asked, grabbing Dani's hand and putting some space between him and Jean.

"It is nothing," Jean said curtly as he looked up at Camille. "Quickly, our time is short. You should dress."

Camille stared down at Jean apprehensively, then to Dani and back again to Jean. She did not understand the connection between these two and it bothered her, but Kaitlin trusts this man. For now, that would have to be enough. She reluctantly released Dani's hand and moved to the closet to dress.

"Yes," Jean said softly to Dani, once Camille entered the closet. "I saw her as well, but dreams do not always come true, Little One."

"Mine do," Dani said sadly.

"Kaitlin's here," Camille said as she looked out the window and pulled up her one-piece, tight jumpsuit and slid on her boots, "I just need a second to dress Luc,--"

Jean raised his hand as he shook his head.

"What do you mean, no?" she hissed as she zipped up her top and moved forward. "I'm not leaving my baby, get out of my,--"

"You must leave Julien something," Jean interrupted. "If you do not, he will hunt you for the rest of his days."

Camille halted, her lips pressed into a thin line as she shot Jean a seething glare. A flood of words surged inside her—none of them pleasant. She was frustrated, disoriented, and scared, but above all, she was angry. Angry because, deep down, she knew he was right. Her defiance wavered as her eyes dropped from his, and her lower lip quivered ever so slightly.

"But..." Her eyes darted to Dani, then over to Luc, "No, I..." She winced as she shook her head. "I can't leave him," she whispered, "I can't." Then, so softly, so faintly that the words barely escaped her lips: "He's my little boy."

"Who will always hate you for stealing him from his father."

Jean truly did understand her pain, but he had no relief to offer her. Nausea overtook Camille as her legs momentarily gave way and she stumbled as if she might fall. Jean reached out to catch her, but she quickly caught herself and shoved him away. For a brief second it looked like she might do more, but instead she turned and took a few steps away from him.

She needed some space. All of a sudden, the room had gotten very small and there didn't seem to be enough air in it. She desperately tried to gulp more in, but it just wasn't working. She needed some time to think, just a few short moments to find a way out of this and make it all work. She was a very smart woman and she knew she could find an acceptable solution in a few seconds if she could just find some air in this room! Jean watched her with little patience. As much as he sympathized with her, they just didn't have time for this. He took a step to reach for her, but Dani quickly grabbed his hand and held onto it tightly with both of his. He looked up to Jean and solemnly shook his head. With a sigh and single nod, Jean agreed.

Camille turned to see Dani holding this man's hand and it infuriated her even more. As much as she tried she couldn't stop looking at it. She took two, very deliberate, angry steps toward Jean then quickly stopped herself, desperately trying to suppress the emotions churning inside her.

"Control, control," she kept repeating to herself, but it was hard because she just couldn't breathe.

She was afraid to look at either one of them in that moment. A part of her, that very dark part she had been in constant battle with since she was fifteen years old, was making her believe that the two of them, Jean and Dani - her own daughter - were purposefully sucking all the air out of the room.

"They don't want you breathe," a voice told her. *"They don't want you to think. They want you to be disoriented and leave Lucien behind."*

This was her battle right now. It was a battle that in the last few years she had always been able to win, but this time, with every passing second, it was becoming infinitely more difficult. Her fists clenched as the roots of her hair began to tingle. She could feel her heart as it pulsated in her chest and the power churned through her veins. She knew what was to come next.

"*No*," she pleaded with herself. "*Stop it! Don't do this. Stay calm. You have to stay calm and breathe.*"

She stopped herself - this time. But what of the next? Another question she could not answer.

"I need to say goodbye to my boy," she said, her body trembling slightly, still afraid to shift her eyes from their hands.

"Camille,--"

"If you don't get out of my way, I swear to whatever God you believe in, I will kill you."

Jean released a not-so-subtle sigh. He too had an inner battle going on that, in ways she would never understand, was just as epic as hers. He stepped aside, pulling Dani with him. Camille put her hand on Dani's chest, stopping her child and Jean released Dani's hand. Camille then gently pushed Dani to the other side of her, away from Jean, then stepped between them to Lucien. Camille's anger began to subside, but it soon gave way to sadness with every inch closer to her first born. As she sat on the bed beside him, that sadness gave way to tears.

"*God,*" she thought. "*Why? Why do you hate me so much?*"

Her tears were the size of marbles. It was a wonder they didn't wake the young boy as they exploded on the sheet below his chin. Finally, she collapsed on top of him, sobbing uncontrollably. He instantly woke as she took him in her arms and held him as tight as his little body could handle. As much pain as she was in, holding him felt so good. She couldn't hug Julien because of what she might do, or better yet, what she might not do. This was so much worse.

"Momma?" Lucien asked, still half asleep. "What's wrong?"

"Shh, it's okay, baby. Everything's fine. I just miss you is all," she said, as she sniffed and wiped away her tears and gently stroked the hair on the side of his head. "Just wanted to come and spend a little time with my baby boy. That's all."

The fact that he was half asleep couldn't stop the young boy from smiling. He loved his mother so much, but for circumstances beyond either one's control, he never got his fair share of time with her. This moment was everything to him.

"Baby… I need you to know that momma loves you very, very, very much, and *I* need to know that you aren't ever gonna forget that. Not ever."

Lucien yawned, then smiled. "I won't, Momma."

"Promise me."

"I promise."

At that moment, Camille gently pressed her right index finger to the center of Lucien's forehead, just above his eyes. Her eyes flickered red as she leaned in, whispering something so soft and wonderful into his ear that his smile grew even wider, a serene, almost entranced expression settling over him. He seemed utterly at peace, completely absorbed in her words. But just as the mysterious connection deepened, Dani rushed over and threw his arms around Lucien in a tight embrace, unintentionally severing the delicate connection between this mother and her son.

Dani kissed his brother on the side of his face as Jean moved to the window where he watched Kaitlin in the car below. It was time. He could wait no longer.

"I love you too, Lucien," Dani said.

"Huh?" Lucien grunted, rubbing his eyes, trying to focus on the fact that his younger brother was fully dressed. "Wh-Where you going? Momma--?" Lucien tried to ask, but before Camille could respond, Jean sprinkled dust over Lucien and he instantly fell backward onto the pillow into a deep sleep, one that, as much as she tried, Camille could not wake him from.

The fragile control Camille had managed to hold onto shattered in an instant, replaced by raw, unfiltered rage. Her eyes blazed a furious red as her hair whipped to life, floating ominously around her head like it had a will of its own. She leapt off the bed, her entire presence radiating fury. Dani gasped—he had seen his mother's mactrouge before, but something was different this time, something darker, and it terrified him. Jean's reaction was swift. Both his hands and eyes flared a glowing blue, pulsating in sync with his steady, controlled breath.

"What did you do to him?!" she asked in a commanding whisper as to not wake the house, her voice was deeper and more resonant than before.

"I will warn you, but once, wiccan,--"

"What did you do?!" Camille again asked as her body floated up, just off the floor.

"You will stand down!" Jean ordered.

Dani was in a panic. He was petrified of what might come next and wanted to close his eyes, but was too scared. Without thinking, he ran in between the two of them.

"Dani, move!" Camille ordered.

"Momma, please stop," Dani pleaded as tears streamed down his face.

"Get out of the way!"

Dani turned and ran to Jean and latched onto his leg with all the strength his little body could muster.

"DANI!" Camille yelled.

"Please don't kill my mom, PLEASE!" Dani begged hysterically, "She doesn't mean it, she's just scared! Please! Please…"

Jean, for whatever reason, seemed surprisingly calm in this very frightening moment. Almost as if it wasn't the first time he had faced a witch in full mactrouge. He remained intensely focused on Camille but allowed the blue to slowly fade from his eyes and hands. He carefully pried the child off of his leg and gently moved the struggling Dani an arm's distance away. Dani fought him the entire time, afraid of what his mom would do to Jean if he weren't there.

"NO! NO! Mommy, pl-please don't do nothing! We're not s-supposed to fight," he said, sobbing hysterically, almost hiccupping the words out. "We're supposed to help each other! Even when we're mad! That's what *you* said! That's what you said!"

Dani struggled with all he had to get back in front of Jean, but the mysterious stranger would not allow it and easily held the child at bay. Camille lowered herself back to the floor, but her eyes remained red, and her hair was working overtime.

"Get over here right now, young lady," Camille ordered as she raised her hand and quickly closed it to a fist. Dani was abruptly yanked away from Jean, a few feet away, and slid across the floor over to Camille. "Don't you *ever* do that again."

Dani stood up next to his mother, snorting and sniffling, both angry and embarrassed at being dragged across the floor that way. Camille powered down, but the intensity and purpose behind those bright green eyes were just as scary as if they were still bright red.

"What did you do to him?" she asked pointedly.

"Sleep sands," Jean said calmly.

"Get it off him. Now, or I,--"

"What? What will you do? Kill me and, in the process, wake everyone in this house? They will probably not harm you or this child – maybe - but they will certainly kill Kait for what she has done. You know this, as well as you know, that this child cannot go with us. Let him sleep. It is better this way for both of you. Now come, it is time. We can stay here no longer."

Camille didn't budge. She couldn't. All she could do was glare into the mysterious stranger's eyes.

"Why do you hate me so much?" she asked.

Jean sighed as he shook his head, "There is no more time for,--"

"Mista, you're either gonna answer me, fight me, or get the hell out of my house right now, but I ain't going anywhere with you until you choose one," Camille said as she held her ground.

Jean's eyes floated to Dani, who gazed back at him. He took a breath and answered the only way he could.

"You know Kaitlin may never have children, yes?" Jean asked.

"I've seen her scars."

"Me too," Dani added. Camille looked at him sharply. "…Well, I did." He meekly murmured.

"Has she told you why?"

Camille shook her head. Jean stared at them, then closed his eyes and exhaled.

"I do not hate *you*, Wiccan," Jean said. "The hate I carry, along with Kaitlin's scars,… are the subtle reminders of,--" Jean paused and took a breath. "My failures."

Camille could tell that this was difficult for him to say, and even though she hated him in that moment, it could not supersede the empathy she felt as he continued.

"It manifests itself unjustly onto you, and for that, I am sorry. Kaitlin is strong. She has mastered the art of forgiveness. I... am trying."

Camille closed her eyes and subtly shook her head. She didn't know what to think of this man anymore.

"Momma, please," Dani begged, "if we stay here we gonna die."

The pause seemed like an eternity, but after what was actually only a second or two, her eyes flashed red, and with a thought, the spell on Dani was released, and Danielle was present - permanently. Camille exhaled so long and so deep that she thought she might faint. She gathered her composure as she set her eyes again on Lucien. She reached down and gently tucked him in, kissed him on his forehead, and closed her eyes tightly to keep any more tears from escaping. She turned and swept Danielle up into her arms as she marched toward the window.

Jean stopped her. "Understand, there will be casualties. People you know and, perhaps, care for."

Camille again hesitated. She was emotionally exhausted, crestfallen, and they hadn't even left the bedroom yet.

"Why didn't you just let me die?" she asked.

"Momma, no!" Dani gasped angrily.

Camille impatiently waited for a response. Jean lowered his eyes and turned away.

"What a coward," she thought. *"He can't even look me in the eye."*

Disgusted, she shook her head and continued to the window.

"One thing more, *Priest*," Camille said with a biting sarcasm. "*Wiccans* are human. Nature worshippers who follow a religion influenced by pre-Christian beliefs and practices." She blinked, and her eyes flashed powerfully to red as her hair came alive. "I'm a witch."

She cast one last, lingering look at Lucien, her heart aching with the weight of her decision. Then, with a single thought, the glass in the window behind her exploded outward in a shower of glittering shards, shattering the night's silence. She knew the window, even fully opened, was far too small for her to escape with Dani in her arms. There wasn't time to hesitate. Without a second thought, she turned and leapt through the jagged frame into the cool night air.

As her body sailed through, the glass shards reversed their course, each piece snapping back into place with eerie precision, reassembling the window perfectly, as if it had never been broken. Camille hit the ground near Kaitlin's car with the grace and agility of a cat, Dani still secure in her arms. She stood there for a moment, her breath heavy and labored, her pulse thrumming in her ears. The night was still, save for the distant hum of crickets and the rustle of leaves in the breeze, along with other things that walk this earth in the darkness of night. She could feel their presence in her bones— there was no turning back now. The wheels had been set in motion.

It had begun.

CHAPTER 40

Tirin's eyes snapped open, abruptly woken by the faint, distant sound of shattering glass. Though it came from the far side of the enormous estate, his heightened senses made it feel as if it were just outside the room. He sniffed the air twice, his nostrils flaring as a low, rumbling growl vibrated from his chest—soft, almost like a purr, but edged with tension. His sharp eyes narrowed in the dim light as he sat up in bed, his muscles coiling with alertness.

The sudden, deliberate movement startled Dane, who lay next to him. He blinked, disoriented and immediately alarmed, sensing that whatever had woken Tirin was serious. They exchanged a brief, knowing glance—no words were needed. Something was wrong, and Tirin was already mentally preparing for whatever was about to unfold.

"What is it?" Dane asked as he watched his partner with peaked curiosity. "What's wrong?"

Tirin seemed confused disoriented, as his nose twitched uncontrollably at a frenzied pace.

"How-w-r-r?" Tirin growled softly to himself, then jumped out of bed and raced to the window with Dane on his heels.

They looked down in the courtyard in awe at Camille as she quickly moved behind Kaitlin's yellow car.

"Camille..." Tirin said softly.

He stood there and watched her from the window, and when she put Dani down, he knew.

Every being consists of a very specific molecular structure. A molecule's size, shape and vibration frequency controls everything from the density of one's bones, down to one's scent. These specifics are the differences between men and women; between humans and Malafecs. Alphas are the only beings whose senses are acute enough to pick up on these frequency changes. They can actually smell the secretion molecules make when vibrating from a cell.

A witch's molecules vibrate at a frequency much higher than any other being on this planet, but like anyone or anything else, witches have very different, very distinct scents. They are unique to the individual, like snowflakes, and their scent cannot be duplicated or changed. Perfume, sweat, filth, musk can all add, enhance, and at times even mask an individual's scent to humans and other Malafecs, but nothing on this planet can hide its true scent from an alpha.

This is what roused Tirin from his bed tonight, narrowed his eyes, and crumpled his already stoic cast. This is what challenged his sanity and confused his soul. This night was the first night in his entire life that he had smelled a witch other than Camille.

"Who is that?" asked an equally perplexed Dane as he watched this tiny stranger run around to the side of the car and enter it.

Tirin could only watch as Camille looked up toward his room from across the courtyard. She knew he would be watching.

"No," Tirin whispered as he subtly shook his head, but he knew she couldn't see it. He placed his right hand on the window, and his fingernails scratched the glass as she ran around the car and entered. "NO!!" he bellowed as he frantically tried to open the window, but it was somehow sealed shut.

Again, he tried, this time with Dane's assistance, but it would not budge.

"The magic man?" Dane asked.

"NO-O-O-O-O!!" Tirin roared the word into a howl as he moved backward, just enough for a running start, then magnificently erupted into his lycan form. "FIND HIM!" he barked.

He then primed himself for what was to come as Dane sped out of the room.

* * *

On the other side of the compound, Jean's hands pressed firmly against the walls. He strained to hold the invisible force field he had set around the entire house, but this was a very big house. His arms quivered from the pressure until he heard a crash from outside, a window being broken.

"*Impossible*," he thought. "*Who?*"

He released the walls, and the force field was lifted. He moved to the children's window and saw the gaping hole in the wall above the courtyard, left by Tirin as he ejected himself through the window. Jean looked down and saw the lycan sniffing around. Finally, Tirin looked up and saw Jean's frame standing in the window.

"Yes. Come to me," Jean said to himself.

Tirin took a step, then sniffed again and abruptly shifted his attention to the car. Tirin roared at the top of his lungs.

"A signal," Jean thought.

Jean's eyes flashed blue, and roots erupted from the stone-paved ground of the courtyard and snaked up Tirin's legs, consuming him. Jean watched Kaitlin's car as it sped toward the gate.

"Faster… Drive faster!" he urged as if she could hear his thoughts.

He could see the malafecs as they began to rouse and close in on the little yellow car from every side, and he knew they would not make it to the gate. Again, his eyes flashed, and with a quick gesture, the sky rumbled, and the wind picked up and forcefully threw the creatures away from the car. Inside the car, Kaitlin sped toward the large iron gate with Camille and Dani huddled in the backseat. Dani watched in awe as the guards were somehow blown away from the speeding car. Camille knew that Jean was behind this. It pained her to watch as most of these malafecs were ones she considered to be friends.

"Camille, the gate!" Kaitlin urged.

Camille's eyes flash red, and with a wave of her hand, the gate flew open, and the little yellow car zoomed through unscathed. With another flick of her wrist, it slammed shut behind them, temporarily impeding anyone or anything that might pursue. Just then, Dane zipped into the kid's room where Jean was. He looked first to the sleeping Lucien, then at Jean, who smiled and spun into the shadow next to the window as Dane lunged for him. Jean passed through the wall in human form and exited another shadow outside, as the raven, as Dane slammed into the wall face first.

Dane looked out the window for Jean but instead saw Tirin across the courtyard, tied up and being swallowed by roots jutting out of the ground. The raven hovered and watched Dane as he broke through the window, somersaulting in the air to the courtyard below. The raven continued to watch from above as Dane and two of the other betas, Teddy and Cree, raced over to Tirin and ripped him from the plants that had engulfed his entire body. Tirin gasped for air when they freed him as the raven watched the little yellow car in the distance.

"Why is she moving so slow?" Jean thought.

She wasn't, really. She just needed more time and it was his job to give it to her. He swooped down into the courtyard and stood up in human form to buy her some. He glanced around the perimeter before he moved toward Tirin and his betas with a calm confidence that seemed misplaced. From the house, vampires approached. Jean stopped, held his ground and looked at each one of them with a smug arrogance no sane being would ever display. Then his focus shifted to Tirin.

"Come on. Come to me," Jean thought as he looked Tirin directly in his eyes, taunting him, daring him to attack.

Tirin rose to his feet, still panting heavily but ever ready for a fight. His betas, alongside ten other vampires, had surrounded Jean, creating a tight, inescapable circle. But Jean wasn't looking for an escape. Suddenly, his eyes flashed blue, and he began spinning rapidly. His movements conjured a mini tornado, whipping dust and wind into a blinding storm that disoriented everyone—everyone except Tirin.

Tirin didn't need his eyes to track a target. Even in the midst of this magical whirlwind, he navigated toward Jean, his heightened senses guiding him through the chaos. Inside, Julien burst from the bedroom, tearing down the hall toward Rayna, who stood calmly at the end of the landing. Draped in a long black robe, Rayna curiously watched the scene unfolding outside through the second-floor bay window. A subtle smile crossed her lips as Tirin closed in on Jean, but just then, the wind howled louder, and the force of the storm threw Tirin and the others backward.

The gale was so powerful that when Julien reached the landing, the front windows exploded inward, sending shards of glass and debris hurtling toward both him and Rayna. In that instant, twenty, maybe thirty warlocks in the world would have had the skill and presence of mind to enter mactrouge, erecting just enough of a force field to protect them from being torn to shreds. Luckily, Julien Dumont Gerard was one of them.

With a deafening boom, the storm abruptly ceased. The wind died down, the dust settled, and when the chaos finally cleared, Jean had vanished.

CHAPTER 41

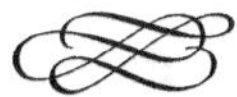

"We don't get to be little girls no more,"

A very nervous Camille sat in the back seat and held Dani tight as Kaitlin raced the little yellow car down the road.

"What about Jean?" Dani asked.

"Don't worry, baby. I'm sure he's not far behind," Kaitlin answered.

Camille pursed her lips, trying to contain her anger and, perhaps, jealousy at Dani's remark.

"Why is she so concerned about him?" she thought as she exhaled deeply.

She was so lost in her own thoughts that she didn't notice the figures on either side of the road darting in and out of the brush at inhuman speeds. Like a shot, one of them emerged from the brush, onto the road and headed straight for the car. Out of the corner of her eye, Camille saw him.

"Watch out!" She shouted, but it was too late.

He rammed into the side of car at full speed, leaving a huge dent in it. The three women screamed as Kaitlin desperately fought to maintain control of the swerving car. She twisted the steering wheel back and forth, continually bumping into the man who was now running along the driver's side of the car, pacing it. He sternly looked into the back window at Camille and their eyes connected. Seconds seemed like minutes as she stared back at the man, a vampire, who was no stranger to her.

Camille had not been very friendly with the vampires around the house or at the office. For the most part they were loners, nomads who never really stuck around long enough for her to develop any kind of relationship with. They also had a standing reputation for not being the most loyal of creatures.

Perhaps it was because they had to actually die before they became their vampire selves. Dying was a singular thing. Even if one died in a group, one still experienced that darkness alone. For betas, it didn't matter, because they didn't die, and even more, their sire was always there, with them, upon their 'awakening' from the change; helping them, teaching them how to survive in this new world. Vampires woke up alone.

Terrence, the man in front of her now, easily the youngest vampire at Gerard industries, seemed different. He had always been polite and considerate of both humans and other Malafecs, and he always had a kind word for her whenever one was needed. As he looked at her now, with blood in his eyes, she was not frightened by him but saddened.

"Do something!" Kaitlin screamed, but Camille just sat there, frozen, unable to respond physically or verbally to the assault being waged against them.

Then, just as Kaitlin thought she had achieved control of the car, another man rocketed himself into the front of the car on the passenger side, sending the car spinning down the middle of the road. He was instantly knocked away as the tail of the spinning car sent him flying back into the brush.

Terrence, on the driver's side of the car, leapt onto the roof of the spinning vehicle and held on until the car came to a screeching stop. Again, the women screamed as Terrence slammed his fist down onto the roof, denting it. A second hit left a much bigger indentation.

"Go, go, go!" Dani screamed.

"Drive!" Camille shouted.

Kaitlin slammed her foot on the accelerator, and the car took off, speeding down the road. But they now had two problems: Terrence was still on the roof, and they were going the wrong way. The last collision had spun the car completely around, and they were now headed back to the Gerard estate, right into the heart of the people chasing them.

"No, no, no!" Dani screamed.

"Camille,--" Kaitlin shouted.

"What are you,--" Camille yelled.

"--get him off the roof! Do something!" Kaitlin cried, but Camille would not mactrouge.

Terrence's fist came down again, this time nearly puncturing through the roof.

"Turn around!" Camille screamed.

Kaitlin slammed on the brakes, which sent Terrence flying off the car. He somersaulted through the air and landed hard on the pavement thirty feet away. At that speed, most humans would have died instantly, but Terrence continued to tumble and roll another ten feet or so before he popped straight up. Not nearly as agile as a lycan, but damn good for a vampire. Terrence turned and looked at them, clothes torn, face bleeding.

"Go!" screamed Camille as Terrence ran straight for them.

Finally, she went into mactrouge, but not to fight. With a thought, she put the car in reverse and forced Kaitlin's foot down on the gas pedal and held it there.

"No!" Kaitlin screamed, but there was nothing she could do to stop it.

Unfortunately, this act of desperation did not matter. There was no way the little yellow car could get up to speed quick enough to outrun Terrence, who was nearly on them. He dove onto the hood as the three women screamed. He pulled himself to his knees and in what looked to be a fit of anger, punched through the windshield, shattering it.

"Camille, enough!" Terrence shouted, his chest throbbing up and down. Vampires don't breathe, but they do tire. They're not built for this much running. "Don't make me kill her," he pleaded.

"Terrence, don't!" Camille yelled.

"Then stop! Now!"

Camille fell out of mactrouge, her eyes brimming with tears as the car screeched to a halt. The intensity of her emotions crashed down on her, overwhelming her senses. Just then, the raven swooped in from behind, seizing Terrence with its long talons and yanking him off the side of the car. Terrence thrashed wildly, desperately trying to break free, making the raven's flight erratic and unsteady. They spun wildly through the air, crashing into the dense brush before the raven finally slammed Terrence against a thick tree branch. The impact pierced through his chest—staking him.

Camille let out a shaky exhale, thick with regret and sorrow. As she watched, Terrence's body disintegrated into dust, vanishing before her eyes. Her face crumpled into her hands, the weight of the moment crushing her spirit. The raven crashed into the tree, knocking Jean back into human form before he tumbled to the ground and disappeared in the brush.

"No!" Kaitlin screamed. "Get out of there!"

The worst place a human could possibly be after the sun goes down was off road, in a wooded area, when vampires were around. Somehow she knew this. It was pitch black and all they could see was the rustling trees and bushes shaking back and forth.

"Jean!" Kaitlin cried.

"Get out of here! Drive!" Jean called out.

"Get in the air!" Kaitlin screamed back at him.

"GO!" Jean yelled.

Kaitlin tried to restart the car, but the engine kept turning over. Suddenly a strange, bright flash of what looked like sunlight to Camille, briefly illuminated the area of the confrontation, then dissipated just as fast. A second later she saw the raven rocket out of the brush, straight up into the night sky. Kaitlin exhaled in relief and tried again to restart the car. Before she could even turn the key around, Gus blazed up to the car, ripped the door off the hinges and threw it behind him. With a swipe he slashed Kaitlin's arm with his nail. The cut was long, but not deep - a warning. Kaitlin screamed from the pain.

"STOP IT!" Dani cried.

Gus then yanked Kaitlin from the car by her throat, silencing her.

"Don't do this, Camille?" Gus begged, not even looking, or caring about Kaitlin, whose toes were barely touching the ground.

"Gussy, let her go!" Camille cried out as Kaitlin watched the raven land behind Gus and transform into Jean as he stood up.

Kaitlin closed her eyes. She knew what was to come next.

"Then stop this!" Gus yelled. "Come back to the house with me and,--"

In a single, brutal breath, Jean grabbed Gus's head and twisted it violently, snapping it completely off. The sickening crack echoed in the air as Kaitlin's eyes flew open, her heels hitting the ground. Camille's piercing scream shattered the moment, horror flooding her senses at the unspeakable act she had just witnessed. He had told her—warned her—that there might be casualties, but never in her wildest nightmares had she imagined this.

When she first left Morgan City for New Orleans, Tirin and his betas—Dane, Teddy, Micah, and Cree—had been assigned to her as her protectors. Gus had been turned a few months later by Tirin, at Teddy's request. These five weren't just her private detail, they were her constant companions. Outside of the house, at least one of them was always physically by her side, never more than a whisper away.

Betas had been, at one point of their life, human, so even after their transformation, they still retained the personalities they had as humans. Unlike their stoic sire, Tirin, these betas were a lively, spirited group. Camille had eaten with them, laughed with them, and shared her deepest burdens with them. When she was down, they were the ones who lifted her up, going out of their way to make her feel like family. They had considered her an honorary member of their pack. To her, they weren't just her protectors—they were her friends, her brothers and sister.

And now, one of them was gone, taken in an instant, and the bond she thought would last forever was shattered.

"OH MY GOD! YOU DIDN'T HAVE TO KILL HIM!" she screamed, sobbing hysterically.

"He was going to kill her!" Jean yelled.

"I could have talked to him! He would have let her go!"

"Camille,--" Kaitlin tried to interject.

"You know Gus would never hurt you!" Camille screamed.

"He *was* hurting me!" Kaitlin screamed back as the tears fell off her cheeks. "I loved Gussy, too,… but he was."

"Get out of the car," Jean ordered Camille.

"What? Wh-What are you doing?" asked Kaitlin.

"This debacle ends now. I will not risk my life or yours one second longer - GET OUT!" He yelled at Camille.

"Stop it! We're not leaving them,--"

"Kaitlin,--"

"--She's just scared. These are her,--"

"We will take the child with us, as we agreed, but,--"

"You're not taking my child anywhere!" Camille said.

"So you would rather she stay here and die with you?!" Jean asked.

"No," Camille sobbed as she begged. "Please! I don't want her to die!"

"THEN FIGHT FOR HER, WITCH!" Jean yelled. "FIGHT!... This is not over! This was not the end, this was just the beginning! They will regroup and come again, this time with more, and if you cannot find the strength to protect Kaitlin and this child, then we shall all die, because I cannot win this battle alone!... DECIDE!"

Camille's eyes found Kaitlin. Her beautiful face was nicked and cut - blood dripped from her arm. Camille looked down at Dani and watched her little girl wipe away her own tears. She seemed to be wiping away her innocence as well.

"We don't get to be little girls no more, Momma," Dani sniffled, quoting her mom's own words back to her.

Camille closed her eyes in embarrassment at the pain she had caused them both. She nodded to Jean and surrendered to what was to come. Dani hugged her tightly as Camille cried quietly to herself. Kaitlin nodded to Jean. He sighed deeply as he checked the cut on her arm. He was unhappy with all of this, but he was a man of his word and would go along with it.

"Can this car continue?" He asked Kaitlin.

Kaitlin entered the car and turned the ignition. It started.

"Then go. I will distract them and try to hold them off for as long as I can."

Kaitlin reached up, pulling Jean's face to hers, and kissed him deeply. For a brief moment, time seemed to stand still. Then, with a soft exhale, Jean took a step back, his eyes lingering on her for just a second longer. In one fluid motion, he leapt into the air, transforming mid-flight into the raven. His dark wings beat against the cool night air, and within seconds, he vanished into the endless black sky.

Kaitlin, made a sharp U-turn, her hands gripping the wheel tightly. The little yellow car rattled and shook, protesting every bump in the road, but she pushed it forward, determined. Slowly, it gained speed, creaking and groaning as it accelerated, finally disappearing into the darkness of the moonless night—swallowed whole by the uncertainty of what lay ahead.

CHAPTER 42

"*Under no circumstances is it okay for them to make it through that pass!*"

Julien sat behind the large desk in the study, his body tense beneath nothing but pajama bottoms and an open robe. A quiet, simmering rage churned beneath his bruised and nicked-up skin, waiting for the right moment to explode. His face and chest bore the marks of the recent chaos—small cuts and bruises from the exploding glass—yet it wasn't the physical wounds that troubled him most.

Rayna, perched on the edge of the desk in her usual spot, cradled a still-sleeping Lucien in her arms. She too wore her robe, her own face and body marked by the glass, but her wounds had already begun to heal—far faster than his. She glanced at Julien, her expression unreadable, as the silence between them thickened, charged with unspoken tension. Even with the boy in her arms, the air felt dangerous, as if the room itself was waiting for Julien's inevitable eruption.

"Why won't he wake?" Julien asked.

"They did something to him to keep him sleeping," she said, as she cradled the young boy as if he were her own. "He's all right, though. Yesss, he's gonna be just fine." She gently stroked Lucien's cheek.

"How could she just leave me like this?" Julien thought, not wanting to believe she actually had.

Just then, he heard the front doors of the house slam open, followed by what seemed to be a violent tussle in the next room. A man screamed as if the life was being torn from his chest. Julien recognized the man's howling cries, and it sent a chill through his body. He lowered his eyes, afraid to look up at the nightmare heading his way.

The doors of the study burst open and Tirin entered. He ripped off what was left of his shirt and threw it to the ground as Dane, with the help of betas Micah and Cree, struggled to restrain a hysterical Teddy. Julien kept his eyes down as the heartbroken beta screamed and frantically tried to free himself from the others.

Finally, Tirin let out a ferocious roar that startled Julien. It was sharp and quick and commanded order amongst the confusion of the moment. Dane, Micah and Cree released Teddy and walked over and stood in line behind Tirin. Teddy quieted himself and took a few more ragged breaths before he staggered over to the others. Tirin stepped in front of him to size up his beta. He tapped Teddy's chin twice, forcing Teddy's head up, and looked him square in his eyes as only a sire could.

"We will find him," Tirin said sternly. "I promise you."

Teddy nodded and lowered his eyes while keeping his chin up. Even in these circumstances it was inappropriate to hold the gaze of his sire for too long. Tirin stepped back and Teddy took his place in line behind Dane, in front of Micah. No one noticed that Julien flinched from Tirin's roar, but this was new even to him. He had never heard his friend communicate with that kind of intensity, but Tirin had also never lost a beta before.

Even Rayna was saddened as twenty of her vampires filed into the room with their heads hanging. Morale was at an all-time low. The Gerard Estate had never taken a defeat like this before. Even on the night of Camille's attack, they felt as if they were tricked more than they were beaten. This was just one battle, though. The first and now, they knew the rules and whom they were fighting against.

The room was quiet. They all stood silently, awaiting the next command from their leader, but he was not yet ready to speak. Instead, he nodded to Rayna. She signaled to Tikesha, otherwise known as Tik, who rushed over and took the still-sleeping Lucien from her arms. Outwardly, Rayna was as calm as ever, but that ever-present smile was uncharacteristically absent. She, too, was angry, just as much as anyone else in the room. At Camille, the destruction of the house, Gussy's death - and her face.

To say that Rayna was an attractive woman is about as big of an understatement as one can make. She knew the appeal she had and the power that it gave her, and she took a great deal of pride in it. Her face had been cut several times, and although it was healing at an exponential rate, someone was going to pay dearly for that.

"Who saw them last?" she asked as she hopped off the desk and headed for the map on the wall. No one answered. "Come on! Who last had eyes on them?!"

"I guess that would be me," one of her vampires said, and the entire room focused on him.

Vampires weren't normally the nervous types, but with Rayna, Tirin, and Julien angry, everyone was a bit uneasy.

"Where?" she asked as she turned her gaze back to the map.

"I followed them out of Belle Chasse, up to Timberlane. Then they turned west onto Lapalco. That's as far as I could keep up."

"West! Fine. Let's go," Tirin grumbled, and everyone moved.

"No!" Rayna said, and everyone stopped.

Tirin whipped around to face her. Even Julien gave her a look. When it came down to it, she was number one in rank, behind Julien, but she had never called out Tirin like that before, not in public.

"Just wait," she said, trying to dial back the tension a few notches. "We've only got one shot at this. Let's just be sure. 'Kay?" she asked him, restoring some of his power back.

Julien's eyes shifted to Tirin, curious how he would take this. Tirin growled under his breath, but he did not leave.

"What's wrong?" Julien said.

"West on Lapalco?" Rayna quietly repeated over and over to herself as she ignored Julien's question. Her eyes flitted back and forth across the map, again and again.

"Rayna," Julien said. The irritation in his voice told everyone in the room that he didn't appreciate being ignored.

"Doesn't make sense." She shook her head.

"Why?"

"Because she'll never get away that way." Her eyes still flitting, back and forth, across the map. "Even with the head start. Kaitlin's no dummy. She knows she can't outrun us going west."

"Then where-r-r-r," Tirin growled as Rayna's eyes continued to flit around the map while she searched for the answer.

"…North!" She exclaimed as she turned to face them. "She'll try to go north, through the pass between Lake Maurepas and Lake Pontchartrain. That's what I would do if I knew a bunch of vampires and lycans were chasing me," she said as she moved toward Tirin.

"Wha--? Why?" Julien asked.

"Because vampires don't swim and alphas can't," she said proudly as she took Tirin's hand, stopping him from leaving and walked him back to the map. "Jimmy Lee, Wyatt, Donte," she called, signaling her lieutenants to the front. "Get your people and take a van. Tirin, we need a beta to go with each of them, to help track."

"We don't need vans," Tirin said, insulted by the notion.

"Baby, my guys can't run around all night like you," she said as a compliment. "They're not built that way."

"Hrrrrr…. Dane. Micah. Cree." He assigned each of them to a group as he called out their names. Teddy was left out.

Julien watched and listened closely as Rayna unfolded her plan.

"Wyatt, follow their trail directly and keep your eyes open for her car. My guess is they boarded the ferry station in Harvey. Take the ferry into the city and fan out. Use the beta to check everything as you make your way to the pass." Wyatt nodded his understanding and she continued. "Jimmy, just in case I'm wrong, which I'm not," she directed toward Julien, "follow Lapalco west, all the way to Butte. If you don't find anything, peel up and head right for this choke point in the pass and wait."

"…For what?" asked Jimmy Lee. "Wh-What are we looking for?"

"The train, baby!" she replied impatiently, then to the entire room, "Find the train, you find them!"

Julien took note of the harshness.

"Wh-What train is it, ma'am?" Jimmy asked.

"I don't know, Jimmy, check them all, damn it!" she snapped. "Donte, you and your boys go with Tirin directly to the train station and start there. If a train left going north - catch it!" She looked over the entire room. "Listen to me, all of you! Under no circumstances is it okay for them to make it through that pass!"

"Teddy," Tirin said. "Tonight, you run with me."

"I suggest you ride with Donte, at least to the station," Rayna said. "I got a feeling tonight you're gonna get a lot more exercise than you think – Tik!" she yelled.

Tik jumped up with Lucien in her arms.

"Where's Taq?" Rayna asked.

Tik's younger brother, Taquan sped over next to her. He was excited and ready to fight.

"You and Taq go with Donte as far as the station, then both of you hit up every place down by the riverfront for any Mal'fec interested in making some extra cash tonight. Send them to Club Dallas."

"Yes, Ms. Rayna," said Tik.

"Then both of you hightail it straight back here to babysit Lucien."

"But,--" Taq tried to express his displeasure, but before he could even get the word out of his mouth, Rayna grabbed him by the collar and pulled him in close.

"This is not the night you want to try me, youngster," she said. "As far as you're concerned, this child is the most important thing in this whole entire world, and if he so much as catches a cold tonight, you will suffer until I deem you worthy enough to kill. You understand me?" Rayna asked.

"Yes, ma'am. Sorry," Taq replied.

"Good boy." Rayna kissed him on the forehead, then took Lucien back from Tik. "Go! What're y'all waiting for?!"

"Wait," Julien said as he rose. Finally, he was ready to talk but there were a few who weren't going to like what he had to say. Two in particular.

"Are you sure?" he asked Rayna.

Rayna twitched her head ever-so-slightly as her lips pursed and her eyebrows furrowed. She stared at him defiantly, unwilling to dignify the question with a response. Seeing this, Julien backed off, turning his attention back to the room.

"Bring them back, all of them. ALIVE," Julien said. Then, he turned his gaze to Tirin, he repeated himself, making absolutely sure there was no misunderstanding. "Alive, Tirin."

Tirin glared at Julien. They held each other's eyes for what seemed like an eternity until Julien let loose all the anger he had been harboring.

"GO!" Julien screamed as a thin line of red glimmered and raced over both his eyes.

The room erupted into chaos as they burst through doors and smashed their way out of the few remaining unbroken windows, each one desperately trying to escape. All but Tirin. He lingered for a moment, holding Julien's gaze with a heavy, unspoken tension before finally turning to leave.

Now, only Julien, Rayna, and Lucien remained in the fractured silence. Rayna, still cradling the ever-slumbering heir in her arms, moved with unsettling calm. She casually walked over to the desk, her eyes landing on the infamous letter opener she had driven into it nearly four years ago.

Julien's eyes tracked the subtle movements of her hand as she gently fondled the handle, her fingers tracing the cold metal like it held a deeper meaning. Something unsaid passed between them, lingering in the room like a storm waiting to break.

"You know, there was a time when my counsel held a certain importance to you. When my words were never questioned, and my impressions garnered a respect I thought I had earned in all our years together."

With a certain ease, she removed the opener from the home it had known for the past forty-seven months and gently placed it on the desk. Julien quietly seethed as she picked up the card, raised it to face level and carefully examined it before her eyes again found his.

"I can only hope that somehow we can find our way back to that time - for both our sakes."

She tossed the card on the desk in front of him, then turned and headed toward the door as she whispered playful nothings in the ear of the sleeping child in her arms. Julien glared at the card. He knew what she was implying and he didn't like it one bit. In a fit of rage, he swept everything off the desk with his arm to let her know just that, but she didn't care or flinch as she continued to the door.

"Rayna!" he hollered as she exited the room. He quickly followed. "God damn it, don't you walk away from--" he said as he rounded the corner and stopped short.

Barrett and Cecil stood in the front doorway. Rayna stood in the middle of the room with a twisted smile on her face in anticipation of the imminent confrontation.

"Where the hell have you two been?" Julien asked. "And what the fuck did you--"

Barrett's eyes flashed red, and Julien was repelled backward into the wall - hard. It was all he could do to remain conscious.

"JULIEN!" screamed Rayna.

That was not the kind of confrontation she had anticipated. She turned to Barrett, her eyes blazing with fury, but before she could take even a single step toward him, two swords from the mantle above the fireplace broke free, soaring to either side of her neck. They hovered ominously, their blades firmly pressed against her skin, yet not quite breaking it.

A surge of panic rose within her, but she quickly focused on Lucien, clutching him tightly to ensure he was out of harm's way. Her heart raced as she found herself trapped in a precarious situation, the weight of danger pressing down on her like the blades poised at her throat.

"Your uppity ass may be able to walk around in the daylight like you ain't got a care in the world, but I don't think you'll be walking very far without that pretty little head on your shoulders. What you think? Hmm?" Barrett asked.

Rayna didn't answer. She was furious, but she knew better than to provoke him any further. Julien tried to move, but Cecil raised his hand and his eyes flashed red, holding Julien down. He was helpless.

"Sit. Down." Barrett ordered Rayna.

Gingerly, she moved to the chair next to the sofa, still holding Lucien, and carefully sat. The blades followed her every movement.

"Never liked you and the influence you had on my boy. I don't know what you did to him to make him bring you home that day, but I should have killed you right then and there, like I wanted to. If you wasn't holding my grandson right now I swear I'd take your fucking head clean off," Barrett said. "Look at her, Ceese,…"

"She, uh, she looks pretty mad," Cecil said. Even now, Cecil was still intimidated by her.

"Yeah, she does," Barrett said. "Her arrogance won't let her be afraid. Just like that alpha of his. Fearless, the both of them! That I can respect."

"Pop,--" Julien said.

"But ain't no one in this house I got more respect for than Camille," Barrett continued. "Going out there alone, knowing what's waiting for her..." he smiled. "Yeah. They gonna remember her name tonight."

"Pop, please don't do this. You promised me,--"

"SHE LIED, JULIEN!" Barrett screamed. "That boy is a girl! She hid that from you, FROM ALL OF US, for four years!" Barrett pointed to Rayna. "This one here told you what the little girl would do and you didn't listen to her! Camille *was* there that day and she heard everything!"

"No," Julien said.

"YES, SHE WAS!!" Barrett spit out with a frightening malignance not even Cecil has seen. "...*She* did this and you made it worse because you weren't warlock enough to fix it. Now I got to."

Two vampires entered the room and stood behind Barrett and Cecil. Rayna saw them and if they had souls, her stare would have bored a hole straight through them.

"Leo," Rayna hissed at one of the vampires.

"Leo's with me now. Should have put him down when I told you," Barrett said, then glanced at Leo. "See, she ain't so tough. You just have to know how to talk to her."

"Stay here with him," Barrett told Rayna. "Protect him, keep him safe as you've done for all these years. He is still my boy. We'll handle everything else from this point on."

Barrett left with Cecil and the two vampires in tow. A few seconds later, the swords dropped to the floor. Simultaneously, Julien was released. Rayna placed the still-sleeping Lucien on the sofa and rushed over to Julien.

"Baby, you okay?" she asked as she checked his head.

Julien cried in her arms, his anguish quickly transforming into a scream of anger that reverberated throughout the room. For a brief moment, Rayna felt a flicker of fear in response to his rage, but that apprehension was short-lived as the absentee smile soon returned to her face. The wild boy who had brought her home all those years ago was back, reminding her of the fierce spirit that had captivated her then and now.

CHAPTER 43

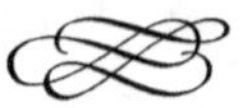

"A crime was committed against me! And I will have my vengeance..."

Kaitlin parked the car at the downtown train station.

"But,… nobody takes the train," Camille said.

"Yeah. That's why we're taking it," Kaitlin said. "We need to minimize the collateral damage of this night, if possible."

"It's a little late for that, don't you think?" Camille said with an edge that did not go unnoticed by Kaitlin.

"Look, we just need to make it to the canal at Pass Manchac. They won't be able to track us so easily past that point. It's your best chance to escape *your* friends," Kaitlin said, equally matching the shade thrown her way by Camille.

Kaitlin turned and entered the station. Camille and Dani followed. Minutes later, the three of them walked through the train to the first empty compartment they saw and quietly took their seats. Kaitlin sat alone in the aisle seat across from Camille and Dani, who sat next to the window. Kaitlin watched as Dani stared at her reflection in the glass from every angle. She could tell that the child was not happy with what she saw. Camille noticed the same thing and seemed aggravated by the fuss as the train started to roll.

"Stop it, you look fine," Camille said.

"But my hair. It's so short," Dani whined.

"It'll grow. It's hair," Camille snapped, already fed up with the ridiculouness of the conversation.

Dani seemed just as aggravated as her mother was about the topic as she slouched back in her seat with her arms crossed over her chest.

"Sit up and uncross yourself," Camille ordered.

Dani obeyed as she uncrossed her arms and pushed herself up.

"I looked better as a boy," she whispered under her breath, just loud enough for her mother to hear.

Camille rolled her eyes and shook her head as the train pulled out of the station.

"Hair's just window dressing, sweetie. I think you look beautiful. You look just like a little girl I used to babysit a long time ago when I was a kid." Kaitlin said as she glanced at Camille then quickly looked away.

Dani frowned. She thought her mom was the most beautiful woman in the world, but on this night, she was not the least bit interested in being compared to her. Camille looked down at Dani and, not so subtly, nudged her.

"Thank you," Dani reluctantly responded.

Camille stared down at her baby girl sitting uncomfortably upright in the seat next to her, then put her arm around her daughter and pulled her in tight. Dani sprawled into her mother's embrace and rested her head on Camille's lap.

"Poor baby," Kaitlin thought as she watched Dani shift around, trying to find comfort. *"All this is so unfair to her."*

Kaitlin glanced up at Camille, who did her best not to look back as she stared out the window and gently stroked her daughter's *short* hair with one hand, while she nervously twisted the Blood Heart with the other.

"…He wouldn't have killed you," Camille finally said while still gazing out the window.

"And you were willing to take that chance?" Kaitlin asked.

"He was just trying to scare you - scare me," Camille answered, still unable to look at her friend.

"Well, it worked. I was scared."

"I'm just saying, your friend didn't have to,--"

"He cut me, Camille! He put his hand around my throat, and you just sat there!" Kaitlin said. She had held that anger in for too long. Camille still couldn't bring herself to look at Kaitlin. Dani laid there trying her best not to hear the argument between the two women of her life.

"You saw the hate in his eyes. You should have done something! You could have stopped it, and maybe he'd still be alive. Instead, you just sat there," Kaitlin cried. "So you don't get to criticize the methods Jean uses… He had his hand around my throat."

Kaitlin knew her words were hurtful to Camille. She loved Camille, but those thoughts were much too heavy for her to carry any further. She needed to release them, and Camille needed to hear them. Kaitlin dabbed at the cut on her arm with a napkin. Camille tentatively reached over to Kaitlin, took her hand, and pulled her close. She placed her hand over Kaitlin's wound as her eyes flashed red for a brief second, then back to normal. The wound was gone.

"I'm so sorry," Camille said.

"I know, baby," said Kaitlin. "I know. But we're all gonna have to fight to get out of this. All of us."

Camille nodded. She finally understood as the two women embraced, crushing Dani between them. A brief moment of peace, but it was fleeting. They heard a loud thump on top of the train. Dani gasped as both Kaitlin and Camille eyed the ceiling. Suddenly, the door to their compartment slid open. Camille's eyes flashed to red, and her hair began to move.

"Tickets?" the ticket man said.

Kaitlin sighed with relief as Camille's hair settled and the red faded. The uniformed man casually approached with his ticket puncher in hand and all seemed normal until Dani noticed something both Kaitlin and Camille had missed.

"Where's your shoes?" Dani curiously asked the man.

Kaitlin and Camille glanced down, both surprised to discover that their ticket puncher seemed to have forgotten to put on his loafers that evening and, apparently, his socks as well. Just then, the man hissed, revealing his fangs as the train entered a small tunnel, plunging them into a brief moment of darkness. When the train emerged, the vampire was nowhere to be seen until suddenly, two arms reached down from the ceiling and snatched Dani up. Her scream pierced the air. In an instant, several windows shattered as a gang of Malafecs leaped through them.

Camille flashed into mactrouge, ready to unleash her fury. Whether strangers or acquaintances, enemies or friends, she was prepared to fight. Meanwhile, Kaitlin lunged for Dani, but they were severely outnumbered. Just then, a raven swooped in with a caw and transformed into Jean, his momentum propelling him through the vampire that had grabbed Dani, staking him in the process.

"I told you, no fighting," he said to Kaitlin.

Kaitlin grabbed Dani as Camille blasted another vampire. She was not just fighting for her life, she now understood she was fighting for both Dani's and Kaitlin's as well. She could not afford to hold back any longer.

"Into the next car! Quickly!" Jean ordered.

Camille ushered them into the next car, moving closer to the engine. When the three women were clear, Jean severed the cables on the train, separating the rear cars, and then stayed behind to hold off the attacking force. Kaitlin watched Jean as he faded into darkness, then moved toward the front of the car with Camille and Dani. Seconds later, she heard the sound of the door sliding closed. She turned back, expecting Jean - but Tirin was there. He hardly seemed winded at all. Kaitlin's anxiety level skyrocketed as Camille jumped in front of her. Kaitlin knew Tirin wanted more than to just take Camille and Dani back as his eyes shifted straight to her. She lowered her eyes, afraid to look at him even now.

"I don't want to hurt you," Camille warned.

"Is that what you told Gus?" Tirin growled. Camille could not respond. "IS IT?!"

It had been a long time since Kaitlin had felt fear like this. Even Camille jumped. They both knew what he was capable of and, at the same time, neither of them knew what he was capable of. He took a step forward. Camille's eyes flashed red as her hair floated wildly about her shoulders.

"Please don't make me do this," Camille pleaded.

"Do what? We both know that you will not kill me," he said as he took another step.

"No, but I'm not gonna let you hurt her, either, now stop!"

Tirin advanced another step.

"Therein lies your problem, witch, because you won't be able to stop me if you don't."

"Please, Tirin," Camille begged. "Please. Don't do this. Just let us go."

"YOU KNOW I CAN'T DO THAT!" Tirin snapped. "Not now. Not after what's been done this night." His eyes were still planted firmly on Kaitlin. "But I know you did not kill Gus,--"

"He had his hand around her throat!" Camille cried.

"--So I make you this promise: as long as I walk this earth, I will let no harm come to you or this child," Tirin said as he looked at Danielle for the first time. "The child you so assiduously hid from me-e-e-e."

He carefully took another step forward.

"Tirin, STOP!"

"Step aside."

"NO!"

"A crime was committed against me!" he scolded her. "And I will have my vengeance against those who committed it."

Kaitlin shuddered as a tear rolled down Camille's face. They both knew there was no way out of this. Easy or hard, someone had to die.

"Step - aside," Tirin ordered one final time. "I will not ask again."

Camille shook her head. He clenched his fists and took another step forward. Talons grew from Camille's fingertips as she levitated off the floor.

"Mmmmm." He almost smiled at his prize student. "You have learned well." He nodded as he again moved forward, unafraid.

Just then, the raven swooped in through a window and landed gracefully between them, transforming back into Jean. Tirin exhaled sharply as his nails elongated into sharp claws, and he charged at Jean with a speed and ferocity that astonished both Kaitlin and Camille. Camille was equally surprised to see Jean not only stand toe to toe with Tirin but match his speed as well—maybe even outpace him by a step.

Jean ducked, deflected, and spun to avoid what would have been lethal blows as the two of them battled fiercely from floor to ceiling in the cramped train car. Neither combatant yielded an inch to the other until, suddenly, the door behind Tirin was bent down to the floor, and The Talisman entered the fray.

"No," Camille gasped.

"No-o-o," Tirin growled.

"…No." Jean deeply sighed.

"Any get in way of Talisman, fall prey to Talisman." The Talisman proclaimed. "Me 'ere for 'dat giiirrrlll," he pointed at Camille.

"I was hoping he was here for you," Jean said to Tirin.

"Make no mistake, our fight is not finished." Tirin glared back at Jean.

With a nod, they silently postponed their fracas for the more imminent danger in front of them.

The Talisman saw Jean and smiled. "Yooou? Standing with a witch?"

Jean nodded, and The Talisman laughed.

"Aaahhh. So be it."

"How do we kill him?" Tirin asked.

"…We can't," Jean said.

The next moments were tense and silent. Everyone was motionless, waiting for the first move. The Talisman took it. He raised his staff, and the four snake eyes turned pitch black. He slammed it down, and blackness swarmed outward from their pupils. Jean looked to Camille, who was still in full mactrouge. She jumped into the air and spun and tried to spit out some kind of spell as the blackness engulfed the passenger car completely. Pitch-blackness. Suffocating silence. Then nothing. Second after second passed as the oxygen was slowly sucked away, but Camille held her concentration and, somehow, in the silence of the void, finished her spell. The blackness reversed back into the cane. She completed her spin and launched an energy blast at him as she collapsed to the floor.

Kaitlin and Dani were on the ground, still conscious, as they gasped for air. Tirin and Jean rose, both winded but ready to fight. Camille's dulled blast exploded on The Talisman as Tirin leapt at him. The Talisman blew a puff of air, sending Tirin flying backward. Jean spun out of the way, avoiding Tirin, who crashed into the back door, his strong body denting it.

Jean completed his spin and, like a warlock, drew from his Qi, releasing energy blasts from both his right and left hand. The Talisman deflected the first one but couldn't get out of the way of the second. With both his hands glowing blue, Jean charged and delivered a left-right combo that rocked The Talisman. The Talisman threw a haymaker. Jean ducked, then delivered another charged combo that rocked The Talisman again.

Tirin sprang up and ran sideways along the train wall, avoiding Camille, who had regained her breath and was, again, ready to fight.

She charged her body with energy and readied herself. The Talisman threw another haymaker that just missed Jean and obliterated the metal seat next to him. Jean threw two more fierce blows.

"JEAN!" Camille shouted, and he dove out of the way.

She threw a powerful blast of energy that hit The Talisman and rocketed him backward. He caught the doorframe, stopping himself from flying out the back end of the train. He tried to pull himself back inside as Tirin shifted into his lycan form and dove into him. They both went tumbling onto the tracks below.

Both Tirin and The Talisman laid on the tracks, Tirin still in full alpha. The Talisman reached up and grabbed Tirin by the neck as the rest of the rolling train rapidly approached. Even at full alpha, Tirin struggled to escape his grasp. He desperately slashed at The Talisman's arm until he was released, then jumped out of the way as the train barreled over The Talisman.

Tirin noticed the train was headed slightly downhill and bending back toward him. It had to slow to make this turn. He howled a call for help, then took off at full alpha speed downhill at an angle for the train.

"Get there, just get there-r-r-r!" he thought to himself.

Halfway down, the vampire Wyatt joined the chase alongside the beta Micah, both trying desperately to keep up with Tirin. They were all fast, but this was a train, and it was gaining speed. They had but one chance.

"The angle! Use the angle!" Tirin roared.

Cutting off the train was their only chance to catch up, but they had to time it just right. Inside, Camille moved over to Jean and offered her hand to help him off the floor. Jean graciously accepted the offer. They took each other in, both with a newfound mutual respect.

"Thank you," Camille said, "for helping us and… for not letting me die the other day."

"You are very welcome, Camille," Jean replied. It was the first time he had called her by name since they met. An acknowledgment that did not go unnoticed by any of the women on the train. Camille smiled. She and Jean looked over to find Kaitlin and Dani proudly beaming at them, but the joyful moment did not last. 'CRASH!' Shards of glass flew through the air as Tirin and Wyatt crashed through the windows. The lycan and the vampire tackled Jean and Camille, then crashed out of two windows on the other side with them, leaving Kaitlin and Dani behind. Jean heard Kaitlin and Dani's screams fade away as he tumbled into the darkness.

The four of them landed hard. Tirin's alpha body shielded Camille, but the impact from the fall was jarring and still knocked her out. Jean tried his best to maintain consciousness as he blasted Wyatt, destroying him. His vision blurred; he caught sight of Micah as he tried to board the train. With the last of his strength, Jean's eyes flashed blue as weeds knifed out of the ground, tied Micah up, and yanked him from the train. Jean smiled as the runaway train sped off into the darkness. Exhausted, Tirin morphed back to his human form. He walked his tired, naked body over to Jean and punched him square in the face. Jean's last thought was of Kaitlin.

CHAPTER 44

"*I had intended on inviting you to brunch in the morning, but I suppose that time has passed.*"

Julien sat in the shoeshine chair at Club Dallas like it was a throne. There was a sense of danger that emanated from him that wasn't there before as he stared at Jean, who was sprawled out on the dance floor, his eyes just beginning to open. Jean was dizzy and disoriented. He touched his face and found a handful of blood as it dripped continuously from his nose. It was obviously broken from Tirin's punch, and it made it difficult for him to breath. He wiped his face with his sleeve and slowly began to make his way to his feet.

What was left of the injured lycans and vampires, plus the new, *paid* recruits, danced wildly around Jean as the song 'Welcome to the Jungle' blasted throughout the Club. Rayna stood to Julien's right in a short, colorful, geisha-style dress. Her hair was in a long ponytail, and she wore wrist and ankle bands that matched her dress. Tirin, now clothed, moved into his spot on Julien's left with Dane, Teddy,

Micah, and Cree next to him. Julien raised his hand, and his troops settled as the music stopped.

"Where is she?" Julien asked.

"Upstairs recovering," Tirin answered. "They were told to bring her down when she wakes."

Julien seemed as if he wanted to respond, but his eyes shifted to Jean as he staggered to his feet.

"Well, well, well. Jean Laveau. Welcome home. I had intended on inviting you to brunch in the morning, but I suppose that time has passed. Too bad. Rayna makes a hell of a Bloody Mary." Julien then addressed his crew. "Seems our friend here's been holding out on us, boys. Apparently, he's what they call a… Houn-gan? Did I say that right?" he asked Rayna.

Rayna nodded and began to read from a slip of paper in her hand.

"A Boku Priest of the highest order, specializing in the practical aspects of voodoo. Powers are organic, stemming from the land, yada, yada, and are heightened between the hours of twelve and six a.m."

She crumpled the paper and tossed it. Jean gave no reaction. He simply wiped more of the dripping blood from his nose.

"Hmph. The Midnight Man," Julien said. "Yeah. Your momma would've been proud." Julien stared at Jean a moment, sizing him up, then continued. "That was some pretty fancy shit you did back at the house." He snapped his fingers. Two men at the front door closed the doors in an attempt to cut Jean off from the elements.

"Now show me what you can do inside," Julien said. "Give him a little something to work with, Mok."

Mokie, the vampire DJ, changed the song to Kool Moe Dee's "I Go to Work." Jean removed his coat and prepared himself to do just that. It was also a stalling tactic. He needed more time, as his head still wasn't quite right. Julien, however, wasn't interested in giving Jean that chance. He nodded to four vampires on the wall, who readied themselves. Jean's eyes faded to blue.

"He's elusive and exceptionally fast," Tirin said.

"For a human?" Julien asked.

"…For anyone," Tirin added with no emotion whatsoever.

Julien didn't respond. He wanted to see what this man could do for himself. Rayna smiled as the first vampire charged. Jean formed a fist-sized energy ball, flipped it in the air, and spun out of the way. It exploded at eye level and released just enough pure sunlight to set the vampire aflame. Two more stupidly charged, and Jean leveled them the same way. Jean moved so fast it was as if he was disappearing and reappearing.

"Mmmmmm. You didn't know he could do that, did you?" Rayna said in a husky, lust-filled voice.

Julien frowned off her comment. Mainly because he didn't know. He continued to watch Jean as he sent the fourth vampire in to die.

"Look closely," Julien said to Tirin. "See! Right there!... He's a Moo-Tone-Wah. The motha-fucka's a shadow dancer."

Tirin looked at Julien, not understanding what that meant. Rayna did.

"Ahhhh," Rayna groaned, almost as if it aroused her. "He moves within the refraction of the light."

Jean broke a table leg and staked the last vampire. He then threw it across the room, staking another for good measure. Julien clapped slowly, unimpressed. He actually was, but he was pissed and being petty. He raised his hands, and the music stopped.

"Mokie. Lose the ball. Raise the lights," Julien ordered.

Mokie did as he was told, and once the disco ball was removed and the lights were raised, nearly all the shadows disappeared from the room.

"Now try," Julien said to Jean. He then looked to Tirin.

Tirin stepped forward, ready to finish what he and Jean had started earlier before The Talisman had interrupted.

"Whoa, whoa, whoa, now. What about me?" Rayna asked. "Don't I get a dance? Tirin's been playing all night."

"This is not a game!" Tirin growled.

"I just want a dance. You can kill him when I'm done."

"Nobody's killing anybody until--" Julien started.

"Julien, you owe me this," Rayna said.

"No, he's mine!" Tirin yelled.

"He cut my face!" Rayna yelled.

"ENOUGH!" Julien commanded, with a strength he had not previously shown.

He glared at Jean for a few seconds while he made up his mind.

"He cut my face," Rayna whispered with a vulnerability that only two in this room had ever seen.

She had gathered herself back from her uncharacteristic emotional outburst, but the anger in her eyes could not be suppressed. Julien sighed as he leaned back in the chair.

"Let her dance a bit."

Rayna clapped like a grade school girl at Julien's decision, and before Tirin could protest, Julien added an amendment to his statement.

"You can cut-in in a minute, but I don't want him dead. Not yet." Julien explained, eyeing Tirin.

Tirin growled softly as he stared Rayna down before moving back to his spot next to Julien. The crowd cheered and Rayna smiled as she stepped out of her heels.

"Awww yeah, y'all!" Mokie said over the microphone. "Give it up for the Momma Bear herself! The Big, Bad Beauty! The one, the only Ms. Ray-na!"

Julien rolled his eyes at the theatrics as the room erupted, He instantly regretted his decision and was about to change his mind until The Cutting Crew's "I Just Died in Your Arms Tonight" started to play. At that point he knew it was too late. He folded his arms across his chest as a bitter grimace washed over his face. Rayna giggled and smiled at Mokie before she turned all of her attention to Jean and slowly moved toward him.

"We do not have to do this," Jean said.

"Awww. But I want to. Besides, this one's my favorite. Come on tall, dark," she said as the smile faded from her face, "dance with me."

She charged with incredible speed and agility, but even without the shadows Jean was still quick enough to form an energy ball and flip it. It exploded inches from her face, but it did not have the same effect as it did on the vampires. It did nothing but make her sneeze. Jean was shocked. Rayna giggled at the burst of sunlight, then she looked at Jean. Her smile was present, but there was fury behind her eyes.

"Pretty," Rayna said, "but that ain't gonna work on me, baby."

She delivered a powerful front kick to his sternum that knocked him across the room. He bounced off a pole on the dance floor and started to fall, but her speed was incredible. She was on him in an instant and caught him by the collar before his body hit the floor.

"When her momma was eight months pregnant, she was bitten by a vampire," Julien said.

Still holding him, she bent over and swung her leg up backward and kicked Jean in the face with a scorpion kick.

"Her mother didn't survive," Julien continued, "but an emergency C-section was performed on the body, and this exquisite creature was brought into this world."

Rayna did a handstand, locked her ankles around Jean's neck and choked him, then threw him across the room.

"Aw, she's something, ain't she?" Julien asked.

While Jean was in the air, Rayna backflipped over to him and kicked him in the chest, sending him further across the room. He bounced off the wall, hit the floor and spit up a mouthful of blood. Julien then nodded to Tirin.

"Time to cut in." Said Julien.

"Teddy," Tirin ordered. "Retribution."

Teddy released a hellacious roar and accelerated. Jean struggled to his feet as Teddy raked his nails across Jean's back. Jean screamed and fell into Rayna's arms. She kissed him, tasted his blood, then spun around and threw him across the room. Jean landed on a table, shattering it. A malafec picked him up and shoved him back into play. Teddy zipped over and engaged Jean again. Jean tried his best to defend himself. He blocked a few good punches and was able to land one or two of his own, but at this point in the game, without access to the elements, he was too weak to cause any real damage. Teddy doubled Jean over with a thunderous left kick to his body. Jean clutched his ribs as he fell.

Rayna sped over and caught him from behind before he could hit ground. She locked up with him and, for the first time, showed her fangs. She sunk them deep into his shoulder, and Jean screamed. He struggled briefly, but it was for naught. Once a vampire locks you up, there is no escape, and she was so much more than an ordinary vampire. She smiled as her eyes rolled back into her head.

"Easy! Not too much," Julien yelled. "He's got a lot of talking to do."

"I will die before I talk to you," Jean stammered.

Rayna guided him to the floor, locked her legs around his arms and lower torso and continued to drink. Julien watched. This was as close to sexual satisfaction as she could ever really get.

CHAPTER 45

"*Look how the wind just strokes her hair and how her eyes catch the sun off the lake and just,... sparkle.*'

Camille heard Julien's voice as they dragged her down the hall, but there was an edge to it that was unfamiliar to her, and she feared she might be the cause of it.

"No, you won't," she heard him say to someone. "You'll cry, scream, beg, maybe even piss your pants, but you won't die. Not until you tell me where my baby girl is."

"No!" Camille screamed as two vampires dragged her into the main room, where she could see Jean being held captive on the dance floor by Rayna.

Manacles bound her wrists and ankles together, making it very difficult for her to move as Leo pulled her into the room with his hand clasped around her neck. She couldn't help but wince as his long, sharp nails dug into her skin around the Blood Heart necklace.

"Leo!" Rayna yelled. The sight of him stoked her anger, and she squeezed Jean a little harder because of it.

Julien appeared calm, but his eyes told a very different story.

"Easy, boss," Leo said. "This ain't me. This is what your father and Mr. Cecil wanted. They the ones told me to do this."

"Where is he?" Julien asked.

"They on they way. They'll be here in a few minutes." Everyone could hear the fear in Leo's voice as his eyes shifted back and forth between Julien and Rayna.

"And you think you gonna survive that long?" asked Julien.

Camille let out a soft gasp as Leo tightened the grip around her neck, his nails making subtle indentations in her skin and putting more tension on the necklace.

"Well, how 'bout I just rip out her neck and you watch her bleed," Leo threatened. The bully in him was still very active and Camille was the only card he had left to play, but it seemed Julien was prepared to call his bluff.

"Then what's gonna stop me from ripping out that heart of yours?"

Julien's eyes flashed red and a mirror on the wall behind Leo cracked loudly. The vampire flinched. Then another mirror to Leo's left shattered and fell to the floor, followed by another on the other side of the room. Jessie, the other vamp holding Camille's arm, released her and slowly backed away.

"Sorry," said Jessie to Julien, as he backed his way into the corridor from whence they came and, like vampires do, disappeared.

"Looks like you done got yourself into quite a predicament," Rayna said to Leo. "Bet you wish you had momma's love now."

"JD, wait, I'm,--"

Before Leo could finish, a large piece of glass dislodged from the wall and barreled across the room, severing his arm from his body. In a flash, Tirin punched through Leo's ribcage and ripped his heart out. It turned to dust, along with Leo, as Tirin crushed it in his hand. Julien stepped forward and caught Camille before she hit the ground. Leo's hand and what was left of his severed arm turned to dust, breaking the necklace and leaving a few blood-stained scratches on her neck. The broken chain slithered around and off her neck. She strained to move her chained hands into position to stop the precious heart from hitting the floor. She caught it and squeezed it as if her very life depended on it.

"I'm sorry, Cher'. You all right?" He whispered.

"Julien, please, let him go," Camille cried. "Let him go. PLEASE!"

Rayna couldn't hide her smile as Julien pushed Camille to a standing position and backed away from her. Confused, he shook his head.

"Please," Camille begged.

"No," Julien answered.

"Let him go!" Camille screamed.

"No!" Julien yelled.

Camille fell to her knees and sobbed uncontrollably in front of him.

"I'm begging you, Julien. PLEASE!"

"You beg for this man's life? This man who has disrespected me? Come into my house and stolen my child from me?!"

"It was my choice to leave," Camille said. "He had nothing to do with that."

That hurt.

"…Why, Cher'?" Julien asked.

"Because I don't want our little girl to die!"

That hurt more. Silence filled the room.

"Our little *girl?*" Julien asked.

He paused a long while. It broke her heart to see the pain and anger in his eyes, knowing she was the one who caused it.

"It's true then? I didn't want to believe it, but… You hid my daughter from me for over three,--"

He couldn't speak the words. He couldn't move. He just stared at her. Silent. Still. A tear rolled down his face. Then another. And another.

"How could you do this to me?" He said softly.

"You lied to me!"

"I told you every,--"

"I know about the prophecy! I know if you let her live, you'll die!"

"No, I,--"

"I heard you!"

"I never believed that," Julien said.

"I heard all of you! I *was* there that day! I was there," she sobbed.

"Baby, I didn't believe it then and I don't believe it now. My daughter would never hurt me. She would have no reason to."

"I heard what you told your father. 'We don't have to do this *now,*"

"Camille,--"

"You could've told me back at Kaitlin's place! I wanted you to! I practically begged you to, and you looked me right in the eye and lied to me - again!"

"Baby, you have to understand I was trying to protect,--"

"LIAR!" she screamed. "You're such a liar-- you're all liars! I don't believe anything you say!"

Julien reached down and picked her up. She struggled with him as he tried to calm her.

"You need to hear me,--"

"Let me go!"

"We were trying to protect you!"

"No! The only reason we're alive now is because I had two boys!"

"Listen to me!"

"You sent Tirin after me! You sent him!" Camille cried.

"CAMILLE!" Tirin boomed and silence again filled the room. "My actions that day did not come from anger, but of concern for a friend who might have overheard the ill-timed misspeaking of an old fool. I have love for only a few in this world. You have ALWAYS been one of them."

"Baby, I'm sorry," Julien said. "I'm so sorry you had to hear what you heard that day. I'd give my right arm if I could go back and somehow fix it. Make it so you never had to carry around the pain you bore all these years. But I can't, and I hate myself for it because I love you so much. Please. Please, forgive me."

"But if she lives, you'll die," Camille said.

"Naw. I'd love that little girl so much that if - if you truly think that I would ever do anything to harm either one of you, then you should just kill me now," Julien said.

His eyes flashed red, and Camille's chains fell off.

"Go on. We both know you can. Strike me down and leave this place. No one will harm you. No one will stop you. Tirin'll see to that." Julien said. He looked at his alpha. "Promise."

Tirin nodded. Julien nodded back, then opened his arms and closed his eyes.

"Go on," Julien said.

"Stop it, you know I won't," Camille said as she squeezed and rolled the Blood Heart between her fingers.

"Why?"

"You know why."

"Because you love me?"

"Yes."

"And trust me?" Julien asked.

Camille hesitated a moment, then, "Yes."

"Then bring her home, and let's be a family once and for all," Julien said. "It don't have to be here. We can leave and go anywhere you want. Just bring my little Peanut back home.

Camille let the tears fall. "I can't."

"Why?"

"Because you cannot protect them," Jean interrupted.

"SPEAK AGAIN AND YOU DIE, YOU SON OF A BITCH!" Julien crazily screamed. "I swear on my momma's soul I will strike you down right here and now!"

Rayna tightened her grip on Jean, silencing him.

"He's right, Julien. You can't," Camille said sadly.

"Camille. Please. Don't do this… Don't. How can you just go and leave me and little Luc like this? I can't even wake my little boy up," Julien said through clenched teeth, his anger beginning to slip through.

"My baby. Where is he?" Camille asked.

"Home."

"You left him alone?!"

Julien's exhale was slight. Unnoticeable to most, but the intensity behind his glare did not escape Camille. The mere thought that he would leave his son alone on any night, let alone one such as this, was distasteful to him and it showed in his eyes. She immediately understood that the remark was disrespectful and seemed to lack any contrition at all, especially after what she had done to him tonight, yet, as a mother, she desperately needed to know and Rayna had a mind to answer her. For whatever reason, the question seemed to catch her ire as well and she lashed out at Camille.

"Of course not! You know I'd never let anything happen to that boy! I left Tik and Taq behind to watch over him in case he woke up while we were traipsing all over town, chasing after you! And you know Tik would die before she'd let anyone or anything threaten a single hair on that boy's head!"

Any other night, Rayna's tone alone—regardless of the remark— would have been more than enough to instigate a fight between the two of them. However, Camille merely looked to Jean, seeking guidance on how to wake her son. Julien shot a glare in his direction as Rayna loosened her grip, allowing Jean to respond.

"Sleep sands… They will wear off in time," Jean responded.

Rayna re-tightened her grip on his broken ribs, almost as punishment for what he had done.

"I know I hurt you and I'm sorry, but,… I can't live this way anymore, Julien. I can't." Camille couldn't look him in the eye. "Whether it's your daddy, or The Council, or this *thing* that's been chasing me. There's always gonna be someone coming. You know that. So, please… if you really love me, just let us go."

"…If I really love you…" Julien said. He sighed deeply as another tear fell off of his face. "Baby girl, I've loved you since the first day I saw you. Before you ever knew. For three days I hid behind that big pecan tree at Lake End Park and waited for you, just to catch a glimpse of you. One day you were just standing there. You was wearing that green dress, the one that matched your eyes so perfectly. I remember you stuck the toes of your right foot in the water and looked off into the distance, and there;" more tears fell from his eyes, "right there,… That's when I knew you were the one."

Tears filled Camille's eyes as she continued to stroke the Blood Heart.

"I said, 'aw na', look at that. Look at that girl, there. Look how the wind just strokes her hair and how her eyes catch the sun off the lake and just,… sparkle. I'd never seen a more beautiful picture than you, standing by the lake, that day. And I just stood there, hiding behind that old pecan tree, watching you. Wondering what you was doing. Who you was waiting for." A tear rolled down his cheek. "Damn fool never showed up."

"That's because I was waiting for you."

Julien moved over to her and took her in his arms, and Camille held on tight.

"Please don't leave me, Camille. Please. Can't nobody harm us if we're together. That's why they try so hard to keep us apart."

Camille looked over to Jean with eyes full of sadness and remorse. She couldn't say the words, but she didn't have to. He knew it was over and he solemnly lowered his head. Just then, Cecil and several vampires burst in through the front door. He saw Julien and wearily shook his head. Displeased that he disobeyed his father's orders.

"Goddamn it, boy. What the hell are you doing here?" Cecil asked.

Julien moved Camille aside, and his eyes and hands flashed red.

"Waiting for you," Julien said as he moved toward Cecil. "I told you a day would come,"

The pannick in Cecil's eyes was quickly outweighed by the booming voice that emanated from the parking lot behind him. A voice he recognized and very much wished he had not heard.

"IT'S YOUR TIME NOW, GIIIIRRL," The Talisman's voice echoed from outside the club, so loud it quaked the room.

Julien stopped in his tracks, and Camille trembled, chilled to the bone.

"TIME FOR YOU TO COME WITH MEEEEE."

"Shit!" Cecil said. "Shit, shit, shit!"

"What the hell was that?" Julien gasped.

"Y-Y-You best step away from her now, boy," Cecil said as he ran and ducked down behind a table for cover.

"What did you and Daddy do?" Julien asked.

"Move away from her, Julien!" Cecil yelled.

Right then, a huge, fiery blast of energy exploded through the doors.

"CAMILLE!" Julien screamed, but it was too late.

Camille released a long, bloodcurdling scream as The Talisman's aim was true and the wave of energy detonated on her. Anguish and silence filled the room, but as the dust settled and the smoke cleared, Camille was still there, standing strong, her feet firmly planted and arms crossed protectively in front of her face. Her eyes pulsed a fierce blood red, mirroring the tension in her clenched fists. Tattered and torn clothing clung to her still-smoldering body, while her hair—now completely white—floated wildly off her shoulders, swirling in sync with the fiery energy and debris from the blast.

Her arms dropped to her sides, and she released another piercing shriek that shattered the windows before it morphed into a wicked cackle. Inhaling deeply, talons erupted from her fingertips, and for the first time, her mildly tanned skin turned a dingy green. She radiated an overwhelming aura of evil.

"Tergum. Tergum. Reverto duos fold." she commanded in a throaty, powerful exhale.

All the energy and debris from The Talisman's blast, gathered and compressed in front of her, then with a thought, she released it back from where it came. It exploded in the parking lot and the building shook. Outside, The Talisman could be heard as he wailed in agony. No one in that room, save Jean, had ever witnessed anything like what they just saw. Camille grinned as she surveyed her surroundings. She could taste their fear. She could feel the call, and this time she did not fight it.

"Kill her! Damn it, somebody kill her now, please!" Cecil cried.

With a flick of her finger, Camille sent a ball of energy at Cecil, just missing him as he dove behind the bar. Julien took a step toward her.

"Cami,--"

She forcefully extended her hand and repelled him backward, out of her way. He bounced hard off the wall. She raised up off the ground as a few of Cecil's vampires tried to attack, but she was way too powerful. She ripped through them and anyone else who opposed her without mercy. Dane moved in an effort to subdue her.

"DANE, NO!" Tirin yelled. "Be stil-l-l-l-l."

Tirin rushed in front of him as Camille zoomed over to attack. She growled at Tirin as blood dripped from her talons and mouth. Tirin remained calm, showing her no fear as he stared deep into her eyes, trying to connect with the woman he once knew. It seemed to be working until she spotted Rayna on the ground, still tied up with Jean. Camille exhaled and released a sinister smile. This time, Rayna was scared.

"STOP!" Julien yelled.

It was a voice she barely recognized, and in the blink of an eye, she darted to him.

"Everyone. Just,… Stop," he said softly.

Ready to strike, she hovered in front of him. Her vision was blurred, so she did not see him as the man she once loved, but his voice was soft and soothing in some strange way and he also showed her no fear as he gazed into those blood red eyes.

"I know you're in there, Cher'. I know you still are. Please," Julien begged, "come back to me."

Dangerous moments passed as she hovered in front of him ready to strike, but for some reason, she did not. Sometimes, in life, the energy returned is equal to that which is given. Perhaps this was the way. Her vision began to clear and she saw him. Her Julien. A tear escaped and rolled down her cheek. Her hair began to settle and the green began to leave her skin as the red left her eyes and her feet touched down on the floor.

"…Julien?" she asked.

"Yeah, Cherie. It's me." He smiled and for a brief moment, they once again found bliss, but, like so many of these moments in life, it was fleeting.

"Now! Kill her now!" Cecil screamed from behind the bar.

"NO!" Julien yelled.

Cecil hurled an energy blast in her direction as two of his vampires charged at her. Julien deflected the blast, which exploded against the bar, splintering the wood and injuring Cecil in the process. As Julien and Tirin fought off the rogue vampires, Camille scanned the room, her heart sinking as she took in the horrifying scene.

She caught sight of the fear in Cecil's eyes from behind the bar and the dust and remnants of both enemies and friends sprawled across the floor. Then, she noticed The Talisman's staff lying on the ground outside the club; it suddenly rose into the air and zipped out of her view. A sense of dread washed over her as she realized he would return again and again. It would never stop unless she found a way to end it. She turn to Tirin and found his eyes across the room and gave him a frail smile.

"*Goodbye, my friend,*" she thought.

Then as Julien prepared to blast another vampire, Camille's eyes flashed red as she rose up off the ground. Tirin saw the finality in her look and charged toward her with all the speed he had as she zipped in front of the attacking vampire. Tirin reached out to grab her; to stop her, but she eluded him exactly the way he had taught her - and he missed. Now, she *was* too fast.

Camille fully absorbed Julien's powerful blast, unprotected, and collapsed to the floor.

"Awh," Tirin painfully gasped.

It was as if he had felt the empathetic death pains of one of his betas and he dropped to his knees and his heartbreaking howl filled the room. Camille could see out the door of the club and smiled as she watched The Talisman tip his hat and walk out of her view. Julien dropped to his knees and cradled Camille in his arms.

"No. I didn't mean--" Julien uttered, barely able to speak.

"It's okay, it's okay," Camille said as she gently touched his face. "They would've,… never let us be."

Her breath was quick and uneven as she swallowed air and blood. Her body trembled in his arms as he squeezed her tighter.

"No, no, no, no, no, please. PLEASE!!" Julien begged.

"Shh-shh-shhhh… I love you," Camille said, her body quivering. She unclenched her fist and revealed the Blood Heart necklace in her palm. She had protected it; saved it for him. Julien smiled as he took it from her hand and kissed it. Camille then turned her head to look at Jean. Sadness filled his face. He had so much respect for this young woman. Learned so much from her in their short time together. In less than one night she had affected him in a way no one ever had. Not even Kaitlin. She smiled and nodded at him. He had affected her as well. She then turned back to Julien.

"I-I-I--" she swallowed. "I'm sorry."

"What for?"

Her eyes flickered red, and with a final surge of energy, she blasted part of the ceiling open and the starry night sky was revealed. She owed Jean a fighting chance and hoped this would be enough. She then set her eyes back on her love and smiled as she took her last breath.

CHAPTER 46

"**G**ive the dog a bone,"

Dani and Kaitlin sat silently on the floor of the train, both in a state of shock. Dani listened to the soothing rhythm of the wheels gliding over the tracks, finding solace in the motion of the train. While they were both deeply concerned about Camille and Jean, there was nothing they could do to help. All they could do was wait and pray. Suddenly, Dani squinted and flinched, as if a sharp, concentrated pain had settled in her chest. She looked up at Kaitlin, tears welling in her eyes, seeking comfort in her presence.

"Baby, don't worry. I know they'll be,--"

"Momma's dead!" Dani screamed.

"Sweetie, you don't know that."

"Yes, I do," she cried, "she's dead, she's dead, SHE'S DEAD!"

Kaitlin squeezed her tight, but before either of them had the chance to mourn, the door from the engineer's car slid open and a man, his lips curled into a sardonic smile, stepped toward them. Two fangs emerged from his mouth.

"Come on, baby," Kaitlin said as she stood up, grabbed Dani, and pushed her toward the back of the train.

Another man leaped through the back door, cutting them off. His breathing was heavy, like someone who had just sprinted down a train. He crouched into a stooped position, raised his nose, and sniffed a few times, releasing a low, sustained growl without ever taking his eyes off them. A black man in a dark suit and sunglasses entered behind the vampire. He wore a large ring on his left pinky, emblazoned with the symbol of The Council, and held a plain manila folder under his right arm.

He stared at Dani for a moment with keen curiosity, then unbuttoned his suit jacket and sat down. Taking a deep breath, he crossed his legs, opened the folder, and began to read from it. No one moved as he patiently examined the contents of the file. No one could. Then, after more than a few uncomfortable moments, he finally spoke.

"Interesting… Well, it appears your uncle Cecil was correct, Daniel. Or should I say Danielle?" the man asked in a British accent. "Unbelievable. I can't believe I had to come all this way - for this."

"How do you want it handled, sir?" the vampire asked.

The man closed the folder and looked at his watch.

"This is utterly ridiculous," the man said. "Kill the child. Do what you want with the woman, but make it quick, Rupert. This train pulls into Ponchatoula in thirty minutes and I do not wish to be on it."

"Aw, this is just a minute steak," Rupert, the vampire, said, looking at Dani. "Kendall?" the vampire asked, addressing the man stooped at the far end of the train. "Who you want?"

Kendall, a lycan, hadn't taken his eyes off of Kaitlin since he entered the car. "You know who I want," he growled.

Dani clutched onto Kaitlin's leg as Kendall rose and took a long sniff. Dani was paralyzed. Kaitlin reached into her pockets and found the "toys" Jean had given her.

"Then come get me," she said.

Kendall obliged. Kaitlin whipped her hands out of her pockets and launched the balls at Rupert while sending the silver jacks flying at the charging Kendall. The balls exploded against Rupert's chest and face, dousing him in holy water. The searing liquid burned through his skin, causing Rupert to scream in agony as he ran and jumped through an open window, leaping off the train.

Kendall, displaying the agility characteristic of an alpha, deftly dodged all the jacks and made it to Kaitlin unscathed. He seized her by the neck, pulling her close as the jacks clattered harmlessly to the floor. She squirmed for a moment, but then her body went limp in his grasp.

"Thanks for the invitation," he whispered. He exhaled and breathed Kaitlin in.

"Ooooh. This is gonna be nice."

The man from The Council, still sitting, watched Dani closely. She felt his eyes on her but, nevertheless, concentrated on the task at hand.

"Knick knack paddy whack," she whispered. "Bring the jacks to his back."

The jacks sprang up before hurtling back like bullets, embedding themselves deep into the lycan's hide. He gasped, instantly releasing Kaitlin, who tumbled to the ground. Flinching, his body stiffened, and he coughed up a mouthful of blood before violently convulsing and collapsing to the floor, lifeless.

The man from The Council rolled his eyes, shaking his head in disgust at the lack of professionalism displayed by his men. Despite his irritation, he couldn't conceal his fascination—perhaps even amusement—at the young child standing before him. He exhaled deeply and refocused his attention on Dani.

"Incantation magic at four years?" he said. "Interesting. You truly are a descendant of Esmerelda, aren't you? Right, then. Let's see what you can do."

He stood, removed his glasses, and his eyes flashed red.

CHAPTER 47

He watched as it emerged, slid down the alphas cheek, and lingered on his chin before falling to the floor.

The crackle of an impending storm echoed above Julien as he cradled his lifeless wife in his arms. He glanced up through the shattered ceiling to see dark clouds unnaturally racing across the sky. Turning his gaze to Jean, he noticed the familiar blue glow had returned to his eyes.

Before Julien could react, two thick vines erupted from the brick wall behind Jean and shot across the dance floor. They intertwined around Rayna's arms, yanking her backward off Jean and slamming her into the far wall. Two additional vines burst through, wrapping around her ankles, while a fifth vine surged from above, encircling her neck like a noose and gradually tightening.

"…Help,--" she hispered, barely able to get the words out of her mouth.

Tirin rushed to her aid. Julien's eyes ignited. Jean saw him and released an energy blast from his Qi. It blew open the floor beneath Julien and Camille, toppling them both into the basement below. Julien blasted himself up through the rubble, back onto the dance floor. He was bruised and bloodied - and angry. He zipped over to Rayna to help Tirin free her as Jean unleashed his wrath.

With incredible speed, Jean formed and released a huge ball of pure sunlight overhead that destroyed all the remaining vampires in the room. He spun, creating a powerful wind, blowing the beta wolves back. Julien was caught in the force of the wind, but both Tirin and Rayna stood strong. Jean saw them. He reached into his pocket and tossed a fistful of dust particles in the air; then, with a puff of his breath, sent them toward Tirin.

The dust was, in actuality, razor-sharp silver filings. They flew toward Tirin, who found himself trapped in the corner with nowhere to go. Rayna grabbed Tirin, spun him around, and huddled over him with her body shielding him from the microprojectiles as her back took the full blow. The filings were not lethal to her, but they were painful just the same. She screamed as her back was shredded. She tossed Tirin over the floored filings to safety. For him to even step on them would be devastating. Dane angrily roared and charged Jean.

"Dane, no!" Tirin yelled, but it was too late.

Jean tossed another handful of dust from his pocket into the air and, like a skilled matador, spun out of the way into a shadow just as Dane charged. He reappeared behind Dane, who blindly ran through the swirling dust.

Tirin let out a horrific scream and fell to the floor, a trickle of blood escaping from his nose. Helpless, he watched as Dane quivered, shook, and then slumped over, collapsing into a bloody mess. Roaring in anguish and pain, Tirin raced over to what remained of Dane. With the dust clinging to his body, Tirin couldn't even lift him into his arms.

Meanwhile, Julien, cut up and bleeding, levitated to confront Jean. His hands glowed red as he pulled energy from his Qi with a speed only a select few had ever witnessed. He shaped the energy and launched it at Jean. Caught off guard, Jean hastily created a matching ball and released it at the last second. Though it deflected Julien's blast, the force sent him stumbling backward, off balance. Julien seized the moment and was on him in an instant, delivering two charged punches that sent Jean crashing into a wall.

Jean was weak and already badly beaten; he couldn't withstand the power and speed Julien displayed for much longer. Julien launched another fatal energy blast Jean's way and, out of desperation, Jean transformed into a swarm of flies just as the blast exploded against the wall. The horde zipped across the room, bouncing off Julien's face, distracting him long enough for the swarm to escape through a hole in the wall. Enraged, Julien released an energy blast through what remained of the ceiling, sending debris crashing down below.

"Get everyone that's not dead and find that son of a bitch! NOW!" he yelled.

"But where,--" asked one of the beta contractors.

Julien blasted the unknown wolf, destroying him.

"GO!" he screamed.

The remaining few contractors scattered as Julien released more blasts in their direction. Rayna sped over and grabbed Julien before he destroyed another. Incensed, he stared at her like she was a stranger.

"Julien, stop! If you kill them, they can't help you."

His eyes faded to normal as he found himself in hers.

"Only he can find him now," she said, indicating Tirin.

The alpha sat on the floor over what was left of Dane, oblivious to all around him. In the last few minutes, he had lost both Dane and Camille. Half his world was gone. Julien limped over and looked down at him. Tirin was taking short, quick breaths as if he were hyperventilating or panting.

"I need you, my friend… Tirin?" Julien said with a strained voice, but Tirin would not look up at him. He couldn't. "TIRIN!" Julien snapped.

In an instant, Tirin was in his face. He growled softly as he glared at him with a crazed look in one eye and murder in the other.

Julien held his stare, and for the first time in all the years they had known one another, he saw something in the left eye of his best friend that he had never before seen: a tear. He watched as it emerged, slid down the alpha's cheek, and lingered on his chin before falling to the floor. Tirin's body quivered. Julien closed his eyes. Already in excruciating emotional torment, the sight of this was just another unbearable coal in the pit.

"I'm sorry," Julien said, "but there'll be time to mourn them later. All of them. Right now, my little girl is still out there somewhere, alone. Maybe in danger, I don't know. But I do know that that man is the only one who knows where and no one can track him, no one can find him, but you." Julien stared at the Blood Heart in his hand. The tears began to flow freely from his own face. "So I'm asking you to help us, to help me find the man responsible for all our pain and make him pay for what he's done." The two men stood there, silent. Tears streamed down both their faces. "Find him," Julien whispered. "Find him, please…. FIND HIM!!"

Tirin roared like never before, allowing the rage and emotion to transform him into full alpha, his face barely a whisker away from Julien's. He paused for a long moment, deliberating what he truly wanted to do in this tense situation. Without uttering a word, he abruptly wheeled around and took off. Cecil climbed out from behind the bar. In a flash, Rayna zipped over and landed a punch square on his face. The force knocked him unconscious and likely broke his nose. They could, and would deal with him later; right now, their focus needed to be elsewhere.

"*Feel it. Feel it down to your core.*"

Kaitlin sprinted toward the back door as the warlock flicked a mild energy blast in her direction. It was akin to flicking a spitball off his thumb—harmless enough not to kill her, but it would certainly leave a mark.

"NO! Dickory dock," Dani screamed, crying. "A shield to block!" Dani threw up a force-field that deflected the blow.

"Good, child," the man said. "Good. But to play with me you'll need more than nursery rhymes."

"Dani, don't listen to,--" Kaitlin tried to stop Dani from succumbing to this bully's taunting, but with a simple thought and a glance from him, she was silenced. It was like an invisible hand had grabbed her by the throat, squeezed and lifted her just a few millimeters off the ground. She struggled for air as she flailed around like a rag doll in the wind. Just when it seemed she would pass out, he released her. She laid on the ground, helpless, trying to suck in more air than her throat would allow. The man gave her a warning look; *next time it would be worse.* Dani was helpless. All she could do was cry.

"Oh, stop crying and concentrate!" he scolded her.

Dani tried to obey for Kaitlin's sake and snorted back her tears.

"Now. Feel the energy around you," the man ordered. "The power. It's part of you. Yes? Feel it. Feel it down to your core."

Dani breathed heavily, rhythmically, as her body trembled.

"Yes. That's it. Now bring it. Come on! Call it! Call for it! BRING IT FORTH!"

Dani's eyes and hands flashed red and if not for the shortness of her sprite-like haircut, her hair would have been floating wildly around her. The man's eyes widened as he gasped at the incredible spectacle he was witnessing.

"Am I seeing this?" he whispered to himself. "Mactrouge at age four?... RELEASE IT! Release it to me!" he shouted.

Dani's chest began to glow. She screamed as she pulled forth a good-sized energy blast and fell to the floor as she launched it at him. It was an incredible strain for her. The blast was not nearly enough to hurt the warlock. It more than likely hurt her more than it did him, but it did push him back a few steps. He was genuinely impressed. Dani watched him as she crawled over to Kaitlin and buried her tiny face in her chest.

"EXCELLENT!" the man shouted. He was truly excited and moved by what he had just witnessed. "Well done! You are truly an amazing little girl, descendent of Esmerelda. Your cognitive skills are equal to that of someone three times your age. You lack power, of course, but that would have come in time. How interesting it would've been to see you in ten years or so…" he said, softly to himself. "Right, then."

He slammed his hands together and created a force so loud and powerful it blew the back wall off the train. Air rushed through the open car, jostling Kaitlin and Dani about the floor. There was nowhere for them to go as the warlock levitated off the floor and prepared himself to strike.

"What a shame," he said.

He launched his blast. Kaitlin closed her eyes, hunching over Dani and squeezing her tightly. The explosion ripped through the back half of the train, completely destroying the area where they had been huddled. They, along with the wreckage, plummeted into the turbulent waters of Lake Maurepas below. As the warlock's eyes returned to their normal hue, he gazed down at the churning waters, finding nothing. With a sigh, he adjusted his glasses and turned away.

CHAPTER 49

A park ranger walked along the perimeter of Bayou Lafitte, his flashlight cutting through the darkness. Suddenly, he heard a rustling in the bushes and approached cautiously, stumbling upon a bloodied and extremely weak Jean Laveau. Before the ranger could react, a vampire swooped in to attack him. In a split second, Jean summoned a tree, its branches thrashing out and driving a stake into the vampire, neutralizing the threat. The ranger, wide-eyed and stunned, could hardly comprehend the chaos unfolding before him.

"The hell was d'at?!" the ranger said, alarmed.

"Vampire. They,--"

"I know 'bout d'em, I'm talkin' 'bout you!" The Ranger yelled.

"I am… human," Jean said. "B-Behind you."

Something was coming. The ranger grabbed Jean and helped him over to his ATV quad as a beta ran into the area. It was Micah. The

Ranger pulled a shotgun from the quad and blasted him. He must have had silver bullets, because he dropped Micah cold. A horrible howl was heard off in the distance. Tirin. The Ranger cringed at the sound of it. He knew he had to get out of there now.

"P-Please. Help me," Jean begged.

The Ranger helped him onto the back of the ATV, then jumped on and took off.

"This ain't safe. We gotta get outta here. How many of 'em did you piss off?" The Ranger asked.

"All of them," Jean said as the ATV took off and plowed through the bayou.

He knew they would pursue him over any mountain, sea or continent for what he had done. He was weak and his powers were fading, but he could still sense the presence of an alpha. Tirin was close. They traveled deep into the bayou until they came across something no one had seen for over two hundred years - a cave. The cave. The Ranger stopped the quad in the muck. Not a wise thing to do this deep in the swamp, but this could not be.

"That's impossible. Ain't no caves out here," the Ranger said.

Almost in response, a vampire tackled Jean and the Ranger, knocking them both off the quad. The vampire broke the gun and went after Jean.

"Go! Get in the cave!" Jean yelled.

The ranger took off, sprinting as fast as an ordinary human could, sloshing and jumping through the thick muck. He scrambled desperately to reach the cave. Just then, a tree sprang to life, its branches lashing out to stake the vampire that was descending on Jean. The ranger reached the cave entrance just in time to see a contract beta in human form splash toward him, but, oddly, the beta wouldn't cross the threshold of the cave. Instead, it turned and charged directly at Jean.

Jean was utterly depleted, fighting against the overwhelming urge to succumb to unconsciousness. Just as the lycan was about to attack, Jean vanished as he fell into the shadow of a giant cypress tree, allowing the beta to slide harmlessly by. He moved through the shadows, inching closer to the cave entrance, but the last ten meters had to be traversed on his own. The beta, recovering from the slippery muck, prepared for a second charge, ready to strike.

"Come on, get outta there! MOVE!" the Ranger screamed, but Jean wasn't going to make it. "Goddamn it!"

The Ranger ran out of the 'supposed' safety of the cave, grabbed Jean and dragged him the remaining distance. The beta leapt toward them, but the Ranger had made it. Both he and Jean were now safely inside. The beta landed awkwardly and nearly injured himself stopping before he slid as much as a millimeter into that cave. For some reason he was afraid to even set a single foot inside.

The beta stood at the entrance, glaring at them. He let out a monstrous roar before he turned and disappeared into the swamp. The Ranger helped Jean deeper into the cave. Then a whisper was heard.

"All who enter here shall die."

The whisper drifted on the night air, so faint the Ranger would have doubted he even heard it if not for the sensation of ice water filling his spine. Unable to go back, he continued forward, helping Jean walk.

"Stop!" Jean ordered. "Do not step on that branch."

"Why?"

"…Because he did," Jean said, pointing to a skeleton on the ground pierced with rusted spikes.

A light, airy cackle began and continued as they moved deeper into the cave. Closer to the source of the whispers; closer to *her* - The Old One. With a wave of his hand, Jean illuminated the space around them. Nothing had changed since Philippe had been there, nearly three hundred years earlier. The skeletons of the dead combatants remain untouched. The Ranger set Jean down against the cave wall.

"What is this place?" the Ranger asked.

"The end of an evil," Jean said.

"*…and the beginning of another,*" Hagatha softly whispered and laughed.

"How's this possible? I've been past here hundreds of times."

Jean frantically searched his pockets, trying to put something together.

"It remains hidden half of the month, revealing itself only during the third and fourth quarter, when the moon is least visible in the sky," he said. "That is how it has gone undetected for so long. We will be safe here for a while, but we must leave this place before tomorrow night, or disappear with it for another twenty-seven days."

"Friend, you may not have twenty-seven minutes. These wounds are bad, and this bite… Vampire?"

"Yes. Do not worry. I have been bitten by a vampire before. I have a serum that will accelerate my healing, but a dose of this magnitude will leave me in a vulnerable state."

"What's d'at mean?"

"Unfiltered, it will leave me virtually comatose. I will be incapable of defending myself or you."

"How long?"

"Twelve hours. Then," he said, holding up a separate vial on a string, "I must ingest this elixir. It will revive me, but I will need someone to administer it."

The ranger nodded. "...I got 'cha you."

Jean drank the serum, then secured the string holding the elixir around his neck. A violent cough erupted from him, forcing blood to spill from his lips. The ranger quickly assisted Jean into a lying position, doing his best to make him comfortable despite the stark, barren surroundings.

"You ain't a warlock," the Ranger stated. "Imogen? Onjeve? Boku?"

"Boku," Jean said, surprised at the knowledge this man possessed.

"A priest?"

Jean nodded and gave him a curious look.

"Hey, you live in New Orleans in this line of work. You best know a little somethin' 'bout everythin'."

Jean smiled in agreement. A howl rang out. The Ranger looked concerned.

"Do not fear," Jean said. "They will not enter. This place is taboo to them."

"Something to do with d'at voice we keep ignorin'?"

"Not a voice. Just a whisper now. She can no longer harm us."

Do not be so sure... Hagatha whispered.

"Thank you," Jean said. "I would not have survived... without..."

Jean felt his consciousness spiraling away. Then darkness.

CHAPTER 50

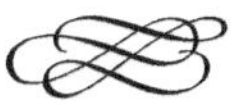

Rayna and Julien stepped off the airboat, the swampy bayou surrounding them. Teddy and Cree dragged Cecil between them, while Tirin stood in the calf-high muck beside the water's edge. A lone vampire and two beta contractors flanked him, the remnants of their group after the disastrous events of the night. The mouth of the cave loomed about fifty meters away, a foreboding presence in the dim light.

"Oh my," Rayna gasped. "Is that what I think it is?"

Tirin nodded.

"He's in there?" Julien asked.

Tirin nodded again.

"Then let's go," Julien said.

"They won't," Tirin said. "They're afraid."

Julien looked toward the contractors with disgust, although the vampire had already made a stealth-worthy exit.

"You're kidding! None of you? I don't believe it! People are supposed to have nightmares about *you!*"

He contemplated killing them, and under different circumstances, he might have gone through with it. However, exhaustion weighed heavily on him, and his powers were nearly depleted. He needed to conserve the little energy he had left; there were still a few important tasks to accomplish that night. With determination, he and Tirin trudged through the muck toward the cave. Cecil stirred awake, his voice barely audible as he began the mumblings of a chant.

"No! Teddy, stop him! Don't let him speak!" Julien shouted.

Teddy silenced Cecil, but too late. A huge bolt of lightning struck the cave, collapsing the entrance. It was completely sealed up.

Julien screamed from sorrow and rage. Tirin turned and grunted at the two contractors, along with Teddy and Cree, then gave each one an angry nod. They slowly began to circle Cecil.

"Julien? Now, I'm sorry, son, but there are things that have been set in motion that just cannot be stopped," Cecil said nervously. "It's better this way. You gotta understand that."

"What things?" Julien whispered. "What did you and my father do?"

The betas began to howl and growl.

"Julien, stop these boys. Please? Julien!" Cecil screamed.

"What did you do, Cecil?" Julien asked.

"The Talisman," Rayna said, putting it together. "They probably sent him after the little girl, too."

Cecil didn't answer. Julien lowered his head, and turned and walked toward the boat as the betas closed in. Cecil's eyes began to glow red, but the betas ripped and scratched at him, making him lose focus each time before he had a chance to charge up.

"No, JD, please," Cecil cried. "Call them off! JD! Call them off! J-DEEEEEE!!!"

Julien turned to Rayna as the betas ripped Cecil apart behind them. She pulled out a fresh deck, shuffled it, and flipped over a single card. She stared at it with a curious look on her face, her eyes flitting back and forth across it, trying to make sense of it.

"What do you see?" Julien asked.

"…Nothing," she answered with a perplexed look.

Rayna showed him the card. There was nothing on it. The card was a blank. Julien closed his eyes and sadly shook his head in despair.

"Come on, baby. Let's go home," Rayna said as she tried to help Julien onto the boat.

Julien looked over his shoulder for Tirin. He saw him standing alone at what was the cave entrance.

"Tirin!" he called out.

Tirin did not respond. He just stood there, staring at the cave. Julien took a step toward him. Rayna gently grabbed his arm.

"Leave him be," she said. "He'll come home when he's ready."

They observed Tirin for a few moments as he clawed and scratched at the cave entrance, but his efforts proved futile. Teddy and Cree soon joined him, attempting to assist in the struggle. Meanwhile, Julien stepped into the boat, and he and Rayna set off for home.

CHAPTER 51

His eyes opened and a spark of red crackled and danced across them before it flickered away.

Julien sat in a chair facing the desk in the study, his head slumped, his eyes closed. His clothes were torn and dirty and there was a mix of dried and fresh blood on his hands and face. He was bruised and sore, but he refused to clean himself up; refused to move. He just sat there and waited. The house looked no better; chairs were busted and overturned, and a shaded desk lamp provided the only illumination, as most of the candles had been extinguished by the wind that moved freely throughout the broken windows and busted front door.

Familiar footsteps approached him from behind, then slowly passed him to the desk. Barrett sat, holding a large manila envelope in his hands. He sighed deeply as he glared at his son, but it wasn't anger that filled his eyes – it was disappointment. Julien didn't see it as he couldn't bring himself to look at him.

"…Responsibility. The word is nefarious. Irreverent," Barrett said. "Puts a stale salty taste in a man's mouth. It's a heavy word that weighs on all of us, at one time, or another. No one, more so, than your great-great-great granddaddy. For thirty years he bore that weight. Thirty - years. Travelling from port to port, city to city. Trying to rid the world of this evil and because of his sacrifice, we get to enjoy the way of life we now lead, but it comes with a price. One that EVERY warlock must pay."

Julien shook his head.

"They're evil, son. Plain and simple. They try and fight it for as long as they can, but, ultimately, it's just who they are. And it's our job, our responsibility, to contain them. We cultivate them and breed with them, but under no circumstances can we allow these women to reach the age of twenty-one."

"She never hurt anybody," Julien said as tears streamed down his face.

"Yet," Barrett replied.

"She was good and you killed her. Just like you killed my mother."

Barrett sighed and shook his head in disgust. Only now could Julien feel the disappointment and shame that emanated in waves from his father.

"Son, your momma died while giving birth to you. It was a horrible accident… As for Camille, well, she had an accident, too," Barrett continued.

"No," Julien angrily interjected.

"She and young Daniel were kidnapped tonight,--"

"Danielle,--"

"Tragically, their bodies will never be found," Barrett said as he tossed the envelope forward. It bore the symbol of The Council on it.

"NO!" Julien yelled as his eyes flashed to red. He clenched his fists and concentrated. He held his helpless father with his stare.

"J-Julien…" Barrett said.

Barrett appeared to struggle with his breathing, but Julien remained unresponsive, continuing to stare right through his father. Just then, Rayna walked into the room, draped in a plush white robe with a towel resting on her shoulders. She perched herself on the corner of the desk, drying her hair while wearing a smile that seemed to lighten the tense atmosphere. Or, perhaps it kindled it even more. Suddenly, Barrett's contempt-filled eyes shifted to her, flickering momentarily before settling into a steady, menacing red.

"Where,… is,… Cecil,… son?…"

"He had an accident, Pop."

"How interesting," Rayna said. "You are a virile old man, aren't you?"

Fascinated by the confrontation, she quietly watched for a moment as Julien and Barrett fought for dominance. Julien obviously had the upper hand, but he had been severely weakened by the night's festivities and Barrett was strong and fresh. He would not simply succumb.

"Knock, knock! Anybody up in here?" Said a voice from the other room.

"Now? Really?" Rayna muttered. She recognized the voice.

"Hello? Mr. Gerard?" Said another equally familiar voice. "It's Mayor Kelvins."

"Unbelievable," Rayna said, still watching Julien and Barrett struggle. "What dumbass let them in?"

"Hate to disturb y'all, but Sheriff Bailey and I need to have a few words with you," the Mayor said.

"Hi, Mr. Mayor!" Rayna yelled into the next room.

"Ms. Rayna?..." the Mayor answered.

"Yeah, uhmm. It's really late! You think we might be able to continue this conversation tomorrow morning in your office?" Rayna asked.

"No, we may not!" Sheriff Bailey yelled back. "I need y'all to come on out here. Now!"

"Ah,… Okay!" She yelled back, then looked at Julien. "Shit! Julien… Julien!" She whispered.

"Or maybe we'll just come on in there," Sheriff Bailey said as if he knew something was going on.

"Honestly, I don't think very much about that, Sheriff Bailey!" Rayna yelled, flustered. "As you can plainly see, the house is in shambles. Please, just give us a moment, and we will be out directly!" She turned to Julien. "What do you want me to do? Julien!" She whispered loudly.

Julien did not respond. His face was flushed, his body quivered from the strain, yet he continued to hold Barrett. The old man had fought and held on much longer than expected - and now seemed to be getting stronger.

"How about I give y'all to the count of ten?" Sheriff Bailey said.

"Sheriff, please," an exasperated Rayna replied.

"One… two…"

"Oh, for Pete's sake!" Rayna moved over to Barrett and snapped his neck.

Julien gasped into a long exhale, sweat dripping from his face. Wearily, after a long, deliberate blink, his eyes faded back to normal. Motionless, he gazed at the body of the only parent he had ever known, almost as if he expected him to rise up and spit a hurtful insult in his direction, or emasculate and embarrass him in a way only he could. Tears quickly filled his eyes when he finally realized, that time had passed and would not come again.

"What did you do?" he whispered as his lip quivered and the tears streamed down his face.

"Julien, we got to,--."

"It was my fight, my moment. MINE!"

"The Mayor and Sheriff Bailey are,--"

"He was for me to kill, not you. ME!"

"Hush, 'fore they hear you!"

"You stole it from me!"

"You were taking too long!" She hissed back at him.

"I was in control!"

"Were you?!" She asked as she yanked him out of the chair like a child. She pushed him into the other room, quietly arguing with him the entire way. Spent, both mentally and emotionally, he had no strength left to fight with her. In the doorway of the study, they fell silent. Looking out into the living room, Julien saw Mayor Kelvins, Sheriff Bailey, two deputies, and another man with whom they were not familiar. The living room was a mess; windows blown out, door nowhere to be found.

"Would have rang the doorbell, but would have had to find the door first," Sheriff Bailey said with a sarcasm this night did not need.

Neither Rayna nor Julien cared for the man, and it was obvious he didn't approve of them either.

"How can we help you, Mr. Mayor?" An exhausted Julien whispered.

"Where's your father at, Julien?" Mayor Kelvins asked. "We need to talk about some of the goings-on this evening."

"I'm sorry, but my father is indisposed at this time."

"Well, maybe you just better get him disposed," Sheriff Bailey said, "and I mean fast!"

"Sheriff, please. Let's try and be civil here?" Mayor Kelvins said.

Bailey quieted himself, but he had a dark sense of mischief about him.

"You know your father and I have been friends for many years, and over time, we've formed a partnership that has been both profitable and mutually satisfactory," Mayor Kelvins stated.

"Well, if I may," said the unassuming, unknown man with the British accent.

"No, sir, you may not!" Mayor Kelvins said, who, for the first time, showed some anger. "Not until I've had my say."

"What do you want, Mr. Mayor?" Julien said wearily.

"Wh-- What do I want?... Well, I want the building housing your nightclub downtown to still be standing. I want my train to not have crashed into the station at Ponchatoula, and I want the twenty-three people who are either dead, maimed, or injured because of this night, not to be! That's what I want!" He took a deep breath, trying to calm down. "But unless you got a time machine, I can't have that, now can I? So now what I want is your father to come in here and tell me why."

"I don't think that's gonna happen, Mayor," Sheriff Bailey said.

"Well, why the hell not?!" Mayor Kelvins yelled.

"What about you, boy? You think that's gonna happen? Huh?" Sheriff Bailey asked as he moved toward Julien. "You think your father's gonna walk past you and stroll up in here and tell us all a sad, sad story of how his ward, your '*sister*', supposedly passed away?" said Bailey, now in Julien's face. "Or should I say your wife? I was always confused about that part. How she died along with her child, your nephew-slash-son, on the train to Ponchatoula?" Bailey tried to look into the study, but Julien blocked his way. "Ooh. Something in there you don't want me to see, boy?"

"Where's your father at, Julien?" Mayor Kelvins asked.

"Yeah, boy, tell us," said Sheriff Bailey. "Where he at?"

"If I were you, Bailey, I'd back up very quickly," Julien said.

"Well, now, that sounded like a threat, didn't it, Randy?" Sheriff Bailey asked. At that moment, an unseen sniper shot through a window, hitting the wall next to Julien. "Tracey?" Another shot through a different window, shattering a vase. "Bobby." Another hit the wall on the other side of them. "Mack?"

Mack answered, speaking through the walkie-talkie on Bailey's belt.

"I got eyes on the old man. He ain't gonna be talking to anybody ever again."

Julien looked down and saw four red dots from the sniper guns converged on his chest.

"Okay, okay. Let's everyone just calm down, please," the British Man said. "Please. Mr. Mayor, my office is willing to take responsibility for everything that has happened tonight, and I promise we will make restitutions to all the families of the deceased and come up with solutions that will not only free you and your office of any responsibility but, perhaps, be the foundation of your campaign for re-election. I'm quite certain that the Gerards will be making a healthy donation to said campaign, both now and summarily in the future," the British Man said as he eyed Julien.

The Mayor quietly contemplated the offer.

"The paper's all over this. I gotta give a press conference by noon."

Julien took all this in but wouldn't back down from his stand-off with Bailey.

"I can have all of this wrapped up and be in your office, with a rather large check for you and your people's trouble, by 11 a.m. at the very latest," the British Man said. "Please. We've worked together for so long. I'd hate to have our allegiance terminated by one minor setback."

"Minor?!" said the outraged Sheriff.

"My office. 11 a.m. And I want him there, too," Mayor Kelvins said, indicating Julien. "As a sign of respect."

"Agreed. And thank you," the British man said.

"Bailey, let's go," said Mayor Kelvins. Sheriff Bailey didn't move. The red dots still hovered on Julien. "Sheriff,"

"Geronimo," Bailey said, and the dots disappeared. "Kelvins ain't always gonna be mayor, boy." He raised his index finger and thumb in the shape of a gun and pointed at Julien. His eyes then shifted to Rayna. "Ms. Rayna," he said with a nod and turned to leave. Just before reaching the door, he stopped. "By the way, your *sister/wife,* or whatever she is, got on that train with the child and a black woman. Nobody got off. Alive, that is."

Sheriff Bailey smiled as he exited with Mayor Kelvins and the two deputies, leaving only the British Man with Rayna and Julien. The British Man walked over to Julien and offered his hand.

"How do you do? I'm Mr. Jeffries. One of the many Top Administrators within The Council."

Julien glared at him and did not accept his hand. Mr. Jeffries smiled and withdrew it.

"I'm extremely honored that The Governors personally selected me for this,... task. I am hopeful that you are educated enough in our ways to know that if I am here - now - it means that all the energies and efforts of the entire Council are here with me, and, right now, we are focused solely on you. Think carefully on how you wish to handle our attention."

Julien was enraged, but he wasn't stupid. He knew that was much more than an idle threat. Taking on The Council was equivalent to a caged tiger taking on a team of big game hunters with laser-sighted rifles, and although perhaps too late, he now understood this.

"I understand," Julien said through his teeth.

"Good. Being angry with me, Mr. Gerard, will not bring your family back or undo any of the harm caused this night by you and your people. It serves as only an obstacle in completing the tasks at hand; so, with less than seven hours before our deadline expires, I would strongly encourage you to lose the attitude and buck up. It's going to be a long night."

Mr. Jefferies walked between Julien and Rayna into the study. He sighed deeply and shook his head. Barrett's body was slumped over the desk.

"Right. Killing your father... Can't say I was prepared for that one. I'm sure my superiors will want to discuss this little gem with you personally. Until then, my team and I will work diligently to make sure that the Gerard name remains unscathed in our history books. In the future, I am optimistically anticipating you will be equally diligent in becoming a better warlock." Jefferies turned to Julien as he continued his impassioned speech. "You are the first family of our race, sir. The scandal of a Gerard falling in love with a witch would be catastrophic, at the very least. It could create an anarchy throughout the lesser warlocks that would spread like a virus, collapsing everything that began with your ancestor nearly three hundred years ago, and neither I nor my superiors will allow that to happen. We understand that you are young, but you should understand that if you weren't a Gerard, you'd be dead for what you've done. You." Jeffries pointed to Rayna. "Move this body, please. I need a place to work."

"What about my daughter?" Julien asked.

"Your daughter's dead," Jefferies said as he picked up the manila envelope from the desk. "As I stated so eloquently in this press release. You'll have time to review it and grieve later. Right now, I need you to gather whatever malafecs you have left. There is much to be done this night and we shall need all the help we can get to try and put things back to normal."

"Normal?" Julien asked bitterly. "Killing innocent witches is normal to you?"

"Define 'innocent,'" Jeffries said.

"She never hurt anybody!"

"Then you should have fought for her!" Jeffries yelled. Julien was stunned as Jeffries continued. "Your ancestor had the impudence to stand in front of The Council and propose genocide on the female of our species, and, out of fear, the fools listened to him."

"Wait, so you don't believe witches are dangerous either?"

"I don't know whether they are or not, but I do know that if you had been brave enough to stand in front of The Council - like he did - and prove what you say you so emphatically believe, your wife might still be alive today."

"I tried to get an audience with you!" Julien said.

"After you unsuccessfully tried to conceal it from us for nearly three years! If you'd have had the courage to stand behind your convictions – from the beginning – they would have eagerly listened to you!" Jeffries said. "You have no idea how many others there are out there that want to believe what you feel is true."

"But why now? After all this time?"

"Because we're dying, you fool! In saving us from these so-called monsters all those years ago, your great-great-great grandfather destroyed our race. There are maybe 1,500 witches left in the world today. In thirty years, that number will be cut in half. Less fortunate warlocks, the ones who cannot afford to pay the ever-increasing price for the next available witch, have been breeding with humans for centuries. Our race has been watered down so much our analysts speculate that both we and our female counterparts will have gone the way of the dodo by the turn of the next century. You could have, perhaps, changed that. Like your ancestor, you had the power to change our destiny. You had the means, the desire, the name, and the witch - a direct descendant of one of the Five Great Ones - and you wasted it!" Jeffries said with an unexpected passion. "You did nothing but draw unwanted attention to our kind by setting off the largest spectacle our slowly diminishing race has experienced since the Esmerelda incident fifty years ago. It took us decades to recover from that, and now, because of your cowardly, poor judgment, The Council will NEVER entertain this subject again. It. Is. Over. We lose. So instead of glaring at me through your self-absorbed, condescending eyes, you might want to turn them inward - if you can stomach it," Jeffries said. "Now get your malafecs together. We have work to do." He glared at Rayna. "AND GET THIS CARCASS OUT OF HERE!"

Even Rayna was intimidated, and she nodded respectfully as Jeffries left the room. She moved over to Julien and tried to put her hand on his shoulder, but Julien jerked away, refusing to look at her.

"Go check on Lucien!" he snapped.

His father's death was still young, and he hadn't quite forgiven her for taking the kill away from him — if that is what he was truly going to do. Perhaps a small part of him never would. She withdrew her hand and removed Barrett's body from the room on her way to see if the mysteriously dormant dreamer had awakened. Julien moved to the window and stared out into the night. He felt cold and alone in a world he didn't want to be in anymore.

"Jeffries was right," he thought. *"All this was my doing."*

He closed his eyes, feeling an emptiness where tears once flowed. His thoughts turned to the daughter he had never met and then to Camille, the enduring source of his strength. Now, more than ever, he needed that strength. He looked up toward the heavens, reaching out for her presence, and asked for it one last time.

"Forgive me, Cher'," he thought to himself. *"Please, give me the strength to live another day without you; to rebuild and to thrive and replace all that was lost, but mostly just to believe that she's still out there; our little girl. And that someday she might find her way back home to me. Give me that strength, and I promise you that I will fight for her like I should have fought for you. God help anyone who gets in my way."*

His eyes opened and a spark of red crackled and danced across them before it flickered away. He slowly exhaled as his brow furrowed and his lips pursed. There was a malevolence in his presence that wasn't there before. It seemed as if Julien Dumont Gerard was on his way to becoming the warlock his father always hoped he would be.

EPILOGUE

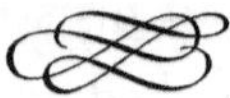

Death has many sounds, but the aftermath remains unchanged: silence. Not the eerie, unsettling kind filled with the anticipation of an even greater catastrophe, but a peaceful, serene calm reminiscent of the soothing relief after a long, hot bath—a cleansing, if you will. In that moment, no sounds pierced the tranquility except the gentle splashing of water against the wreckage floating across the still, dark waters of Lake Maurepas. From within that silence emerged the strong, familiar voice of witch, a friend, a mother. A hero.

"This is not my story. It was never meant to be about me," the voice whispered.

The debris in the water shifted from the small edge of a dome that began to crown. Water and debris sheeted off the object, which grew as it emerged. Then, with a buoyant splash, the lake released a translucent bubble to the air above. As the bubble splashed back

420

down to the water's surface, the pearlescent coating on it began to fade to clear glass, revealing Dani and Kaitlin encased within the force-field.

"THIS... is her story."

Kaitlin sat, awestruck, as she watched the young child, her eyes glowing red and hands outstretched, fiercely holding onto a spell she should never have been able to cast. How perfectly beautiful the child was, yet the strain in her face was evident. Her body began to tremble; her tiny arms quivered as if she were holding the weight of the world. Her breath was rapid, almost resembling panting, but in reality, she was hyperventilating. Her blood was filling with carbon dioxide faster than her small body could expel it.

Suddenly, her eyes flickered, then faded to normal and rolled back in her head as her body went limp. The force field dissolved instantly as Dani collapsed, sinking beneath the welcoming waves. Kaitlin dove after her, shoving through the water and debris in a desperate attempt to reach the rapidly descending child. After what felt like an eternity, she emerged with an unconscious Dani in her arms.

Without hesitation, she administered mouth-to-mouth resuscitation, followed by a firm squeeze. Dani convulsed and coughed up the excess water from her lungs. Kaitlin listened intently, her ear close to Dani's face. She could hear and feel the breath returning to the child. Dani was breathing on her own; she was going to be all right. With care, Kaitlin gently tipped Dani onto her back in the water and slowly paddled through the debris toward the north shore of Canal Pass Manchac with the child in tow.

THE END

ACKNOWLEDGMENTS

To my two boys, Dillon Anthony and Dakarai Ajay. For all the times I yelled at you to turn the TV down so I could concentrate. Thank you for your patience, understanding and gradual acceptance of the insanity that lives within your father. Know that it resides within you as well... and that may not be such a bad thing. To the big B. P. (Bronson Picket!) for being – the Big B. P. Only you could be crazy enough to stand outside in the rain until three O' clock in the morning, listening to foolish tales about a Witch, a Warlock and a Voodoo Priest. The support you've given cannot be put into words. Lastly, to my twelfth grade English teacher, Mr. Joseph Geiger, for igniting the spark and lighting the way. If not for you, I can most assuredly say I would not be here today. Thank you.

ABOUT THE AUTHOR

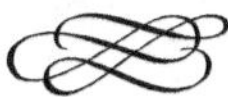

D. A. BARNEY was born and raised in Cleveland Heights, Ohio and for as far back as he could remember, there was a voice constantly whispering strange things to him. Beautiful things; amazing things and sometimes, even scary things. He began to write the voice down, and the rest is history. He and The Voice received a BFA in Film from The Ohio State University, where they specialized in writing and directing. Since then their scripts have won eleven awards in competitions and film festivals around the world. This is their first foray into the surrealistic world of book publication. It will not be their last. Stay tuned. Check out the website for definitions, profiles and other cool stuff at:

https://thewiccanchronicles.com/

https://www.facebook.com/TheWiccanChronicles

https://www.instagram.com/the.wiccan.chronicles/

https://www.tiktok.com/@the_wiccan_chronicles?lang=en

The Wiccan Chronicles
D.A. BARNEY
THE MIDNIGHT MAN

BOOK II: THE MIDNIGHT MAN

Prologue

July 15, 1999 – New Orleans, Louisiana

"This is bullshit!" Taq, a young vampire in his late teens, said as he moved from the foot of Lucien's bed to the window. He scanned the empty courtyard below, then turned and retraced his steps back to the bed, where the sole heir to the Gerard fortune helplessly lay in an unwakeable sleep. "We should be out there."

"Taq, I swear, if you wake this boy," threatened his older sister Tik, who sat on the bed next to Lucien, stroking his head with a concerned hand.

She was only a few years older than her brother, but she had the maternal instincts of a lioness and the nurturing skills to match. Most female vampires are cursed with 'The Wanting' if they've never had a child. It's an ever-constant call from deep inside their bodies that can never be answered. Tik's call was strong.

"No one can! That's the point!" Taq yelled.

Tik gave her younger brother a look that, even though he was physically bigger than her, made him take pause. He pushed off the bed and trekked back to the window.

"He did this," Taq said, gesturing toward the window, "he's the one that should be punished, not us."

"You think this is punishment?"

"I think I should be out there fighting with the rest of them, not stuck here babysitting with you."

Before Taq could even blink, Tik was off the bed and across the room. She slammed her brother into the wall and pinned him there.

"I was in the courtyard tonight. I saw what he's capable of; felt it. So trust me when I tell you that staying here with me tonight is no punishment," she said.

Just then, Lucien abruptly woke from his sleep and sat straight up. Tik sped over and sat next to him, with Taq taking his place at the foot of the bed.

"What is it, Luc? You okay, baby?" Tik asked.

His body quivered as he stared off in the distance, trying his best to hold back a wave of tears with his rapidly-blinking eyelids. He was unsuccessful and one by one, they escaped.

"Baby, what's wrong?" Tik asked as she tried to brush the tears from his face.

"My momma's dead!"

He knew it. He somehow felt it in every bone, every muscle, every molecule. Tik picked him up and held him tight as he cried on her shoulder. Taq's anger steeped as he watched, knowing there was nothing he could do. Just then, the window to the courtyard blew open and spilled an unearthly cold wind into the room.

"Taq!" Tik ordered.

Taq sped over to the window and closed it. He paused a moment as he stared at the handle because he knew he had checked and secured it before. As he pondered this window conundrum, he felt some kind of force press up against him and violate his personal space before it moved right through him. He shivered and turned, only to see his sister, with Luc's head resting comfortably on her shoulder. He scanned the room with a stilled apprehensiveness uncharacteristic of a vampire and although he saw nothing strange or out of the ordinary, he knew they were no longer alone.

9 798893 246469